THE SUN CHILD

"Open," Joog said, but the girl didn't respond. "Open your mouth and I will pour," he said.

Joog waited a moment, then opened his own mouth, held the pouch above it, and poured a thin stream of water into his mouth. "Now you," he said.

He put his index finger in her mouth and pulled down on the lower jaw. "Leave it open," he said, slowly withdrawing his finger, then tilting her chin up. Without any sudden moves that could frighten her, he lifted the pouch and slowly dribbled water into her mouth.

The girl eagerly swallowed, and when Joog started to upright the pouch, her hand was suddenly over his, encouraging him to give her more water.

"I was right," he said. "You are thirsty."

When she was done drinking, she flopped down, short of breath.

"Your journey must have been long," Joog said.

The girl's eyes closed. She coughed weakly several times, then drifted into sleep.

Joog sat at her side, staring at her. Who was this wonder child? He glanced at the sun, then back at her. "Sun child," he said. "Is that your name?"

Daughter
of the
Fifth Moon

Lynn
Armistead
McKee

A SIGNET BOOK

SIGNET
Published by New American Library, a division of
Penguin Putnam Inc., 375 Hudson Street,
New York, New York 10014, U.S.A.
Penguin Books Ltd, 27 Wrights Lane,
London W8 5TZ, England
Penguin Books Australia Ltd, Ringwood,
Victoria, Australia
Penguin Books Canada Ltd, 10 Alcorn Avenue,
Toronto, Ontario, Canada M4V 3B2
Penguin Books (N.Z.) Ltd, 182–190 Wairau Road,
Auckland 10, New Zealand

Penguin Books Ltd, Registered Offices:
Harmondsworth, Middlesex, England

First published by Signet, an imprint of New American Library,
a division of Penguin Putnam Inc.

First Printing, June 2001
10 9 8 7 6 5 4 3 2 1

For Tatum Madison Oliver.
The circle of life goes on.

1

Mixya's onyx eyes flashed open. It wasn't the wind or the cry of some nocturnal creature that awakened her. She knew those sounds of the island. Those were the sounds that lulled her to sleep, that kept her company through long nights. No, something else moved, stirred the air, even instinctively made her nostrils flare as if she were an animal that could detect another by scent. To her east she heard the surf, the dark blue waves with jewels of moonlight riding their crests crashing over the white sand. Mixya turned to her side and the skin on her neck prickled. Her sleeping hammock swayed. She sensed something . . . something threatening. Fear rippled through her, making her shudder. She tapped her husband's shoulder. His lids raised, but not as wide as hers. The woman's black eyes shone with fright in the slice of moonlight that pricked through the thatch.

"Listen," she whispered, pressing a finger to his lips before he could speak.

Obaec cocked his head and propped up on his elbows. He stared out the opening of their round hut, searching in the darkness for the source of his wife's alarm. He saw nothing. Obaec comfortingly smoothed her hair against her head with a gentle hand. "There is nothing," he said. "Did you have a bad dream?" The night would slip away soon, and with it would fade all the dark mysteries. When morning came, Mixya would be fine. Father sun would rise, and the small village would begin to stir with activity.

The woman shook her head. There was something out there. She was certain. "Carib?" Mixya whispered on a trembling breath. Her skin broke with cold sweat.

Obaec squeezed his wife's hand to reassure her as he climbed out of the hammock. He would look about, convince her there was nothing to be afraid of, and then she would sleep again, her head tucked in the crook of his arm, his hand lying lovingly across her warm and full breast.

Obaec gazed at his sleeping daughter. She was their only child, despite years of effort to have other children. Nyna had been conceived immediately after the marriage and was delivered with no problem, but Mixya had not borne any children after that.

Obaec would do anything for either of them. He knew Mixya and Nyna depended on him to protect and provide for them. Though he was certain Mixya had only been awakened by a bad dream, there was a thread of uncertainty that seeped through his veins. He could not name what the feeling was that made his blood heat inside him. In his head he knew there was nothing to fear, but his gut felt something else. Obaec ducked through the opening of their hut, hiding the fear that burned inside his belly. "Carib," she had said. Just the word made his skin crawl. He knew the Carib too well, and there was good reason to fear them.

As a boy Obaec had survived a Carib attack, and the memory of it remained clear in his head. He conjured the vivid image of the Carib warriors ravaging his village. Horrifying even in appearance, with their black-stained eyes and eyebrows and flowing hair, the Caribs terrified Obaec's people. The most contemptible thing he knew of the Caribs was that they ate the flesh of men. They were known to take the young Taino women, keep them as slaves and concubines, allowing them no meat other than that of lizards, snakes, and rats. When a woman gave birth to an infant spawned by the men, the child was murdered and eaten. The Caribs raised no offspring except those by their own women.

Obaec had heard the Caribs believed there was nothing in the world as flavorful as the flesh of men—better than that of boys or women. They abducted Taino boys, cut off their manparts, and fattened them up to feast upon later. Obaec was certain that if his mother had not made him climb a tree and hide during the Carib attack, he would have been castrated on the spot and one day his bones gnawed as were his father's and older brother's that very day.

Obaec's stomach soured, and the contents rose in his throat as he recalled watching those despicable men butcher and roast human flesh, then feast on it there on the beach before loading their ocean-going piraguas with the young women, men, and boys of his village, then sailing off into the sea. Old men and old women lay strewn in blood about the village. The small bodies of female children and infants also lay murdered. The Caribs did not want them, as it would take too long for the little girls to become mature and satisfying to them. Obaec's mother, too old to be considered for a captive, lay slain beneath the tree in which he roosted.

For days Obaec had stayed perched in the tree, even after other Taino survivors had begun the task of clearing the village of bodies and attempting to recover.

His uncle spotted him and called to him. At first Obaec refused to come down, but his uncle convinced him that he needed to eat and to rest if he wanted to grow into a man. His uncle told him his mother would want to see him do that.

Obaec had felt the rage burning inside him. Why did the Taino have no weapons to fight off the enemy—weapons like the Caribs'—arrows with sharp tortoiseshell and jagged fish-bone points? Why did they not have bludgeons edged with slivers of shells and sharks' teeth tipped with manioc poison? The Taino never used the poison. They took great care in extracting the toxin from the manioc so they could make delicious cassava cakes. How different the Taino were from the Carib!

Slowly, Obaec descended the tree, all the while vowing that he would fashion a weapon, one that was sharp and deadly, and if the Caribs ever came back, it would be their flesh that would run blood. He would dismember them and throw them in a stew pot and make the surviving enemy men swallow the meat of their brothers!

Obaec thought of that weapon now as he stared into the darkness. He glanced at the back of his hut where he hid the shell knife in a basket. Only Mixya knew of it, as war was not the Taino way, and the men would disapprove. He had shown his wife the knife on their wedding night, puffing out his chest as he told her how he would defend her with his life if he needed to.

Obaec looked at Mixya. If he retrieved the knife now it would cause her alarm and demonstrate his fear. He did not want to act too hastily. After all, he had heard nothing, no sounds at all other than those of the forest and sea. It was probably nothing. He would investigate.

Obaec stepped out of the hut and looked around, then disappeared in the darkness.

This was the hot season, the season of great storms, yet Mixya suddenly felt as if cold water ran down her spine and limbs. She gathered her arms around herself, rubbing the peculiar chill from her upper arms. There was little saliva in her mouth, yet the urge to swallow was compelling. In her mind she tried to identify the dull sound that had awakened her, but she was not successful. And why, she wondered, had she immediately thought of the Caribs? She had never even seen one of them. She had only heard the stories, the dreadful tales of their bestial ways.

Suddenly she was sorry she had awakened her husband. He would find her foolish. She wished for the sun to come up and wash away her fears with its light. She prayed for daylight and the resumption of routine chores. It was time for manioc planting and there were baskets to be made—

Suddenly the village gushed with noise. War whoops filled the air, a sound Mixya had never heard before. Nyna sat up, startled. Mixya grabbed her from the hammock and carried her on her hip. "Shh," she said, pulling her daughter close.

Shocked awake by the Carib attack, the Taino men scrambled to desperately defend themselves and their families. The wind carried their shouts.

Mixya stiffened. If they stayed in the hut, they would certainly be found and killed. Mixya crawled to the rear of the hut and fluttered her hand inside the basket. She felt the blade of the sharp knife and grasped it.

Listening to her heart pound in her chest, she held Nyna, crept out the door, and ran into the forest. Darker here, with the moonlight obscured by the thick canopy of trees, mother and daughter scrunched down in a brush thicket. They could still hear the cries and commotion in the village. Nyna put her hands over her ears and rocked. "Mother, Mother, Mother," she whimpered.

A shadow lumbered through the forest, darting in and out of the diffuse light. The figure was difficult to track, appearing and disappearing in the trees.

Nyna's whimpering grew louder, her eyes flickering with terror.

Mixya put her down, but kept an arm wrapped around her. "Quiet, little one. Quiet." She knew the Caribs were going to find them. Her hands shook as she thought of the savages and how they would kill her beloved daughter.

The silhouette appeared closer, and she could feel the vibration of the earth as his feet pounded the ground. The brush rattled. He was here!

With a sudden rush of courage, Mixya sprang to her feet and ran at the figure. She held the knife firmly in her hand. She lunged at the man and plunged the knife into him. She aimed at his throat, but at the last moment the man lurched to the side, and she wounded him in the shoulder.

Her victim grunted in pain and reeled backward, clutching the knife that protruded from his shoulder. He stopped, breathed a ragged breath, and staggered toward her.

"Oh, no!" Mixya cried.

Nyna screamed.

2

"Obaec!" Mixya's hands flew to her mouth. She had stabbed her husband!

"No! No!" she wailed.

"You and Nyna have to get away," he said, blood spilling through his fingers. "Before the sun rises. Follow me," he said.

"I am so sorry," she said, embracing him. "I thought you were a Carib." Blood smeared across her cheek as she pressed her head on his chest.

Nyna wrapped her arms around the legs of her parents and cried softly. Obaec touched the top of her head comfortingly.

"There is no time," he said. "They will kill you both. Come."

Obaec led them around the village and down the beach, stumbling now and again as he grew weaker. He tripped over a piece of driftwood and fell onto the sand, staining the white beach a deep scarlet. Nyna covered her mouth to silence her cries as her mother helped Obaec to his feet.

"There," he said, pointing to the flotilla of Carib piraguas. The Taino canoes were beached in full view of the village. They would be spotted easily if they risked taking a piragua of their own. A Carib dugout was the only choice. "Hurry," he said.

When they reached the large canoes, Obaec directed his wife to get in one. He lifted Nyna and put her in the

piragua, then turned to Mixya. The woman saw something in her husband's face. She saw the pain from his
wound cloud his eyes, but she witnessed something else
even more disturbing.

"You are not going with us, are you?" she asked. Her
blood turned cold as it ran through her veins.

"Get in, woman."

"We will all go," Mixya said, "or none of us will go.
We will stay and hide in the forest together."

Obaec swayed with dizziness. Blood slicked the right
side of his body. "No," he said. "We would be found."

Mixya put her hand over the bleeding hole in his
shoulder. "I have done this to you, husband. I will take
care of you, heal you, love you."

Obaec pushed her away. "You are wasting time. Get
in."

She stared into her husband's eyes and touched her
palm to his cheek. "Then you will go with us."

Obaec looked down at his wound. "I cannot. I would
be a burden. You must go with Nyna to take care of
her," Obaec said. "Our daughter needs you."

Mixya reluctantly got in the canoe.

Suddenly she arched her back and grunted. Mixya
twisted back to look at her husband and fell forward,
her chest thumping on the side of the dugout. A long
shaft stuck out of her back.

"Mother!" Nyna screamed.

Obaec looked behind them. The moonlight shone on
a single Carib kicking up sand as he ran down the beach
toward them. Mixya lay still. With a swift yank Obaec
pulled the Carib lance from her back. Carefully he
turned her and held her head up. Her eyes stared
aimlessly . . . no focus . . . no spirit. She was gone.

Obaec shoved the piragua into the water, groaning
with the pain. He heaved again, and the canoe slid without a ripple into the surf. "Lay flat in the bottom," he
told Nyna, pushing the dugout deeper. He was winded,

and the pain and bleeding quickly sapped his strength. His voice rattled like dead palms.

Nyna's only chance of survival was to have the piragua catch a current that would carry her to another Taino island. Even if she made it to an uninhabited island, she would at least have a chance at survival. Here she would surely perish at the torturous hands of the Carib. The evil ones only let the young women live, not the older ones, nor the children. They killed everyone except the women they took away with them to serve as slaves and concubines. Obaec's whole family was doomed to die at the foul hands of the savages! He prayed he could save his young daughter.

Water above his waist now, he pulled Mixya's body from the piragua. It splashed into the sea.

"They will not have you, too!" he said to Nyna.

Nyna sobbed, the sound blending with the pounding of the surf.

The Carib reached the water. Obaec could not permit him to get to Nyna.

Images of the Carib attack so long ago skidded across his mind, the horror of it all.

"Father!" Nyna wailed as he let go of the canoe.

"Take the paddle," he yelled. "You have seen me do it. Take the paddle!"

She was so young, so small, he thought. He wasn't even sure she could use the paddle. With the last of his strength, Obaec pulled himself proudly erect and ran at the Carib. Hot, shooting pain ripped through his wounded shoulder as he thrust both arms toward the sky.

"Here I am!" he shouted. "Come for me!"

Nyna shrunk into the bottom of the boat, but kept her head just high enough so her eyes peered over the rim of the dugout. Tears distorting her vision, she watched her brave father buckle under the blow of a Carib war club. He sank in the shallow moonlit water, and Nyna's mouth opened and let out a cry. Her chest crushed with fear and anguish, her stomach knotted. Then Obaec slowly rose from the sea, water sliding in sheets off his body. The Carib struck again. Obaec warded off the blow with his right forearm. But the Carib was strong and full of feral energy. He came at her father once more, swinging wildly, powerfully, striking the side of Obaec's head. Again he slumped into the sea.

"Father!" Nyna screamed. "Get up! No! No!"

She waited for him to rise out of the surf as he did before, but as the dugout rocked in the sea, Nyna finally realized her father was not going to stand again. He was with her mother, silent, still, beneath the blue water. Nyna looked at the long wooden paddle. She didn't want to touch it, put her hands where *their* sweaty hands had been.

She called out for her father and mother, crying at the sky. She heard the shrieks of the Carib as he came for her, trudging through the water.

Finally she picked up the paddle. It was heavy and awkward. She lowered the wide end into the sea and pushed the water with the paddle, as hard and fast as she could. The piragua moved more swiftly, riding the waves, until finally the Carib and the shore vanished in darkness.

It was not long before her arms ached and she felt sick, as though she might vomit. She lost her grip on the paddle, and it slipped silently into the ocean. She reached over the edge, stretching for it. Her fingertips barely touched the tip of the paddle. Instead of drawing the paddle to her, her touch edged the paddle farther away. She watched as it drifted farther and farther. Nyna lay down and shriveled into a ball in the bottom of the canoe. She put her hands over her head and cried. She cried from sorrow and heartache, and she cried from desperation and fear. Her face was wet with tears and her nose ran. Even though she knew her mother was dead and couldn't hear her, Nyna cried for her. Mother always made things better, took the hurts away, and stilled her fears. She wanted her now, wanted her mother's soft voice to assure her everything would be all right. Nyna wanted to feel Mother's hand stroke her hair. She lay there, shaking and whimpering, afraid to lift her head to see if the Carib was swimming after her. At this moment he could be only an arm's length from the piragua, his evil black eyes glowing with wild excitement. He would latch on to the side of the canoe, turn it over, and spill her into the ocean. Then he would dive for her and slash her with his knife before returning to the shore. She would be food for the sharks. Perhaps close by there was even a large dugout filled with the savages, all of them with wicked eyes!

She cried until too exhausted to continue. Sleep came to her just before dawn. She didn't dream.

When the sun lapped its hot tongue across her back, Nyna awakened. She was gritty and sticky from the sea's salt and the tears that had dried on her skin. Cautiously she reared her head, and the wind took her hair, whisking it gently off her shoulders. All about her was blue sea, darker than she had ever seen the water before, almost black. Nyna looked in all directions, but there was no land, no sandy beach or trees. She was alone.

When the sun was high above her, Nyna's throat grew dry. Her stomach grumbled, and she wished she had some cassava bread to nibble on.

Later in the day, the sun straight ahead of her, Nyna propped her head on the side of the piragua. She wanted to go home. Her eyes stung as if ready to fill with tears. She sniffed and swiped her nose with the back of her hand. She missed her mother and father. She was hungry and thirsty, and so alone.

3

The sun kept at her, searing her with its scalding sheets of heat. Her lips fissured and stung with the dusting of salt. Her eyes burned.

So thirsty, so terribly thirsty.

Nyna crawled onto her knees. How long had she been floating in this terrible canoe? She recalled at least three days, but after that her memory was hazy. She wanted to go home. She whimpered.

The water sparkled with the blinding sun. Nyna stared, thinking she could see the reflection of her father's face. She cupped her hands and dipped them in the beautiful blue water. The piragua rocked, threatening to tip. Nyna held her breath until the dugout settled. Again she made a bowl with her hands, then slowly lifted the water to her lips. Most of the water drained between her fingers, but there was enough to wet her mouth.

More. So thirsty.

The seawater burned her lips and throat, but for an instant it satisfied the powerful thirst. Her stomach did not fare as well, and she retched. Her mother had always told her not to drink the seawater. Was it poison? She had never questioned why. It didn't taste good.

Nyna folded herself back into the bottom of the dugout. A thin veil of white salt coated her golden brown body and dulled her thick black hair. She wanted to cry, but didn't have the strength.

By dusk, she wasn't sure if another day had passed or

not. Was the twilight dawn or sundown? She had slept on and off, sometimes waking and thinking she was home, then jerking awake when she remembered the truth.

The canoe suddenly bucked. Except for the gentle rocking, movement ceased. The canoe was grounded. Nyna lifted her head. Dizziness swept over her, and her torso swayed as she raised up on her knees.

White beach stretched as far as she could see, beautiful trailing flowers, tall dune reeds, and thickets of brush, green trees. Nyna blinked, thinking the image would disappear. When it didn't, she opened her mouth to call out, but then pressed her lips together, sealing out any sound she might have made. This was not home.

Carib? she wondered, sinking lower in the piragua. The dugout rocked with the waves. She had to hide. Nyna pulled herself up. Her arms felt weighted and her legs light, knees unable to withstand her own weight. Her small muscles trembled as she got to her feet and struggled out of the canoe. The cool water washed across her calves. Nyna made her way to the beach, twice falling with weakness before stepping on dry land.

The sand was still warm from the afternoon sun, and it stuck to her sweaty body. She heard herself grunting and crying as her little feet struggled to move her over the dune into the thick brush.

She cried softly for her mother, her face scrunching from the muscle pain and exertion.

Finally over the sandy hill, Nyna crawled into the dense brush. Her small chest heaved for breath. A drizzle of rain began as she coiled into a ball. The wind picked up, and she shuddered with a chill. Her shoulders shook with her crying.

"Take me," she whispered. If she died she could be with her mother and father . . . safe . . . warm.

Heavier rain fell, soaking her, washing the salt away. She opened her mouth.

*   *   *

At the change of the tide, as quietly as it had arrived, the Carib piragua drifted away on the current.

Even during the periods of rain, Nyna slept through the night. She didn't wake until the early sunlight struck her face. She partially opened one eye. Towering puffs of white clouds floated in the bright blue sky. Nyna tucked her arms and legs even closer to her body. The hunger was gone, but the thirst remained. Her mother would have brought her water to remedy her parched throat. What would she do with no mother and no father?

"Mother," she whispered, her voice scratching her throat. A soft wind rustled the brush. Mother's breath.

Slowly, Nyna drifted into part sleep, part dream.

Joog crawled out of his hut, careful not to wake his mother. It was early enough, he thought.

The boy stretched in the pale yellow light of the sunrise. If he hurried, he might collect some conchs in the shallow water and bring them back to his mother. She would be pleased. He would provide well for her, even if he was young.

He thought of the lines that channeled the skin about his mother's eyes. She still missed his father. Her hair had grown long again, but her heart still ached. It was the custom to cut the hair short as a symbol of grief when a loved one died. Nihapu had taken her husband's knife and sawed through her hair when she learned of his death. Now her hair was long again, and the grieving period should have ended. It had not.

Joog breathed in a lungful of the morning air. He would greet the day later when he returned with the conch. He picked up a basket and trotted through the village, through the palmetto-rich scrub pine forest and onto the beach.

Ankle-deep in water, Joog traveled up the shoreline.

He found three conchs right away and put them in the basket. The sun was getting higher. Maybe it was not as early as he thought. He'd take a shortcut through the woods to get back. Joog's brown calves tightened as he walked through the sand and up the dune.

Surprised by movement caught from the corner of his eye, Joog dropped to a crouch. A raccoon waddled through the brush. Ah, if I only had my bola, he thought.

He put down the basket and went to all fours. This was a good time to practice hunting, he thought. Quietly, lightly touching each hand and knee to the ground before applying weight, he crept closer to the raccoon. How close could he get? he wondered.

The raccoon stopped and looked behind him. Joog froze, not even blinking. He thought about his breathing, concentrating on slow, shallow breaths that did not flare his nostrils, nor cause his chest to move much.

The raccoon sniffed the air and looked around, but did not appear to see him. Joog's heart beat faster with the small victory. Then the raccoon was on the move again.

The boy slowly lifted his right hand from the ground, continuing to stalk the animal. A noise distracted him. It came from his left, and he cocked his head in that direction. But he didn't want to lose the raccoon. He was sure he could get very, very close. It was a game . . . one his grandfather, the cacique, had taught him. "Be one with the soil, the air, the trees," he had told Joog. "A good hunter can get almost close enough to capture the prey with his hands. Be close enough that the kill is clean. A good hunter does not wound an animal so that it gets away and suffers until its death. Man owes the animal for giving up his flesh."

Joog's grandfather, Chogatis, took him to the woods and taught him what the words meant. He showed Joog the way to communicate with the spirits of the trees, the stones, the earth. He showed him how to be one with all those things. No wonder Chogatis was the cacique, the chief. He seemed to know everything!

His grandfather told him that a good hunter practices all the time, perfecting his skills. So, here was an opportunity to practice, Joog thought. How very close he was to the raccoon already. Would not his mother and Chogatis be surprised if along with the conch he brought home a raccoon he had caught with his bare hands!

He looked back toward the animal. But then there was that noise again. A worthy hunter should be curious and careful, also, he thought. The sound he heard was like a soft cry. Perhaps there was a hurt animal hiding in the clump of brush. Or suppose it was a warrior, an enemy? He was obligated to investigate.

Joog continued on his hands and knees, silently approaching the thicket. Before pushing away any of the undergrowth, he stopped and waited, listening, using all his senses. There were no more sounds, no smells to help him determine what was hiding.

Cautiously he took his right hand and pulled down some grasses. As the grass bent, some of the wiry blades split open. The scent was the same as if he had walked upon the grass, crushing it. He noted the sweet aroma.

Joog gazed through the tangle of scrub. His breath seized up in his chest. He squinted and changed his angle. Like a rush of cold water streaming through his body, his arms tingled. There, nestled in the brush was a child, a girl. She wore a kind of short apron suspended from a belt about her hips. It was not made from a hide or any plant that he knew. On one arm was a bracelet made of a most remarkable substance. He had never seen anything like it before. The color was that of the sun and when the light hit it, the brilliance flashed back in his eyes.

Joog inspected the girl. Definitely younger than he. Her hair was long and as black as the night sky when it rained, though it was tangled and full of snarls. Entwined in the mat of hair were several feathers. Though worn and frayed, they were of incredible colors. Brilliant green, yellow, and scarlet. What bird could this have come from? He noticed another peculiar feature. Her forehead was strangely shaped, somehow flattened. So odd. Where had she come from? She was not Ais, not from this clan, nor any other Ais clan. Nor was she like any other people he had ever seen or heard of, and he knew of many peoples. She was not Jeaga, not Tequesta, Jororo, Mayaca, Tocobaga, Calusa, nor any of the other people that lived in the region. Had she fallen from the sky, maybe even from the sun itself? The bracelet drew his eyes back once again. Perhaps it was even made of the sun.

She lay still, and her eyelids, with their long dark lashes, were closed. The girl breathed out a sigh. Ah, that was the noise he had heard. He had to hurry back to the village and tell his grandfather. Chogatis would know what to do.

Quickly, Joog grabbed the basket of conch, then ran home full speed.

"Grandfather," he called, entering the village. The people were just beginning to stir. The sweet smell of berry cakes wafted through the village, carried on cook fire smoke. He was surely waking those who still slept. "Grandfather!"

Chogatis sat in front of his shelter, which was larger than other dwellings in the village. His legs were crossed, his back straight, his chin tilted so slightly upward. His eyes were closed. Chogatis greeted the day.

Joog dashed across the main plaza, nearly losing his footing in the sudden stop before his grandfather.

Chogatis opened his eyes and stared at the boy. "One does not disturb another when he is greeting the day."

"Sorry, Grandfather," Joog said, breathless from the run. He attempted to control his panting, but still spoke on short breaths. "I have found something."

Chogatis peered in the basket. "Conch? Why do they excite you?"

Joog shook his head, his dark hair whipping across his shoulders. "No, no, no. Not conch."

"Catch your breath, boy. In through the nose." Chogatis demonstrated, breathing in deeply. He exhaled through his mouth, blowing through pursed lips. "Out through the mouth."

Joog imitated his grandfather.

"Now, sit and tell me what has you so excited."

Joog lowered himself to the ground. He glanced about to see if anyone was watching. He already knew he had attracted attention, and now he thought better of it. Chogatis might prefer this to be a secret. He spoke quietly, almost in a whisper. "I went for conch for Mother this morning . . . very early. On my return I found something. A girl."

"What do you mean? Who has a lost child?"

"No, she is not one of us. She is not Ais."

"You found a girl, a child, and she is not Ais?"

Joog nodded vigorously. "Yes, she was sleeping in a thick clump of brush. Hiding there. I think she comes from the sun!"

Chogatis arched his brows. "A girl from the sun. How interesting." The grandfather held back a smile, but Joog still saw the skepticism in Chogatis's eyes.

"You can see her for yourself," he said. "Her forehead is unusual." Joog ran his hand from his eyebrows to the top of his head trying to illustrate the shape. "And, Grandfather, she wears this most incredible bracelet on her arm! It is made from something the color of the sun, and shines just as brightly. And there are feathers from birds I have never seen." Joog sprang to his feet. "Come see. I will show you!"

Chogatis stood. "Get your mother," he said. "If this girl is hurt or ill, she will need a woman who is a healer."

Joog grabbed the basket and sprinted through the village. Nihapu sat by her small fire, fanning the coals. The air was damp, and the fire did not want to cooperate.

"Where have you been?" she asked, aggravation tinting her voice.

"Look," he said, handing her the basket. "I wanted to surprise you this morning. I will always provide for you."

"You make me age with worry. I wake and my son is not anywhere."

"I would have been back earlier," he said. "Mother, I was stalking a raccoon, and I found something. I told Grandfather, and he told me to get you."

"What did you find?" Nihapu asked.

"You have to go with us," Joog said. "I found a girl . . . an incredible girl."

Nihapu rose. Her son had passion for whatever he discovered or did. If he fashioned a tool, he did nothing except concentrate on that task for days. Then he would make more, modifying them, finding more excitement in each one. Then several moon phases later, he would be on to something else with equal intensity. The child was filled with so much zest and fire. His genuine enthusiasm and the thrill he found in simple things always charmed the elders. She looked at her boy's face, and her heart filled with love.

"Where? What kind of girl?"

"By the beach," he said, turning away, anxious for her to follow. "You will see," he said. "I will take you and Chogatis to see her. Hurry."

Chogatis and Nihapu followed the boy down the shore. He stopped twice, searching the beach, appearing unsure of his location. Finally he pointed to the spot where he believed the girl to be.

"There," he whispered. "Follow me. Be very quiet."

Chogatis nodded at Joog and then followed, Nihapu just behind.

Joog stopped short of the clump of brush. "In there."

Chogatis stooped and tried to see through the vegetation.

"Get closer," Joog whispered.

Chogatis went down on his hands and knees. He pushed aside a sheaf of grass and weed. There, just as Joog had said, was the small girl. He gazed at the bracelet. It did indeed shine with the color of the sun. He backed away.

Nihapu took a peek and covered her mouth with her hand in surprise.

"Where is she from?" Joog asked in a whisper.

Chogatis shook his head. "She is a strange one."

"Did you see the bracelet and the feathers?" the boy asked.

Both Chogatis and Nihapu nodded.

"Remarkable," Chogatis said.

"I think the child is ill," Nihapu said. "And she appears burned from the sun. I will prepare some medicines."

"No," Chogatis said sharply. "Not yet. Let me consult Uxaam. The shaman may be able to determine who this girl is."

"But look at her," Nihapu said. "She needs help. She is frail and sick. She sleeps a sick sleep." She took a step toward the thicket. "I will carry her back."

Chogatis firmly laid a hand on her shoulder. "No, you will not."

4

Joog hid behind the dune, peeking over the sandy hill to watch as Chogatis and Uxaam inspected his find. He wished he could see more clearly.

Uxaam crawled next to the peculiar, sleeping child. He looked at her, studying the shape of her head, the feathers, and especially the bracelet. There was nothing strange about the shape of her eyes. Her skin color and hair were also similar to the Ais's. He held his outstretched hands over her, detecting the body heat. From this he hoped to gather a sense of her spirit. He moved his hands in unison, sweeping the length of her body. He closed his eyes and waited, expecting his senses to tell him something.

A few moments later he looked back at Chogatis and shrugged.

Chogatis urged him on.

Cautiously the shaman allowed one finger to touch her hair and then her cheek. The child moaned and fluttered her eyelids. Uxaam drew back and sat very still and quiet. The child mumbled something, but the words were unintelligible. What kind of language was that? He had never heard it before.

When the girl settled back into sleep, the shaman touched the bracelet she wore. How extraordinarily beautiful. And those feathers, such magnificent colors.

Uxaam plucked a hair from her head, backed away, and stood up, beckoning Chogatis to take a look.

Chogatis stooped and gazed through the brush. When the cacique finished studying the girl again, he and Uxaam moved a short distance away.

"Do you think the ocean has spit her up onto the shore?" Chogatis asked.

"No. She is not from this world," Uxaam said. "Chogatis, she wears such amazing ornaments! The bracelet. It is not true yellow as the ocher of the earth, but more like the blazing yellow that streaks the clouds at sunrise and sunset. It is like the sun itself!" Uxaam paused, then said, "She comes from there." He pointed to the sky.

"Maybe she has fallen," Chogatis said.

"I am perplexed," the shaman said. "I have never seen someone with a head shaped like hers. Wherever she comes from, it is far, far away. I have an uneasy feeling about this." Uxaam glanced back toward the clump of brush where the girl lay. "I could not feel her spirit. My instinct says let her be. I will call on the spirits for help." He dangled the piece of the girl's hair in front of the cacique. "Until we know more, leave her there. If she is cast out of the heavens, we should not interfere."

"Nihapu is willing to take her. If she wakes and is lucid, we could learn more."

"Not yet," Uxaam said.

When Uxaam and Chogatis left, Joog ran over the dune and crept up on the sleeping girl. She was so small, he thought. What could be dangerous about this little child? The bracelet, the feathers, they were things of beauty. Maybe where she came from a head like hers was also considered beautiful.

The girl moved and moaned.

Joog watched her, fascinated. "Are you awake?" he asked. He would ask her where she was from and how she had gotten here. Why didn't Chogatis and Uxaam do that? It seemed so simple.

"Can you hear me?" he asked. He reached to touch her, then pulled back. If he touched her, would something happen to him? Was she a shapeshifter that might turn into a bear, a bear with a huge head and ferocious teeth and powerful claws? Did she have that kind of magic? he wondered. The brilliance of the bracelet made him blink.

Joog sat beside the girl, watching her sleep. The child captivated him. What if she were not cast out of the heavens, what if she had lost her way?

He recalled the time when his father was killed and the Jeaga captured him. He had been so afraid. Perhaps this girl needed just one friend, as he had.

Joog gently shook her shoulder.

Nothing happened to him. Her skin was slightly cool and damp, but pleasingly smooth. He leaned close and sniffed. She smelled of the rain and the sea.

The girl's eyelids slowly raised. He could see she took a minute to focus. When she saw him, she whimpered, her mouth screwing up as if she were going to cry.

When he had been captured, he was strong and he had fought. He felt she might do the same if she had had the strength. But she was too weak, and too young. Yet, still, she had to feel the same kind of fear he had.

Joog smiled in an effort to reassure her. He cocked his head. "Who are you?"

The child coiled more tightly.

"Do not be afraid," he said. "I will not hurt you."

The girl put her hands over her face. Joog stroked the backs of her hands. "Do not be afraid, little one."

Her skin was dry and burned. "Did you burn yourself living so close to the sun?" He stared at her cracked lips. She needed water.

"I will be back," he said, scooting away. He ran to the village. In his shelter he grabbed a water pouch made from an otter's stomach. Next he picked up a large whelk shell he could use as a drinking cup.

"What are you doing?" Nihapu asked, coming up behind him.

Joog flinched. "Water from the cenote—"

Nihapu looked at the shell dipper. "Why do you need that to get the water? You have the water pouch."

Joog smelled the fish stew his mother brewed. "I was going to sneak a dip of the stew," he said, letting a wide grin wash over his face. "You are the finest cook," he said. "It smells so good."

"I would have fixed you a bowl, boy."

"No, no. Go about your chores," he said. "Just a swallow will do."

Joog brushed past her, stopped at the pot steeping over the fire. He dipped the shell in the stew, then sipped it. "Delicious," he said, putting down the ladle. Without giving his mother a chance to ask any more questions, he sprinted off.

After gathering water from the sinkhole, he went straight to the girl and crawled next to her.

"I am back," he said, touching her arm just below the bracelet. "I have brought you some water."

Nyna opened her eyes at his touch.

"Water," Joog said. "You must be thirsty."

He put some water on his fingers and touched them to her mouth, wetting her lips.

She cringed, the water burning the cracks in her lips. Joog drew his hand back, but she reached for it. The girl said something, but the language was different.

"More," he said. "More water?"

The child's black eyes stared at him. He didn't see as much fear in them now.

"Here," he said, lifting her head with one hand. "Pick up your head." He let go and the child propped herself on an elbow. He brought the pouch near her mouth. This was going to be difficult without the cup.

"Open," he said, but the girl didn't respond. "Open your mouth and I will pour," he said.

Joog waited a moment, then opened his own mouth,

held the pouch above it, and poured a thin stream of water into his mouth. "Now, you," he said.

He pried his index finger in her mouth and pulled down on the lower jaw. "Leave it open," he said, slowly withdrawing his finger, then tilting her chin up. Without any sudden moves that could frighten her, he lifted the pouch and slowly dribbled water into her mouth.

The girl eagerly swallowed, and when Joog started to upright the pouch, her hand was suddenly over his, encouraging him to give her more water.

"I was right," he said. "You are thirsty."

When she was done drinking, she flopped down, short of breath.

"Your journey must have been long," Joog said.

The girl's eyes closed. She coughed weakly several times, then drifted into sleep.

Joog sat at her side, staring at her. Who was this wonder child? He glanced at the sun, then back at her. "Sun child," he said. "Is that your name?"

Night fell over the village in a sudden heavy curtain of blackness. Storm clouds rushed over the setting sun, then later obliterated the stars and moon. Thunder convulsed the thatch roofs, and the ground quaked. Uxaam sat cross-legged in the center of a raised, open-sided platform. He stirred a small fire with a stick and watched the smoke funnel up to the roof. This was a ceremonial place, a place the shaman talked to the spirits. A sacred place.

Tonight he was troubled. The girl child, the one who carried a piece of the sun, could appear to be something she was not. She could be a witch, one who could steal the soul and power of another's life and add what she stole to her own power. Witches fed on the weak and feeble. They could change into any person or animal living on the ground. And if they were especially powerful, they could take on the shapes and flight of birds. The feathers, he thought.

Lightning fractured the sky, and the rain pounded harder. The wind thrashed, stripping leaves from the trees, twisting off whole branches, blowing the rain through the platform, pelting the shaman's naked back.

The floor of the platform reverberated like drumbeats beneath the spirit man's haunches. He chanted, calling out even above the howl of the wind and the beat of rain. His words were those of the ancient forgotten tongue, the language of the shaman, the voice of the spirits. His chant rang with a mystical rhythm, a fluency that bordered on melody. He complemented his chant with the counter rhythm of his turtle-shell rattle.

The cup of water before him seethed with aromas of magical plants and herbs. Taken from the fire just before the rain, the potion still steamed. He held the strange girl's piece of hair over the bowl, then let it drop into the mixture. Uxaam gathered his own hair to the back of his neck, twisted it into a cord, and used two curved bone pins to hold it there.

The rain-chilled air made the shaman shiver. Uxaam loosened the drawstring of the pouch he wore at his waist. He pulled out several smaller packets, then decided on one. He untied the cordage that bound the rolled leaf into a neat pack. Inside was a small amount of pulverized plant parts. He pinched up a bit, and then put it under his tongue. Uxaam's chant muted to a mere hum.

He turned to the damp fire that burned inside his shelter. He waved his rattle over it and spoke softly, leaning in to the fire so it could hear his voice. The coals erupted into small flames.

Uxaam straightened and threw a fistful of green pine needles onto the flames. The fire hissed. Thick smoke rose.

He lifted the bowl with the potion in both hands, cradling the container beneath his nose. He sniffed, breathing in deeply. It was good. He raised the bowl over the fire and chanted, the words strong, riding the storm wind.

"Hay-ya, hay-ya. Ho. Hay-ya, hay-ya. Ho."

He followed the bowl with his eyes as he brought it to his lips and sipped. As he swallowed, he felt the liquid glide down his throat and land in his fasting belly. Again he put his mouth to the bowl and this time took a larger drink. Enough.

The shaman's head dropped, then slowly, as if struggling, he raised it up. Flashes of light and color danced before his eyes. Here, in the spirit realm, the world was distorted, as if he watched through a lens of gently moving water. Sounds were louder, echoing like the warped visual perception that rippled in front of him. But even through this distorted illusion, a man of the spirits could see other things more clearly. Though physical images were convoluted and became more obscure, the intangible things became more distinct. The shaman could detect fear, anger, love, most powerful emotions. He could sense truth and deception. And in this state, if the spirits chose to, they could evoke visions.

A swirling white mist clouded his eyes for a moment. When it lifted, blowing away like smoke in the wind, the shaman was far away. Ghostly, deep-toned cries echoed in his ears. Rich crimson blood trickled through white sand, forming a web of fine thready streams. A woman sank into the water, her blood seeping out, oozing into a surrounding circle that dyed the water red. And in the distance there rose peaks of earth unlike anything he had ever seen. What place could this be?

Uxaam's attention turned to a dark silhouette. A man, he thought, running down the beach, stumbling and shouting words Uxaam could not make out.

Then suddenly, the smell of deep sea spiraled up his nostrils. He rocked with waves. His focus blurred and faded, the haze and mist vanished, and the shaman's vision ended.

Early, just after greeting the day, Chogatis called upon Joog. "Come with me, Grandson," he said.

Joog put down his bowl and jumped to his feet. He loved outings with his grandfather. Chogatis showed him the ways, the secrets that made a man a good hunter, a good warrior. "Where are we going?" he asked.

"Follow me," Chogatis said.

Cetisa, Nihapu's sister, stood in front of her hut. "You spend a lot of time with that boy," she called out. "Seems a cacique's time could be better spent."

"Wipe your chin, woman," Chogatis said.

Cetisa looked confused, but touched her chin with her finger.

"I thought I saw rattlesnake venom dribble from your mouth as you spoke," Chogatis said.

Cetisa turned on her heel and disappeared inside.

"Why is she so hateful?" Joog asked. "Sometimes my mother cries over the things she says to her."

"She is a disgruntled woman. Your mother has the healing gift and Cetisa does not. And Nihapu has you. The spirits have not seen fit to give Cetisa a child."

"Because she is too mean!" Joog said, then laughed. The boy walked backward in front of Chogatis. "What lesson do you teach me today?"

"Patience," Chogatis said.

By the shallow stream, Chogatis sat. "Sit as I do."

Joog crossed his legs and rested his hands in his lap.

"There is a special place an Ais man can go if he has the patience to travel far. In this place there is oneness with the rest of the earth. A man can become one with nature."

"How far is it?" Joog asked.

"Patience, boy. Patience. Pick up a stone and hold it in your hand." Joog picked up a rock and Chogatis did the same. "Take your time and explore it. Feel it with your hands, smell it, taste it. Listen to what it says."

Joog fondled the rock.

"Let the stone speak to you."

Joog sniffed the rock, then put his tongue on it. He held it to his ear, then looked at Chogatis.

"Do not hurry it," Chogatis said, "or you will not hear the stone when it speaks."

Chogatis rolled his rock over in his hands, concentrating. Joog copied his grandfather.

After a while, Chogatis put down his rock. "The place I spoke of is not a place I can take you. You must go yourself."

"How will I find it?"

Chogatis swept his hand in front of his face. "You cannot see them, but there are curtains you must pass through. To reach this place of oneness you must pass through four curtains. These are very special passageways, each one taking you closer and farther than the one before."

Joog's eyes widened and filled with wonder.

"You live now in the world of the first curtain. Your vision of things is limited here, distracted by movement and conversation, activity. You must find your way from this world and pass through the second curtain. There you will be relaxed and at peace."

"Then will I be there?" Joog asked.

Chogatis smiled. "Oh, no. Remember, patience. You must pass through all four curtains before you enter the place where there is no separation between yourself and everything else."

Chogatis stared straight ahead, his long dark hair catching the soft breeze that swept it to his back. "A good hunter must find his way through those curtains. Then he can see and hear, smell every raccoon, deer, rabbit, lizard that moves through the forest. He can sit in the middle of the forest and blend with everything around him, even have creatures of all kinds come to him and sit beside him. Those who cannot pass through the curtains are discontent, moving through the woods, seeing nothing. They jump from one thought to the next, never able to concentrate on their surroundings. They are poor hunters."

"I want to be a good hunter! How?"

"First you must learn to pass through the second curtain. Close your eyes," Chogatis said.

The man and the boy closed their eyes.

"Take four deep breaths," the grandfather said. "One from each of the directions. Through your nose, out your mouth."

Joog did as he was told.

"Tense your feet," Chogatis said. "Make all the muscles in your feet hard. Squeeze. Let go. Do that again, squeeze harder this time."

Joog tensed his feet so much that he grimaced.

"Let go. Deep breath. Breathe out. Now tense your calf muscles. Hold them tight. Let go. Breathe."

Chogatis led the boy up through all the parts of his body, ending with his scalp.

"This time tense your whole body. Make it as hard as the stone you held."

Joog tightened all his muscles, holding his breath. Finally Chogatis said, "Release."

Joog blew out his pent-up breath.

"Let yourself sink into the earth. Feel there is no beginning or ending of you. Relax and melt into your surroundings. Hear even the wind stirred by a butterfly's wings. Experience all the sensations around you. If any thoughts come into your head, acknowledge them and then let them go."

The two sat quietly for a few moments. At last Chogatis told Joog to open his eyes. "Practice often. When you get very good at passing through this second curtain, you will be able to do it with your eyes open, even when you are doing other things."

Chogatis stood.

"Wait," Joog said. "What about the other curtains, the place of oneness?"

"Patience. The day you took your first step you did not go right on to running."

Joog nodded that he understood. Patience was a difficult thing. He had wanted to check on the sun child when he first awakened, but knew he could not just run off so quickly. Patience. Patience. He would check on the girl after they returned to the village.

5

Joog crouched next to the child. "Water," he said. "Drink some."

The girl's mouth opened, and Joog poured water into it. She choked when she swallowed, coughing and spewing.

He lifted her head. When she stopped choking, Joog laid her down. "Are you hungry?"

The boy pulled a piece of berry cake from his pouch. "I saved this for you," he said. "Here." He pushed the cake toward her, but the girl just stared.

"Food," Joog said, taking a taste of the cake. "Good."

He offered the cake to the girl again. Maybe it was too big. He tore off a small piece and put it to her lips. The child finally opened her mouth. She chewed weakly.

The girl looked worse today. How was he going to keep coming here to bring her water and food? He was afraid for her.

Joog pointed to himself and said his name. He repeated it several times, then pointed to her.

"Nyna," she whispered.

A big grin wrapped itself around Joog's mouth. "Nyna. A nice name. I have never heard that before. Want some more water?" He held up the water pouch. Her lips came apart, and she attempted to sit up, but was too weak. Joog lifted her head and positioned the spout to her mouth. He let the water dribble out slowly. Some of it ran down her chin.

When she finished drinking, Joog covered her with a small hide blanket. Nyna's eyes followed the boy. He did not like the way they appeared deeper in her head, with a dull glaze covering them. He would bring her some fish-stew broth. That would be easier for her to eat than the berry cake.

Joog gathered his things and left.

"I have had a vision," Uxaam said to the Council. They sat in a circle. Chogatis held the Talking Stick in case they needed it. In heated discussions, whoever held the Talking Stick was given the right to speak without interruption. The rules dictated that the Stick be passed to anyone who wanted to speak.

A few moments before Uxaam announced his vision, Chogatis had informed the Council of the girl on the beach. Everyone was curious, and now looked to Uxaam for explanations.

"You consulted the spirits?" Chogatis asked.

"Yes," Uxaam confirmed. "During the storm."

Etac, Cetisa's husband, who was the War Chief, shifted restlessly. "What have the spirits shown you?" he asked.

"Carnage. Some kind of butchery. Blood ran like small rivers through the sand. I am convinced this girl child has been cast out of her world. There is bloodshed surrounding her. She could be a sorcerer or even a spirit."

"Bloodshed?" another man asked.

"I saw the blood spilling on white sand, a woman slain, a man running on the beach," Uxaam said. "I heard cries. And the land spiked up in enormous peaks in the distance. I know of no place like that."

"Maybe she escaped from this place," Chogatis said. "Perhaps she fled from something."

"But where would she have come from?" Etac asked. "And how would she have gotten here? She is but a small child!"

"That is right," Uxaam said. "It could be that she is

an outcast, hurled out of her world. We cannot interfere. She did not come to us, she was found by accident."

Another man, squatting rather than sitting, rocked back. "Could it be that she is not alone? How would a small child from a far land come here alone?"

Chogatis fanned a mosquito from his face as he heard the collective gulping of breath at the thought that others accompanied this girl.

"My point," Uxaam said. "We have found no one else. No one looks after her. She is alone, and it would be impossible for a child so small to travel alone any great distance."

Chogatis tapped a stick in the dirt. "Then your advice is to leave her where she is. We should not help her in any way, help her so she might restore her health and tell us where she is from?"

Uxaam's eyes blinked with the challenge. "I only tell you what the spirits chose to show me in a vision."

"I understand," Chogatis said. "But as we have said, she is only a child. We must be certain we do the right thing. Could she be a test? Might the spirits test our goodness and charity?"

"I suppose that is another possibility," Uxaam said.

Chogatis tilted his head to the side. "I am not sure what they have shown you."

The cacique rose to his feet, ending the Council meeting.

"If you were asked to care for that strange girl on the beach, what would you do for her?" Joog asked his mother.

"Small amounts of food . . . often. She would need to build her strength. Teas and broths. Medicines."

"What kind of medicines?"

Nihapu used a stick to push aside the stew pot's flat rock cover. Picking up another stick, she tweezed a hot stone from the fire and dropped it in her brew. She pushed the cover back over the top of the pot.

"Let me see," Nihapu said, putting her index finger over her lips in thought. "Medicines that would keep bad spirits away from wounds, medicines that would encourage her appetite and speed her recovery."

Nihapu looked at her son. "Why do you ask these questions? Why do you not run along and play?"

Joog fidgeted. She would know his plan if he pursued this line of questioning. How was he to give Nyna the right medicines, the right nourishment?

"Go play," his mother said again.

Buhgo! he thought. He would ask Buhgo!

Joog hopped up. "Yes, Mother," he said.

Joog looked about the village. Buhgo was a boy about his own age, but Buhgo was different. He preferred to play the games of girls, and it was whispered that he had the healing gift, like Nihapu. Women were healers. The boys teased him that he was really a girl snared inside a boy's body.

Buhgo sat next to his mother, Zinni, outside their shelter. Both had clay on their hands as they formed new pots.

"Good day, Joog," Zinni said.

"Good day," Joog returned. "Buhgo, do you want to play? I will get my hoop."

Buhgo stared at Joog. "You want me to play the hoop game?"

Joog shrugged. "I thought it would be fun."

Buhgo poured water over his hands to clean them.

"Meet me by the courtyard," Joog said. "I will go get my hoop and lance."

Joog rolled the hoop and Buhgo lifted his lance. He held it shoulder high, aiming as carefully as he could before releasing it. The lance flew through the air, but missed the hoop, clattering to the ground. It was the fifth time he had missed.

"I am no good at this," Buhgo said.

Guacana, another boy of the village, paused as he passed with a friend. He pointed at Buhgo and whispered to his friend. Both boys broke out in laughter and then ran off.

"I do not feel much like playing," Joog said. "Maybe we could explore the stream."

Buhgo agreed and they walked away, leaving the hoop and lances on the ground.

As they walked, Joog tried to relax, to pass through the second curtain as Chogatis had taught him. Finally he gave up. He was not skilled yet. It would take a lot more practice, just as Chogatis had said.

They made their way to a fish weir that Joog and Chogatis had set up several days before. It was Joog's job to check it and collect the fish it trapped.

"It is said you have the healing gift like my mother," Joog said. "Do you think that is true?"

Buhgo stiffened.

"I do not think that is a bad thing, Buhgo. I think it is interesting."

"Really?" Buhgo said.

"What if someone had made a long trip, a very long journey without food or water and was very weak, what medicines would you give her?"

"You are speaking of the girl the men are talking about, right? The sun child?"

"No, no. I am just curious."

Buhgo turned away and started walking back toward the village.

"Wait," Joog said. He glared at the boy for a few moments. "I am sorry I did not tell the truth. Come with me," he said.

"You must not tell anyone," Joog said, crouching.

"No one," Buhgo said. "You are my friend."

"Come closer," Joog said. "Her name is Nyna."

Buhgo sucked in a breath.

Nyna's lids fluttered, and she turned to see them.

"She is different," Joog said. "But just look at her. She means no harm."

"What is that?" Buhgo asked, looking at the bracelet. Joog shook his head.

"No one knows. Uxaam thinks it is made of the sun."

Buhgo studied the girl, looking at her small hands, the beautiful feathers in her hair, the brilliant bracelet.

"I have to help her, Buhgo. Tell me what to do."

Buhgo touched the girl's chapped lower lip. "Have you given her water?"

"Some," Joog said.

"She needs shelter and medicine. If not, I think she will die soon."

"Can you help her?" Joog asked.

"Nihapu knows the medicines."

"But you do, too, they say."

"Not like your mother. Somehow you have to convince your grandfather to let Nihapu care for her. I do not think she has many days left."

"How?" Joog shook his head.

"Why is this so important?" Buhgo asked.

"I remember the journey with my father and another man."

"I have heard some of the story," Buhgo said.

"The Jeaga killed my father and his friend. I hid, scared they would kill me, but I was willing to die for the Ais. When they found me, one man who was their cacique wanted me dead, too. The other man persuaded the cacique to let me live. This man was named Banabas. He spared my life, took me to live with him and his wife. They treated me as their own, yet I was the enemy. They put aside their fears and ideas of the Ais, and cared for me. When they could, they returned me home, to the Hawk clan of Ais. Because of them there is less hatred between the Ais and the Jeaga. Perhaps this girl has been sent to build a trust between two peoples. Maybe someone should not be afraid and help her."

"Who are her people?"

"I do not think anyone knows. No one agrees on anything about her."

"Nyna," Buhgo said, "can you hear us?"

The girl moaned softly.

"If she is to get help, it needs to be soon," Buhgo said. "She does not even open her eyes now."

"You have to see her again," Joog said to his mother. "She is so small, it is not right. How do grown men fear such a little girl?"

"Uxaam believes she is cast out of another world. The spirits showed him a vision."

"Please," Joog pleaded. He turned to his friend. "Buhgo also thinks she will die soon without your help."

"You took Buhgo to see her? You should not have done that."

"I hoped he could help her. But he says he does not know the medicines like you do."

"Chogatis will not allow anyone to interfere with what the spirits have done with this girl."

"Do not tell him. Just come with me one more time."

Joog took his mother's hand. "Come," he said. "You are the healer of the Hawk clan of the Ais. Only you can spare her. Is that not what Banabas and Talli did for me?"

Nihapu and the two boys visited the child again.

"Buhgo is right," Nihapu said. "She is dying."

Nyna mumbled something at Nihapu's touch and a tear rolled out of her eye.

"I will do my best," Nihapu said. "I cannot let her suffer like this."

Joog plucked one of the red feathers from Nyna's hair.

As they went back to the village, he thanked his mother. "You do a good thing," he said.

"I will speak to your grandfather," she said. "But Joog, we must respect what he decides."

"I know. I will come with you."

Chogatis saw them approaching and dismissed Uxaam.

"Grandfather," Joog began, "I have been to see the girl again. I made my mother go, and also Buhgo. They fear she is dying."

Chogatis patted the ground for them to sit. "That may be. We cannot intervene."

Nihapu looked into Chogatis's eyes. "She is only a little girl. What harm can she do?"

"You are the nurturing one, Nihapu," Chogatis said. "I know it is difficult for you to see anyone suffer. That is not your way. You are a healer."

"Remember how grateful we were that someone took care of Joog, even though he was the enemy? This child is not a warrior. She is a little girl who is separated from her family. She needs our help."

"And what if she is a bad thing, as Uxaam suggests? His vision showed him much bloodshed."

"And there was bloodshed surrounding Joog when the Jeaga killed his father. But Joog was not a warrior, only a boy."

"Look," Joog said, bringing the feather from behind his back.

Cetisa came up behind them. "What is all the stir?" she asked. "And what is that?" she asked, eyeing the feather. Then her eyebrows arched. "Ah, the girl Uxaam has warned us about."

"She needs help," Nihapu said.

6

"What is that feather you have?" Cetisa asked.

"Is it not beautiful? It belongs to Nyna," Joog said.

"Who?" Cetisa asked.

"The girl," Joog answered.

"What has your son been doing?" Cetisa asked Nihapu. "Seems he has been disobeying."

Joog looked at his mother and then his grandfather. "I gave her water and tried to get her to eat, but she is too weak. She cannot harm anyone. She is dying. We need to help her!"

Chogatis eyed the feather, and Joog held it up as he continued his argument. "Where could such a feather come from?"

"Perhaps she is a witch and can change into any form as the raven can," Chogatis replied.

"Such a beautiful feather could only come from a spirit world, not a witches' world. And you have seen the bracelet! I think the spirits have shown us their signs and now test us to see if we are courageous and good."

Cetisa clucked her tongue. "He is so fanciful. Really, Nihapu, you should control your son better. First he defies his grandfather's authority, spends enough time with the forbidden child to learn her name, and now he makes up such outrageous stories."

Chogatis took the frayed feather. "I have wondered the same as you, Grandson."

"What?" Cetisa yelped. "I cannot believe you would entertain such a ridiculous idea!"

"And what if the child is a wounded spirit, Cetisa?" Nihapu asked. "If we ignore this child who is so in need, perhaps the wrath of the spirits will be cast upon the Hawk clan."

"If she is evil, we will learn soon enough," Chogatis said. "If you can bring her to good health, Nihapu, then we can learn more about her. Then I will make my decision of what to do about her. Retrieve the child. Bring her to your home and take care of her."

Cetisa huffed. "The others will not be pleased, Chogatis."

"I am the cacique, and I have made the decision."

Chogatis dismissed them all with a wave of his hand.

Nihapu carried Nyna in her arms. Both women and men stopped what they were doing and glared. Nihapu could feel all their eyes on her. The village became still and quiet as she passed, Joog and Buhgo just behind her.

Zinni's face squirmed with concern for her son.

Uxaam walked across the plaza and stood in front of Nihapu. "What is this?" he asked.

"Chogatis has given permission," she answered.

"I do not believe that. We had this discussion this very day."

Nihapu turned in Chogatis's direction. Uxaam also looked at the cacique.

Chogatis nodded. "Let her pass," he said.

Uxaam backed away. "I hope we will not regret this," he said.

Inside the hut, Nihapu said, "Put some nut grass beneath the mat before I lay her on it." Joog took some of the dried tubers from a basket and put them beneath the mat. The perennial would serve as an insect repellent.

"Now, hand me that bowl of water and the cloth," she said.

Joog set the water and the small hide cloth next to her.
Nyna opened her eyes at the touch of the water to
her skin.

"It is all right," Nihapu said in a soft voice. "I am just
cleaning you up a little. It will make you feel better."

Nyna gazed at her and then at Joog. Her hazy eyes
filled with fear. Joog knelt next to her.

"Do not be afraid, Nyna. My mother will tend to you
and make you well."

Nyna looked about the square hut as Nihapu inspected her.

"The child has no wounds, that is good," Nihapu said.
"When she is stronger, we will wash her hair, but for
now we will just pull it back from her face." Nihapu
removed the other two feathers and gathered Nyna's
hair, twisted it at the back of her neck, then tied a thin
leather lace around it. "There, that will keep your hair
from your face," she said, smiling at the child.

Nihapu took the child's old skirt and dressed the girl
in a skirt made from the plaited soft tendrils of the air
plant that gracefully decorated so many of the trees. She
held the old skirt in her hands. What could this be made
of? she wondered. "Stay with her while I gather the medicine plants," she said.

As Nihapu entered one of the trails, she heard something behind her. She turned around to see Buhgo.

"Can I go with you?" he asked. "I want to learn."

Nihapu looked in the distance behind him. His mother
stood far back.

"All right," Nihapu said.

She first stopped at a tree with light gray bark. It bore
a yellowish-brown fruit.

"Persimmon," Buhgo said, reaching for a branch to
climb on.

"We do not want the fruit this time. We want the
green leaves to brew. It will give her strength."

Buhgo stripped the leaves, then put them in Nihapu's basket. "What do we look for now?" he asked.

"Smooth snakebark. You will recognize it by—"

"I know," he said. "The bark is orange-brown and flakes. Steep the bark for a tea that soothes the stomach and makes you hungry."

"Yes," Nihapu said. "Who has taught you?"

The boy shook his head and shrugged. "Some things I just know. It is in here," he said, touching his head.

Nihapu stared curiously at the boy. She, too, had some of the knowledge in her head from birth. Other things she had to learn. As a child she was recognized as having the healing gift. The attention this gift brought to her also estranged her older sister.

"I am not supposed to know those things," Buhgo said, his mouth turning down. "But I cannot help it. The healing gift is a woman's art."

"No, you cannot help it," she said. "But it is not shameful. The spirits chose you for the gift. In the past it has always been a woman who heals. People fear what they do not understand. New ideas are frightening sometimes."

After collecting the snakebark, Nihapu told the boy they should look for bracken fern. When they found it, she stooped next to the stiff, wiry plant.

"The mature fern is tough and poisonous. But these," she said, unfurling a new shoot, "are good. They have to be cooked for half a day."

"What are they used for?"

"It is a rich medicine to help restore health. It feeds the body things that have become depleted."

Buhgo fingered the velvety stem of the older plant. "Strange how some parts of a plant can be helpful, and other parts of the same plant can be so harmful. The spurge nettle is like that, even the coontie," he said.

"You do know many things," she said.

"I want to learn more. Will you teach me?"

"I will share what I know," she said. "If it pleases your mother."

Buhgo hung his head. "I bring her heartache."

Cetisa slid next to Etac on the sleeping mat. She trailed her finger down the center of his chest. "What do you think of that girl being brought into the village?" she asked.

Etac shifted. "It was Chogatis's decision."

"But Uxaam has warned that she might be evil . . . so evil that she was cast out of her world."

"Chogatis says we do not know that yet."

Cetisa rolled to her back and stared at the roof through the darkness. "And of course my sister will tend to the child and help her recover. If the girl is evil, the people will resent Nihapu's intervention."

"And what if the child is only a child?"

"Then everyone will be grateful to the wonderful, remarkable, gifted healing woman!"

Etac put his arm under his wife's head to cradle her. "You cannot be so bitter because she was born a healer. Nihapu did not choose it."

"I have value, too," Cetisa said. "Even as a child Nihapu got all the attention. Everyone knew she was a healer even then. There was such a fuss about her all the time. Sometimes I felt like I was not even there."

"Snuggle closer," Etac said. "Relax. Your body is so tense. Think of how lucky you are and how unfortunate Nihapu has been."

Cetisa rested her head in the crook of his arm and closed her eyes. Even when bad things happened to her sister, it still brought attention to Nihapu. Nihapu married Chogatis's son, Tsalochee, the son of the cacique! Yes, he had been killed, but he was considered a hero, and everyone worried about Nihapu. And of course Joog was a great matter of concern when the Jeaga captured him. Nihapu had lost her husband, but she had a son.

Why did the spirits not see fit to give her and Etac a child? Always, the attention was on Nihapu. Always.

"Where are you going?" Zinni asked her husband, Ochopee.

"I am going to meet Uxaam," he answered.

"Why? What cannot wait until the morning?"

Buhgo's younger sister stirred on her mat, but was not awake as Buhgo was.

"We have things to discuss," Ochopee said and left. He could see Uxaam sitting at his hearth, keeping the fire alive. The night was dark, the sky clouded over. The fire would be their only light.

"What is your concern?" Uxaam asked.

Ochopee rubbed his chin. "You think the girl will bring misfortune to the Hawk?"

"I am uncertain," Uxaam said. "Clearly she is not from this world. But nothing has shown me signs of impending danger."

"Chogatis has not been the same for a long time. He has become soft."

"He is not as aggressive as he once was," Uxaam said.

Ochopee tossed a twig into the fire. "I think he really changed when the Jeaga returned Joog. He lets the boy speak kindly of the Jeaga. The Jeaga are our enemy! They still hold the river. Chogatis has forgotten how we suffered during the drought. Once he sought to take the river, but he no longer challenges the Jeaga."

"But he is the cacique," Uxaam said. "We must trust that he makes wise decisions."

"I fear even a drought will not bring back the old Chogatis. Just look what he has done with this girl. He has put us all in danger. If she is a child of the spirits, then let the spirits tend to her. We do not know what he has brought into this village!"

"It sounds as if you want him to step down. He will not do that now."

"What if he is waiting for Joog to be old enough to take his place? If we think Chogatis has become soft on the Jeaga, think of how the boy talks of the Jeaga. He speaks fondly of them! He even keeps the name the Jeaga gave him, Joog. Chogatis says it is in respect for the man and woman who cared for him."

For many days Nihapu stayed at Nyna's side. She fed the child and gave her water and medicines. Buhgo visited often, helping Nihapu prepare the medicines and collecting the plants and fruits for her.

Joog practiced passing through the second curtain, becoming more skilled each time. Soon he knew he would be ready for another lesson.

Nyna slowly gained her strength and in recent days made efforts to communicate. She was bright and learned the Ais words quickly.

Chogatis came to Nihapu's hearth. Joog sat outside making anther hoop. He looked up as his grandfather addressed Nihapu.

"Tell me how she is," Chogatis said.

"The child will recover," Nihapu said. "And she is quick!"

"What have you learned about her?"

"Not too much. She has come a long way from her home."

"Has she told you from where she comes?"

"She spent days on the sea on her journey here. When asked who her people were, she said they were *Taino*."

"I want to see her," Chogatis said.

"She is awake," Nihapu said.

Nyna sipped on a bowl of turtle soup. Chogatis stood at her side.

"Sit next to her. You are so tall, and she is so little. You will be less threatening."

Chogatis lowered himself to the ground.

"Nyna," he said. "An unusual name for us to hear,

yet I find it pleasing to the ear." He touched her armlet and put a curious expression on his face. "What is this that looks like the sun?"

"Canoa," Nyna said, revealing the Tainan word for the brilliant substance.

"Why have you come here?"

Nyna looked at Nihapu, unable to understand Chogatis's question.

"Joog, come in here," Chogatis called.

The boy put down his hoop.

Chogatis pointed to the boy, then at Nihapu. "Mother," he said. He repeated his pointing, this time saying, "Son. Mother."

He pointed to Nyna and then held his hands open in question.

Nyna's face saddened. She spoke a string of words, but no one understood. She stood up, and with a flurry of words in her language she told the story of how her mother and father had been killed. She fidgeted and flitted about, her voice rising, all the time gibbering hysterically. She acted out the moment of being awakened in the darkness, the hiding in the brush with her mother, the running down the beach, and crying. She pretended to stab herself in the back and fell to the ground. "Carib!" she cried out. "Carib!"

"She is too upset," Nihapu said, stooping and putting her arm around the girl. "Do not ask her anything else."

Nyna suddenly grasped an invisible paddle and demonstrated how she had paddled the piragua away, out into the sea. She let her eyes focus as if she could still see the Carib who came after her. She pointed, and cried out a fearful noise. "Carib," she said again.

"Carib?" Chogatis asked.

Nyna nodded vigorously.

The cacique touched the top of the girl's head. "Who are these Carib?" he said aloud. "So where in the sea did she come from?" He touched the canoa bracelet. It was cool. How had she gotten a piece of the sun and tamed the heat from it?

Chogatis got to his feet. "Joog," he said, "have you been practicing?"

"Yes," he answered.

"Good. Then it is time I teach you more."

Chogatis led Joog to the beach. He stood on the white sand and looked out over the water. "Where do you think she came from? How far away? We have big canoes and have traveled deep in the sea. Why have we never seen her people or these Carib? What lies out there, Joog? How much is there that we do not know?"

Joog watched his grandfather's eyes. There were creases about his face, lines formed from living a long time, crinkles etched from pain and wisdom.

"We think we are so important," Chogatis said. "But how small are we really?" He picked up a handful of sand, then let it trickle through his fingers and blow away. "How big is the sea? How many things are there that we know nothing about? This young girl, this Nyna, has already seen more than I have in my long lifetime."

Chogatis sat on the sand and closed his eyes. He did not have to ask Joog to do the same. The boy understood it was time for the lesson.

After some time of 'quiet, Chogatis spoke. "Think of your mind as the sea. Most of the time our minds are like the choppy surface being whipped by the wind. We are so busy taking care of the waves and wind; we think that is all there is. We must stop and look deep beneath the ocean. There we will find the place of oneness. To pierce the surface of the ocean we must focus our minds, concentrate. Find something that pleases you," Chogatis said.

Joog chose a shell that sparkled in the sunlight.

"Have you found something?" Chogatis asked.

"Yes, Grandfather."

"Let that object occupy all your thoughts. Think of

nothing else. If wandering thoughts find their way into your head, simply acknowledge them, and then let them go. If you try to fight them, your concentration will be broken. Your mind may not want to stay so focused and may resist, but you are learning to control your mind. When those rebellious thoughts give up, you will pass through the third curtain, a realm of total peace. Words will have no meaning."

Joog stared hard at the shell. At first he heard the rush of the ocean, the bird songs, and other sounds around him. He pushed harder, seeing only the shell. He would think he was about to pass through the curtain and a sudden unwanted thought would come to mind. His leg would itch, his stomach grumble with hunger. He listened to his grandfather's slow and rhythmic breathing.

Finally Chogatis took a long deep breath, then turned to Joog. "Do not be disappointed if you are not successful this first time. The third curtain is hard to pass through, but if you do not give up, you will find it worth the effort. It will get easier each time. You are training your mind."

Joog smiled, but was still disappointed that he did not learn as quickly as he would like.

On the way back, Chogatis spoke of times he spent alone in the woods. "Once you control your mind, you will be able to pick up things that go beyond your eyes, and ears. You will sense the presence of an animal before you can see or hear it. You will be close to being one with everything. I have been walking through the woods and suddenly felt compelled to turn in a direction, only to stare in the face of a deer or rabbit. It is as if the animal called out to me with his spirit."

As the moon went through its phases, Nyna's strength grew. She was gradually learning the Ais language, though hand signs and expressions aided most communication.

This morning a dry nagging cough awakened Nihapu. Her eyes stung. She hoped she was not getting sick. Who would minister to her if she were the one who was ill? Uxaam was the only other person in the village who knew much of anything about potions, but his were mostly magical medicines, not used to cure sickness.

Just as she sat up rubbing her eyes, she caught a glimpse of Joog and Nyna slipping out of the hut. He was probably taking the girl to collect something Nihapu needed. He wanted so to be a man. He knew that since his father died they depended on the donations of the people. He wanted to help provide for his mother and himself, and of course now Nyna.

The two ran off, finally stopping beneath a small geiger tree. The beautiful red flowers were gone, replaced by small pale fruits. Nyna picked one and bit into it. Quickly she spat it out and screwed up her mouth.

Joog laughed. "They are not so good raw. You have to cook them."

Nyna wiped her mouth with the back of her hand and started to laugh. She looked up in the tree. Images of her home drifted in her mind.

"Hammock," she said. She pretended to suspend a hammock from the trees, then feigned sleep.

"Your bed is hung from the trees!" Joog looked up at the tree. He had an idea.

Nyna coughed several times and rubbed her eyes.

"Come with me," he said, taking off in a run. "Etac!" he called sprinting into the village. Etac was a good fisherman and was always making and repairing traps and nets.

Etac turned.

"Can I have a fish net?" Joog asked.

"You are taking Nyna fishing?" he asked. "I cannot give you my good net as I am going to use it today. I am readying to go at this very moment."

"Do you have an old one?"

"Yes, but it has holes I have not mended."

Joog grinned at Nyna. "That is all right. I am not using it for fishing anyway."

Etac rummaged through a pile of goods, finally extracting a tangled net. "Will this do?"

"Yes," Joog said. "Perfect. Thank you!"

Joog draped the net over his shoulder. It dragged the ground behind him, and he found it was quite heavy.

"Come on," he said, taking Nyna by the hand.

Her irritated eyes teared as they scampered across the village, and she coughed again.

Joog stopped and asked her if she was all right. Nyna nodded that she was.

Buhgo caught up with the pair. "What are you doing?" he asked, running alongside.

"Buhgo!" It was Ochopee.

"Yes, Father," he answered.

"Come here," he said. "What have I told you?"

Zinni came next to her husband. "Let the boy play," she said.

"There is enough talk about him. He does not need to associate with that girl."

"Even the cacique's grandson has befriended her," Zinni argued.

"Our son will not," he said.

Buhgo turned to his friends. "I am sorry," he said.

Joog and Nyna continued on. He stopped at his mother's hut. "I need some cordage," he said, gathering up a coil of rope and giving it to Nyna.

"What are you doing?" Nihapu asked.

"Making a bed," he said.

Joog led Nyna behind the village and sat beneath a tree. He spread the fish net on the ground. They worked for a long time to untangle it. Joog noted the tears in the net, but decided the holes were not large enough to worry about. He cut a piece of the rope and handed it to Nyna. "Thread it through this end of the net," he said, giving a brief demonstration.

Nyna caught on quickly. "A hammock," she said with a broad smile.

After threading the ropes through both ends of the net, Joog shimmied up the tree and crawled out on a branch. Nyna watched, her eyes wide. He tied one end of the sling to the branch, then crept farther out and tied the other.

The hammock gently swayed. Nyna clapped her hands and jumped up and down in excitement. A cough interrupted her giggling.

Joog looked down at her. Was she ill? Then his attention turned. From his vantage point he could see over the brush and huts. There was a commotion in the village. Etac stood in the center of the plaza. He dumped a large basket of fish on the ground. Something was wrong!

Joog climbed down from the tree. Nyna followed him into the center of the village.

The plaza clamored with noise. Ochopee spotted them first and boldly pointed, shouting, "That girl! She is to blame!"

—

7

"The beach is covered with dead fish," Etac said. "All kinds, even a porpoise. The air stings the eyes and chokes you."

Ochopee looked around the gathered crowd. "It begins already! The spirits punish us."

A few men mumbled in agreement.

Chogatis bent and picked up a dead fish. "I have heard of massive fish kills. The Calusa have experienced—"

"But we have not," Ochopee interrupted. "I find it a peculiar coincidence just after bringing this girl into the village."

"She has a name," Nihapu said. "Nyna."

"And what kind of name is that?" Ochopee said. "Just look at her. She is different."

"Just look at her head!" Guacana said and laughed. Some of the other children joined in his laughter.

"Stop it," Joog said, the cords in his neck standing out.

"Yes," Buhgo said. "Stop."

Ochopee threw his hands in the air. "Look at the dissension she has caused, even amongst our children!"

"Flathead," Guacana said, another giggle bursting from him.

Joog stepped forward, hands wrapped into tight fists.

"No," Nihapu said, putting her hand on his shoulder. "Do not lower yourself."

Ochopee took Buhgo by the upper arm. "Our children

quarrel, ready to fight with one another. We are Ais. She is the outsider. We cannot permit this to happen!''

Nyna reached out and took Joog's hand.

Cetisa folded her arms across her chest. "You should take a lesson from Ochopee and keep your son under control, Nihapu.''

Nyna looked from face to face, trying to interpret. She caught a few words, but the expressions told her the most. Guacana still laughed. Her stomach clenched. There were some angry, hateful faces, all staring at her. Her throat tightened.

She let go of Joog's hand and ran off. She ran hard, through the woods, away from the village and the people who hated her, the ones who thought her so ugly. She wanted to go home, wanted her mother, her father! She sobbed as she ran, dodging the thick palmettos, the pine scrub, over the dune onto the sandy beach. Were any of her people left anywhere? The Taino were a kind and gentle people, not like these Ais!

Suddenly, Nyna came to a stop. The beach was littered with dead sea life. Rotting fish lay everywhere, all sizes and kinds. She looked out over the endless sea. The air stung her nose and throat and made her cough. Her eyes burned. "Mother," she cried, sinking to her knees.

Joog's hand came to rest on her shoulder. The air strangled him and the stinging in his eyes was irritating. "I am sorry, Nyna," he said squatting next to her. "Ochopee starts trouble. He is afraid. His displays are how he hides his fear. Everyone fears things they do not understand. Look at this," he said, sweeping his arm in front of him at the incredible scene on the beach. "Who can understand why something like this happens? Ones like Ochopee need to have someone or something to accuse. That is how they make sense of things or their panic would take hold.''

Nyna did not understand all the words, but Joog's voice was soft and reassuring. Did he understand that she had not killed the fish? Why would they think she did this terrible thing?

Nyna looked at all the dead fish. "Nyna . . . no," she said.

"No, you did not make the fish die. I know that. Chogatis knows of other fish kills."

She wiped her eyes and cheeks, then touched her hand to Joog's face. He was a handsome boy. The Ais thought she was ugly. She palmed his cheek. She took his hand and placed it on her forehead. The shape of her forehead was part of the Taino way. Mothers shaped their baby girls' foreheads to make them more beautiful, but these people thought she was ugly and misshapen. Joog must, too. Her hurt eyes filled with tears again.

The Ais were fisherfolk and relied heavily on the sea for their nourishment. The fish kill put an extraordinary strain on them. Afraid to catch or harvest anything in the sea in fear that if they ate it, they, too, would die, they abandoned the ocean, the source that provided the main staple of their diet. So afraid that the fish would poison them, they refrained from taking fish, even from the freshwater streams, and sinkholes, and ponds. Upon Uxaam's recommendation, they resisted eating the animals that preyed upon the fish. It was a trying time for the Hawk Clan of the Ais, bringing back even more intensely the recollection of the drought and the war with the Jeaga.

Every morning as they greeted the day, the Ais asked the spirits to remove this terrible curse from them. Uxaam's voice rang loudly every evening, calling to the spirits, making offerings and supplications. He sent runners to request the shamans of two neighboring Ais clans to come and pray with him. Several days later both the visiting shamans stood with Uxaam, sprinkling their magic powders and offerings into the sea.

"I recall the drought," the shaman from the Osprey Clan said. "We were unable to help the Hawk. Our water is only enough to support ourselves. I hope that we help you now."

"The Ais are united," Uxaam said. "We are thankful for your support."

Nyna prayed for the end of the fish kill, also. She had Joog teach her the Ais way of imploring the spirits. The ways were different from the Taino, and she questioned if the Ais spirits listened to a Taino girl. But still she petitioned them every morning, and silently at night before she slept.

Many days passed before the fish stopped washing up on the beach. The visiting shamans returned to their clans with the profuse gratitude of the Hawk Clan.

Each day Chogatis notched his stick. Every so often he laid his hand on the stick, matching fingers with notches. He had marched both his hands up the stick twice before the fish stopped washing up on the beach. Finally the air cleared, and the people stopped coughing, their eyes stopped burning, and at last the beach remained clean of rotting carcasses. Uxaam took credit for the cure, claiming it was his prayers to the spirits that ended the disaster. He sent word to the other clans to join the Hawk in their celebration for the return of healthy fish.

It had been a full cycle of the moon since the last fish lay dead and rotting on the sand. The men sat in Council and Uxaam took the opportunity to boast. "It was not easy pleading to the spirits as I had to do. And we owe thanks to the other clans who prayed with us."

"We are thankful," Etac said.

"Tomorrow night we will celebrate our good fortune," Chogatis said. "The hunting has been good and the sea is clean again. Uxaam, do you think it safe to eat the fish? And the mollusks?"

"The beach has been clear since the last full moon. The moon is full again. I think it safe."

"Good," Chogatis said.

The cacique commenced to dismiss Council when Ochopee spoke up. "I have a concern."

"What would that be?" Chogatis asked.

"The girl, Nyna, is still with us. The spirits may not be done with the Ais. There may be other consequences for our interference. We may celebrate prematurely."

Chogatis smiled. "But Uxaam has just told us how successful he was in his plea. The fish no longer die, a sign that he is most powerful and respected by spirits."

Chogatis looked over the faces of the men. He was sure some agreed with Ochopee, but he felt secure he had squelched further discussion at this time.

"Any other concerns, Ochopee?" Chogatis asked.

"One other. I know that since your son's death we have all contributed to providing for Nihapu and Joog. It is time for Nihapu to find a mate. Until then, who will provide for the outsider girl?"

"Nihapu shares provisions with her," Chogatis said.

"So we are to contribute even more so that girl is taken care of?"

"If you see fit. But I will make certain she has enough," Chogatis said.

"I mean no offense, Cacique, but you are not a young man. When you die, who then will provide for the girl?"

"Tell me, Ochopee, do you expect me to die soon?"

Nervous laughter broke out among the men.

"If not," Chogatis added, "then we have a long time to come up with a solution. At least I hope we have a long time."

Again the men laughed. Chogatis was sharp.

When the men dispersed, the cacique walked alone along the shallow stream. He supposed the others believed he had forgotten when the drought had come and the streambed became dry. But he had not forgotten. It was a hard time for the Ais, much like what they had just been through. Little water, little food. The deer fled in search of water, their throats as dry as the Ais'. Fires swept the land, scorching deep layers of soil, preventing the sprouting of new shoots on which the deer loved to feed. The air had grown thick with ash, and the streambed cracked and crumbled. No, a man could not forget such a time. The Big Water, the sea, had furtively crept into one of their sinkholes, contaminating it so the water was not potable.

Chogatis picked up a stone and skipped it over the water. The Ais and Jeaga had a long history of struggle. Even in the worst droughts, the river always had water. Desperately Chogatis had led his people against the Jeaga, hoping to take part of the river so his people would not thirst and starve at the will of the rains. That was when Tsalochee had been killed and Joog captured.

Even after the rains returned, there remained much hatred of the Jeaga amongst the Ais.

Life was not easy, he thought. So many complications colored a man's thinking. Chogatis recalled the pain of losing his wife, their only son, and Joog. The day the Jeaga man and woman dared to walk into the Ais village to bring his grandson home was the day Chogatis changed. That was the day the spirits chose to open his eyes so that he might see more clearly. The Jeaga were not really so different from the Ais. From that day his people accused him rightly. His heart had softened. All men suffered, and all men had goodness in their hearts. He saw that so clearly and wished his people did. There would never be peace until all men understood that. There even existed hatred so far away as where Nyna had come from. When would it end?

Chogatis sat on the ground. He needed a solution to the concerns Ochopee had brought up in Council. They were valid concerns and Chogatis was sure that Ochopee was not alone in his misgivings. The Ais needed harmony, and that was his responsibility. That was what a cacique did for his people. He was the father, and the Ais his children.

Chogatis focused on a slender blade of grass and quietly slipped through the curtains to the place of oneness.

Sometime later Chogatis breathed in four deep breaths. He was refreshed and knew what he must do.

Ochopee paced inside his hut. Buhgo and his sister, Laira, sat outside by the fire, pounding berries to mix with fat and the deer meat Ochopee had brought home from his early-morning hunt.

"How can this be?" Ochopee asked his wife.

"You know how this can be," she said. "My moon cycle has not come three times in a row."

"Does Nihapu have medicine?"

Zinni's head dropped. She knew Ochopee did not want any more children. When Laira was born, Buhgo was still too young to display his feminine traits. But as Buhgo grew, he became an embarrassment to his father, and Ochopee wanted no more embarrassments.

"I suppose she may know of something," Zinni finally said.

"Go talk to her," Ochopee said. "End this pregnancy before your stomach grows large. We do not want to have to explain to anyone."

Zinni stroked her abdomen. Though her form was thin, her stomach was not as flat as before she had carried Buhgo and Laira. Her belly had a subtle but distinct roundness to it, a tribute to her ability to birth big, strong, healthy babies.

"There is nothing wrong with Laira," she said. "And Buhgo should not make you feel so shamed. He is a good boy."

"He is a girl in a boy's body. He will never be a man, a hunter, a provider, a warrior. He will play with his medicines and sew and cook and chatter with the women! He is not a son . . . not my son."

"This child does not have to be like Buhgo," she said.

"Get rid of it." Ochopee walked out.

8

The next morning the village filled with excitement. Men and women, even the children, scurried about to make ready for the celebration that would begin at sundown. Tonight they would give thanks for the end of the fish kill. Their activities and laughter would ring long into the night.

Members of both the Bobcat and Osprey clans arrived before the sun was straight overhead. The men gathered about the central hearth and the women helped with preparation of the food. The children played their hoop and ball games.

Nyna and Laira followed Joog into the woods. He took with him his small bola.

"Maybe I can get a squirrel or a rabbit," he said. "You know soon I will be ready to become a man, and so Chogatis says I should practice all the skills I will need as a hunter and a warrior."

Nyna watched Joog, picking up some of the meaning, relying heavily on his hand gestures and expressions.

"Warrior," Nyna repeated. She recalled the fearsome Carib warriors and their weapons. Her people had no such weapons, no horrid murdering clubs. They only had weapons for hunting of small animals. They were no match for the Carib. She would have Joog show her the Ais weapons.

Suddenly the boy crouched. "Get down," he said. "There," he whispered. "See him?"

Nyna and Laira crouched behind a wax myrtle.

A fat raccoon waddled through the woods.

"Stay here," the boy told his companions. Joog tried to clear his mind and concentrate. He wanted to see only the raccoon. Then he would be able to anticipate what the animal would do. He focused unblinkingly. Slowly, with all the stealth he could muster, he raised one foot and carefully brought it forward, stepping down quietly. Still he could hear the crush of the forest floor beneath his foot. The raccoon stopped sharply and looked in Joog's direction. The boy did not move, trying to blend with the trees and shrub. The raccoon sniffed the air, then, as if satisfied, waddled on.

Nyna raised up to see better. She made no noise, sensing the intensity of the moment.

Joog brought his other foot forward, stalking his prey. As he got closer, his focus sharpened even more. He could smell the musky scent of the coon's fur, the smell of oysters on his paws. Closer he crept, keeping his form compatible with his surroundings.

Suddenly the raccoon halted and looked back. His nose wrinkled as he sniffed. Joog could see the markings on the raccoon's face, and for a moment their eyes locked. The boy felt the fear, the confusion that swam inside the small animal. Then quickly, the raccoon bolted and scurried up a tree.

Nyna squealed behind Joog, and he laughed aloud. Laira clapped her hands.

"I almost had him," Joog said. "Just a little closer!" He squatted in thought. What had just happened? He would have to ask his grandfather.

Joog ran back to the girls. "I will be a good provider one day," he said. He liked the way Nyna was looking at him. She had seen how close he had gotten. She appeared impressed with his skills. That made him feel good.

*　　*　　*

Chogatis asked Nihapu if she needed anything so she would be ready for the festivities.

"Joog and Nyna have helped me," she said. "I cannot think of anything I need."

Nihapu went about her chores, expecting Chogatis to leave, but he kept watching her, following her with his eyes.

Nihapu turned so she would face him squarely. "What is it, Chogatis?"

"You are a good woman," he said. "My son was wise choosing you as a wife," he told her.

"Thank you," she said, sliding a stick under the lash of a pot that hung over the fire. She moved the pot to the side, away from the direct heat.

She looked at him again, tilting her head to the side. "You seem as if you want to say something else."

Chogatis leaned against a tree. His shape and structure did not give away his age. His skin was still tight over his muscles, and his hair thick and black as soot. "I need to speak with you," he said. "I want to tell you something."

"But of course," she said, putting down the stick and giving him her full attention.

"You never knew my wife," he said. "She was kind and beautiful. The night she died lives in my mind as if it were just yesterday."

"No, I am sorry, I did not know her. Tsalochee told me she died giving birth to him."

Chogatis nodded, and Nihapu saw him swallow as if the words were hard coming. "We knew the time was close for the child to be born. Pawopu was so happy, as was I."

The cacique swiped a hand over his face.

"I see it is painful for you to remember."

"The rain pounded the village. Lightning. Thunder. Great winds. The surf roared. It was difficult to sleep.

Storms are noisy, but I still think that if she had called out to me, I would have heard her."

Chogatis rubbed his forehead, then continued. "She lay on her side, her back to me, one hand beneath her head. I wondered how she slept so soundly with all that noise. I moved closer to her and let my arm fall across her so I could hold her as she slept. I remember how her hair felt, cool and sleek against me. I can still smell the sweetness of it. But then I felt something warm seep beneath me. I sat up to look, thinking it run off from the rain, but the warmth of it puzzled me. In the bright flash of lightning I saw that it was not rainwater at all. A pool of blood, still warm from her, spread in all directions. I turned her face so I could see her eyes. They were open, but vacant. I shook her, then embraced her, calling her name, but she was gone. I held her close, as if by pressing her to me, my spirit might call hers back."

Chogatis paused. Nihapu thought he did so to wait for the strain to leave his voice. "That must have been so terrible," she said.

"I heard her voice, as clearly as if she spoke right in my ear. 'The baby,' she said to me. 'Save the baby.' Then I remembered the unborn child still inside her. I laid her down on her back and I took my knife and slit open her belly. I was crying like an old woman, my hands trembling, my shoulders shaking, and my eyes nearly unable to see for the cloak of tears. When air hit his face, our son cried, even before I had lifted him from the womb."

Nihapu thought of her husband, Chogatis's son, and how she had loved him. "And he is gone from us now, also."

"Nihapu, in all this time I have not considered taking another wife. I have not and will not ever feel for any woman what I felt for Pawopu. But something has happened. . . ."

"There is a woman in your life?" Nihapu said. She

smiled at the cacique. "You have kept quite a secret. I am happy for you. Tell me," she said, her expression displaying her eagerness to be let in on the secret. Her eyes twinkled, and her lips curled playfully.

Chogatis pushed away from the tree. "I am not certain how to go about this. The Hawk provide for you and Joog because Tsalochee was your husband, Joog's father, and my son. And he died at the hands of the Jeaga. But the people expect you to find another husband, and then they will not need to continue to give up portions of their food and supplies. And they strongly object to providing for Nyna."

"She does not need much," Nihapu said. "I will share whatever I have with her. I promise, she will not be a burden. They need not give any more than they already do. Joog and I will eat less. I have no interest in another man, another husband. I am not ready."

"I understand," he said. "But I have come up with a solution for all of us. I think the only way to solve all these problems is for you to be my wife.'

"What?" Nihapu said. "I—"

"I do not expect you to be my woman. We do not have to perform those kinds of marital obligations. But this way I can become solely responsible for you and Joog, and for Nyna, also. There will be no pressure on you to find another husband. I need a wife, someone to do a woman's chores about my hearth. Men are so inept at sewing, cooking, pot making, weaving. I rely too much on others. I am tired, and I grow old. The people will keep the custom of providing for the cacique's family after death . . . even Nyna, because she will live as my daughter."

"I am dumbfounded," Nihapu said. "I do not know what to say."

"I have given it thought. Conversation amongst some has made me think. I want what is best for my son's wife, my grandchild, and Nyna as well. I am the one who made the decision for her to live among us. I am responsible."

Zinni approached, ending the conversation.

"Think about what I have said," Chogatis said.

"Good day," Zinni said as she passed him. She stood in front of Nihapu. "Can I talk with you?"

Nihapu could not take her eyes from Chogatis's back. His flowing hair stirred about his shoulders, moved by the breeze he created as he walked. His gait was not an old man's gait, nor was it a young man's stride. Confident, wise, experienced were the words that came to mind. Tsalochee had looked much like his father. How she missed him.

"Nihapu?" Zinni said. "Can I talk with you?"

"Yes," she answered in a flat monotone, her mind still swirling elsewhere.

Zinni sat. "Are you all right?"

Nihapu finally turned and faced her visitor. "What?"

"Are you all right?" Zinni asked again.

"Yes, I am fine. I was just thinking hard about something."

The young woman wrung her hands. Her face was thin, with hollows in her cheeks beneath lovely defined cheekbones. She had a delicateness to her structure that made her appear fragile. "I need your help," Zinni said.

"Is something wrong?" Nihapu asked.

Zinni nervously looked about. "Not really."

Buhgo spotted his mother with Nihapu and sprinted over to them. Zinni gave her son a hug. "Go and play," she said. "I have to speak woman-talk with Nihapu."

"There is nothing to do," Buhgo said. "Everyone is busy preparing for the festivities."

"We have things to prepare, also. You can be very helpful to me if you gather some cocoplums and sea grapes. And by the beach, get some sea purslane."

"All right," Buhgo said. "Nihapu, are there plants you wish me to gather also?"

"I have everything," she answered.

"He is such a good child," Zinni said, watching her son trot away. "Ochopee is humiliated by him."

"It is sad his father feels that way," Nihapu said.

There was a pause in the conversation. Finally Zinni's head shot up. "I am pregnant," she said.

Nihapu's face brightened. "How wonder—"

"No," Zinni interrupted. "Ochopee fears he will have another child like Buhgo. Is there a medicine?"

Nihapu shook her head. "I know of no medicine that can make a child either like Buhgo or not like Buhgo."

"No," Zinni said, squirming. "Is there a medicine that can get rid of this baby?" She looked down and rested her hand on her belly.

Nihapu rocked back. "You do not want to do that," she said. "Spirits give us children. Only they can take them away."

"Is there a medicine?" she asked again.

"Zinni, think of what you are asking."

"Ochopee will throw me out. He will claim I have been unfaithful and that this child is not his. I know he will."

"Perhaps you are better without him, then," Nihapu said.

"I love him so. I could not bear to be without him. And Buhgo and Laira need a father, and so will this child. How would I ever care for three children on my own?"

She knew Zinni was right. If Ochopee threw her out and claimed adultery, no one would help her. She and her children would be outcasts. Zinni and her children would have to leave the village and they would surely perish. A woman and children in the wilderness were guaranteed death.

"There is a medicine," Nihapu said. "Sometimes it works and sometimes it does not. It is not a reliable thing."

"I must try. Surely you must understand. Please," Zinni said, her voice cracking. She swept her hair back with her hand. "I want to do this soon, get it behind me. Ochopee will turn from me if I do not take care of this."

"All right," Nihapu said. "These are the things you must bring to me. Some of them I will use and some I will not. Other things I will gather myself. I do not want you to know the ingredients. This is not a medicine for women to take just because they do not feel like having a child. It is dangerous and undependable."

"I know. I know," Zinni said.

"Bring me leaves of the silver leaf, kernels from the tallowwood plum, young shoots of the pokeberry, but cut it a safe distance from the roots. We want to solve your problem, not kill you outright. Bring also some blackberries and several talinum leaves. Can you remember them all?"

Zinni repeated the list, but left out one ingredient.

"The blackberries," Nihapu reminded.

When Zinni left, Nihapu searched her baskets. She kept dried herbs, fruits, and plant parts to make her medicines. She had cures for stomachaches, rashes, many sicknesses. But she had not found a medicine that cured the coughing disease, nor a cure for the one that caused the awful slow death. What a hideous sickness that is, she thought. It begins with only a simple unpleasant chancre in a personal area that soon heals on its own. But at the end, which could be many, many seasons later, repulsive ulcerating lesions appear, especially on the palate, in the nose, the throat, the leg just below the knee, most anywhere on the body. She had even seen some who shook with severe tremors of the mouth and hand, even the tongue. They went mad. It was a terrible disease.

From the fire, Uxaam removed the earthen pot filled with roasted leaves and twigs of the yaupon tree. He put them in another large pot, added water, and said the ritual chants as the strong cassina brewed. Only the men would consume this black drink. Women and children were not allowed to taste the ritual tea.

Chogatis spoke with Uxaam as he stirred the brew.

"What children will receive their totems tonight?" the cacique asked. "Who are ready?"

"There are several," Uxaam answered. "And there is one new child to name."

"Nyna will need a totem to protect her."

"She has her own spirits," Uxaam answered. "Taino spirits."

"But we do not know what they are. When you look at the sky tonight, those stars are the hearths of Ais spirits and ancestors, not Taino. She needs their protection. Her spirits cannot see her here."

Uxaam let go of the stirring stick. "You want me to give this girl an Ais totem. You think the spirits would even make a totem known to me?"

"Ask them," Chogatis said. Uxaam was difficult and stubborn, but above all he was a man of the spirits and would do as they directed.

"It is short notice," Uxaam complained.

"Not for you," Chogatis said. "We have our differences, but I do not let that blind me to what a gifted shaman you are. I trust you can do it." Chogatis started to walk away. He and Uxaam often disagreed, but Chogatis had the greatest respect for him. "My words are not flattery," he added. "I speak only the truth."

The flaming tongues of the fire in the pit in the center of the plaza leaped high in the darkness. All day, food had been prepared and now it was spread beside the fire for all to partake. There was coontie bread, roasting and smoking meat, freshwater and saltwater fish, shellfish, roasted turkeys, ibis, turtle and gophers, succulent berries and fruits, teas, and cooked greens of all kinds. This time of abundant richness would pass when the air grew cooler. In preparation for that time, along with the food prepared for today's feast, they started the process of drying fruits and other foodstuffs.

Over a drying rack, Cetisa hung long strips of meat. After the roasts and steaks had been taken from the larger animals, she had sliced along the length of the muscle, cutting thin strips of meat that would dry quickly. Some of these strips she would use in soups and stews, and some she would mix with fat and partially dried and pounded berries. The fat was the trick. Because it went rancid so quickly the fat had to be heated until it became liquid, then filtered several times through dried grasses. Finally there would be a pure tallow. When it cooled, that was when she would mix the dried meat and berries with it. This food source would last a long time. When the process was complete, the product would be stored in airtight intestines.

The air filled with sweet and hearty aromas as the people of the village gathered by the fire, waiting for Uxaam to appear.

"First he will tell the story of creation," Joog said to Nyna. Her face told him she did not understand. "Uxaam will recall how people first came to earth." Joog talked with his hands as well as his words.

"Taino came from Cacibagiuagua and Amaiauba," she said. How could she explain the two caves from which her people emerged? She had not seen any caves in this new land. The nobles and wealthy came from Cacibagiuagua, and the common people out of Amaiauba. Where were the Ais caves?

Nyna used her finger to draw a picture of the two caves in the dirt. The drawing was not easy to make out with only the firelight and moonlight. And the concept of a cave was completely unknown to Joog.

She drew a figure of a man that appeared to guard the caves. "Marocael," she said.

Nyna continued the story drawn in the dirt. Marocael protected the caves. But one day he forgot to close the caves, and the sun escaped from it and along with it, some of the first people.

"Understand?" she asked. She knew he didn't comprehend all that she said, but maybe he understood most of it from the drawings. Joog was good, working hard to make himself understood, to teach her this strange language, and he made an effort to learn some of her words, too.

A sudden howl from the shaman initiated the ceremonies. Uxaam's lime-whitened face stood out in the darkness. Charcoal mixed with grease provided the color for a line down the middle of his face, from forehead, over his nose, down his lips, and past his chin. Three short black lines slanted sharply upward across each of his cheekbones. Draped down the center of his forehead was a fox skin, the nose of the animal resting between Uxaam's eyes. The fox headdress covered his head, and the tail ran down his back.

"Wa hay ah ha! Wa hay ah ha!" he sang into the night air. From a pouch about his waist he took a handful of a magic substance and hurled it into the fire. The fire spit, and sparks flew up in a great halo, brightening the night with flickering orange light.

The women backed away in a circle around the fire, and the men came forward. Uxaam led them in song, some rhythmically striking sticks together, others slamming their palms on the skin drumheads.

Nyna peered around Nihapu's leg. The voices grew louder and louder, the earth rumbling beneath her feet with the beat of the drums. Like a powerful heartbeat, the drums vibrated in the ground, communicating their mystical rhythm to Nyna. She soon found her head bobbing, hands moving.

The men danced in a way that magically made them seem part of the music, their heads dipping and lifting, their feet barely coming off the ground as they moved, their waists and knees bending deep, and torsos twisting gracefully.

Nihapu lifted Nyna so she could see more clearly.

The music abruptly ended, the singers, musicians, and dancers arresting at the same moment. The village hushed.

Uxaam's face glowed with the fire. He stood on a wooden stool, reminding Nyna of the Taino *duhos*, small chairs used for ceremonies. The shaman outstretched his arms, lifting his standard that bore a single white egret feather in its crest. The feather waved in the fire-born wind, and Uxaam seemed to tower above the others, like some supernatural being.

In one last incantation, his voice alone echoed over the village. When he quieted, the breeze, as if somehow summoned, swept over him, bringing alive the sound of the shell anklets, armlets, and necklaces that dripped from his body.

The children, intimidated by the awesome sight and sound, bunched closer to their mothers, or if being held, nestled their heads in the crooks of their mothers' necks.

Uxaam stepped down on the ground. "Laira," he called. "Come forward."

Ochopee's mouth opened with pleasant surprise. Uxaam was going to give his daughter a totem!

"The otter has chosen you," Uxaam said. "Come forward."

Uxaam had observed Laira for several seasons. She possessed many of the otter's characteristics. She was certainly playful and a good swimmer. She relished all seafood, never tiring of it. The otter was appropriate. He held out the small leather pouch necklace that held an otter claw and tooth that he was to place over Laira's head.

Ochopee scanned the crowd for his daughter and the rest of his family. His face slowly changed as he realized none of them was there. The crowd began to mumble. Something was very wrong!

9

"Hurry! Hurry!" Buhgo cried, leading Nihapu away from the plaza and all the celebration.

Nihapu trotted behind the boy, carrying Nyna on her hip. Joog ran alongside her.

Laira's wailing could be heard before they reached the hut.

"Inside," Buhgo said.

"Joog, stay with Nyna," Nihapu said.

In the darkness it was difficult to see. "Buhgo, bring a pitch torch," she said.

From what she could tell, Zinni lay on the bare ground, trembling all over. Her eyes rolled about in her head.

From the rear of the hut, Laira cried again, a long baleful whine.

Buhgo entered with the torch and Nihapu could see better. Laira suddenly silenced, her outstretched body stiffened, arching her back off the ground. The child's body shook and contorted.

"What has happened?" Nihapu asked.

"Help them, help them," Buhgo said. He started crying. "Do something!"

Nihapu turned to the boy and grabbed his arm. "Tell me what has happened?"

"I do not know," the boy wailed. "Help them!"

Nihapu jerked Buhgo's arm. "I cannot help them if I do not know what is wrong. Think, boy. Think."

Buhgo's bottom lip trembled. "Mother did not feel well. She complained and wanted Laira and me to go to the ceremonies without her. But then, Laira started not to feel well either. I thought she just wanted to stay with Mother."

"What else, Buhgo? When did Zinni get sick?"

"Today. Late."

Nihapu looked around. She saw the pouch of medicine she had prepared for Zinni. The parfleche lay open and empty.

"What did she do with this?" she asked.

"She made some tea for herself. She said it was a woman's tea and that I was not to drink it."

"She used it all?"

Buhgo shrugged. "I think so."

Nihapu looked at the mother and daughter, both writhing in seizures.

"Turn your sister on her side and hold her there. Do not fight her, just help her stay on her side."

Nihapu pushed Zinni onto her side, just in time. Zinni retched and vomited. "We do not want them to choke," she said. "Get Laira on her side."

Buhgo did as he was told. He heard his sister's stomach lurch, but nothing came up.

"Did your mother also tell Laira not to drink the tea?"

"Laira was not with me when Mother told me not to drink it. What is it? What is wrong with them? The tea?"

Nihapu had told Zinni to take the medicine over several days, sipping it in tea at each meal. It appeared that in her anxiety, Zinni had brewed the entire medicine packet and drunk it all today. Laira must have gotten into it by accident.

"Get out, Buhgo!" Ochopee stood in the doorway. "Wait outside with your sister."

Buhgo loosened his grip on Laira.

"Nightshade and thorn apple," Nihapu said. "Do you know them?"

"Yes!" Buhgo answered.

"Bring them and boil them. Be swift."

"No," Ochopee said. "My son does no woman's work!"

"Do you want your wife and daughter to live?"

"Send someone else. Your boy, Joog."

"Joog does not know the plants like Buhgo. Buhgo *knows*. He has the gift. Let him hurry or they will die."

Ochopee hesitated, and Buhgo bore his eyes into his father's. Finally Ochopee jerked his head toward the doorway and stepped aside. Buhgo scrambled out of the hut.

"Hold your daughter on her side so when she begins to shake again you can keep her from hurting herself."

Ochopee lifted Laira into his lap. His expression changed to solid worry. "What is wrong?"

Nihapu did not wish to enter into family matters, but this time she would make her feelings known. "Zinni carries your child, is that not correct?"

Ochopee didn't respond.

"You told her to come to me for a medicine to rid herself of this baby. I advised her against it, telling her the medicine was unreliable and dangerous. She was so afraid that you would turn her out if she birthed this child that she was willing to do anything. So I made her the medicine."

"What kind of medicine did you make?" His voice was suspicious and verged on angry.

"I made the only medicine I know that can do what she asked. It appears she did not follow my directions."

"But Laira," he said. "What about her?"

Zinni began to convulse again, and Nihapu dropped the conversation until the seizure passed.

"I told your wife how to take this medicine and told her that even used with caution, this was a dangerous potion. She should have taken this medicine over a period of several days, but from what I can tell she brewed all the tea and apparently Laira got hold of it and drank some herself."

"Will they be all right?" Ochopee asked, his eyebrows dipping.

"I do not know. This is a very bad thing."

Nyna, Joog, and Buhgo stayed in Nihapu's hut for the night. Nihapu and Ochopee treated Zinni and Laira with the decoction Nihapu brewed.

Joog saw that Buhgo remained distressed, and so he began to tell stories. Nyna joined in, intriguing the boys with her tales of exotic plants and animals that were native to her homeland. She told her stories with a mixture of mime and words. She told them about *hutias*, small furry animals they hunted and ate, and about the pepper pot spiced with *aji* that kept food from going rancid too quickly. And the birds, some of the exquisite birds, like *perdices*.

She explained how they used to catch large water birds. The hunters would throw big calabashes into the water where large water birds swam. They would do this for a long time until the birds became accustomed to seeing the gourds on the water. Then one day some men would clean out several large gourds, put eye-holes in them and put them over their heads. They would wade in the water up to their chins and walk around like a drifting calabash, until close enough to the waterfowl to grab it by the feet and draw it underwater. The other birds believed their companion had just merely dove for food. When they came nearer the disguised man, they were caught in the same manner. The water birds stayed because they never sensed danger nor witnessed the killing of one of their species. So the Taino had a constant supply of these birds.

It took Nyna a long time to tell the story. When she walked around, pretending to have the gourd over her head, the boys laughed.

They stayed awake late into the night, until Buhgo began to yawn. Then Joog suggested that they sleep.

When morning came, Buhgo awakened first. He hurried to his mother and sister's side. He stood in the entranceway, waiting to see if he would be allowed in.

Ochopee saw him, but ignored his son.

"Come in," Nihapu said. "Your mother would like to see you."

Zinni fluttered her eyelids and held out her hand to her son. Buhgo moved inside and grasped his mother's sweaty palm.

"Will you and Laira be all right?" he asked.

Zinni did not speak, but she squeezed his hand. He looked at Nihapu.

"The worst is over, I think," she said. "But she must have a lot of rest and a lot of attention."

"What made them sick?" Buhgo asked.

Nihapu glanced at Ochopee. "Perhaps your father should explain," she said.

Ochopee clenched his jaw and grated his teeth. "You would be better at that," he said. Ochopee moved past them and exited the hut.

Buhgo was clearly confused.

"Wait until your mother is feeling better. I'm sure she will want to explain everything to you," Nihapu said.

"Why is it such a secret? Did they do something wrong?"

"No, no, they did nothing wrong. It is a parent's privilege to explain some things to their children. Be patient. Now," she said, "I should tend to my family. Joog and Nyna must be hungry. And you have dark rims beneath your eyes. You children stayed awake too late."

Buhgo smiled his confession. "They kept my mind off my mother and sister."

"Zinni and Laira are lucky. If you did not know the healing ways, they might have died. Who else could have gone for the ingredients I needed for their medicines?"

Buhgo grinned in earnest. "Do you think I saved their lives?"

"I certainly do. There is no doubt about it."

Nihapu patted the boy's head. "Watch over them. I will be back later to check. Give them plenty of water to drink. Do not worry about them eating just yet. Remember, plenty of water."

"Medicine?"

"No medicines," Nihapu said as she left.

Chogatis stopped her as she made her way to her hearth.

"Are they going to be all right?" he asked.

"It appears so," she said.

"Ochopee is unclear. Should we fear a sickness spreading through the village?"

Nihapu shook her head. "Nothing to worry about."

Chogatis tipped her chin up so she would look at him. "What is it?"

"That is between Ochopee and Zinni," she said.

"How can that be? That does not make sense."

"You will have to ask Ochopee these questions," she said.

"But you assure me there is no danger to the others in the village?"

"I am sure," she said.

"That is good. Have you given thought to my proposition?"

"Oh, Chogatis, it is a kind thing you do, and I would be proud to be the wife of the cacique!" Nihapu hung her head. "But I do not love you. One day a woman will come into your life and set fire in your heart again, the way Pawopu did."

Chogatis rocked back his head. "There will never be another fire in my heart," he said.

Nihapu looked up. "You cannot say that. You are a most desirable man, handsome, noble, and a powerful leader of the Hawk. You may be taken with some woman, as there are plenty to choose from."

"Are you sparing my feelings?" he asked. "Do you find it such a distasteful idea to be my wife that you try to flatter me?"

Nihapu's mouth opened. "Oh, no. I have offended you. That is not the meaning of my argument at all."

"You speak the truth to me? Do not spare my feelings. I must know."

"I did not say those things to spare your feelings. I meant them."

"Then there is no argument, no disagreement. It is decided. I will make the announcement in Council."

Chogatis turned his back and walked away.

"Wait," she said, her voice drifting off at the end.

Chogatis sounded the conch-shell horn, declaring that a meeting of Council was to take place.

He watched as the men gathered. He was sure none of them guessed all the things that were on his mind. They probably expected a few discussions, but not the one about his proposal to Nihapu. And, he thought, over that, he would allow no discussion.

Their oiled bodies shone in the sunlight and their shell ornaments winked and glittered. Most of the men gathered their hair in a knot behind their heads, pulled back from their faces.

Chogatis surveyed the group, then lifted the Talking Stick. "I have inquired about Ochopee's wife and daughter," he started. "We have nothing to fear. This is not a sickness that will spread through the village."

A man to Chogatis's left signaled that he wished to speak. Chogatis acknowledged him.

"Can you tell us more? How can two in the same family have this sickness, whatever it is, and then it be said that the sickness does not spread?"

"I have Nihapu's assurance."

"But that is not enough. Two are ill! Is this another curse brought by the girl?"

"It has nothing to do with Nyna," Chogatis said.

Uxaam asked for the Talking Stick and Chogatis relinquished it.

"These are important questions. Chogatis, you must not speak in circles."

Chogatis looked across at Ochopee, whose face dripped with perspiration. "Ochopee, do you wish to speak?"

"Yes, tell us, Ochopee," Uxaam said, followed by collective sounds of agreement.

"Chogatis has said all there is to say," Ochopee mumbled.

Uxaam's eyebrows angled down. "Speak clearly, Ochopee."

Ochopee cleared his throat. "I know no more than Chogatis."

Chogatis gestured for the Talking Stick to be returned. Uxaam held on to it for an extra few moments, looking between Chogatis and Ochopee. Finally he handed it to the cacique.

"Uxaam, because the ceremonies were interrupted last night I think we should continue this night. We should finish what we started," Chogatis said.

Uxaam kept his silence, but nodded agreement.

"There is another thing of which I wish to speak," Chogatis said. "Nihapu will be my wife."

An immediate muttering of surprise started amongst the group.

"I know this comes as a surprise," Chogatis said, "but I have thought it out. She pleases me. She was a good wife to my son. There need not be any more concern about Nihapu's provisions."

Chogatis read the expressions of the men. They thought his notion odd, indeed. They were so surprised that many of them sat with mouths agape. Eventually they would come to terms with it.

Uxaam asked Nihapu if he could bring Nyna to his ceremonial platform.

"When Chogatis asked that Nyna be given a totem, I did my best to study the girl," he said. "Then, with caution I approached the spirits, hoping my petition to be shown a totem for this outlander would not be offensive. They showed me nothing, gave me no vision. I would not have been able to give her a totem during last night's ceremony."

"What do you want with the child?" Nihapu asked.

"Perhaps I go to the spirits again, and if she is with me, they will see her. Maybe they will be persuaded to listen."

"Do not frighten her," Nihapu said.

Uxaam led Nyna to the platform. He helped her up and sat her in the center near the small smoldering embers.

Nyna watched as the shaman prepared. He spread a white powder around them in a circle. Then he sat across from her.

"I am a man of the spirits, the shaman," he said, in his effort to explain what he was doing.

"Behique," Nyna said.

"Shaman," Uxaam repeated.

"Yes, shaman . . . *behique.* The same."

"Ah," Uxaam said. *"Behique."*

Nyna smiled at her first communication with this man.

"I must talk to the spirits," he said, dancing his hands toward the heavens. He chanted a small incantation so she could hear what it sounded like.

"Zemis," she said.

Uxaam sighed. How were the spirits going to help him find a totem for someone who worshipped *zemis*? What a strange-sounding name. *Zemis. Zemis* could be birds, or fish, or lizards. Who knew what these people with the bizarre-shaped heads believed in!

Uxaam took a bundle of green pine needles and touched the coals with them. They sizzled, and when they burned sufficiently, they emitted a pungent thick smoke. Uxaam waved the smoking pine, smudging the air to cleanse it.

At first he closed only one eye, keeping the other on the girl. Nyna cocked her head and looked at him curiously. She closed one eye in imitation. Finally Uxaam closed both his eyes and began his song.

In a moment he heard a trill, a high-pitched mimic of his song. His eyes opened. Nyna was smiling.

"No, no, no," he said. "Do not sing. This is a shaman's song, it is a special prayer to call the spirits."

He started his melody again, and again she joined in.

Uxaam grunted and put the pine bundle on the ground. His expression was clearly filled with exasperation. He pointed to himself. "Shaman," he said.

"Behique," she replied.

Uxaam reluctantly nodded. "My song. *Behique's* song." He poked his finger to his chest several times. "I sing. You are quiet." He put his hand over her mouth and shook his head. "Quiet."

He sang half a verse, then opened one eye to see what she was doing. The girl was sitting, hands in her lap, her eyes closed, head tilted slightly back. Uxaam's taut lips relaxed a bit.

He held the smudge pine in the air again and waved it. Satisfied, he meditated for a moment, taking himself to the spirit world. Then he chanted again, softly, quietly. Slowly the gray behind his closed eyes vanished like the pine smoke.

He flew on the wings of the great eagle, high over a land surrounded by water. Huge spikes of earth jutted into the air, rising from the back of beautiful white beaches and turquoise waters, a sight which he had never seen before. The land was covered with thick lush foliage, some of which was so foreign to his bank of knowledge that he wondered if he had the words to explain them to others.

This was her land. How had the spirits known to take him there, to the Taino, who did not even know the same spirits?

The wind rushed past his face as the eagle came closer to the island. He saw a small village, houses built round, surrounding a central court, slings hanging from trees, baskets heavily laden with fruits, women with flattened foreheads like the child's. The men banded their hair in tufts, barren between, with forelocks cut in a fringe nearly to their eyebrows. Their foreheads were tattooed. One man stood out amongst the rest. He wore a headband of green cylindrical beads with an ornament made of the beaten and flattened substance the girl wore in her bracelet. He wore earplugs of the same. The cacique.

Then the eagle dipped one wing and turned, soaring back out over the sea. A pod of porpoises swam ahead of the eagle's shadow, rolling in the blinding sunlit water.

He heard a whoosh and felt his skin prickle. A cold wind splashed his face, and suddenly the gray behind his closed eyes returned.

Slowly he lifted his lids. Nyna, too, opened her eyes. She smiled at him.

Uxaam shuddered.

"Go," he said, pointing to the short ladder.

Nyna climbed down.

In the afternoon a thunderhead moved from the west to the east, the underbelly of the clouds swollen and dark. Low rumbles of thunder preceded the storm, and the animal sounds grew quiet. At last, when the heavens could hold no more, great sheets of rain were purged, soaking the Hawk village. The rain extinguished the cook fires, streamed through the thatch of the huts, and soaked everything and everyone.

When dusk fell over the coastal village, the rain had finally ceased. The Fire Keeper rekindled the central hearth with tinder he kept protected from the elements. When the fire was suitable, the Hawk clan gathered and Uxaam again initiated the ceremony with his chants and songs. The humid air hung over them like soggy hides. The food, so crisp and fresh yesterday, lay sodden in the plaza.

"Nyna come forward," Uxaam said.

The crowd stirred with agitation just as Uxaam and Chogatis had anticipated. Giving the child a totem was an implication of acceptance.

"The child lives with Ais and needs a totem spirit to look after her," Uxaam said. "The spirits spoke to me today."

The people settled down and turned toward the girl.

Nyna held Nihapu's hand tightly.

"Go on," Joog whispered. "It is good. He gives you your totem."

Nyna let go of Nihapu's hand and walked forward. She looked up at the faces of the people who parted so she could pass. They questioned, still unsure of her. Some, like Ochopee, she was sure still distrusted her.

She knew Uxaam was completely confused by her, especially after his spirit journey this afternoon. Standing just in front of him, Uxaam held out a small pouch on a leather cord. He put the necklace over her neck. "The porpoise speaks for the girl, Nyna."

The sound of enlightenment rumbled through the crowd. They had heard she came on a long journey over the Big Water. Yes, the porpoise was a likely totem.

He turned Nyna by the shoulders so she faced the crowd, the sea of faces with so many questions written on them.

Uxaam went on to give names to two newborns of the

village. He announced that when Laira was well, he would give her her totem.

A group of men gathered in front of the fire, the plaza their stage. They had fought the Jeaga, and like the reenactment of a hunt, these men decided to once again tell the story of a battle with the enemy.

They began with Etac calling out the battle cry. Immediately the others who participated whooped and shrieked, wielding their weapons, striking and killing the phantom enemy. So profound was their performance they sometimes forgot for a moment that this was a dramatization. Their hearts beat heavily in their chests, and sweat slicked their bodies.

At first Nyna backed away, reminded of the Carib attack on her people. She had not seen much that terrible night, but it was enough, and she had heard her father's story many times. Her stomach soured. Then suddenly her eyes converged on Ochopee's weapon. He held a war club, a piece of wood with shark teeth embedded in it. Then her eyes jumped to another who sliced his sharp, beveled shell knife through an imaginary throat. There were clubs embedded with sharp shell fragments, shields to defend themselves from blows, lances and sticks with stingray spines in the end that one of the performers pretended to jab up an enemy's nose into his brain.

Nyna's eyes darted from weapon to weapon. Her people possessed none of these killing weapons. Her people had weapons for hunting, but there existed only small animals on her island—*hutias*, snakes, rodents—nothing the size of the deer and bear that lived in the land of the Ais.

The dancing and feasting lasted until well after the moon was high in the sky. The men drank the hot cassina, the black tea. It made them break into heavy sweats and purge everything from their stomachs. The man who drank the most and was the last to empty his stomach was considered the champion for the night. Tonight that man was Etac. He was celebrated. The men were cleansed and ready to start anew. This was a time for thanksgiving and celebration! For one night, conflicts and concerns were put aside.

Word had spread that Nihapu would marry the cacique, and the women gathered around her full of questions and excitement. Every time Nihapu had a chance to glance up, she saw Chogatis watching and smiling from a distance. Their eyes caught through small spaces between dancers, men whose raucous laughter belted in the night, bevies of women who clustered to gossip . . . glimpses here and there. Nihapu felt a little tingle that made one corner of her mouth lift in a flirtatious curve.

Zinni listened to the music and laughter from inside her hut. Unexpectedly she flinched. Immediately her hand touched her belly. Tears quickly pooled in her eyes.

10

The next morning Nihapu stopped in to check on Zinni and Laira. The air was crisp and clean, the sky already a blinding blue.

"Are you feeling well?" she asked.

Zinni nodded that she was. "I need more medicine. It did not work," she said. "Last night I felt the baby move."

"I told you the medicine was not reliable. Besides, you need to give it time. Something may still happen yet."

"But if it does not, Ochopee will be so angry. Please prepare more of the medicine. I will follow your advice this time."

Nihapu rubbed her upper arms to ease a slight chill. "If it did not work the first time, it should not be repeated. I hope you have done no damage with your foolishness."

Zinni's head shot up. "What do you mean?"

"Do you not realize what you have done? The potion is a kind of poison. Taken in small doses it has one effect, in large doses another. As you were poisoned by the medicine, so was Laira, and so was the unborn child inside you. I only hope the baby has faired as well as the two of you. But that is a difficult call."

"You think the child might be damaged? There might be something wrong?" Zinni's voice trembled.

"We know there are certain things an expectant mother cannot eat or do or it affects the baby or the birth. Eating animal heart and liver will discolor your face, and if you stand in the doorway to look out, you will have hard labor. There are so many of those simple things. This was a powerful medicine. I do not know what it might do. If it did not kill the baby, what has it done?"

Zinni's voice strangled on her fear. "I may have made all my husband's fears come true! What will I do if there is something wrong with this child? What will I do?" She was crying now, and Nihapu stroked her hair.

Nihapu felt sympathy for the desperate woman. "All happens because the spirits deem it to be," she said. "Sometimes we are careless, and it seems we have intervened in the great plan for us, but I think in the end, we find ourselves on the path the spirits designed for us no matter what detours we take. There is nothing you can do, Zinni. If the spirits want the baby healthy, then he will be. If he is to be damaged, that is their will, and you must accept it."

Several days passed after the celebration. Nyna wore her totem about her neck. Often she touched it with her fingers hoping to gain some sense of what it was all about. She didn't quite understand its significance, but she did know that it made her more acceptable to the Ais.

Joog told her to open the pouch and look inside. They sat together in the hammock. Nyna had shown him how to hang the fish net correctly so it was more a hammock than the sling he had initially prepared. Her fingers nimbly urged the drawstring of her totem pouch to loosen. Then she held the pouch upside down. Two articles tumbled out into her waiting hand. She pushed one of them around on her palm.

"What is this?" she asked.

"It's a piece of porpoise bone," Joog said. "It has been fire polished."

Nyna inspected it, curious at why she should wear an animal bone around her neck.

As if he could read her mind, Joog explained. "The spirit of the porpoise protects you and guides you."

Nyna accepted Joog's explanation. She supposed the idea was a nice one. The other article was a small, rolled-up hairless piece of hide. It was tied with palm fiber.

"Open it," Joog said.

Nyna worked the fiber string loose and slowly unrolled the palm-sized hide. Inside was the tip of a small eagle feather. It caught in the wind and floated away.

Nyna started to run after it. "No," Joog said. "The feather is meant to be free. Uxaam only wanted you to see it and then it would be free. Do you know why he wants you to think of the eagle?"

"Yes, I think so," she said, recalling the spirit journey she had accompanied him on over her village in the sea. She wondered if Uxaam knew she had been with him. Perhaps that was the meaning of the eagle feather, to let her know that he was aware of her presence.

Nyna laid the small hide swatch out straight. Etched on it was a fine drawing. She sucked in a breath and gingerly touched it.

There it was before her, a sketch of her homeland—the beach with its gentle waves and palms, the round huts, the court, the corrals, the mountains that jutted into the sky.

She thought she might cry. She ached to return home. She wanted to eat *batatas*, peanuts, beans, sweet guayaba, and savory *perdices*. She wanted cassava cakes and food from the pepper pot, tasty and spiced with *aji*. And she did not want to sleep on the hard ground with the insects.

Joog stared, amazed by the black-line etching Uxaam had done with stain and the fine tip of a shark's tooth. Joog watched Nyna, how she gazed at the miniature drawing in wonder and remembrance. One day she would decide to go home.

"Is that what it looks like?" Joog asked.

"More beautiful," Nyna answered. She smiled and hugged the hide to her chest.

"Let us show Buhgo!" Joog said.

The two jumped down. Nyna stuffed her things back into her totem pouch. As they sprinted across the village, she spotted Uxaam. Nyna paused, grabbing Joog's arm to make him wait. They stared at one another for a moment, then Uxaam nodded, almost imperceptibly.

"Will you tell me now?" Buhgo asked his mother. "Tell me what happened to you and Laira."

Zinni put down the paddle she used to press into clay pots. The paddle had a design incised on it, and when she pressed it on wet clay, it left a stamped design on the pot.

"Nihapu made a tea for me, a woman's tea," she began. "She instructed me to take it over several days, but I ignored her directions."

"Why would you ignore what she told you?"

"I was anxious, in too much of a hurry. I brewed a tea with all the medicine in it and sipped on it all day. When I was not watching, Laira drank some also. That is why she got sick, too."

"What kind of medicine was it?"

Zinni turned from him and picked up the paddle and began to stamp the design into a wet pot. "I told you," she said. "A woman's tea."

Buhgo realized he was prying. Perhaps his mother did not want to discuss *women's* issues. Still, he was haunted by her mysteriousness.

Suddenly, Zinni turned to her son. "A new baby grows inside me."

"A baby!" Buhgo shouted with excitement.

"Shh, I have told no one else, but Nihapu."

"Father knows?"

Zinni's finger's knuckle pressed against her teeth. "Not really," she said.

"Why have you not told him?"

"I wait for the right moment. For now it is our secret."

Someone called Buhgo's name. Both Zinni and her son turned.

Buhgo sprang to his feet. Nyna and Joog ran up to him.

"You will not believe what Nyna has in her totem pouch," Joog said. "Wait until you see. Zinni, you will want to see, also. Show them."

Nyna extracted the rolled-up hide and unfurled it. Small as it was, Uxaam had taken much time in etching the finest detail on this very small rectangle.

"Look close," Joog said. "See the trees on the beach, the land and how it rises in giant peaks."

"Ooh," Buhgo said, totally fascinated.

Zinni stared at the sketch. "This is where you come from?"

"Taino," Nyna said. "My home."

Zinni struggled to understand. "How does Uxaam know such about a land he has never seen?"

"Yes," Buhgo said. "How does Uxaam know?"

"Spirit man," Nyna answered.

Buhgo and Zinni sat back. They knew Uxaam was a powerful shaman, but this was incredible. Their respect for him swelled.

Laira came over to see, craning her neck. Zinni held the drawing closer. She pointed to a small tree, smaller than the ones Uxaam had drawn on the beach. The tree had wide leaves and what appeared to be a stalk loaded with long, cylindrical curving fruit.

Nyna looked closer and her eyes lit up. "*Abanoa*," she said. Then she pretended to peel and eat one of the fruits. First she held it up and peeled the skin down in three long sections, then put the fruit in her mouth. She smacked her lips.

"How far away?" Zinni asked. She had never seen or heard of fruit like this. The girl had to have come from a very faraway land. And also unknown to her were the skinny trees that lined the beach, with their arcing trunks, clusters of enormous nuts, and drooping fronds at the crown.

Joog answered for Nyna. "She was in a canoe for quite a few days before washing up on our beach."

"Such a long journey for such a small one," Zinni said. If Nihapu was right, if they always ended up on the path that took them where the spirits wanted them to go, then why had this path been chosen for Nyna?

The Ais believed that the winter cold wind was the breath of ancient beasts that once roamed the earth. Their spirits still dwelled in another world, a place where the air was cold. So large were these creatures that it was said the earth had trembled beneath their footfalls. There were animals like the panther, only twice the size, with enormous incisors that slashed and pierced its prey. Bears and wolves, lions, animals that existed only in legends. Uxaam claimed to have the remains of the largest beast of all. It was an animal that staggered the imagination, tall as three men, with fanning, flapping ears and a wrinkled snout that looked like a fat snake that hung to the ground. This beast had round, tree trunk–like legs and circular feet larger than a man's head. Tusks curled up out of its mouth in gigantic graceful arcs.

It was said it was part of a tusk that had been passed down to Uxaam through generations. The legend said it was magic and for the shaman's eyes only. Uxaam shared the stories and descriptions of all the colossal creatures that lived so long ago, but he did not let anyone look upon that sacred piece of tusk. It was used in the most solemn of rituals and always under cover of a specially cured and softened hide cloth.

The Ais regarded the northern winds with great trepidation. The cold wind on their necks was a reminder that perhaps those fearsome animals of long ago might return again. Men were at the mercy of the spirits and had best please them!

Winter was the dry season and always there was the fear of the drought. It was the time that the old ones suffered. Their knobby bones ached, and many got sick and died. Neither was it a good time for infants. Like the old ones, they did not tolerate the cold.

Even though winter was short, now that it ended, the Ais and all the people of the region were grateful.

Zinni had not been able to keep her secret very long. Her belly swelled, and the pregnancy became obvious. Ochopee was livid. She explained over and over again how she had attempted to satisfy his demands.

"But you did not take the medicine as you were told," he yelled. "Now you are still with child and what kind of child will it be? You have made things even worse. When this child is born, it is yours, not mine. I will have nothing to do with it."

"But it is your child, Ochopee, you know that. What will people think if you disown this baby? They will think I was unfaithful and you are kind enough not to turn me out."

"I do not care what they think!"

Zinni sat at the hearth, her face in her hands. She had seen that villagers looked up at her husband's ravings. She knew she and Ochopee were the topic of many conversations, especially the gossipy old women.

Cetisa had come to a complete stop as she walked by. She did not even look away when Zinni noticed her. The woman watched their argument with no shame.

Zinni felt sick. She knew it was obvious to all that Ochopee was displeased with his wife, and she knew the speculation was that she had been unfaithful. No one knew that Ochopee had demanded that she rid herself of the child, and that she had tried to obey his wishes. She was the object of scorn.

She feared for her unborn child and prayed that he be born with no defects. Perhaps when Ochopee saw the baby, and saw that it was normal, he would take pride in the child and things would return to the way they used to be. Zinni wanted her husband back. She wanted him to hold her in the night, touch her again. Since she had told him of the pregnancy, he slept away from her and denied all affection.

Cetisa bathed in the stream. The water was high, and she was able to immerse much of her body in it. This winter had been exceptionally wet, and the Ais and wildlife flourished.

She lathered the crushed fruit of the soapberry tree in her hands and over her body.

Her sister was going to marry the cacique today. The thought riled her. Nihapu had everything. Cetisa wanted a child, something of her own to love that would love her back unequivocally. She had been with Etac all this time and still no child grew in her womb.

Cetisa rinsed and came out of the water. She used the frayed woody stem of the gouania vine to clean her teeth. The stem was aromatic but a little bitter. Nevertheless it left the mouth clean and toughened the gums. She crushed a berry from the rouge plant and dipped her finger in it. Usually used as a paint, Cetisa was careful to use the red juice only as a faint stain on her cheeks. Her face appeared slightly aglow, as if excited, or as it did when in the midst of joining with Etac. When a man would look at her, might it make him think of such a moment? she wondered. That was her intent.

After she dressed, Cetisa returned to the village. Her wet hair shone in the sunlight. Her body smelled sweet and clean, and of course there was the very subtle provocative flush to her face.

Etac glared at her when she entered the village. She smiled at him and passed by. Cetisa had exceptionally long legs for an Ais woman, her long strides were graceful and her whole body moved with her legs, arms gently swinging at her side, hips swaying.

Ochopee stood at the central hearth, chatting with a few men. Cetisa came close, slowed as she passed him, tossing her hair, a barely discernable sensual smile forming at the corners of her mouth and in her eyes. With her mouth only slightly open, she tasted her lips with her tongue. Her eyes paused on Ochopee as she wiped away the dew between her breasts with a single finger. Delighting in the look of awe on Ochopee's face, she moved on.

At first there was silence behind her, but then she heard Ochopee and his friends. Yes, she had brought some attention to herself. Cetisa was pleased, and now that the men could not see her face, a broad grin came over her.

Tonight there would be much celebration. The crescent moon overhead, the flicker of firelight, and the mood of the moment would benefit her plan.

11

Before dusk the men gathered on one side of the village to feast with Chogatis. Nihapu and the women gathered on the other side. The tittering of the women added to Nihapu's nervousness. She wondered, as she had done so many times, if she was doing the right thing. She did not love Chogatis, not the way she loved Tsalochee. But over the last few turnings of the moon, she had spent more time with him. While they walked and talked, she often found her mind wandering, thinking of what it would be like to be his wife and especially the wife of a cacique.

There were things about him that Nihapu found pleasing. He was gentle in both speech and demeanor. He was fair, wise, compassionate. He was patient, and certainly spent devoted time with Joog.

This would be the best thing for the Ais and for her family. She did not want to have to find a man to marry her and provide for them. And who would take Nyna? Chogatis was right.

The sound of the conch horn called the men and women together. The oldest married men formed a semicircle around half the central hearth, behind them the next oldest married men. The women did the same on the other side of the fire. They waited for the appearance of Chogatis and Nihapu.

First Uxaam went for Chogatis. "You are ready, Cacique?" he asked.

Chogatis was dressed in his finest buckskin breechclout and vest. Bands of shells covered his legs from ankle to knee. His body was washed with lime, and he carried a sleeping-skin blanket neatly folded over his arm.

"I am ready," Chogatis said.

Uxaam led the cacique to the center of the gathered crowd where he waited while the shaman fetched the bride.

"Chogatis awaits you," Uxaam said to Nihapu.

She followed Uxaam, head demurely bowed, the snowy egret feathers entwined in her hair, floating on the breeze. About her neck she wore a shell gorget on a necklace that Chogatis had made for her, and on her arm, she, too, carried a sleeping blanket.

Uxaam led her next to Chogatis, and the groom and bride stood quietly before the people.

Nihapu found it difficult to look up, but Chogatis took her hand and patted it, reassuring and calming her. Then he took her blanket and folded it inside his.

The women giggled and sighed, covering their mouths with their hands in hopes of muffling the sound.

Uxaam chanted a prayer, then looked at the couple. "You will be as one flesh," he said.

The crowd clamored with excitement. There was no doubt this was a strange uniting, but still there was much to celebrate when their cacique took a wife, especially after he had been without one for so long. It was his privilege to take as many wives as he wished. At least, now, he had one.

Chogatis led Nihapu away to his lodge, as was the tradition. The crowd grew even noisier. The celebration began.

Inside Chogatis's hut, he lay the blankets on the floor, one atop the other. Nihapu stared at him.

Chogatis bent again and moved the blankets side by side.

Nihapu moved to the dark side of the hut, where little

light leaked in. She turned her back and took the feathers from her hair.

Chogatis sat on a blanket and watched.

Her hair undone, it cascaded down her back to her waist. Nihapu's fingers slowly unknotted the waistband of her skirt. She waited a moment, then the skirt slowly slid from her waist, down her thighs and calves to her ankles, pooling around her feet.

Chogatis let out a deep breath. He had not looked at a woman in too many seasons to count. His eyes feasted on every swell and indentation of the woman before him. Warmth gushed into his groin and he heard himself sigh.

He had promised Nihapu that she did not need to fulfill *those* kinds of wifely duties. This was a marriage of convenience for both of them.

Chogatis lay down on the blanket fully dressed and rolled to his side. He closed his eyes, but when he felt Nihapu's warmth as she lay next to him, his eyes opened and stared in the darkness. He hadn't realized just how much he had missed a woman until now.

The joyful noise of celebration echoed in the village. Cetisa stayed in the background, keeping her eye on Ochopee. Zinni retired with the children, but Ochopee stayed for more festivities. The men ladled drink from large bowls, and the women danced with each other.

Late in the night some of the men swept their arms under their women and carried them off, all to the riotous applause of the other men. Etac came for Cetisa.

"Come on, woman," he said, biting her neck.

Cetisa gently pushed him away. "You go on," she said.

Etac pulled back and looked at her. "You smell sweet. Do you know what you do to me?"

"Stop, Etac," she said.

Etac stepped back, then looked about to see if others had noticed his wife's spurning.

"You go ahead to bed," Cetisa said. "I will be along."

"The marriage of your sister eats at you," he said.

"Yes," Cetisa answered. "I just want to be alone. Do you understand?"

"All right," he said, moving away from her. "If that is what you want."

"Go," she said. "Do not wait for me. Go ahead and sleep."

Etac briefly joined the other men who remained by the fire, then retired.

When Ochopee excused himself from the group and headed toward his hut, Cetisa intercepted him.

With a fluid movement she threaded her hair behind her ear. "What is your hurry?" she asked. "The moon is still high."

"I have gorged myself on food and drink," he said. "My head is light. I should sleep."

"You are not that old," she said, coquettishly tilting her head to one side and biting her bottom lip.

Ochopee took a step, but Cetisa blocked him. "Do you not think I look all right? Is there something you do not like?" she asked.

Ochopee looked her up and down. "You look fine," he said.

"Good," Cetisa whispered, touching her fingertip to his lips. "Why do you not take a walk with me? I am not ready to sleep."

She reached around his neck and massaged it. "It will be worth your while," she said. "Come." She took his hand and led him into the darkness.

A safe distance from the village, she stopped and turned to face him. She put both hands on his chest. "You are a strong man," she said, feathering her hands down his torso, then up his sides. "I know what a man like you needs. Zinni does not please you."

Ochopee grasped her hands and held them aside. "You have a husband," he said. "And I—"

"And perhaps he does not please me the way I need

to be pleased." Her eyes darted over his body. "You could please me." She stepped closer, her hands caressing the outside of his thighs, moving teasingly closer to the inside.

She went to her knees and looked at him. "There are no demands," she said. "But we both need . . ."

Her mouth was wet and hot on his legs. She trailed her tongue behind his knee and up his inner thigh.

Ochopee reached for himself, feeling the swelling and surging need for touch. Cetisa brushed his hand away. "Does she satisfy you?" she asked.

Cetisa released the belt of her skirt and slid it down.

She reached beneath his breechclout and took his man-part in her hands and pressed it between her breasts. With vexingly light touches she stroked him, keeping him locked in the cleavage of her breasts.

Ochopee arched backward, and his knees buckled. He groaned when she took him in her mouth.

"Yes," Cetisa whispered, her breath hot on his skin.

Ochopee sank to his knees. Cetisa lay back, and he fell on top of her.

He pumped into her in a delirium brought on by the drink and the raw need inside him. His body was quickly drenched in sweat as the frenzy peaked. He bucked, then stiffened, paralyzed by the pleasure and explosion.

When it was over, he slumped, his groaning muffled by the flesh of her shoulder.

"Yes," she whispered.

She let him rest a moment, then slid from beneath him, dressed and left.

By the time Cetisa entered her hut and lay down on her mat, Ochopee was asleep on the ground where she had left him.

The adults were late to rise, but the children already played. Joog sent his hoop rolling across the plaza. He quickly took aim, then hurled his long pointed stick.

He jumped and whooped as he saw his stick whoosh through the center of the hoop and clatter to the ground. The hoop finally wobbled and fell to the side.

Joog thrust one arm in the air with victory.

Guacana slapped him on the back. "Your aim is perfect," he said.

"I want to try," Nyna said.

"This is a boy's game," Guacana reminded her. "For warriors, not women. Go and weave your baskets that I hear you are so good at making."

Nyna looked at Joog. "You can watch," he said. "I will teach you the game later."

Buhgo retrieved Joog's hoop as Guacana rolled his own. Guacana, too, centered his stick through the hoop.

"Ais are the best warriors!" Joog cried.

It was Buhgo's turn. He balanced his hoop, then swiftly ran his hand over the top to begin its roll. The hoop wobbled a short distance and fell over.

"Try again," Joog said. "As my grandfather says, everything takes practice and patience."

"He will never do it right," Guacana said.

Joog ignored him. "Do it again, Buhgo."

The boy ran out and picked up his hoop. This time he closed his eyes tightly as he righted the hoop and balanced it. Finally he dared to open his eyes and stare at the hoop in concentration. He sent it rolling.

The hoop rolled successfully, and Buhgo quickly took aim with his stick. Hurriedly he sent it flying through the air, sailing way above the hoop and behind it. The stick skittered in the dirt in what seemed a deafening and unending clatter.

Guacana roared back in laughter. "I told you," he said. "His wife will starve . . . but then he is a wife," he said, clutching his sides as he laughed.

"Be quiet," Joog said. "He is learning."

Guacana's laughter heightened. Barely able to get the

words out he said, "Go weave baskets with Nyna. You are nothing but a girl. A girl!"

Guacana suddenly lunged at Buhgo. He reached out, grabbing for the boy's breechclout. "Let me see underneath. I bet you have no manpart. Let me see!" He was laughing so hard he was spitting as he talked. Tears rolled down his cheeks.

Buhgo was horrified. He pushed Guacana's hand away as it clutched his breechcloth.

Suddenly Nyna was on Guacana's back. "Stop," she yelled, slapping his face with one hand and wrapping her arm around his neck. She pounded and kicked Guacana, hanging on with her elbow crooked around his throat.

Guacana fell to the ground and Nyna went down with him. She sat on his back and held his head in the dirt. "Say sorry!" she screamed.

Guacana struggled to get free, and Nyna pushed his face harder in the dirt. Guacana sputtered.

"Tell him, sorry."

When Guacana did not respond, she took a hank of his hair and yanked his head back. With her other hand she twisted one of his arms free and bent it up against his back. She jabbed his elbow, threatening to snatch his shoulder out of the socket. Her knees squeezed his sides.

Guacana grunted.

"Say it," she said.

"I am sorry," Guacana whispered.

"Loud!" Nyna demanded.

Guacana apologized louder, and Nyna nudged his arm up even higher.

Guacana let out a shriek.

"Now who is girl?" she said.

The crowd of gathered children laughed deafeningly loud.

Buhgo put his hand on Nyna's back. "Let him go," he said.

"He is mean!" Nyna said. To her, Buhgo was the

Taino, her people, gentle, easy, caring, defenseless. Guacana was the Carib. A sense of exhilaration swept over her. It felt good to smash his face in the dirt, to shove his arm nearly out of the socket. She wished he had not said he was sorry yet, then she could have pushed his arm up even farther!

"Do not hurt him more," Buhgo said.

"For my mother and father," she said with one last thump at his elbow. Nyna slowly released the pressure on Guacana's arm. When she let go of his hair, his head dropped as if tied to a weight. She climbed off the boy and dusted her knees.

Nyna straightened up and grinned at Joog. "That was good!" she said.

Ochopee felt a knock in his side. Groggily he lifted his head. Chogatis stood over him, nudging him with his foot.

"Zinni looks for you," Chogatis said.

The sun burned Ochopee's eyes. He raised up on one elbow, shaded his eyes with his hand, and squinted. "It is morning?"

"Not so early, but yes, morning."

Ochopee got to his feet and rubbed his face. "Tell her I have gone for a bath."

"I think that better come from you. She wondered where her husband has been all night."

"Umm," Ochopee muttered.

At the stream he splashed water on his face and hair. He shook his head, sending out a halo of water droplets. He rinsed his mouth, then sat back on the bank.

"Cetisa," he said aloud. What was she after anyway? Had she had an eye for him all this time, and had he not noticed?"

Ochopee recalled her boldness. It was certainly exciting, he thought. Zinni had never been so aggressive. Yes, he liked it. Maybe she would see him again.

Ochopee returned to the village. Zinni did not look up at him as he took his atlatl and lance.

"What do you hunt?" she asked.

"Whatever I find," he said.

"Why do you not take your son along? Teach him."

"It is women's stuff he wants to learn, not men's."

"He is your son, and he needs a father."

"He has a mother," Ochopee said as he left. He passed the central hearth where several of the men gathered. He looked for Etac and saw that he was with the group. He continued on, hoping to find Cetisa. Finally he spotted her scraping the inside of a rabbit skin.

"I want to talk to you," he said, gesturing with his head for her to follow him.

Cetisa put down the fur. She waited a moment, looked around, then took the same path as Ochopee. They met in the cover of the woods.

"Tell me," he said.

"Tell you what?" she asked.

"What was your cause last night?"

Cetisa put on a wry face. "Did you not like it?" She smoothed her hand over one breast.

Ochopee gazed at her. She was being playful and seductive. "I liked it," he said.

Cetisa took his hand and cupped it around her breast. "I think you did," she said, bending her head and touching her lips to his hand.

"I do not understand," Ochopee said.

"There is nothing to understand. It is obvious to everyone that Zinni does not satisfy you, and Etac does not know how to please me."

Ochopee moved closer. She did make it sound so simple. He clutched a handful of her hair and pulled her head back, exposing her long neck. He bit her just below her ear. Her whimper of pleasure sent torrents of heat through him. If she wanted to be satisfied, she had chosen the right man.

Ochopee tore away his breechclout and lifted her by the hips.

Cetisa laughed and nibbled his earlobe as he slid her down over his erect manpart.

He groaned with the warmth and wetness of her. He took a few steps forward, carrying her, her legs wrapped about him, and leaned her back against a tree.

He could wait no longer, her soft moans of pleasure feeding the fire inside him. He buried his face in her shoulder and plunged into her over and over.

Cetisa's fingers clawed at Ochopee's sweaty back.

In a moment he was done, the weight of his gratified body pressing her into the tree. He could not move for a moment. Finally, as his manpart gave up its staggering rigidity, he slowly withdrew.

"You see," she whispered.

A rustle in the brush made them both look.

"Who is there?" Ochopee called.

12

Nyna thought about the scuffle with Guacana as she gathered reeds. She cut another rush with Nihapu's woman's knife. Guacana was a mean-spirited child. Perhaps he would leave Buhgo alone now. She was glad that Joog had found her and not that boy.

Where was Joog? she wondered. He had taken her to this place near the cenote, the sinkhole, so she could gather reeds. Then he had said he wanted to check a trap and would be right back.

Nyna bundled the reeds she had collected and laid them on the ground. She moved to a clear spot where the villagers came for water and bathing if they did not use the stream. The sinkhole, fed by an underground spring, was quite beautiful. The water was sparkling clear and tinted the most incredible aquamarine.

Nyna put her foot on the ledge and edged out to the water. The sun was warm on her back, and the cool water covered her feet. Looking at her reflection, she touched her forehead. All the Taino women had flattened foreheads. Mothers kept their sleeping female infants' heads pushed against a cushion. If Nyna had been older, she would have had red-colored, x-shaped tattoos on her forehead, too. She wondered what Joog would have thought of that.

Suddenly Joog ran up behind her, breathless.

"Joog?" she said, bustling out of the water. His face was red, and he panted. "What is wrong?"

"Nothing," he said. "Nothing for you to worry about."

"The trap?"

"The trap was empty. There is nothing to worry about."

"You breathe hard," she said.

Joog and Nyna carried their things to Chogatis's hut. It was rectangular and bigger than the other huts, much longer, much wider, befitting a cacique.

"There is so much space," Joog said, putting down his armload of possessions. He wandered around. Rooms were separated by partitions. He entered one room, where low benches formed seating platforms. This was a place of important meetings . . . by invitation. Few had ever been inside the cacique's home.

"Why so many rooms?" Nyna asked.

"The cacique can take many wives. He needs room for all his family. Chogatis chooses not to take many wives."

Joog continued to look around, fascinated by the large house. A few moments later he realized Nyna had wandered away.

He found her in the area where Chogatis stored his weapons. She lifted a lance.

"No!" Joog said.

Nyna jumped and dropped the spear.

"Women do not touch weapons," Joog said.

"Can I look?" she asked.

He shrugged. "You can look. Why are you so interested in war weapons?" he asked.

Nyna did not hear his question. Her focus centered on the weaponry. Her father had only a knife, hidden away in the back of their small hut. She had heard the Ais word *war* and realized her people had no such word.

The weapons she stared at were not for hunting. These were not designed for such clean kills as that. These were the instruments of murder. There were large and small spears tipped with stingray tail spines, horseshoe crab tails, bone and antler points, stone points, and sharks' teeth.

Several atlatls were bunched together. There was one made from oak and another from red mangrove. Oak and mulberry bows hung from support posts, along with an array of arrows with feather flights. On the ground were spools of twine and cord wound around wooden pegs. She looked at the different kinds of rope, four-ply, two-ply. Some rope Chogatis had made from sabal palm trunk fiber, some from agave, mulberry bark, and some from sabal palm leaf split fiber. She knelt next to a basket that contained two bolas.

"Come," Joog said.

When the boy turned his back, Nyna reached up and stroked the shaft of one of the arrows. Her finger slid down the smooth wood.

"Tend the fire," Chogatis told Joog as he poled his canoe through the water.

Joog scooted closer to the elevated clay-lined basin that cradled the fire. He fanned it and fed it more light wood. The boy watched the sparks fly into the clear night air. Stars covered the sky and only wisps of white clouds slid past the moon.

"There," Chogatis said, pointing to a swirl in the water. "Get your spear."

Joog grabbed the shaft of his spear that lay in the bottom of the piragua.

"Slowly," Chogatis said, reminding Joog to be careful and quiet as he got to his feet.

Joog gradually straightened. "I see them," he said, spotting the fish in the moonlight. "Snook!" His voice was soft so as not to startle the fish, but yet filled with excitement.

"Remember, the water is distorting," Chogatis whispered. "Concentrate. Patience."

Joog perched in the bow of the dugout. Patience, he

said to himself. He lifted the long-shafted harpoon, wrapped the end of the attached cord about his wrist, and held the spear ready.

Joog singled out a fish, focusing on his target. Then with a flowing movement, as if his arm were part of the weapon, he thrust the harpoon into the water.

The spear entered the water cleanly, hardly leaving a ripple. Joog flipped his hand so he could hold the cord. The line went taut with the fish's short-lived attempt at escape.

"I have him!" Joog shouted.

Joog pulled in the cord, retrieving his spear and his prize, a large thigh-thick snook.

"A good catch," Chogatis said.

Joog held the fish down with his foot and pulled out his harpoon. It was a fine fish, one that would make a satisfying meal for his family. Nihapu would be proud.

On their return, Chogatis asked, "Have you been practicing?"

"Yes," Joog answered. "I think I am getting better. I find that I can cross the third curtain, but I have trouble staying there."

"That is the challenge," Chogatis said. "The mind wants to do as it pleases. You are taming it, training it to do as you command. Do not get discouraged."

Joog sat quietly in the piragua, watching his grandfather pole the canoe. Chogatis seemed to belong there, to be a part of the sea, the wind, even the sky. His grandfather was a wise man. There was something he should ask Chogatis, but he did not want to bring trouble to anyone.

"Grandfather," he finally said, "if you were to see something, something you happened upon by accident, and what you witnessed you knew was wrong, what would you do?"

"I suppose it would depend on the circumstances. What kind of wrong thing?"

The image of Cetisa and Ochopee together fluttered through his mind.

"Have you witnessed something?" Chogatis asked.

Joog could not lie to his grandfather, so he chose not to answer, and Chogatis let it be.

"When you are ready," Chogatis said. "Perhaps that is what keeps you from the world past the third curtain. Troubling thoughts have ways of interfering."

Yes, Joog thought, perhaps that was what was hampering his success. He could not get to the place of oneness if he could not pass through the third curtain because he anguished over the decision to tell someone about Ochopee and Cetisa.

But then, he thought, what Ochopee and Cetisa chose to do was not his business.

Another cycle of the moon passed. Every time Joog was around Ochopee or Cetisa he was uncomfortable. Several times he noticed Ochopee disappear and Cetisa would soon follow. Yet, in the village no one seemed suspicious, and the two of them paid no attention to each other when people were around.

What was this joining attraction? He did not understand. As he got older he realized there were more things he did not understand than those that he did.

"Mother," he said one day. "Why do men and women join?"

Nihapu's head popped up. She hesitated, then said, "To have children. Just as the birds and rabbits, a husband and wife want children."

"Yes, but something is different with people," he said.

"What do you mean?"

"Animals have seasons for breeding. I do not think that is so for men and women."

Nihapu combed her hair back from her forehead with her fingers. "You are correct."

"Why would a man and woman join if it were not to have children?"

"It can be a pleasant thing when the man and woman love each other."

"So it is done either to make children or because a man and woman love each other?"

"You will understand better when you are older," she said.

"I am not sure it appeals to me," he said.

Nihapu laughed. "Wait to make that judgment when you are a little older. Soon you will understand. What has prompted this interest?"

"I just wondered," he said.

"Well, if it is on your mind, that is evidence that the time is coming that you will soon experience these feelings you wonder about . . . feelings a man has."

Joog was still confused. Did Ochopee and Cetisa want children? Did they love each other? But they were married to others.

Joog shook his head. This was a curious thing.

Nyna stood on the beach, looking out over the sea as she often did. The wind blew in her ears, and the waves crashed on the shore. She did not hear Guacana come behind her.

Suddenly, one of his hands was over her mouth and the other yanking her arm up behind her.

"How is that?" he said. He knocked her feet from under her, forcing her to the ground. Nyna thrashed wildly, swinging her free arm and kicking. She hit the ground with a thud. Guacana sat on her chest, pinning her arms down with his knees.

"Get off me!" Nyna yelled.

Guacana lifted his weight and flipped her over. "Eat the sand," he said. "Let me see you eat the sand."

His hand held her face on its side, her cheek flat on the beach.

Guacana then turned her so she was facedown. The grit crept into her eyes and nostrils.

"Do it!" he said, yanking her hair to lift her head.

Nyna did not respond.

The boy grabbed a handful of sand and slapped it against her mouth. The broken edge of a shell sliced her lip. Guacana rubbed the sand hard on her mouth, abrading her lips.

He pushed her face back down in the sand. "Enough," he said. "Do not ever come near me again or I will shove dirt down your throat until you choke!"

Suddenly he was off her and gone. Nyna lay still on the beach. Her shoulder ached, her scalp was sore, her lips burned, and it hurt to open her eyes, they were so full of sand.

Finally she sat up, brushing her face. She crawled to the water and rinsed her face. The salt stung all the little cuts and especially her eyes, but at least she washed the sand out of them.

She tasted blood and licked her lip, then pressed on it with her finger so it would not bleed.

Joog saw her as soon as she came up the trail to the village.

"What happened?" he asked. He pulled her hand from her mouth.

"Guacana," Nyna said.

Joog took her to Nihapu. "Guacana did this to her," he said.

Nihapu held the girl's face in her hands. It was etched with scratches, and her lip was slightly swollen. Nihapu tousled Nyna's hair, shaking loose the sand.

When Nihapu's hand roughed up the spot where Guacana had pulled her hair, Nyna flinched.

Joog looked around the village. "Where is he? I will take care of Guacana!"

"No," Nyna said. "It is over."

Joog's temper continued to flare. "He did this because

you defended Buhgo, and he was humiliated. He deserves to be humiliated . . . again!"

"Let it end," Nyna said.

"She is right," Nihapu said. "If you retaliate, then this will go on and on, and he will hurt Nyna again."

Joog knew his mother was right. Ais had laws that encompassed severe punishment for a man who harmed another. But children were given freedom . . . freedom to get hurt and learn from it. Guacana had learned there might be a consequence for taunting another, and Nyna had learned that there were consequences when one humiliated another. Chogatis would say the matter was ended.

"It is a decent thing to want to defend your friend," Nihapu said. "It comes from here," she said, putting her fist over her heart.

"Guacana is unkind to everyone," Joog said.

"Then he will be taken care of," Nihapu said. "The spirits see to that. It is not your place."

Joog wished the spirits would do something right now, and do it so he could witness. But that was not the way they worked.

"Rest for a while," Nihapu said to Nyna. "Lie on your mat. Let your shoulder rest."

Nihapu led Joog outside. She spoke softly so her voice did not travel inside. "Do not forget that Nyna is not Ais. Many still think that she may be a witch. There are only a few of us who truly accept her. The people let her stay because of Chogatis. No matter how evil Guacana is, if there are sides to be taken, the Ais will side with Guacana. If you pursue the issue, it will only make it worse on Nyna. The people might be forced to choose. Do you understand?"

Again his mother was right. Nyna was still not accepted. That was clearly evident by all the mumbling when Uxaam had given her a totem. He supposed it was better to keep this incident quiet.

Nihapu touched her son's cheek. "The only reason there was no outcry over the first scuttle between Nyna and Guacana is because the episode was so humiliating. Guacana was overpowered by a girl younger than he. He wanted that kept quiet."

"Sister," Cetisa said, walking up. "Or should I address you more formally since you are the cacique's wife?"

"Good day," Nihapu replied.

Cetisa glared at Joog.

Joog fidgeted.

Nihapu glanced back and forth between her sister and her son. "What is this about?" she asked.

"The boy is growing up, right?" Cetisa said. "Then he should be setting traps and procuring food."

"He does."

"Some time ago I noticed a trap there," she said, pointing. "Close to the cenote. Was that yours?"

"I have had one there," he said.

Cetisa glared at the boy. "I suppose you checked it often."

"Yes," Joog said.

"What have you come for?" Nihapu asked.

"Just to pay a visit," Cetisa said. "We are sisters . . . family. I only wanted to make sure you were faring well in your new marriage. Family must look out for each other and protect each other. Is that not right, Joog?"

"Yes," the boy answered.

Nihapu shook her head. "Cetisa, this is a peculiar visit. Speak the truth. What brings you here today?"

"I told you," she said. "Where is the spirit girl? The sun child?"

"She is resting," Nihapu said.

"You know there is still much gossip about her."

"Yes," Nihapu said. "Idle talk with no truth in it."

With the passing of many days, Zinni grew ready to deliver her child. Cetisa heard the news that Zinni's labor pains had started. She touched her own barren belly. Ochopee had not given her a child either. She would have to end it with him. Joog knew, and he would always be watching. She was tired of Ochopee anyway.

Cetisa looked across at the birthing hut. The birthing huts, or women's huts, were used for both delivering babies and for menstruating women who had to stay isolated from the others. Cetisa wondered what it would be like to visit one of those huts for the purpose of having a baby instead of having to go because her womb was empty. Why did Zinni deserve another child while she had none?

Ochopee was coming her way. When he passed her, he gestured for her to follow and meet him.

Cetisa caught a glimpse of Joog by the central hearth. He was watching, just as she knew he would be. This would be the last time she met Ochopee. It was much too dangerous. She waited for the boy to busy himself with something. At last he turned away from her.

Cetisa hurried into the forest. Ochopee stepped from behind a tree, one hand firmly grabbing her breast, the other running up under her skirt.

Cetisa pushed him away. "Joog was watching," she said. "And you should be waiting outside the birthing hut."

Ochopee pushed his pelvis against her. "This is what I should be doing."

"No," Cetisa said, squirming away. "I think this has become too risky. We should not do this anymore."

Ochopee grabbed the back of her head. "What do you mean?"

"We cannot keep on. Joog saw us together, and now he watches. One day he will tell."

"You are his mother's sister. He will say nothing that will bring harm to you."

"I cannot take that chance. We must end it."

"No," Ochopee said, clutching her upper arm. "Joog

would have told already if he was going to. If you are so afraid, then leave your husband," Ochopee said, squeezing her arm tight.

"You are hurting me," she said.

"There is no shame brought to you if you have no husband."

"And you would leave Zinni? You have problems in your marriage, but in your heart you love her or you would be without a wife already. We pleasure each other, but I do not love you, and you do not love me. I love Etac, and I do not want our marriage endangered."

Ochopee's face wormed into a look of disbelief. "What are you saying?"

Cetisa backed away. "We gave pleasure to one another, and that was good. Now it is done."

Ochopee stood rooted, watching her turn her back to him and leave.

Zinni held on to the pole to keep herself balanced as she squatted. Nihapu stroked Zinni's belly.

"The contractions are hard," she said, feeling the muscles beneath her hand tighten.

"Yes," Zinni grunted. "They have gone on since mid-morning."

Nihapu sponged Zinni's body with cool water.

Zinni's knuckles grew white as she gripped the pole. She leaned her head to rest on the post. This one was stronger still, starting in the small of her back like a flame, then circling her in a band of raging fire, taking her breath from her. She bore down, pushing until her face reddened.

"Good," Nihapu said, reaching under Zinni to examine her. The bag of waters was still intact. She probed with her finger, poking the sack until it broke, a splash of water hitting the ground. "Not long now."

Zinni's breath exploded from her at the end of the

next contraction. She panted. "Another," she said, feeling the heat begin again in her back.

"They will come harder and more quickly now," Nihapu said. She pushed down on Zinni's belly, helping the baby find its way. "Push hard," she said.

Zinni drew in a deep breath and held it, bearing down until she thought the pressure would split her open.

"I feel the head," Nihapu said. "You are doing a good job. Just a few more pushes and you will cradle this new life in your arms."

"No more. No more," Zinni cried at the end of the last pain.

"The baby waits to be sure you want it. He pauses at the door of life. Show him how much you love him. Push him out into this world so you can show him. Push! Push!"

Zinni gathered all her strength, pushing down, eyes squeezed shut, cheeks blown up with air.

"Good, good," Nihapu said. "He comes."

"Aiyee," Zinni screamed on the burst of breath that rushed from her.

Nihapu caught the baby in her hands. "A boy," she said.

"Let me see," Zinni cried. "Is he all right? Tell me he is."

"Lay back," Nihapu directed.

"Give me the baby," Zinni said.

Nihapu did not answer. She cleaned the baby's face, and the child wailed.

Zinni reached out her arms.

Nihapu looked down at the child. She swaddled him in soft buckskin, then laid him on his mother's belly. "The afterbirth still comes," Nihapu said.

Zinni touched the top of the baby's head. "Is he beautiful?" she asked.

When the afterbirth was delivered, Nihapu took the child again, cut the cord, and tied it off with sinew. "Put him to suckle," she said, giving Zinni the blanketed newborn again.

Zinni looked into the face of her son and put her finger in his tiny palm. His hand curled around it. "He is beautiful," she said. "Look at him. All this time I worried for nothing."

Nihapu stood up and went to the entrance of the birthing hut. Ochopee was not there, only several of the village women.

She spoke quietly so as not to upset Zinni. "Someone go get Uxaam, and hurry," she said.

13

"Why is he here?" Zinni asked Nihapu, seeing Uxaam come in. She looked down at her baby. "There is nothing wrong," she said. "He is beautiful."

Uxaam bent next to her. "Let me have him, Zinni," he said.

Uxaam lifted the child from Zinni's arms.

"Look at his back," Nihapu said.

Uxaam opened the buckskin blanket and turned the infant over. At the base of the child's spine was a pouch, skin covering an opening of the spine.

"What is wrong with him?" Zinni asked. She sat up. "Tell me!"

"I have heard of this," Uxaam said, "but I have never seen it." He crouched next to Zinni. "Here," he said, lightly touching the defect. "Do you see? This must be protected at all times. I think he may not live," Uxaam said. "I will do what I can."

Zinni began crying. "Where is Ochopee? Does he know?"

"I have not seem him," Nihapu said.

"Do not tell him! Please! Give me the blanket," she said tugging at the buckskin tucked beneath Uxaam's arm.

"You cannot keep this from your husband," the shaman said. "That will be impossible."

Zinni's attention turned sharply to the doorway.

"Keep what from me?" Ochopee asked.

Silence filled the room, sagging heavy in the air as if it had weight.

"There is something wrong with the child," Ochopee said, his voice flat. He stood for a moment, looking from person to person before deciding to leave.

Ochopee's silhouette passed through the doorway. Why did the spirits torture him so? he wondered. First Buhgo, and now another. This is exactly what he feared, and Zinni had botched the chance to get rid of it.

He wandered to the beach and sat on a rocky out-cropping. The waves spilled over the rocks where he rested his feet. He had not even asked what was wrong with the baby, or looked at it. It didn't matter if it was a boy or a girl. Something was wrong . . . imperfect. Maybe the child's head was misshapen like that girl's. Bad things had happened since her arrival. There was the fish kill, now the baby. And Cetisa?

Ochopee got up and tromped back to the village.

He found the cacique. "I want to see you, Chogatis."

"I have heard the bad news," Chogatis said.

"No, you have not," Ochopee said. "But you need to hear it! This girl, this Nyna, that you have allowed to live among us, she brings bad luck!"

"You think Nyna is the reason for the child's defect?"

"I think we are seeing effects from our interference with the spirits. She was cast out of some other world."

"Bad things happen all the time," Chogatis said. "Sometimes we understand why and sometimes we do not. We did not understand why we suffered the drought. Were we punished then? For what?"

"As you say, sometimes we do not understand. But sometimes we do, and this time we *do* understand."

"You are upset now Ochopee. Do not say anything more. Let some time pass."

Joog sat on the ground on the north side of Chogatis's house. Nyna was drawing a picture of a manioc plant in the dirt. He could hear the conversation between Ochopee and Chogatis. He wondered why Ochopee did not suspect he was being punished for something he did, for being with Cetisa when he should not have been.

He heard Ochopee leave, then saw him as he crossed the plaza. Joog feared he was going to start trouble again for Nyna.

"I will be back," he said to Nyna as he stood.

Keeping out of sight, Joog trailed Ochopee to a small group of men.

"The child is defective," Ochopee said.

Joog thought his choice of words odd. *Defective* sounded as if he spoke of a tool, not a baby.

"Think about it," Ochopee was saying. "How many of you have had bad luck since Chogatis permitted Nyna to live with us. I tell you, the Ais spirits are angry."

Joog felt sick. He knew he would have to do something.

For days Joog pondered what to do. He watched Nyna at play. She seemed so innocent. There was so much good in her heart. He thought of how she had come to Buhgo's defense.

As he watched her now, he was intrigued with the way she entertained herself. She stood, feet planted firmly apart. She whirled her hand over her head as if she were readying to cast a bola. Yes, she looked exactly as if she were hurling a bola. She had accompanied him often enough as he hunted raccoons and rabbits with his bola. On those occasions he noticed how she studied him.

"What are you doing?" he asked her. "What do you play?"

Nyna smiled at him. "I am like Joog. I hunt."

Joog grinned. "What do you hunt?" he asked.

Nyna spun the make-believe bola over her head again. "Carib," she answered.

Joog took her whirling arm. "Nyna, women are not

hunters, nor are they warriors. If others see you do this—"

"I cause trouble?" she asked.

"Yes," he said. "The Ais do not understand you."

Nyna sat on the ground and reached inside her totem pouch. She pulled out the drawing and looked at it. "I want to go home," she said.

"I know," Joog said. "One day when you are old enough, then maybe you can find your people."

"When I am old?" she said, misunderstanding.

"Older, not old."

Joog squatted next to her. He needed for her to understand how she had to be careful not to make herself any more curious or misunderstood than she already was. She could not play that she hunted, or that she wielded any kind of weapon. She had to avoid the taboos of their culture.

"Nyna, Zinni has a new baby." He held his arms as if rocking a baby.

"Baby," she said.

"Yes, but something is wrong with the baby."

Nyna's face saddened.

"Ochopee is so disturbed, he must find a reason . . . something to blame. His pain confuses him. He goes about saying that the Ais spirits are angered by your presence. He feels Chogatis should not have interfered."

"Ochopee thinks I am bad," she said.

"Yes," Joog answered. "You must not even pretend you play with weapons or do other things the Ais would think strange. You must be careful."

"Oh," she said. She looked away for a moment, then back at Joog. He saw deep hurt buried in her dark eyes. She was so young to have suffered so much pain, both before she arrived and after she had come to live with them

"Does Joog think I am bad?" she asked, tears beginning to well in her eyes.

"No," Joog said. "Nyna is good." His heart ached for her. He hoped that one day she would be able to return to her people. The Jeaga woman, Talli, and her husband Banabas, had done all they could to make his life pleasant when he lived with them. But no matter how much they came to love one another as a family, they all knew that he was an outsider, Ais, the enemy. He could never be Jeaga any more than Nyna could be Ais.

Chogatis lay on his mat, eyes open, listening to the night sounds. He spoke softly so only Nihapu could hear. "Ochopee will not let the issues surrounding Nyna rest. He is sour inside."

Nihapu turned on her side to face her husband. "His heart is crushed by this baby," she said.

"That is his disposition, with or without this new child. When he was a boy, he was determined to be the fiercest warrior of the Ais. He tortured himself, held burning sticks to his skin, and pierced his flesh with thorns, all to make him resistant to pain. An unusual boy and man. I hope his focus on Nyna will deteriorate, but I think it will not."

"You made the right decision, Chogatis," Nihapu said. "Nyna comes from so far away that no one knows her people. If she was Calusa, the Ais would not want her, but she would not be feared."

"You are right," Chogatis said. "Like most men, Ochopee fears what he does not know. He cannot believe that there are people so far away that we do not even know of them, that the earth is so large that we cannot imagine how much we do not know. Even Uxaam, in all his wisdom, knows only the Ais spirits . . . and only what those spirits choose for him to know."

Nihapu touched Chogatis's face. "I think it is you who has the wisdom."

"Sometimes I stand on the shore and look as far as I can. I see where the sea ends in the flat line against the sky. But as far as we have gone in our dugouts, we get no closer to that place where the water meets the heavens. I think no man can go that far."

"How do you think of such things?" she asked.

"I suppose serious contemplations are part of aging. When I was young, I thought I was wise. Now as I grow old, I know I am not."

Nihapu laughed and put her head on his chest. "That in itself is wisdom."

Chogatis stroked her hair. Nihapu's show of affection warmed him.

Joog scooted outside at the break of dawn. Unable to sleep, he had waited for the first sliver of tawny light to come through the trees. He wanted to catch Ochopee early.

Mosquitoes still swarmed, not yet intimidated by the pale light. At least when it was cold they were not such pests. With the return of the warm weather they multiplied. Even the oil that made his body gleam in the light did not ward them all off. He slapped at a large insect on his arm.

"Ha!" he said, seeing he had flattened the bug. He wiped the smear of blood away.

Ochopee emerged from his hut and stretched. Joog waited as Ochopee faced the east and sat with his legs crossed to greet the day. When the man finished, Joog took the advantage.

"Buhgo is sleeping," Ochopee said when Joog came to him. "He will wake soon."

"It is not Buhgo I wish to see."

"Oh," Ochopee said. "Then who?"

"I come to say to you that I am sorry about the baby." Joog stopped. He had practiced this speech all night in his head, now he stumbled on the words.

Ochopee's hand swept over his brow.

Before Ochopee could say anything, Joog found his

voice again. "It is a sad thing that has happened, but Nyna is not to blame."

Ochopee heaved out a stale breath. "So that is why you come to speak to me so early."

"She is only a little girl who has come here from far away. Her people were attacked by Caribs and she was set out to sea."

"Caribs," Ochopee said. "Have you ever seen or heard of a Carib . . . or a, what does she call her people?"

"Taino," Joog said. "Her people are Taino. But you do not have to see one for them to be real."

"And this dugout that came from so far, where is that?"

"The tide and current took it away."

"You are a foolish boy, but I expected more of your grandfather. There are those of us who talk. We will confront Chogatis about this girl."

"No!" Joog said. "Think of this before you speak. I saw you and Cetisa and I think the spirits punish only you for what you have done. If there is trouble for Nyna, then I will have to tell the truth."

"That would be bad for Cetisa," Ochopee said. "The Ais show no sympathy for unfaithful women."

"It would also be bad for you. You now hold high ranking in Council. You have betrayed Etac, the War Chief. You would lose your status."

Ochopee forced a smile. "They will not believe you."

"Chogatis will, but even if others do not, it will give them something to think about . . . there will always be that doubt."

14

The seasons turned with predictability, coming and going, hot and wet, dry and cold. Little ones grew, and old folk died. As it should be. Times were good for the Ais. For many seasons the rains came as needed, and life was an ostentatious pageant of fertility and abundance. But the old ones did not forget the time of drought, the time thirst parched their throats and hunger pangs pained their gut. They still talked of approaching their southern neighbors, the Jeaga, for territory along the river. Joog, they decided, should be their emissary, as he had lived among them. When the boy at last became a man, and skilled with the finesse of persuasion and the mastery of command, then he should present their request to the Jeaga. As long as the spirits remained good to the Ais, the weather cooperative, they would be able to wait until that time came.

As time went on, Joog assumed that his conversation with Ochopee had made a difference, as the talk about Nyna quieted just after. For some time now there had been little dissension concerning the girl. She was still not truly accepted and trusted by the Ais, but she was tolerated. Joog often stood back and watched Nyna. He found he liked the newly forming curves of her body and the sound of her maturing voice. He recalled asking his mother so many seasons ago about the reasons a man and woman joined. He thought he now understood, just as she said he would.

Guacana did not change as he grew older. He found ways to harass Nyna, never forgiving her for humiliating him. Nyna did her best to ignore him, but as he aged, his aggression became more brazen and bold.

Zinni cared for her new child dutifully and, remarkably, he lived. Uxaam gave him the name Taska, warrior, for he was a fighter. Zinni watched over the child day and night. The first four days she had no sleep, afraid that an ancestor ghost would come and hold the child and take him away. Buhgo and Nihapu convinced her that if a ghost came for him, there would be nothing she could do, and by being so tired, she could not tend to the baby as she should. Finally, Zinni relinquished and slept when the baby slept.

So that Taska would teethe properly she asked Yixala, an old man of the village, to rub the child's gums. When Yixala was young, he was bitten by a snake and nearly died. Because of that incident, he was given the gift of the *snake that wants to bite* and therefore was responsible for the Ais children's teeth coming in properly.

There were other rituals to ensure a new child's future. As deer never get sick, Uxaam burned deer hair and held the child over the smoke so he might keep well like the deer. Joog brought the baby his offering, a snared mockingbird. Its tongue was boiled to form a broth, and a gray-and-white feather put in the baby's blanket. Zinni dipped her finger in the broth and then put her finger in the baby's mouth. The family ate the small amount of bird breast. This pledged that the child would talk well.

Another custom had yet to be performed. This custom was the father's responsibility. "You must do this," Zinni told Ochopee. "You do not want your son to be afraid of the dark." She lifted the wooden bowl of water-soaked embers. "It is a father's duty."

"I told you he is not my child."

"But he is. He is your son. He is our son." She held out the bowl. "Rub it on his chest, over his heart."

Ochopee hesitated.

"He needs his father's courage. I cannot give him a man's bravery. Please."

Ochopee reached in the bowl and took one of the embers. Zinni took up the baby and unwrapped his blanket, exposing his chest.

Ochopee smeared the wet black soot over his son's heart.

"You will be proud of him," Zinni said.

Ochopee paid the child little attention and gave Zinni no help in his care. Because Taska could not walk, his mother carried him everywhere, and as the boy grew larger, she found it increasingly difficult. Still Ochopee offered no aid.

Buhgo moved gracefully, and his hands talked like a woman's hands, but much to everyone's surprise his body grew muscular and powerful. To his father's disgrace, he continued to study the medicines with Nihapu, and others had begun to take notice of his healing skills. Many eyes grew blind to the aberration and now saw the gift he possessed. Some had even summoned Buhgo to a sick loved one's bedside. He had always helped his mother care for Taska, and now he took on the chore of carrying his brother most of the time. Buhgo built a litter that two could carry, and he also built a small travois that could be propped up. Despite Taska's physical anomaly, he was bright, cheerful, intuitive, and wise beyond his years, another surprise to all. He talked remarkably early and could converse on subjects much beyond his age. His inquisitiveness was incessant. He asked questions and then questioned the answers he was given. Ochopee saw these deviations as faults, just more conditions that made Taska different.

As Taska grew, some noticed a unique look in his eyes, as if sometimes he were really somewhere else. Though he was mostly happy and joyful, he occasionally had terrible dreams. Those dreams did not come frequently, but when they did, no one in his house slept well. His mother would wake him from the dream with his heart pounding and his body drenched in sweat. Though she prodded, and he tried, he could not recall the exact nature of the dreams. Buhgo was the first to notice that Taska's nightmares usually preceded a tragedy in the village. The first one had come when a young woman had her baby too early. The child lived only a day. Another dream preceded a sickness that swept through the village youngsters, leaving one of them deaf. And then he had had the terrible nightmare the night before the oldest woman in the village died.

Taska had other bad dreams, and Buhgo could always match them with incidents in the village. Zinni and Buhgo began to expect there was some mysterious magic in Taska, but Ochopee only saw the imperfection.

Ochopee refused to sleep with his wife and in general neglected his family. The only one he paid any attention to was Laira, but as she saw her father's resentment of the rest of the family, she had little time for him. He lived with them and provided for them, but his days of being a good husband and father had nearly been forgotten by his wife and children.

Cetisa was still without a child, and she grew more bitter with each day. She resented her sister more deeply than ever and rarely spoke a kind word to her or her family. She was openly critical and harsh, something that did not go unnoticed by others in the village. Etac cajoled his wife and comforted her. Most men would have thrown her out or taken another wife if the first wife bore him no children and behaved as poorly as she did. But Etac did not entertain that idea. He loved Cetisa, understood her, and that was enough. If the spirits deemed they should not have children, then it would be so.

Joog had come of age, and it was time for him to enter manhood, just as Nyna stood on the brink of becoming a woman. Even though she was younger than Joog, she would acquire the status of woman at about the same time he participated in the rites of manhood. Girls became women earlier in their lives than boys became men. Nihapu spoke to her often, teaching her the Ais customs surrounding the onset of the first menses. Nyna could not recall the Taino tradition. The memories of her people and even her native language slipped through the tiny holes in her mind that time put there. She fought to recall all that she was able to, recounting the routine of Taino daily life as often as she could. Today she told Joog and Laira about a way of fishing.

"Remoras," she said. "The fish that stick onto sharks with suction-cup mouths. Our fishermen hook those through the tail and attach fishing string. Then they are turned loose in the water. The remoras seek out sharks and turtles, fasten themselves to them, and when the fishermen pull them up—"

"What a clever idea," Joog said.

"Whatever would make them think of such a thing?" Laira asked.

"The Taino like to relax," Nyna said. "No hurry. So they let the remoras do the work for them." She whisked her hair from her face. "One day I want to go home again," she said. "But when I do, I want to take my people something. I will need your help."

"What?" Joog asked.

"I know this is a difficult thing I request, but you are the only one I can ask."

"Go ahead," Joog said. "Tell me what you want."

"My people have no weapons. They do not know how to defend themselves."

Joog found such a concept hard to believe. "But they hunt. They have weapons for that, do they not?"

"There are no large animals, only small ones. The weapons for hunting are not good for defense against the Carib. We do not hunt large animals. We eat mostly fruits and nuts, fish and manioc." She tried to explain *batatas*, sweet potatoes.

"A root, like coontie?" Laira asked.

"Not exactly," Nyna said. "It is orange and sweet when roasted."

"No deer or bear where you come from?" Joog asked.

"No."

Joog circled a stick in the dirt. "And do the Taino not have neighbors they have fought against?"

"No," she said, "not until the Carib. When they come, they destroy the village, all the people. There is nothing much left. The Taino are gentle people and are unprepared for warfare. The Carib have been savage for all their time. The Taino cannot make up those generations of learning weaponry and warfare and catch up with the Carib. They need help." Nyna shuddered. The Taino would give anyone anything they asked for, but the Carib asked the only thing they could not give. "They only want to rape and abduct young women and feast on the flesh of men."

Laira gasped. "Where do they come from? Will they come here?"

"They spread across the sea," Nyna answered. "But I do not know their origin."

"I am afraid," Laira said. "What if they come here?"

Nyna shivered with the thought. "At least the Ais know how to defend themselves. My people need this knowledge." She reached and touched the top of Joog's hand. "Will you help me? Teach me how to make and use the fiercest of weapons?"

"That is forbidden," Laira said. "Women do not touch weapons. Never! It could render a weapon useless."

"I would not touch anyone else's. Joog would teach me to make my own."

"It is time for the last lesson," Chogatis said to his grandson. "In a while Uxaam will direct you to go on your first vision quest so that you can become a man. This time alone will be an intimate time, a time you determine the image of yourself. You must be ready."

Joog sat next to his grandfather and took the four deep breaths, in through the nose, out through the mouth. He had progressed from having to concentrate on a real object to finding a focus inside his head with his eyes closed.

Joog relaxed his body, starting with his feet and ending with his scalp, feeling the tension wash out. He sank inside himself, down the steps deeper and deeper inside, letting go of the outside world. No stray thoughts entered his mind, just absolute darkness. Instead of interpreting the sound of the surf, the squawk of the bluejays, the background noise became a blur with no meaning and no definition.

The blackness was overwhelming, blanketing all thoughts.

Chogatis's voice spoke in his head. "You are nearly there, boy, in the place of oneness, where you can see with the eye in your heart rather than with the eyes in your head. The time is at hand."

Joog felt himself drifting up and out, back into his conscious self. He did not rush the process, but let his mind return to the world on its own time. He opened his eyes.

"You are ready," Chogatis said, his voice melodic.

Joog's hair prickled on the back of his neck. "Are you certain?" he asked.

"The fasting will purify you. Then as you pass through the last curtain, the vision will come. You will be one with all. You will be part of the wind, the soil, all life blended into one Great Spirit. You will see."

Joog was eager to begin his journey and at the same time apprehensive. This time was what a boy strove for all his life.

"Mark your face with this charcoal," Chogatis said.

"Make solid lines across your face, evidence that you fast and purify yourself."

Joog took the burned stick and dragged it across his face, the first line cutting across his forehead, the next beginning at the temple smudging across the corners of his eyes, over the bridge of his nose and across the other eye to the opposite temple. Then again he drew a line just beneath his nose and another across his mouth.

"Good," Chogatis said. "All will see that you fast, that you are ready."

Nyna watched as Joog prepared. She feigned to tend to some sewing, but her eyes settled on the stick as he drew the lines. She noted the sharp edge of the bones of his face, the strong square jaw. Indeed, Joog was no longer just a boy, but someone balanced on the precipice of manhood.

A hank of Joog's black hair hung in a braid at the side of his head, a leather thong with white shell beads woven in it. A scarlet cardinal's feather dripped from the end. He was quite a handsome sight.

Buhgo and Taska also watched the preparations. During the last full moon, Guacana had been sent on his vision quest. Buhgo would be next, Uxaam decided.

"Will I be a man?" Taska asked.

Buhgo didn't know how to answer.

"Probably not," Taska said, answering himself. "I cannot go on a vision quest."

"But I think there are exceptions, different ways of becoming a man, because of your condition. There will be other rites, other ways. Uxaam will know when the time comes."

Taska looked up at the sky. "Do you feel something?" he asked.

"Why?"

"The air is different. The birds talk. The tree spirits talk."

"I do not hear them."

"I do . . . the bird and tree spirits. They whisper today."

"Why do you not tell these things to Uxaam and let him help you interpret them? This happens to you often." Buhgo's attention turned to the central hearth. "Look," he said. "I think Uxaam is ready."

Taska stretched his neck to see better. He glanced at the shaman and then across at Joog.

Joog stood tall in front of his grandfather. Chogatis pressed a white bead in his hand. "My father gave me this when I went on my first vision quest. I gave it to your father on his first quest. He carried it in his totem pouch until he died. I believe he would have passed it on to you." He opened the boy's pouch and dropped the bead inside.

Joog clasped the pouch with his hand. It was good to have something of tradition, something passed from generation to generation. The oyster bead would bring him good luck.

"Uxaam awaits," Chogatis said.

The cacique and his grandson trod to the central hearth where the shaman and the men of the village gathered. The women and children stood back at a distance, not allowed within this sacred circle of men.

Uxaam took a handful of ash and spread it over Joog's chest, then his arms and legs. "Man has a scent all animals fear. The ash washes it away, allows you to walk among them."

Uxaam implored the spirits. "All the powers of the universe, the ancient ones, the four directions, all things that move in the universe, hear me. All waters, all trees, all the sacred ones, hear me. This young man comes to you so he may know how he and his future generations are to live as you wish. Hear me then." Uxaam held a worn leather satchel up over his head so all could see.

Buhgo's eyes were glued to the shaman and Joog. He felt no enthusiasm for his first vision quest as other boys did. A shudder ran down his spine. He deeply feared that he would fail and bring his father more shame.

Suddenly, Buhgo noticed something moving just out of the corner of his eye. Taska held his arms in the air. His eyes were closed, but his mouth moved, mimicking Uxaam's every move and word.

"Taska!" Buhgo said. "Stop. You make a mockery of the spirits."

Taska's eyes flew open. "This will be a dangerous journey for Joog," he said.

"All quests are dangerous."

"This one especially," Taska said.

"Uxaam does all he can to keep him safe," Buhgo said. "The rest is up to the spirits."

Joog's body tightened as Uxaam lowered the satchel and withdrew the shell knife, its edge beveled and sharpened, glittering in the sun. Uxaam took Joog's hand in his and turned it palm up. He drew the knife on the inside of Joog's palm, slicing the skin in a shallow straight line. Everyone watched to see if the boy flinched. He did not.

Blood beaded along the cut. Uxaam squeezed Joog's hand, and a droplet of blood spilled on the ground.

"Mother Earth," Uxaam called. "Here is the blood of this boy who becomes a man. Recognize him wherever he might be."

Then the shaman spoke to Joog. "Now Mother Earth breathes inside you, and you inside her. She is your friend. Hear her voice and listen to what she says in all that you do."

Uxaam produced another small pouch and removed a thorn. On Joog's upper arm he pierced a series of dots and lines, forming a unique geometric design. He took his black paste of charcoal and bear grease and smeared it deep in the design, then with a cloth he wiped away the excess. When Joog's arm healed, a black tattoo proving his entrance to manhood would remain.

With no weapons or provisions of any kind, Uxaam
sent Joog alone into the forest.

Nihapu and Nyna watched from a respectable woman's
distance away, both their hearts beating swiftly. The men
remained solemn. This was a sober occasion. It would
not be time to celebrate until the young man returned
in victory. As always, when a boy disappeared into the
trees in quest of his first vision, a tinge of apprehension
hung in the hearts of the people. Uxaam said a quick
prayer for Joog's safe return.

Joog followed his instinct, his bare feet light on the
ground. The spirits would guide his direction and lead
him. He watched the sun, noticing whether it was to his
right shoulder, or left, behind him or straight ahead. By
late afternoon his stomach grumbled, and he feared he
would grow hungry and show weakness.

With the sun at his face, the horizon glowed, shining
through the pines with its furious fire. The sky was
streaked in magnificent oranges, yellows as bright as the
sea daisy's petals, purples as deep as the cocoplum, and
reds as crimson as fresh blood. Fanning rays of light, the
color of Nyna's armlet, stretched into the sky, through
pink clouds and into the darkening heavens.

He sensed he was near and stopped to say a prayer.
He knew the place for his quest was to be far from the
village so he would be self-dependent, and it had to be
an area of risk.

Joog stood erect to make sure the spirits could see
him so deep in the pines. "I have come in humility, with
only my breechclout. I bring no worldly possessions. I
have come to lament that I might understand who I am.
My body has been made pure, and my blood has been
sacrificed to Mother Earth."

The pine needles crunched beneath his feet as he continued on. A sudden wind soughed through the trees.

Joog stopped and looked up at the rustling pines. The wind whispered, then seemed to murmur his name.

Joog turned in circles, looking for the source that sighed his name. The breeze brushed his face, cold and eerie, and the sound of faint music carried through the pines.

This was the place, he realized. From this time, when the rim of the sun barely held on to the sky, nightfall would come quickly. He gathered armfuls of pine needles and then covered them with soft ferns to make a bed. He would spend the night with an empty belly, alone, with no fire, no tools, no weapons, at the mercy of the spirits. He prayed he was worthy of their charity and they would see fit to soon give him a vision.

Joog waited in the darkness, crouching for a long while, chanting, saying prayers, calling to the spirits. The mosquitoes were incessant, stinging, fluttering in his nose and eyes. His skin dampened with anxious perspiration. Clearly he heard the cry of a panther nearby. He kept watch for the eyes. Bears also wandered these woods. He had seen a rub just before he came upon this place. Deer liked it here amongst the pine and oak, rich with berries and nuts to eat and thickets in which to hide . . . and they made good prey. That meant the predators would search this ground for a nightly meal.

Though the bed Joog prepared was enticing as he grew more tired, his instinct told him not to sleep. If he had fire, he would have napped, because the flames would deter predators. But if he chose to sleep so vulnerably, he would be taking a great risk. And what if that was a sign the spirits looked for, what if they tested his endurance?

By morning his throat was dry from lack of water and all the praying and chanting. When the first rays of light stung his eyes, Joog celebrated. The spirits had found grace in him for this first night. Perhaps today the vision would come. He had heard the stories of boys who waited for their vision and it did not come. If the spirits found no reason to give the boy a vision, his life ended in slow starvation and thirst, or by the bite of a snake, or other attack.

No boy could return to the village without a vision—that would bring too much disgrace to him and his family. And surely the shaman would see through a vision invented by a boy.

Joog's pulse sped up at the thought of an entire day passing and he had not had a vision yet. Most boys took three days, he knew that, but still the passing of one day made him anxious.

By late afternoon Joog's stomach growled with hunger. The temperature climbed, and the air stood still. Even in the shade of the trees his body oozed sweat. His mouth dried out, and when he prayed out loud, his words sounded sticky.

Joog stood tall, his arms stretched high over his head. "See me!" he shouted. "I am Joog, a boy who is ready to become a man. I come with no weapons, no food, no water, putting my trust in you. I leave myself vulnerable, defenseless, knowing you see me. Give me a sign!"

Joog prayed aloud over and over, his hair sticking to his sweaty head, neck, and shoulders. His voice grew weak, and his body slack with exhaustion. As evening came and passed, Joog still stood amidst the trees, calling out, now crying, for the spirits to receive him.

Finally, before daybreak, he sat back on his heels. "Why can you not see me?" he screamed. "I am Joog of the Ais, a boy ready to become a man. I come unarmed, defenseless, putting my trust in you! My spirit is not broken. I hunger and I thirst, but I do not quit. I am Joog of the Ais, a boy who is ready to become a man!"

He repeated his call over and over until his head became dizzy. He had been without food, water, or sleep for a full two days.

The morning of the third day, Joog noticed he no

longer felt hungry. Now he only felt weak and ill. If the vision did not come soon, he knew he would perish alone in these woods, an embarrassment to his mother, his grandfather, and his people

The air, heavy laden with moisture, hung over him like a sodden hide. Tears left streaks through the dirt on his face. The soil clung to his legs and feet, and every part of him that touched it.

Joog finally sank onto the bed he had prepared when he first arrived. How still the trees seemed, he thought. Nothing rustled and even the birds were quiet. Then in the distance he heard a buzzing. It grew louder, coming closer. Joog watched through the trees. Something moved, covering the ground as far as he could see. Whatever it was, was coming at him . . . for him . . . the whirring sound roaring louder and louder.

15

The ground itself seemed to flutter and vibrate in the distance, coming closer all the time. The air became hazy as if a great fog had settled in.

Joog got up, his eyes boring ahead. Is this it? he wondered. Was this real or a vision?

As the line of thundering earth came closer, Joog's mouth dropped open. Through the mist he saw grasshoppers, so many he knew there was no number that could count them. They covered the earth, marching toward him in a yellow, black, and red legion. Waves of the large creatures moved over the land, hiding in the fog, stirring up the soil and debris beneath them. They moved as if time slowed down, and he could see every movement of their legs, every flutter of their wings.

"Yes," Joog whispered, realizing this was indeed a vision. He frantically emptied his mind of distracting thoughts. He closed his eyes to help him pass through the curtains. He forced himself to acknowledge and then let go of the interfering thoughts, going deep inside himself. He summoned all his concentration. He could not fail now! He felt his energy and tension pass through his body and out the top of his head, leaving him relaxed and focused . . . through the third curtain. Down, down, down. At last, the fourth curtain.

Slowly Joog opened his eyes so he could see his spirit messengers. To his surprise the land was still, the mist vanishing as he watched, and with it the grasshoppers also faded right into the air.

He felt wind at his back, blowing his hair. Joog turned to look. Great white wings beat the air as an enormous and beautiful egret settled to earth. The bird gazed at him, its eyes clear and brilliant like raindrops. There in the egret's eyes he saw the image of himself. Then silently the majestic bird lifted into the air, a single feather floating down into Joog's hands.

The vision ended, but the wind continued. Joog looked at the darkening sky. A storm brewed, and from the looks of it, a bad one. A drizzle of rain already fell. Exhilarated and exhausted, Joog sank to his knees, lifted his face and arms to the sky in thanksgiving, the rain falling gently on his face. He would return to the village a man!

"I do not like it," Uxaam said. He and Chogatis stood on the shore. The waves were high, crashing over rock, the wind a steady scream. He bent and touched the water. "It is warm," he said. "Too warm."

Chogatis cupped a handful of the water. It seeped through his fingers, the gale catching it. "The weather has been too hot. The sea brews like tea over the fire."

Uxaam stared across the ocean. "The signs are not good," he said. "The wind grows worse, the squalls coming closer together. Mother earth births a storm the same way a woman brings forth life. This storm comes soon."

"Joog," Chogatis said. "He has not returned."

Uxaam did not answer. Joog had not yet returned from his vision quest. This was the end of the third day. No one stayed longer than four days . . . if they were to return.

The morning had been blustery and drizzle had fallen. The squalls began mid-afternoon. Chances were good Joog would be caught in the storm that brewed.

Chogatis and Uxaam had seen these kinds of storms,

bred and nourished deep at sea. They happened in the warm season, especially when the heat was severe. Storms, such as the one they suspected was coming, had wiped out entire villages, swept them clean away as if they had never existed. The Hawk had been spared many seasons. Perhaps it was time.

"You know what will be said," Uxaam said. "They will blame the girl."

"I know," Chogatis said.

Uxaam opened his arms in the wind. He began a chant in the ancient tongue used only by shamans. Chogatis left him on the beach and returned to the village.

"Husband," Nihapu said, greeting him, "I see worry in your eyes."

Chogatis leaned his head back and looked at the clouds. "A storm comes. It is time to warn everyone." He took her hand in his and looked at her face. "It has been a good life with you, Nihapu. You are a good wife."

"You sound as if you do not expect our good life to continue. This storm has you worried."

"Yes," he said.

"And Joog?"

"I especially fear for him."

"What can we do?"

Chogatis rubbed the top of her hand. "Wait."

Joog knew he was close to the village. He could not be that far now. He had ended up far to the west, now he tracked back east.

Dusk would be upon him soon, and the weather grew increasingly worse. The fierce wind howled through the trees, and bursts of rain drenched him. As each moment passed, the storm grew worse.

With no visible sun to guide him, Joog pressed on, hoping he headed in the right direction. Lightning fractured the sky and was immediately followed by a crack of thunder. The clouds opened up with driving rain that stung his skin. Sheets of rain glided over his face, making it impossible to keep his eyes open. A gust of wind snapped a large branch and sent it hurling through the air. Pockets of debris-ridden air blasted through the trees with a furious roar.

Joog took refuge behind a large oak, huddling at its base. At times the lightning kept the sky as brilliant with light as if the sun shone. And always the barrage of thunder, the bellowing and howling of the wind hammered the earth. The ground reverberated beneath his feet. Green leaves, stripped from the trees, flew through the air.

On and on the storm blustered, mauling every tree and plant in its track.

A twig, not as big around as Joog's little finger, catapulted through the air. Then like a well-aimed dart, it stabbed Joog's calf. At first he didn't realize that the twig had actually skewered his leg. With both ends of the spike exposed, he was uncertain which was the entry point and which was the exit. His leg was red, awash with rain-diluted blood. Joog grabbed one end of the twig and pulled. The stick broke off.

He rested the back of his head against the tree and he glanced back at the wound. At least the bleeding was not terrible, though the pain radiated up his leg and into his hip.

The thatch rattled wildly, and as the wind shrieked, some of it came loose and blew away.

Nihapu huddled close to Chogatis and Nyna.

"Do you hear that?" Nihapu asked.

"The wind," Chogatis said.

"No, I hear someone," she said.

Chogatis shook his head. "Nothing."

"I hear," Nyna said. She scooted past Chogatis and Nihapu, shielding her eyes from the rain and wind.

She looked about, searching through the obscurity of the storm.

The voice called again. "Help me!"

Through the blinding rain, she saw someone standing in the middle of the plaza.

"Someone help me!"

Nyna ducked her head and pushed against the strong wind, moving toward the figure that called for help.

"No!" Nihapu yelled. "Come back!"

"Please help me! Please!" Zinni screamed over the roaring wind.

"What? What?" Nyna asked.

Zinni grabbed Nyna's arm. "Ochopee is dead! Taska is buried beneath the rubble. A beam pins him. Help me."

Zinni led Nyna to the place where her hut once stood. Buhgo held Taska's head up out of a muddy pool of water. Ochopee lay facedown, a gash on the back of his head spilling blood. Laira rocked back and forth, crying.

Chogatis and Nihapu appeared. "We need to lift the beam," Chogatis said. "Let me get this end, and Buhgo, you take the upper end and shove toward me. Push it upright. Nyna, give him some help."

Nihapu knelt by Taska. "When they move the beam, the release of the pressure may cause some pain. Be ready," she said.

"Now," Chogatis said.

Buhgo and Nyna lifted the end and shoved it, standing the pole on its end. Chogatis held firm so the post wouldn't slip. He moved to the side, and they pushed the beam away. It landed with a boom and rolled in the mud.

Zinni pulled Taska's head into her lap.

"I am all right," he said.

When the beam had fallen, it smacked Ochopee in the back of the head, then landed at an angle. The weight of the end that pinned Taska was supported by the end wedged in the ground.

"Take him to my lodge," Chogatis said. He moved beside Ochopee and turned him over. Ochopee made a gurgling sound.

"Wait!" Chogatis yelled. "Ochopee is alive!"

Zinni bit her trembling bottom lip. Buhgo helped Chogatis lift Ochopee over his shoulder. Ochopee's head hung down the cacique's back. "Let's go," Chogatis said.

Nyna lagged behind, trying to salvage a few things for Zinni. She threw Zinni's sewing kit and some of Buhgo's medicine kits in her arms and hurried across the plaza.

Another incredible gust of wind howled. The cracking of a tree trunk startled her as she ran. Her foot slipped in the mud, twisting her ankle. Down she crashed to the ground, Zinni and Buhgo's belongings splattering in the mud.

She tried to get up, but the pain in her ankle stopped her.

Guacana suddenly appeared in front of her.

"I hurt my ankle," she called, trying to be heard over the storm.

Guacana stared at her and a sick smile spread over his face.

"Can you help me up?" she asked.

Guacana turned and sprinted away.

In a moment, Buhgo clutched her arm and pulled her up. "Lean on me," he said.

Nyna looked behind her, but there was no sign of Guacana. He had disappeared in the storm.

Inside the lodge, Nihapu and Buhgo examined Nyna's ankle. "It is not broken," Nihapu said. "Maybe a little swelling, but it will heal quickly if you rest it."

Through the night the wind screeched, and the rain pounded. Buhgo and Nihapu cleaned and bandaged Ochopee's head, but Ochopee did not wake.

Near dawn the wind died down, and the rain stopped.

With first light the villagers wandered about, surveying the damage. Buhgo, Laira, and Zinni stood where their hut once was. The support posts lay on the ground, and their belongings were strewn about or completely gone. "What will we do?" Zinni whispered. "What will we do?"

"We will be all right," Buhgo said.

"What if your father dies or never wakens?"

"You must look at this a different way," Buhgo said. "The spirits have blessed us. We are still alive. Ochopee is alive. Taska was not hurt. We could have been killed."

Zinni held her face in her hands and cried.

Chogatis and Uxaam passed as they inspected the village. "We will all help you," Chogatis said. "By tonight you will have a new house."

Zinni looked at the cacique. She opened her mouth to speak, but her throat was too tight.

Etac joined Chogatis and Uxaam as they continued the examination of the village. "We were spared," Etac said.

"You are right," Uxaam said. "We have seen worse."

Only a few of the huts were blown away. All had lost a lot of thatch, but that was easy to repair. No lives appeared to have been lost.

Nihapu stood in the lodge doorway. "I worry about Joog," she said to Nyna.

Nyna hobbled next to Nihapu. "He will be back," she said. "He is strong."

"I pray for him," Nihapu said.

Joog broke off the other end of the twig near his leg so it did not stick out too far. A few feet away he saw a branch on the ground that would make a good walking stick.

Joog pulled himself up, grimacing with the pain in his calf. He dragged the injured leg and picked up the stick, stripping the remaining leaves. It was crooked but sturdy. Slowly he continued his journey back to the village.

There were so many downed trees and so much debris that Joog found the trek a struggle. He was already weak and exhausted, and the wound made the journey even more difficult.

Before the sun was overhead, the territory became familiar. Finally he stood by the cenote. Tired and thirsty, he stopped for a drink. The water slid down into his empty stomach.

He balanced himself with the walking stick and moved on, smelling the smoke and aromas of cook fires as he entered the village.

Nyna was the first to spot him. "Look!" she yelled. "It's Joog!"

Nihapu's hand flew to her mouth, her eyes filling with tears.

Nyna started to run, but the pain in her ankle quickly slowed her down. Buhgo was next to see Joog. He and Nihapu both sped across the village. "Put one arm around my neck and the other over your mother's shoulder," Buhgo said.

Joog dropped the walking stick, and Buhgo and Nihapu helped him to the central hearth. He sat propped against a log bench, his wounded leg outstretched.

Nyna limped next to him.

"You are hurt," Joog said.

"Only a sprain," she answered.

His eyes sought his mother for confirmation.

"She twisted it. She will be fine," Nihapu said.

Joog eyed the village and the destruction. "Was anyone else hurt?" he asked.

"Ochopee," Buhgo answered.

Nihapu knelt and examined her son's wound. "The stick must be removed," she said. "Buhgo, go find prickly pear. Take the mature joints and remove the thorns."

The news spread quickly that Joog had returned. The men gathered around him and welcomed him.

Taska was especially relieved, as he had feared his

dream was a premonition of Joog's death. Now he knew the dream only foretold the storm and Joog's difficult journey.

"We will delay the celebration for a few days," Chogatis said.

Nihapu fed Joog fish stew and a special tea. When Buhgo returned with the prickly pear, she left to prepare the medicine.

Uxaam put his hand on Chogatis's shoulder. "The boy is a man," he said.

"Yes," Chogatis said. "He returns to us safely . . . once more."

"Tell me about Ochopee," Joog said.

"He has a head injury. He does not wake," Chogatis said.

"We do all we can," Uxaam said.

"Anyone else?" Joog asked.

"Small things, bruises and cuts. We are fortunate," Chogatis said.

Nihapu returned with Buhgo, and the men left. "Have him sip this elixir," Nihapu said. Nyna stooped next to Joog and put the shell dipper to his lips. "Have him drink it all," Nihapu said. "It will help dull the pain."

Nihapu wiped the wound with clean water. She added snakebark leaves to the bowl of water and stirred until it foamed. She lathered the leg, then wiped it dry.

"He has finished the medicine," Nyna said.

Nihapu rolled a hide beneath the leg to elevate it. "Take your knife," she told Buhgo. "Cut away the torn flesh."

Joog groaned as Buhgo cut. Nihapu dabbed the blood away. "All right," she said.

Deftly she pinched the stick between thumb and forefinger. "I have it," she said. "I am going to take it out."

Joog looked at his leg and nodded, then leaned back. Nihapu pulled the stick slowly and steadily. Sweat broke out across Joog's forehead and ran down into his eyes.

Nihapu laid the bloody stick on the ground. "I have it all," she said. She poured the soapy water into the wound from both sides. "Let it bleed," Nihapu said. "The blood will help wash out dirt and bad spirits."

After a few moments Nihapu sliced open a pad of the prickly pear cactus. She laid the pulpy side of each piece of cactus over the entrance and exit wounds. Then she bound it all with a strip of hide.

"I am so happy you are home," Nyna whispered, patting the sweat from his face with a swatch of soft deerskin.

Joog felt himself relaxing. He was tired and wanted to sleep.

Zinni sponged Ochopee's forehead. They were alone in the lodge, so she took a moment to study her husband. Buhgo looked so much like his father, the same bones in his face as if it had been chiseled and hewn from stone. Zinni tilted her head to admire his profile. How long had it been since he had *been* with her?

She smoothed his hair back from his face, enjoying the moment, savoring it by closing her eyes and remembering how it used to be. She ached to be able to show him this kind of affection again, if he would only allow it. Zinni sighed, then looked at her husband's face. What she saw stunned her.

Zinni gulped a breath and jumped to her feet and out the doorway.

"Nihapu, hurry!" she cried.

16

Etac wiped the sweat from his brow, then continued to lash new thatch where the storm had done damage to his house. Cetisa handed him a new sabal palm frond. The hut took on a patchwork appearance, the fresh green thatch spotting the old brown fronds.

"Would you like some water?" Cetisa asked.

"Yes," he said. He turned to her. "I think we should rest awhile. The heat of the day is not the best time to labor."

"Have you seen Joog?" she asked.

"Briefly."

"Everyone is chattering about his return. I do not understand why."

Etac put down the palm leaf. "Of course you do. If it were anyone else you would have no problem." He lifted her chin. "You know I am right."

He took her hand and led her inside the hut. He came behind her and put his hands on her shoulders, gently massaging. "You are too tense," he said. "Relax. Lay down on the mat."

"No, I—"

"Do not argue with me," he said.

Cetisa sank to her knees, then stretched out facedown. Etac sat beside her. Softly he stroked her back. He rubbed her temples, then the base of her neck.

"That is better," he said. "Your bitterness is going to destroy you. It can bring no good to you or anyone else, only bad things. If you do not let it go, the spirits will find a way to strip it from you. I do not want to see that."

Nihapu jumped up.

"Hurry!" Zinni called.

"What is it?" Nihapu said, flying inside the lodge.

"He is awake. He opened his eyes!"

Nihapu crouched next to Ochopee and called his name. There was no response.

"He did open his eyes. He looked up at me." Zinni squatted. "Open your eyes, Ochopee. Open your eyes."

"Sometimes people open their eyes, but are still in the deep sleep. It happens."

"No," Zinni said. "He looked at me. He did!" She picked up the damp hide and wiped his face with it. "Ochopee."

His eyes fluttered.

"You see!" Zinni said. "He hears me." She wiped his face some more. "Open your eyes, husband."

Slowly Ochopee's eyes opened.

Zinni touched the cloth to his mouth. She squeezed it and a dribble of water fell into his mouth.

"Not too fast," Nihapu said. "You do not want him to choke."

"Can you hear me?" Zinni asked.

Ochopee did not speak, but he lifted his hand.

"Let him rest," Nihapu said. "This is a very good sign."

The men and women of the village patched their homes and by dark had erected a new house for Ochopee. Uxaam purified it with pine smoke. Buhgo and Chogatis carried Ochopee on a litter and laid him on a new mat inside the hut. As they carried him, Ochopee appeared to be awake. He looked about, but was too weak to speak.

Uxaam sat with Joog by the central hearth.

"I thought the vision would not come," Joog said. "Then finally, when I thought I could bear no more, it began. But I do not understand any of it. Will you help me?"

"Tell me what you saw."

"At first there was noise, a whirring sound that grew louder and louder, and the earth seemed to vibrate. A great cloud settled over the land. And then, when it was close enough, I saw what it was. Grasshoppers, a multitude of them, more than any man has a number for. Like grains of sand cover the beach, these creatures covered the earth, all coming toward me."

Uxaam's forehead frowned. "Grasshoppers," he said. "A large gathering of them."

"Yes," Joog said. "And then everything slowed down, as if my eyes could see every movement. When their wings fluttered, I could see them move so slowly."

"Did any of them speak to you. Did you hear a voice?"

"No," Joog said. "I centered my spirit, emptied my mind, but I heard nothing. When I opened my eyes, the fog was vanishing and with it went all the grasshoppers. Just disappeared, faded. It is hard to explain."

"I understand," Uxaam said.

"The way everything moved, so slow, so unnatural, like this," he said, waving his hand very slowly. "And the way they disappeared. That was slow, too, like I said, they faded away."

Uxaam smiled. "I understand."

"It was so incredible. I will never forget it."

"Was that all?" Uxaam asked.

"No," Joog said, pulling the egret feather from his waistband. "I felt wind at my back, and when I looked, I saw a great white egret. His wings beat slowly, like the way the grasshoppers moved. Gently he settled to earth and looked at me."

"Did it speak?" Uxaam asked.

"No, but the bird's eyes were like small pools of clear water. My reflection was there, but—"

"What did you see?"

"It was me, but I was older. I had lines in my face and gray in my hair."

"Ah," Uxaam said. "Anything else?"

"Just the feather that fell as the bird took wing."

"The egret is a good sign. He is the peacemaker and fisherman. He is a good sign when fishing or during conflict." Uxaam took the feather. "These are used in healing ceremonies to take away anger and negative thoughts, and to bring harmony."

"What does it mean?" Joog asked.

"And you saw yourself in the egret's eye. That is special," Uxaam said. "The spirits see that you will be remembered as a peacemaker, one who brings harmony."

Uxaam handed back the feather. "Keep this in a safe place. When the time comes, you will need to pray over this feather."

"How will I know the time?"

"When you can bring harmony to a situation, pray first over the egret's gift. This is not for trivial conflicts."

"I understand," Joog said. "What can you tell me about the grasshoppers?"

Uxaam wiped his hand over his face. "Not a good sign. When you see grasshoppers congregate, they warn of bad weather."

"The storm!" Joog said.

Uxaam shook his head. "I do not think so. We have been given good luck in regard to the storm. You saw many grasshoppers in one area."

"More than a man could count."

"Yes," Uxaam said, staring in the distance. "Grasshoppers can warn us of droughts. When too many are in one area, it means dry weather for a long time.

"How soon?" Joog asked.

"That we do not know."

"Then what good is the warning? It might come tomorrow or not come until I am an old man."

"Perhaps," Uxaam said. "But Grasshopper warns us to prepare."

"How do we prepare for something that may not happen for a lifetime?"

Uxaam closed his eyes and hummed.

The lessons from the spirits were difficult to interpret, Joog thought.

"The grasshopper and the egret together," Uxaam said. "Some way you must see your way clear to bring harmony or prevent conflict over the drought. That is the image you must see of yourself. Your destiny."

Uxaam could see the confusion still on Joog's face.

"I do not understand it all, yet," Joog said.

"But you will. All the mysteries reveal themselves in time."

Several days later Chogatis announced that the celebration for Joog would begin at sundown.

Nyna and Nihapu prepared special foods to offer the villagers. Zinni and Laira helped them.

"I need to check on Ochopee," Zinni said.

"Has he spoken yet?" Nihapu asked.

"No. He looks about with this expression of confusion. But he stays awake longer each day."

"Head wounds are very strange. They take their time. Cannot be rushed," Nihapu said.

Laira cut her eyes toward Nihapu. "He does not take his medicine as he should."

"Oh?" Nihapu said.

Zinni wiped the sweat from her forehead with the back of her hand. "I think he feels weak, not in his body, but in his head. He does not like to think he is dependent on me or Laira, or especially Buhgo."

"Pride can do a lot to a man," Nihapu said.

"That he has too much of," Zinni said.

"I do not understand men," Nyna said. She appeared deep in thought for a moment. "I wonder if Taino men are the same. How much I do not know about my own people," she said.

Zinni got up. "I will see how he is doing and try to give him your medicine again," she said.

Nyna and Laira went to get more water from the cenote. The water there was spiritual water with mysterious qualities, unlike the stream water. Water from the spring was appropriate for ceremonies, rituals, and feasts.

Nearby, in the dense brushwood of reeds and rushes, Nyna stopped. "I want to show you something," she said. "But you must promise not to tell."

"A secret?" Laira asked.

"Yes," Nyna said. "Joog does not even know yet."

Suddenly Nyna was on her knees, crawling through the tall brush. In a moment she emerged.

Laira put her hand over her mouth to stifle her surprise. "What have you done?" she asked.

17

Zinni entered her new house. Ochopee lay on his mat, his head elevated on a hide roll.

"Husband, I have spoken to Nihapu and she says you must take your medicine. How do you expect to get well if you do not?"

She dipped a small shell in the potion, then held it to Ochopee's mouth. He turned his head.

"Take this," she said. "Nihapu has made this medicine to help you get well. Is that not what you want? Do you want to lie here like this day after day? Do you not want to get up, go outside, feel the sunshine on your back?"

Ochopee looked at her, his eyes dull but piercing, reaching deep inside her.

"What do you see?" she asked. "What is it that has you so troubled? Taking medicine from your wife does not make you less of a man. I cannot help you if you do not let me."

Ochopee continued to gaze at her. He parted his lips, and Zinni put the shell to his mouth. "Good," she said as he swallowed.

Laira could not believe what she saw. "Oh, my," she said. "And Joog does not know?"

Nyna held out the first weapon she had created. She had detached the lip from a queen conch shell, then hafted it on a short stout laurel oak stick.

"An ax!" Laira said. "How did you know how to do this?"

"I watched Joog and the others." Nyna held it out for Laira to hold, but the girl recoiled.

"No, no, no," she said.

"It is mine, not a man's. There is nothing to fear."

"But women do not make weapons. They cannot."

"The men say *Ais* women cannot. I am not Ais. Go on, touch it."

Laira wavered, then hesitantly extended one finger. She touched the sinew that bound the conch lip to the stick. She pulled back and looked at her friend.

"I kept the sinew wet as I tied it, and when it dried, it shrank and became very tight." Nyna held the ax upright, her elbow flexing back and forth as if she was going to throw it. "I have practiced throwing it, but I am not very good. But if a Carib came close, I could swing it hard and split his skull!"

"If anyone finds out, there will be great trouble for you."

Nyna offered Laira the ax. "Want to try?"

"I do not think so," she answered.

"I am saving things to make different tools and weapons, shark teeth, more conch, antler. There," she said, pointing in the brush. "I have a basket."

Nyna got on her knees, pushed the ax back into hiding and pulled out the basket. "See all the things I have collected."

Laira sat next to her.

Nyna removed the drawing of her village from her totem bag. "I will show my people how to make these things," she said. "One day I will go home." Delicately, as if caressing the picture, Nyna moved her fingertips over the hide.

Laira sat with her hands in her lap. "These are not weapons," Nyna said. "You can touch them. Pick them up and look close."

Laira lifted a sand shark's tooth. "Sharp. Oh," she said, seeing another she liked better. She sawed her finger gently with the tiger shark tooth.

"I am going to make a different weapon with this one," Nyna said, lifting another queen conch. She held it up by putting her finger through the hole she had tapped in the top of the shell to dislodge the creature that had lived inside.

"You have such amazing ideas," Laira said. "So daring."

Nyna stuffed the things back in the basket and shoved it in the brush. "I will still need Joog to help me."

They collected the water and returned to the village. Just as they set down the water beside Nihapu, Nyna clutched her totem bag.

"Oh, no," she said. "I left the drawing."

She turned quickly and ran back to the cenote. It lay just as she had left it, open on the ground. Nyna lifted it and held it to her cheek, feeling the softness of the buckskin. She rolled it up tightly and tied it closed, then packed it back in her totem bag.

Suddenly she felt eyes on her, even though she heard and saw nothing. Very slowly she turned around.

Guacana smiled at her, his evil eyes aglow.

Nyna nodded and attempted to pass him, but Guacana grabbed her by the arm.

He fondled her armlet. "I know you are not from this world. You fool others, but not me."

"Let me by," Nyna said.

Guacana squeezed her arm. He jerked her in front of him and shoved her to the ground.

"You are not a boy anymore," Nyna said. "You are a man. Ais men do not harm other Ais."

"They do not harm *Ais*, is correct. And you are right, I am a man. So," he said, saliva pooling in the corners of his mouth, "I think that is exactly what you should deal with . . . a man."

Nyna started to get up, but Guacana pushed the heel of his foot into her chest.

"Turn over," he said. "On your hands and knees."

"I am leaving," Nyna said, pushing his foot off her.

Guacana kicked her in the stomach as she attempted to get up. Nyna folded her arms over her belly and gasped for air. Again he kicked her. She fell to her knees.

Guacana was quickly on her, whipping her over so she lay facedown. His arm went around her, lifting her hips.

Nyna twisted, but his grip around her was too firm. He wedged his hand between her thighs, ripping them apart, one of his nails gouging her soft flesh.

The initial violent stab of his manpart made her shriek.

"If you scream, I will slit your throat!" Guacana said.

Nyna struggled to loosen herself from his grip, but it was to no avail. He pounded into her, thrusts so vicious and fierce that he grunted with each one.

Nyna sobbed, still trying to jab him with her elbows. The pain inside her was searing, splitting her, ripping her. "No, no," she cried.

Suddenly he stopped, and the weight of him collapsing on her back flattened her to the ground. Her nose sucked in dirt, and her tongue tasted it.

In a moment she felt the air on her back as he withdrew. "If you tell anyone, you will be sorry."

"I do not care if you hurt me . . . kill me," she said.

"It is not you I will hurt. Your friend, Buhgo, will pay." One last blow with his foot to her side, and he was gone.

Nyna lay in the dirt for a long time, whimpering. Even though he was no longer inside her, that part of her throbbed in pain. She wished he had killed her. As she lay with the side of her face flat on the ground, she saw through the stalks of the reeds and the other brush. She caught a glimpse of her basket.

Nyna closed her eyes and pictured what she could recall of her village. She imagined the ocean breeze on her face. She could smell the cassava bread and taste the sweet juicy fruits and succulent fish. She could hear the songs of the birds and even a song her mother used to sing to her.

One day she would go home to help her people. She wiped her nose. "No, he will not kill me," she said aloud.

Then she imagined herself holding the ax she had made, swinging it wildly, connecting with Guacana's head, and splitting it open like a ripe gourd. She reveled in that moment, striking his head . . . the Carib's head.

Nyna finally got up. Filth clung to her body, and the stickiness between her legs made her think she was going to vomit. She crawled to the cenote, removed her skirt, and carefully lowered herself in the water. She splashed her face several times, then leaned her hair back into the water. Gradually she scrubbed her body, not neglecting any minute bit of her flesh, the stench of Guacana finally washing away. Beneath the water she let out a scream.

Nyna climbed out of the water. Her skirt needed mending. That was easy enough to do. She gathered some of the airplant hanging from the trees, plaited one and wove it into the shredded areas. It was not perfect, but good enough. Again, as she sat, skirt finished, she burst into tears. What had she done? What could she have done when she was so little to deserve this punishment, this horrible life with people who hated her? Why?

Nyna cried out for her mother. There was no one on this earth that loved her like her mother had. There was a gaping chasm in her heart. There was no one she could go to, no matter what she had done and still be safe. Suddenly she realized she had trouble picturing her mother's face. She closed her eyes and fought to remember. She tried to feel the warmth of her mother when she held her and consoled her. She listened for her voice that had been soft like the breeze. She never felt more alone since the days adrift in the canoe.

Nyna laced the waistband around her, and as she did, she noticed something on her leg that made her swallow a mouthful of air.

18

Uxaam checked the pot in which he collected stran-
gler fig sap. Earlier he had cut several slashes in the
bark and then a center vertical groove that connected
the cuts. At the base of the groove he affixed a shell
spout. Uxaam was pleased. The milky sap had oozed
from the cuts and collected in the pot.

He removed the pot and carried it home. There was
enough to make several paints. He diluted the sap with
water and in one large quahog clamshell he poured some
of the diluted sap. To that he added finely powdered
shell, making a white paint. In other shells he made black
paint with charcoal and sap, and purple he made by add-
ing crushed pokeberries. For red he used the rouge plant
berries. His palette ready, he chewed the end of a red
cedar stem until it frayed, forming a nice brush.

Uxaam took his wood mask, carved from gumbo-
limbo, and began to paint the face. Around the small
open mouth he painted red, then added a fine outline of
black. The sappy paint adhered to the wood. He painted
white around the circular cut-out eyes and then outlined
them in deep black. He chose to streak rays of red and
black fanning out from the eyes. On the forehead he
painted a white triangle with red wings emanating from
it.

He admired the mask. The sun would dry it quickly,
and it would be ready for tonight.

* * *

Nihapu's voice rang out, calling Nyna's name.

"Nyna," she called again. "Where are you?"

"Here," Nyna said. She stepped onto the trail.

"Oh my goodness," Nihapu said. "What has happened? I was worried when you did not return."

Leaves and twigs tangled in Nyna's dripping hair. She stood with her head bowed. "Look," she said, touching her leg. Nyna rubbed her hand down her leg smearing a trickle of blood. She whimpered as another thin watery red stripe dribbled down her thigh.

"You are a woman!" Nihapu said. "This is wonderful!"

Nyna could say nothing. Had Guacana hurt her, torn her just as it had felt like, or was this her first moon cycle? How was she to know? She was sore and ached there. How badly had he hurt her? She cringed with fear.

"You do not look happy. This is a wonderful event. You gain the status of womanhood."

"But . . ."

If she told of Guacana's assault, Joog's celebration would be ruined. What would Guacana do to Buhgo? And Nihapu could be right; this might be her moon cycle.

"Smile," Nihapu said. "I have a leather strap and the stuffing for you." Nihapu pulled the pieces of rubbish from Nyna's wet hair. "Did you think you could wash it away?" she asked, humor tilting her voice.

"Yes," Nyna said.

"It is not that easy," she said and laughed. "Women wish it were so."

Nihapu looked the girl over. Her side was abraded. "What is this?"

"I bumped into a tree. I was not watching where I was going. I would not make a good hunter," she said. "Men know best."

"Sometimes," she said. "Not always. You know men think moon-cycle blood is magical. They are afraid of it,

and the woman who has it. It is a great mystery to them.
To us it is just a nuisance. We have to stay by ourselves
in one of the women's huts, eat special foods, and stay
away from hunting trails. Our life is interrupted every
turning of the moon. I think long ago a great-great-
grandfather made up the rules for women on their moon.
I do not think the spirits had anything to do with it."
Nihapu thought for a moment. "No, it was a man so
afraid of something he did not understand."

"I wonder what rules my people have."

"Probably the same," Nihapu said, smoothing Nyna's
hair. "Let us go make the announcement to Chogatis."

"Must we? What if this is not moon blood?"

"Of course it is. What else could it be?"

Nyna wanted to reveal to Nihapu what Guacana had
done to her. She wanted Nihapu to tell her for sure what
this blood was. Nihapu would keep her secret. But what
if she did not? What if she whispered it to Chogatis? She
had to think of Buhgo. Nyna thought she might cry again
and fought the tears. How badly was she hurt? If she
went unattended, would she get sick and die?

"Come," Nihapu said. "This is important news. More
reason to celebrate. Chogatis will choose a woman to
teach Joog the ways of joining, and a grandmother to
stay with you, all in one night!"

Just before they entered the village Nyna wiped the
inside of her thigh again. Just a small film of blood
stained her hand.

"Go inside," Nihapu said. "I will be right there."

Nyna did as she was told. At least no one had stopped
them to talk. She did not think she could carry on a
conversation.

Nihapu went for Chogatis. He was helping Uxaam get
ready for the celebration.

It was not polite for a woman to interrupt a man's
conversation so she waited for a break in their talk.
"May I speak with you?" she asked Chogatis.

"Of course," he said.

"It is a private matter."

"I will be there in a moment," he said.

Nihapu lowered her head in respect and returned to Nyna.

"Here it is," Nihapu said, extracting a leather strap from a basket. "Pad it with this," she said, handing her some soft cattail fluff.

Nihapu studied Nyna's face. "Does your belly cramp?" she asked.

"No."

"Does your head or back ache or your belly feel uncomfortably heavy?"

Nyna shook her head.

"Then what is it? You should be filled with excitement."

"I am," Nyna said, forcing a smile that only curved one side of her mouth.

Chogatis entered the lodge. "You need me?" he asked.

Nihapu got to her feet. "Wonderful news. Nyna has her first moon blood! She is a woman."

"Ah," Chogatis said, his face brightening. "That is good news. I will ask Uxaam for his advice on the grandmother."

Several young men from the Bobcat and Osprey clans arrived in the village. They, too, had recently passed through the rites of manhood. They sat with Joog, boasting about their most recent adventure, their vision quests, and the lessons they had learned in how to please a woman.

"Of all the rituals, the time with the woman was the best," the youngest man, Chitola, said. "While I am here, I am looking at your women," he said.

All of them laughed.

"Wait until the woman teacher is done with you," another said to Joog. "You will never be the same."

"I look forward to it," Joog said.

"Have you had those dreams?" Chitola asked. "You know the ones I mean. Well, it is so much better than that! Incredible."

One of the others slapped him on the back. "I think he needs a wife soon," he said.

"Show me about," Chitola said. "We have a little time."

Joog escorted the visitors around the village, introducing them to others. When they happened upon Ochopee's lodge, Laira sat outside with Nyna.

"Who is that strange one," Chitola asked.

"Nyna," Joog answered. "She has come from far across the sea. She is Taino."

"Interesting," Chitola said. "And the pretty one with her?"

"Laira."

"They are too young for you," one of them said.

"I like her," Chitola said. "Introduce me."

Joog called Nyna and Laira over.

Uxaam dressed in a feather cape, his hair tied near the top of his head, which was covered in an antler headdress. His body, gleaming with oil, dripped with bands of plinking shells.

"So you are ready," Chogatis said.

"Almost."

"Who have you selected to teach my grandson?"

"Qitce. She should teach him well."

"Ah," Chogatis said, rubbing his chin. "A good choice. She is not too old." He pondered a moment. "Yes, not too old, not too young. The woman who gets Joog will be pleased with what Qitce will teach him."

"She was very honored when I told her she was my choice."

"I have another request," Chogatis said. "Nyna needs a grandmother."

Uxaam's head shot up. "She has her first moon blood?"

"Yes," Chogatis said.

Uxaam paced. "I think we should bring it to Council," he said. "If we do this without discussion, there will be more trouble. The girl is tolerated, not welcomed."

"You are probably right," Chogatis said. "I hate to do this, but I will call them together now."

After the sounding of the conch horn, the men gathered, curious as to the reason for this meeting called just before the celebration.

Chogatis held the Talking Stick. "Nyna is a woman," he began. "It is the time for Uxaam to select a grandmother to stay with her this first time. However, we knew there might be concerns. So as not to have divisiveness, we thought it best talked about in an open forum."

A man near Etac shifted his weight and signaled he wished to speak. Chogatis acknowledged him.

"She is not Ais," the man said. "No grandmother should be expected to take on this responsibility."

A mumbling of agreement spread among the men.

"I agree," another man spoke. "Think of what you ask of Nyna, also. A grandmother instructs the new woman in *Ais* traditions and ways. Why would she want to learn these things?"

Chogatis blinked rapidly with irritation. "Because she lives with Ais, has grown up Ais, is now an Ais woman."

Guacana signaled to speak. Chogatis was slow in recognizing him.

"She is not Ais! Some of us still think she is an outcast, unsuitable for her world. It is enough that Uxaam gave her a totem. If not for Chogatis, we would have left her on the beach to die. It was apparent she was sent there by the spirits to do that, but we intervened. We have experienced a lot of misfortune since she has been among us." Guacana looked around at the others, reading their faces, testing the strength of his argument by their expressions.

Etac asked to interrupt. "You are new to Council, Guacana. There is no need to rile anyone. In Council we do what is best for the Ais."

"Well said," Chogatis said. "The girl has become a woman, and we must decide if it is appropriate to give her a grandmother and train her in Ais ways. She may be with us forever. I think it fair we share the customs with her."

Guacana spoke again. "Again, I say, she is not Ais. There are no laws or traditions for those not Ais. Why do you think Joog was returned to you? The Jeaga recognized that Joog could never be Jeaga, never pass through the rituals that would make him a man if not with his own people. Certainly we are as wise as the Jeaga!"

A stronger agreement rumbled through the assembly.

He continued. "The Ais spirits do not recognize her, just as the Jeaga did not recognize Joog." Guacana knew he had struck a weakness in Chogatis.

Uxaam drew a line in the dirt. "We must decide. Those who stand with Guacana, stand on this side with him," he said, tapping the ground with a stick. "Those who do not stand with Guacana, come to the other side."

The men glanced at one another as they took their places on either side of the line. Custom was that the cacique and shaman could not choose a side, and so Uxaam and Chogatis stood where they were. When all the men had lined up, it was clear that more stood with Guacana. Only Etac and a few others took the side opposite Guacana.

"It is decided," Uxaam said.

The men dispersed, and Chogatis returned to his lodge. Guacana was rancid inside, like Ochopee.

Nihapu waited beside the lodge. "Well," she said, "I think I can tell from your face that there is bad news."

Chogatis nodded. "Council recommends there be no rites and rituals, no grandmother for Nyna."

The lines in Nihapu's face seemed to sag just as her heart did.

"I am sorry," Chogatis said.

Nihapu scored her bottom lip as she thought. "Then I will do it," she said. "I will teach her on my own. I am not as old and wise and experienced as the grandmothers, but I can do it."

"Nyna," Nihapu said as they entered the lodge. "I have good news."

Buhgo finished lacing the cleaned deer hide to a frame constructed of saplings. Etac had provided the deer. A tripod of poles suspended thin strips of the meat and some of it smoked on grates. Buhgo had scraped the hair off and saved the antlers and hooves. Now over a low fire he pulverized the brains into a slimy paste.

He stirred the mixture waiting for it to boil, and as he did he thought of his friend Joog. He wished he were like Joog, brave and smart. Buhgo did not want to go on a vision quest. He was afraid of what might happen to him, and as always he feared failure that would bring more humiliation to his father. But he saw no way of getting out of it. All boys passed through this rite into manhood. Every time he thought about it, his stomach knotted.

Satisfied that the tanning solution was ready, he removed the pot from the fire. He let it cool a few moments, then began the process of painting both sides of the translucent skin with the emulsion.

"Buhgo, come here," Zinni called.

Buhgo went into the hut.

"Check your father's head before I rebandage it," she said.

He knelt and examined Ochopee's wound. "It is healing nicely," he said. He took his knife and cut away more hair from the injury. As he did, he saw that Ochopee stared at him, fixed on his face. It was a peculiar gaze he thought, as if he had a difficult time grasping what was going on.

"Does it hurt you?" Buhgo asked.

Ochopee nodded, but never took his eyes off Buhgo.

"Give me the bandages," the boy said. He dabbed a medicinal paste on Ochopee's wound and then wrapped the bandage around his father's head, tying it firmly.

Ochopee's stare made him uncomfortable. He sat back, his father's eyes following him.

"What is it?" Buhgo said. "Can you speak? Can you hear?"

Ochopee swallowed and squinted as if looking into bright sunlight. His voice was low and hollow sounding. "Who are you?"

19

Zinni could not believe what she heard. Buhgo looked up at his mother.

"He does not know Buhgo," Taska said. "He has forgotten."

Zinni stooped next to Ochopee. "Buhgo is your son." She pointed to Taska. "And he is also your son."

Ochopee maintained a blank expression.

"His head injury has taken his memory," Taska said.

"How can you not remember your son?" Zinni asked. "Do you know me?"

Ochopee stared at her, studying her. "No," he finally said.

"I am your wife," Zinni said. She took his hand and pressed his palm to her cheek. "Do you not recognize me?"

Ochopee shook his head.

"Have you lost all your memory? Can you recall anything?"

"No," he said. "Who am I?"

Tears streamed down Zinni's face. "You are Ochopee, my husband, father of Laira, Buhgo, and Taska."

"Ochopee," he said, rolling the name in his mouth as if tasting it, seeing how it sounded.

The sound of drums and Uxaam's distinct voice summoned the villagers. The celebration was to begin.

"Take your brother and Laira," Zinni said. "I will stay with Ochopee."

*   *   *

Joog stood on one foot, balanced with a walking stick, on Uxaam's platform. Nihapu had treated his wound with the greatest attention. Already it was healing, though quite sore. His back was to the people who gathered to watch.

Uxaam held the painted mask over his face as he spoke. "Ancestors, spirits of all creatures, Mother Earth, all living things, recognize this man, Joog. He has fulfilled all requirements to become a worthy man of the Ais. Receive him with respect for his station."

Uxaam held out Joog's first dipper of the black drink. He took it and drank down the hot bitter liquid. When the dipper was empty, he turned to face the crowd. He held the dipper high and turned it upside down to show that he had emptied it. The men whooped and cheered.

The golden light of the sunset splattered the village. Nyna stood far behind the crowd, as did Cetisa.

"He is quite handsome," Nyna said.

"I suppose," Cetisa said.

"The other men will respect his counsel. He is just and fair."

"Yes, but he speaks too kindly of the Jeaga. The men do not forget that. The Jeaga are our enemy."

"I thought that ended when the Jeaga returned Joog to the Ais."

"They still hold the river. The Ais do not forget that just because of one simple kindness. The others think differently than Chogatis and Joog."

The fire in the central hearth leaped into the air as the evening descended.

Cetisa walked into the crowd, leaving Nyna alone. Nihapu had warned Nyna not to circulate because of her moon cycle. When the festivities quieted she would take her to the woman's hut, but Nihapu did not want to do that in front of everyone. Nyna agreed, especially because it might cause a disturbance and ruin Joog's special night.

Across the way, through the throng of men and women, her eyes snagged on Guacana. His corrupt smile parted over white teeth. She shivered and again felt sick to her stomach. He slapped a hand on the man's shoulder he was talking to, and then started strolling in her direction.

Nyna backed into the shadows, then stepped behind a tree.

"I know you are there," he said, so close to her she was sure she could smell him. After this afternoon she knew his scent, like prey knows the scent of the predator. He came around the tree.

"What do you want?" she asked. She realized she had made a mistake moving away from the crowd. She would have been better if she had walked right into the gathering and surrounded herself with others.

"You know what I want. And I will have it again," he said.

"I will scream," she said. "I will run screaming, straight to Chogatis."

Guacana laughed, rocking back his head. "Go," he said. "Your little friend will not be happy with your decision."

"Leave me alone," she said.

Guacana reached forward and flipped her long hair aside. "Not to worry," he said. "Not tonight." He bit the air as if he might nibble her throat.

His gesture made her skin crawl. "I told you I will scream." She backed away.

"Not tonight," he repeated. "Tonight I just look. And tell me," he said, stepping closer, "where does that armlet come from?" He slicked his finger over the amazing ornament.

Nyna twisted away and lifted her head with pride as she took a deep breath. She refused to look at him.

"You will not say, because if you do, it will give away who you are. Is that not right?"

Again Nyna did not answer.

"Oh," Guacana said as if suddenly remembering something. "I hear that you are now a woman. I am pleased. Yes," he said. "I like that idea. So, as I said, not tonight. Men do not touch the women on their moon. They are unclean and defile men. You are lucky this time. But you will see me again . . . and again. Do not close your eyes," he said, a sweeping, disgusting grin coursing over his face.

Behind Guacana, Nyna could see Buhgo coming.

"I may not see you, but I will always smell you," she said.

"Guacana," Buhgo called. "Can you never leave the girl be?"

"There is no girl here. Take another look. Here stands a man, a woman, and a boy . . . oh, sorry I was confused for a moment. A man, a woman, and a girl."

"Come on, Buhgo," Nyna said. "Let us leave. Where he thinks there is a man is only a fool."

Nyna joined Buhgo, and they walked away from Guacana.

"What did he do?" Buhgo asked.

"He just makes stupid talk."

Buhgo looked at her as they walked. "How does it feel?"

"What do you mean?"

"To be a woman."

"I guess that is the talk of the village. I feel no different.

"I am sorry they decided not to give you a grandmother."

"But Nihapu said she would be the grandmother. She will teach me everything and tend to me." Nyna felt that in a way she was lying to her friend. Yet, she told no specific lie. Still, if this was not her moon blood, then she had not been exactly truthful with him.

They proceeded to where Taska and Laira were sitting. Buhgo had designed a portable chair that relieved pressure from the base of Taska's spine. Now he could sit with others and enjoy the festivities.

Chitola swaggered up to them.

"You have an interest in my sister?" Buhgo asked.

"She has a pretty face."

"She is not eligible for marriage yet," Taska said.

"But soon," Chitola said, letting his eyes trail over her body. "The signs are all there."

Laira grinned at the attention. "I will be a woman soon." She sat up straighter, pulling her shoulders back.

"Where is your father," Chitola asked. "Perhaps I could get permission to court you when the time comes."

Laira grimaced. "He is ill," she said. "Perhaps when you come again."

"Perhaps," Chitola said, then left.

"So our friend Joog is at last a man," Taska said. Even though he spoke of Joog, Taska could not take his eyes from Nyna. "Something is wrong," he said.

Buhgo looked at Nyna.

"No, nothing is wrong," she said.

"I do not like the feeling that is radiating from you," Taska said.

"My brother's talent is powerful. So, tell us what it is he is sensing."

"I do not know what he is talking about," she said.

"You must," Taska said. "The feeling is strong."

Nyna wrung her hands. "Maybe you sense the confrontation I just had with Guacana. But that was nothing serious."

"Strange," Taska said. "But if that is what you say."

Nyna let out a deep breath. She was afraid Taska would keep prying. "I should not be here," she said.

"Nihapu advised me not to wander." She backed away. "Enjoy the evening," she said.

Nyna joined Nihapu. "Is it still too early to go to the woman's hut?" she asked.

"I think we should wait until everyone sleeps. We will avoid problems that way."

"All right," Nyna said.

Nihapu took another basket of food to the central hearth, leaving Nyna alone in front of the lodge to watch from afar.

The drumming started, and the men's voices began their songs. One man sang out, his voice high and resounding. The other men followed, repeating the first man's words and melody. They danced in a circle around the fire, toe down first, then heel, jingling the shells banded about their legs and ankles. Some carried rattles made of mud turtle shells filled with hard seeds and mounted on sticks. The rattles kept their own rhythm, complementing the drums with their counterpart.

Chitola found his place in the circle. He danced proudly, glancing out of the corner of his eye to see if Laira watched him. She did.

The voices grew louder and louder, echoing, warbling, trilling, filling the air. The women danced in an outer circle in the opposite direction of the men. Nihapu put down the basket and found herself a place in the procession. She carried a hawk wing in her right hand that she held just at her left shoulder.

Magically, when the last drumbeat sounded, everyone stopped. The rattles were instantly quiet, the voices mute, and even the dance ceased all at one time. That was the game of the dance and the music, for everything to stop sharply.

There was a moment of silence, then the uproar of men and women pleased with their achievement.

Chogatis found Nihapu and stood next to her. He nod-

ded at Uxaam, who raised his stave to gather everyone's attention.

"Joog, come forward," Uxaam said.

The crowd looked about, finally settling on Joog as he
made his way to Uxaam. The shaman put his hand on
Joog's shoulder.

"You now begin your first journey as a man," the shaman said. "Learn well over these next few days. Unlike
the other lessons of manhood, this is the only time these
lessons will be taught."

The group buzzed. Nihapu glanced at her husband and
put her arm through his.

"I name Qitce as your teacher."

The woman who would be Joog's teacher had been
kept a secret until this moment. A burst of approval
circulated through the crowd. The men laughed and
spoke to each other, many recalling their first journey as
a man. The women huddled and discussed how privileged
Qitce was to teach the cacique's grandson.

Qitce stood alone in her finest garb and jewelry.

"Your teacher awaits," Uxaam said.

Nyna stretched to see farther in the distance. The people separated to give Joog a path to his teacher.

As Joog left with Qitce, Nyna was surprised at her
feelings. This was an important event for Joog. She had
watched boys come of age before and had seen the moment they were sent off with their teachers. Those times
she was filled with a sense of joy. But that was not the
feeling she had tonight. It was a new feeling, unpleasant,
deep inside. She didn't even know Qitce, but for some
mysterious reason, she had a negative feeling toward her.
Nyna couldn't describe the feeling as dislike, it was something else. She thought and thought, wondering what this
was all about.

The embers in the central hearth quit flaming, but still
glowed in the dark. The firekeeper would feed it just

enough to keep it alive until morning. The central hearth never went out. It was from this hearth that all fires were started in the village. The fire represented the life of the Ais, and if it were to go out, it would be a bad omen.

Nyna and Nihapu stood just outside the lodge. "It seems nearly everyone has left the plaza," Nihapu said. "Get your things and I will collect several of mine and we will go to the woman's hut."

The two entered the lodge, Nyna going to her sleeping room and Nihapu to the main room.

"I am taking Nyna now," Nihapu said to Chogatis.

He pushed his wife's hair behind her ear. "I think I do not like it."

"Someone must do this for her," she said. "It is not right that she becomes a woman and has no guidance."

Chogatis smiled at her. "That is not what I mean. I think I will not like sleeping alone. I will miss you."

His words made Nihapu smile back. It felt good inside to know someone would miss her if she were not there. And she would miss Chogatis, also. Over time his goodness had found its way into her heart.

"I will miss my husband."

"Those are good words to my ears," he said. "With Joog gone, and you off with Nyna, this big lodge will be empty. I have grown accustomed to not being alone."

Nihapu lowered her eyes. "I am glad my words please you, and I am sorry you will be lonesome."

Chogatis touched his palm to Nihapu's cheek. His hand slid to her neck and up under her hair, pulling her delicately toward him. She felt his chest against hers and warmth, like thick tea, flow through her.

"I am ready," Nyna said, coming from her partitioned room. "Oh—"

Chogatis dropped his hand, and Nihapu jumped.

"We, um . . . we, uh . . . we do not have to go now," Nyna said, stumbling nervously over her words.

"No, no," Nihapu said. "This is a good time. My basket, where is it?" She flit about, finally retrieving a basket she had prepared earlier. "Ah," she said. "I have it."

Nihapu ducked through the doorway and Nyna followed to a set of isolated huts that were upwind of the village. "The men even fear some evil something might drift on the wind to them . . . they might breathe the same air that has passed over us," Nihapu said.

The first hut they came upon was occupied, evidenced by the smoldering embers of a small fire in front of it. Three or four menstruating women would stay together in a single hut, but those with their first moon stayed only with the grandmother.

"Here," Nihapu said. "This one is good."

Nyna glanced over the huts. "This is the same one in which Zinni gave birth to Taska."

"Yes," Nihapu said. "I think you are right."

The inside was plain, no decorations or articles hanging from posts other than the few that would be necessary. Nyna dragged her finger down the post that stood alone in the center. It was smooth and shiny, worn with the oils of many hands that had gripped it while giving birth.

Nyna and Nihapu unrolled their sleeping mats.

"Do you believe in all the taboos?" Nyna asked.

"You mean about the moon blood? Most I do, but I still believe an old grandfather added his own to the spirits'. Like the huts being upwind," she said. "The wind does not always blow the same way. And what about the time we gather our things before we come to the isolation huts. Does not the air pass over us then? Nothing happens. But it is the tradition, the custom, the old beliefs, and so we honor them."

"I wonder if it was the same for my mother and all the Taino women."

Nihapu sat next to her basket. "Perhaps you will have the opportunity to find out one day."

Nyna gazed at Nih

Whatever would have become of her if not for Nihapu, Joog, and Chogatis? "I am sorry you must bring me here. I think you would have preferred to be with Chogatis."

Nihapu's head dipped and Nyna detected a flush in her cheeks.

"Something is happening between you and Chogatis. I have seen it growing slowly, slowly."

Nihapu looked up. "Have you now?" she said.

"Do you love him?"

Nihapu was not quick to answer. She stopped fumbling through the basket and looked up to the roof searching for an answer. "I think so, in a way. It is not the same as Tsalochee. A different kind of love."

"I want to love."

"Oh, Nyna, you will," Nihapu said, stroking Nyna's hair.

Nyna hung her head. The picture of Joog going off with Qitce fluttered into her mind.

Qitce led Joog to the retreat where older women taught boys who had just become men the ways to please a woman. The hut was near the cenote and was never approached except on these occasions.

"Do not be nervous," Qitce said. "You may not have done this before, but I have. That is why I am chosen. I have experience. This is my task, my responsibility."

Qitce removed the jewelry from her arms, then turned her back to Joog. "Lift my necklace over my head," she said.

When he had removed the necklace, she took it from him and then held out one leg. "Slide this band from my thigh" she said.

Joog pulled on the band that dangled rows of shell beads. As he did, Qitce pushed her fingers through his hair.

"Kneel," she said. "It will be easier."

Joog got to his knees and glided the band down her leg and off her foot.

"Good," she whispered, stepping closer.

She untied the waistband of her skirt and let it drop to the ground. "Now, look at me," she said. Joog sat back. She turned around for him, slowly, so he could study her from all angles.

She smiled, recognizing the obvious sign of his arousal beneath his breechclout.

Joog reached to loosen his breechclout, but Qitce stopped him.

"No," she said. "Not yet. A man must have patience to please a woman."

Qitce knelt in front of him and placed his hand on her breast. "We will begin here," she said.

For the next two days Qitce taught Joog the things that would please a woman. With every lesson he thought he might explode, and eagerly he attempted to join with her. Each time she reminded him about patience. If he could learn to control himself now, when he had a wife, he would bring her great satisfaction and his gratification would be even more pleasurable.

When he touched Qitce the right way, she rewarded him with light stroking, but never enough to give him release. On the third day, Joog was caressing Qitce's body, nibbling, tasting, rubbing, stroking at the right times, with the right pressure, all those sensitive places she had shown him. The ache in his groin was intense, and his body trembled. Gently she urged him atop her and guided him into her.

Today his patience was rewarded.

20

Early in the morning Nihapu woke Nyna. "Get up, child," she said. "Father Sun awaits you."

Nyna sat straight up and rubbed her eyes.

"You must make your run to the east to present yourself to Father Sun."

"How far?" Nyna asked. "I will not know when to stop."

Traditionally the grandmother designated the spot to run to. She would place a basket there filled with good totems. Other girls of the village who had not experienced their first moon cycle would run with her, trailing behind, being careful not to overtake the menstruant. But Nyna had no grandmother, and no one would run with her.

Nihapu grinned. "I awoke very early. I have put a basket where you should stop. Every day I will move it closer. On the morning of the fourth day, the basket will be close. Go now. This is your first day!"

Nyna stood and stretched.

Nihapu pointed. "Through the woods that way," she said. "Keep on a straight path toward the beach until you come to the basket. It is not that far. When you return, you will bathe in the stream."

Nyna stared at the forest ahead of her. She still ached in that part of her that Guacana had violated. When she walked she could feel the discomfort, so how would it be when she ran?

"Hurry," Nihapu said. "You must see Father Sun while he still sits close to the water."

Nyna began to trot through the woods. The path was clear, pounded down by generations of young women. At the same time that Nyna caught sound of the surf, she spotted the basket. She stood beside it, and through a clearing in the trees, she could clearly see the sun.

"I am here," she said. She did not know what to expect. She waited a few moments, then turned around and headed back to the hut.

Buhgo stood in front with Nihapu. He had brought Taska with him.

"You should not be here," Nyna said.

"Taska has something for you."

"Uxaam would have made one of these, but—"

"I know," Nyna said. "I am not Ais."

Taska held out a leg bone of an ibis. "I have cleaned it and said prayers over it, just as Uxaam would have done. It is tradition that you use it to drink the special teas Nihapu will brew."

Nyna thought she might cry. "You are so kind to me," she said.

"Take it," Buhgo said.

Nyna took the bird bone and held it to her chest. "Thank you. I hope no one will make trouble for you."

"No one knows," Taska said. "But if they asked, I would tell them. I do not care."

Nihapu cleared her throat. "That is courageous of you, Taska. But it is also wise not to share what you have done with others as they may take it out on Nyna."

"You are right," Taska said. "I was thinking only of myself."

"I did not mean it that way," Nihapu said. "You have done something charitable."

"I am glad you approve," Taska said.

Buhgo hoisted the travois. "We had better hurry along."

Nihapu took the bird bone from Nyna and put it inside the hut. "I am glad Taska fashioned this for you," she said. "Come. It is time to bathe."

There was a special place in the stream for menstruating women to bathe. It was southeast of the village so the contaminated water flowed away.

Nyna stood behind a bush and removed the leather strap. The inside was clean, no sign of blood. She bit her bottom lip. Her fear was realized. It was not moon blood, but blood from the damage Guacana had done to her. Her throat tightened, and her heart pounded. If she could tell Nihapu what had happened, then Nihapu could tell her if she would be all right. She could give her medicines if she needed them.

"You are so modest today," Nihapu said, stepping into the water.

"Sorry. I was daydreaming," Nyna said, moving out of cover and into the water.

"Lean your head back," Nihapu said. "Soak your hair and I will wash it."

"Is that part of the grandmother's duty?"

"Yes," Nihapu answered. "I have special soap." Nihapu lathered the paste she had made. To the crushed flower petals of the blue lobelia, marsh pinks, stargrass, and sweet bay magnolia, she had added pure tallow, ash, and lime to form an aromatic paste.

"It smells sweet," Nyna said.

Nihapu lifted her palm closer to Nyna so she could smell it better. Nyna inhaled and sighed at the delightful fragrance.

Nihapu began at Nyna's crown, working in the rich lather. The girl closed her eyes. For a moment she thought she caught scent of something, the sweet aroma of a fruit that grew in her homeland. Her mouth watered in response. But hard as she tried, she could not picture the fruit or recall its name. How could her mouth remember so well?

"Do you remember much about when you were a little girl?" Nyna asked.

"Some," she answered.

"I do not want to forget, and yet it is happening," Nyna said.

"Do not worry about things you cannot do anything about. That is time ill spent."

Nihapu leaned Nyna's head back into the water to rinse it.

Two other women showed up to bathe in the stream, but when they saw it was Nyna in the water, they moved further downstream.

"Maybe I should not be learning the Ais ways. Council is right, I am not Ais," Nyna said.

"Quiet," Nihapu said. "That is foolish talk. You have become a woman. There are privileges that go with that. If you live amongst the Ais, then the Ais spirits see you. The Jeaga, our fiercest enemy, took care of my Joog."

"But we know why they returned him to you."

"Yes," Nihapu said. "Because they cared about him, loved him."

"That is right. And they knew he could not go through the Jeaga rites and rituals that would declare him a man." Nyna twisted her hair into a thick cable, wringing the water from it. She stood up. "You are wasting your time on me," Nyna said. "I am Taino. I am glad I am Taino. I will never be Ais."

"But—"

Nyna was up and out of the water. She dressed, putting on the leather strap so as not to become suspect.

"You need the cattail fluff to go inside," Nihapu said.

"Oh . . . yes," Nyna said. "I forgot."

"While you are here in the woman's hut, let me teach you," Nihapu said. "If you never find your people, at least you will be comfortable with Ais ways."

"But I will find them," she said.

"How? Do you think you can just set out in a canoe? Which way would you go?"

"I do not know," Nyna said. "But I will. I will. I have to."

Nihapu reached out and stroked Nyna's cheek. "I think you are the daughter of the fifth moon."

Nyna tilted her head in curiosity. "What do you mean?"

Nihapu's lips curled into a gentle smile. "Long ago there were thirteen original clan mothers . . . one for each of the thirteen moons that appear before a season returns. Each clan mother had a special lesson to teach us."

Nyna wrung her hair as she listened.

Nihapu continued. "The clan mother of the fifth moon reminds us that we hear our very first sound while still inside our mother's womb, long before we are born. We hear two heartbeats . . . our own and that of our mother. The second heartbeat gives us a sense of tranquillity and safe refuge. When we come into the world, the second heartbeat disappears. Some of us go through life searching for that missing heartbeat, never finding it because we look in the wrong places. And some do not even know what it is that they search for. I think that is you."

Nyna drew in a deep breath.

"Until one finds that second heartbeat there is no inner peace," Nihapu said. "The clan mother of the fifth moon tells us that the second heartbeat we all yearn to hear is Earth Mother's heartbeat. We are never alone. All we must do is stop and listen for it."

Nyna hung her head. Nihapu bent and lifted Nyna's chin so she could look in the young woman's eyes while she spoke. "The emptiness you feel is not because you are lost from the Taino. It is the hollow deep inside that waits to be filled with the second heartbeat. But I think you will not rest until you find your people again. Until then you cannot stop and listen. Until then you cannot hear Earth Mother's heartbeat and find the contentment you long for."

The four days in the woman's hut passed slowly. Nihapu used the time to discuss a woman's role amongst the Ais, and to tell the legends and stories about Ais women. Nyna gleaned from Nihapu's stories that women were actually more powerful than the men thought. They had great influence over their husbands. The art was making the man think he was the most powerful.

To appease Nihapu, every morning Nyna ran to the east, to the basket, then returned. On the last morning there was a very short distance to run. She presented herself to Father Sun, then bathed. Nihapu dressed her in a new skirt.

"You do not bleed much," Nihapu said.

"Not much," Nyna said, wondering how much a woman bled during her moon cycle. "How do you know?"

"You do not need to change the strap very often. You are a lucky woman."

Nyna smiled.

As they walked the trail to the village, Cetisa came up to them. "I want to talk to you, sister."

"Come to my lodge," Nihapu said.

"No. I want to speak to you alone. Send the girl on."

"Nyna is not a girl anymore," Nihapu corrected.

"Send the woman on then," Cetisa said.

"Let us get settled first," Nihapu said.

"I want to speak to you now."

"All right," Nihapu said. She handed Nyna her basket and gestured for her to go on alone back to the lodge.

With Nyna out of earshot, Nihapu asked, "What is it?"

Cetisa paced, clearly uncomfortable. "You are lucky, sister. The spirits have always chosen you."

"Let us not go over this again."

"But it is true. You were given the healing gift, you

have a son, and you are the wife of the cacique. And me? I am only a wife. No gift, no child, no nobility."

"What do you want?" Nihapu asked. "We have discussed this over and over. Why again?"

"Have I ever asked for help?" Cetisa asked.

"Never. But I believe that is because of your pride. Even when you are sick, you do not ask."

"Well, I come to you now." Cetisa fumbled with her shell gorget necklace. "I want a child and I need your help. After all this time with Etac we still have no children."

"Perhaps that is the way the spirits wish it to be."

"No!" Cetisa looked away. "You can help. You have the gift. You know medicines."

"You want me to make a medicine that will help you conceive a child?"

Cetisa spun around. "Yes. Will you? But do not tell Etac," she added.

"Why would you keep this from your husband? He wants children, also."

Cetisa shook her head. "Because." She considered her answer for a moment. "I do not want him to think I needed special help."

"Because it comes from me? You do not want him to know you have come to your sister for help. Somehow in your head that demeans you."

Cetisa sucked in a big breath. "Yes."

Nihapu turned on her heel.

"Wait," Cetisa said. "This is hard for me to do."

Nihapu looked over her shoulder. "We are sisters. It should not be difficult to ask a sister for help."

"Please," Cetisa begged.

"All right," Nihapu said. "I will prepare a medicine, but it is only the spirits who breathe life into you."

Cetisa wrapped her arms around herself and watched her sister's back as she walked away.

When Nihapu arrived at the lodge, Nyna had already put everything away. Chogatis embraced each of them.

"Has Joog returned?" Nyna asked.

"Yes," Chogatis answered. "But he has gone on a hunt."

"Is that the house built for him?" Nihapu asked, looking across the village at a new hut.

"Yes," Chogatis said. "Uxaam has already purified it. When Joog returns, he will move his things."

Ochopee passed them. "I see he has recovered," Nihapu said.

"All but his memory. He takes long walks every day, but he seems confused sometimes."

Nihapu watched Ochopee. "I do not suppose it is easy to have lost your memory. I think his left side sags."

Chogatis nodded. "I think you are right. There is a faint limp."

"And how is Joog?" Nihapu said, turning back to Chogatis. "Did he talk to you?"

"He said that Qitce was an excellent teacher, and Qitce says he was a quick and dedicated learner."

Nihapu laughed softly.

Nyna again experienced that strange feeling she had when she watched Qitce and Joog go off together. She wondered if Guacana was taught to do what he did to her. If that was joining, she wanted no part of it. Why would a woman teach a man that? How could that be pleasurable? She conjured images of Qitce and Joog, and it made her shudder.

21

Nyna took a coal from the fire and set it inside a quahog shell that lay in a small basket. She checked to see that no one noticed what she was doing. Satisfied, she stood up and followed the trail to the cenote. There she pulled her hidden basket from beneath the rushes. She took out the ax and shoved it back beneath the brush. Then she held up the club she had made. It was only a piece of wood, but soon it would be much more. This was not a good place to work on it, she thought, and so she carried her things deep in the woods.

Nyna cleared a space on the ground, brushing away leaves and sticks until there was only dirt. She dug out a shallow depression, with sloping sides about as wide as the length of her arm. She surrounded it with rocks she collected. Then in the center she made a small pile of dry grass and dead pine needles. She gathered small twigs and slivers of wood and bark and put them in a heap next to larger pieces of wood.

Nyna blew on the coal in the shell and it flared. With two sticks she tweezed the coal and placed it on the tinder in the center of the fire pit. She leaned in and gently blew, watching the leaves and needles catch fire. When it burned brightly, Nyna added the twigs and then arranged the larger pieces in a cone over the small fire. The smoke and sparks channeled straight up.

When done, Nyna sat back and waited for the fire to burn down to coals. Meanwhile she prepared the wood.

She put the tip of an antler against the wood at an angle and tapped it with a rock. The antler chiseled a narrow trough down the shaft of the wood. At about one third of the way down the wood she quit, rotated it, and started another groove. Nyna continued encircling the top third of the wood club with these channels.

She brushed off the wood and cleaned out the grooves. "Yes," she said aloud, pleased with the first part of her task.

The fire burned low, just as she wanted it. Nyna took the quahog shell and put it on the coals. Then from her basket she took out a ball of pitch on the end of a stick that she had collected from a pine and rested it in the shell. She watched the pitch liquefy and bubble. The smell of turpentine saturated the air around her as it evaporated, leaving only the viscid resin behind. Nyna took some of the ash from the fire and sprinkled it in the pitch, then stirred it with a stick to mix it well.

Now came the important part. She laid a handful of sharks' teeth out in front of her. She tried one out, slipping the base of the tooth into one of the grooves in the wood club. It fit nicely!

Nyna held the club near the fire. The glue adhered to the stick enough that she could lift it from the shell and dribble it inside one of the grooves. Carefully she placed sharks' teeth in the gooey channel. In just a moment it was set fast.

Nyna began to gather the pitch glue on the stick again when she heard something. It could just be an old raccoon, or deer, she thought. But then it could be someone.

She doused the fire with dirt and was covering it when she realized someone was standing in front of her.

"Ochopee," she said. "You startled me."

"Who are you?" he asked.

"Nyna," she said. "I am Nyna."

"Your head. You are not Ais."

His eyes fell on the club. "What are you doing?"

Ochopee picked up the club and looked at it. He turned it in his hands. "Put everything in the basket and get up," he said.

Nyna gathered the sharks' teeth and antler and put them in the basket. She looked at Ochopee.

"Get up," he said, grabbing her by the upper arm.

"I am Nyna," she said again. "I live with Chogatis and Nihapu."

"I do not know who you are," he said, dragging her along. "But I know you are not Ais!" He yanked her arm.

Ochopee jerked and pulled her all the way back to the village. Uxaam was the first to see them.

"Ochopee, what are you doing?" Uxaam called out.

"Who is this?" Ochopee asked.

"Let her go," Uxaam said. "I will explain."

Ochopee dropped her arm and snatched the basket from her. "She is not Ais."

"No, she is not," Uxaam said.

Others began to gather around. Nyna edged away.

"Do not let her go yet," Ochopee said. "Look at this," he said, holding up the club. "I found her deep in the woods making this club. What woman fashions weapons?"

The crowd gasped and mumbled.

"Nyna," Uxaam said. "Is this true?"

Nyna stopped. It felt as if cold water were poured down her spine and arms.

"Tell them," Ochopee said. "You were making this weapon when I came upon you. And look in this basket, more things for more weapons!"

Chogatis joined the group. "Come here, Nyna," he said.

Nyna bowed her head and walked to the cacique.

"Is what Ochopee says, true?"

"Yes," she answered in almost a whisper.

Chogatis wiped his face with his hand. "Go then," he said. "Stay inside the lodge until I come for you."

Nyna backed away.

"Council needs to gather," Uxaam said.

Chogatis picked up the conch horn by the central hearth and blew it. The women scattered as the men formed about the hearth.

"What will we do about this woman who has made a weapon?" Uxaam asked.

Guacana chewed on a blade of grass.

"Do you wish to speak, Guacana?" Chogatis asked.

"I have said before what I think of the Taino woman. She does not belong with us. I think that is clear now. And what do you suppose she was going to do with that club. Murder one of us in our sleep?"

"Come now, Guacana," Uxaam said. "You do not believe that."

"I do," Guacana said.

Chogatis rubbed the back of his neck. "She has lived with us all this time."

Guacana wadded the grass in his hand, then flicked it away. "Perhaps now that she is a woman things will change."

Joog entered the village, carrying a deer carcass over his shoulders. When he saw Council gathered, he laid the deer on the ground.

"Join us," Uxaam said.

Joog chose a place next to Etac and sat with his legs crossed.

Uxaam explained why they were meeting.

"Nyna has told me so many times how her people have no weapons, how the Carib slaughter the Taino. She wants to take the knowledge of weapons to her people," Joog said.

"But she is a woman," another man said. "It is not permitted."

"She should be cast out," Guacana said. "She has broken Ais law."

"Yes," another man said. "We cannot allow it."

Then several were speaking at the same time, all agreeing that she should be punished.

Chogatis held up the Talking Stick and silenced them.

Joog signaled that he wished to speak. Chogatis handed him the Stick. "This is my first Council," he said. "But you have met many times before concerning Nyna. The last was very recent. I am sure each of you recalls your decision."

The men were nodding.

"Did you decide that Nyna was not Ais, and therefore not entitled to participate in Ais traditions? She was not permitted a grandmother nor any of the rites that accompany an Ais girl when she becomes a woman."

"Right!" Guacana called out. "She is not Ais!"

"Quiet," Chogatis scolded. "You will abide by the rules of the Talking Stick or you are not welcome in Council."

Guacana grumbled.

Ochopee signaled to speak, and Chogatis gestured for Joog to pass the Stick.

"We cannot allow this woman to go unpunished. She has clearly broken Ais law."

Joog smiled and motioned for the Stick. The Stick passed around the circle to him. "You have confirmed my point. She is not Ais, and therefore not subject to either Ais privilege nor law. She is Taino, and so she has broken no law."

Chogatis held back a broad smile. His grandson was smart.

Guacana lifted his hand for the Stick. "Then you are saying Ais laws do not apply to her in any way. I want to make sure we all understand exactly what you are saying."

Chogatis took the Talking Stick. "I am not certain

what you are getting at, Guacana. I believe you have something in mind."

Guacana shook his head and shrugged. "No," he said.

Chogatis glared at him. The cacique did not know what Guacana's intentions were, but he was sure they were corrupt.

"Then how does Council decide?" Uxaam asked. He drew a line in the dirt. "If you agree with Joog, that Ais law does not pertain to Nyna, stand on this side."

Joog took his place on the side of the line.

"And if you disagree, stand on the opposite side."

Slowly the men took their places. They could not say that Nyna was Ais—they had already fervently declared that she was not when she was denied the grandmother. And so they had no choice but to stand with Joog. All except Ochopee who defiantly stood opposite.

"I was not part of the previous decision," Ochopee said.

The last man to declare his decision was Guacana. Chogatis clenched his jaw as Guacana stood on Joog's side. The cacique did not like the smug smile on the man's face. He wished he knew what was going on inside Guacana's head. Whatever it was, was not good.

"Council has decided," Chogatis said. "And so it shall be."

After the men dispersed, Chogatis remained with Uxaam. "I do not like whatever Guacana is thinking," he said.

"Yes," Uxaam said. "It is as if he has some kind of plan."

"Exactly," Chogatis said. "I think we have been set up somehow, and he plans to use this decision in some way to hurt Nyna."

"I believe your instincts are right."

Another full moon came and went. Laira entered womanhood with all the pomp that went with the occasion. For the celebration Ochopee provided an enormous feast for all before sending his daughter off with a grandmother to the woman's hut. Zinni was happy to see her husband's chest puff with pride. It had been so long since she had seen him take any pride in his children. Chitolo would be interested to know that Laira was now of age to marry. His next visit would be interesting.

Uxaam noted that since the big storm there had been no rain, and he was becoming concerned, especially considering Joog's vision. The water level in the cenote had dropped and the stream seemed narrower, the banks sticking out above the water. He prayed the dry weather was not a pattern that would remain.

Nyna was permitted to work on her weapons. The women frowned on it, and the men stayed clear, her activity leaving them extremely uncomfortable. She was relieved that she could now work openly on the weapons and tools. Chogatis and Joog helped with their expertise. But, so as not to plague the village with what she did, when she practiced using the weapons, she did that in the woods, out of sight.

This morning she planned to practice hurling a large five-weight bola. She admired her latest work. Instead of rocks, she had filled wet rawhide pouches with sand. As the rawhide dried, it shrank. This way she was sure the pouches were equally weighted and nearly as hard as rocks. She dangled three of the pouches in her hand, then felt the other two. They were perfect. Thrown accurately it would tangle a man's legs and bring him down just as it would a deer. Then he would certainly be at the disadvantage.

Nyna hiked to the beach to practice. She did not feel well today. Her head ached and she felt more tired than usual. But if she was going to learn to use the weapons she made, she had to practice. She wanted to learn to throw the bola with some precision. The beach was a good place to practice as there was no brush to interfere.

The labyrinth of prop roots of a mangrove served as her target. She stood in the water, twirling the bola overhead. She let go, sending the bola whipping through the air into the mangrove roots.

"Good work!" It was Joog.

"You were watching . . . hiding?"

"I did not want to distract you," he said as both of them walked to the mangrove.

Nyna bent and untangled the leather thongs from the roots. Joog took the bola from her. "Come, and I will show you another way," he said.

From the same spot she had thrown before, Joog showed her how to throw it sidearm. "This way is good in the open, like the beach," he said.

He demonstrated, but didn't let go. He handed the bola to Nyna. "Try it."

Nyna practiced first. Joog stood snuggly behind her and put his hands on her bare shoulders. "Keep your shoulders square," he said, breathing through her hair. Nyna straightened, letting his hands guide her. She tried the swing again.

"When you let go, snap your wrist," he said.

In one flowing motion, Nyna flung the bola. In an instant it wrapped around the mangrove prop roots.

"That was great," Joog said.

"That would hurt a man's ankles," she said. "If he was running, it would bring him down. And then," she said, "I could be on him with my club!"

Joog gave her a fascinated smile. "A woman who makes and uses weapons," he said.

"I want to practice some more," she said. "You go ahead back."

"Remember, shoulders square and snap your wrist."

After Joog left, she threw the bola repeatedly, each time having to untangle it from the roots. She rested for a while, rubbing her temples. In her gut she wanted immediate improvement, though in her mind she knew it would take many sessions like this, throwing the bola over and over, before she would get noticeably better. Joog had done it since he was very small and so he was an expert. It would take her people a long time to learn, just like her.

Nyna bundled her bola and proceeded back to the village. On the way she deviated from the trail, thinking she might catch sight of a deer and really have an opportunity to use the bola. In an area thick with palmettos and oaks she stopped. The deer were known to feed in this area and rest in the shade of the palmetto thickets in the middle of the day.

Since it was late afternoon, she thought perhaps the deer would begin to feed again. She leaned quietly against a tree and waited. She began to think it was getting too late to stay any longer when her patience was rewarded.

She saw a deer moving nearly silently through the forest. She stood very still as the animal continued to move in her direction. Not too far from her it suddenly stopped, lifted its head and looked around. The deer's ears twitched skittishly.

Nyna was close enough to see the large brown eyes and the fear that sparked in them. The bola hung from her hand ready to be swung. The deer was a doe, its fur a beautiful dun velvet. Its eyes were wide apart, characteristic of prey, whereas predators' eyes were closer together.

Nyna bunched up the bola. She couldn't bring herself to hurt the animal just for the sake of throwing the bola. As soon as the deer detected sound and movement, it bolted into the forest.

Without warning a voice boomed behind her. "You think you are a hunter but you are not!"

"Guacana!"

"I had to watch to see if you had the courage, and just as I thought, you did not."

"No," Nyna said, taking a step.

"You do not want me to hurt your little boy-girl friend, do you?"

Nyna clenched the bola in her fist. She would have no problem throwing the bola at this *animal*. "Step aside," she said.

"You know what I am here for."

Nyna dipped her head so she would not have to look at him. She walked forward.

"Why do you do this each time? We both know you will not let Buhgo be hurt. You do care about him, do you not?"

Her fingers twitched around the leather in her hand. How easy to send it flying around Guacana's legs, the pouches hitting with enough force to shatter his ankle. But then what would his vengeance be on her innocent friend?

A horrid taste developed in her mouth, and her stomach churned. How her head still ached!

"All right," Nyna finally said. "Get it over with."

"Down on the ground," he said.

Nyna dropped to the earth and turned over to her hands and knees. She hiked her skirt, not bothering to remove it.

"Is that the way you like it?" Guacana asked.

"That is what you want, is it not? You cannot bear to look me in the face. Who is the coward?"

"You think you stop me with your talk?"

Nyna peered behind her. "What are you afraid of, Guacana? What do you think you will see in my face."

"You do not make any sense," he said, dropping his breechclout.

"You do it like an animal. You cannot do it any other way, can you?"

He got to his knees and took himself in his hand.

"Your manpart would fail you any other way," she muttered.

Guacana thrust into her.

Nyna did not move or make a noise. There was no reason to fight him; it only got her hurt even more.

"You filthy slime!" Guacana cried out, jumping off her.

Nyna looked behind her. He stared down at his rapidly deflating manpart. It was smeared with blood.

"You have tricked me! Defiled me with your filth!" he cried.

Suddenly, Nyna realized what had happened. "Moon blood!" she said. "The most potent blood of all!" Now she knew why her head ached all day and she felt so sluggish. At last her first real moon cycle! What a perfect time!

Guacana picked up his breechclout from the ground and fled to the stream to wash. Nyna was sure he would not taint the cenote with her abomination! The sight of him retreating in such horror that he fled unclothed gave her a sense of being avenged.

She lay back on the ground and sank into the leaves. The coolness of twilight was quickly approaching. Even though the sun had not set, the moon was already up. Perhaps the Ais spirits did look after her. Or maybe there was a Taino grandmother that watched over her. A sense of euphoria swept over Nyna. Nihapu was right. There was grand power in being a woman. Even the bola was no match!

22

Nyna treasured the time in the woman's hut. It was the one place she was away from Guacana. Somehow she now appreciated Nihapu's stories about women even more because they meant something.

She spent the day grinding coontie root, thoroughly washing it until the water ran clear and the poison was rinsed away. It reminded her of manioc. She closed her eyes as she ground the root in her mortar with the oak pestle. She could nearly see her mother, sitting just as she did, on her heels, grinding manioc. Nyna strained, wanting so to see her mother's face, but it was too vague.

On the sixth day of isolation, she packed her basket. There was no moon blood today, which meant she would go home. Nyna bathed in the stream, said the Ais prayers as if Nihapu were watching, and dressed in a freshly made skirt. Once again she was clean.

As she made her way back to the village, she passed Guacana. He spat on the ground. "I am not finished with you," he said.

Nyna kept on without acknowledging that he spoke to her. What she did not understand was that if he hated her so, if he feared she was evil, why did he want to join with her? If you disliked or distrusted someone, you stayed away. At least she thought that was the way it was for most people.

Ochopee and Joog sat at Chogatis's hearth as she entered to put her things away. They were speaking of the recent lack of rain. She listened from inside.

"Some of us have been talking," Ochopee was saying. "I cannot recall specifics, but deep inside I know what it is to suffer a drought. There are those of us who are becoming concerned."

"Yes," Chogatis said. "You are not alone. But it is much too early to say that a drought is looming."

"Grandfather," Joog said. "I am concerned also. The grasshoppers. Uxaam interprets the grasshoppers of my vision to indicate a coming drought."

"It is still too early," Chogatis said. "We should not get excited yet."

"Perhaps it is time for Joog to visit the Jeaga and work on negotiations," Ochopee said.

Chogatis gazed at his grandson. "When the time is right. It is a lot to ask."

"But I have no fear of the Jeaga," Joog said. "Perhaps Ochopee is right. We should keep in mind that a drought will come again . . . sometime. Uxaam says the egret and the grasshoppers determine my destiny."

"I suppose you could open some negotiations with them. It does not need to be specific at this time. Perhaps renew old friendships you had."

"Actually, I would like to visit the Jeaga," Joog said.

"It has been a long time," the cacique said. "Before this gray began to streak my hair."

"Then it is time," Joog said. "No more time should pass or they will forget me."

Night fell in a hush over the village. Yixala, the old man who had the gift of the *snake that wants to bite,* lay on his mat. In the middle of the night, the aggravation of incessant mosquitoes brought him up from his deep sleep. He was surprised because the lack of recent rain should have discouraged more mosquitoes. He sat up and swatted at them. He intended to move both hands and fan, but found he could only lift his left arm. The other arm did not respond, and his fingers of his right hand were curled into a claw. The right side of his face seemed peculiar. He touched it. His mouth sagged on the right side and so did his eyelid.

Just as he was thinking how strange this was, a large raven, black as the rich dark loam, flew into his house and perched at his feet.

Yixala knew the raven was the harbinger of both good and bad signs. It was the raven that had the power to fight bad signs, like those of the owl. But also, it was a trickster and shapechanger. Raven was one of the few spirits that was both natural and supernatural, with the ability to cross over into the spirit world. It could bring a person's spirit back from the land of the deceased and back to life. Raven could also escort a spirit into the land of the dead.

Yixala drew back and felt a chill run down his spine. "Why do you visit me in the middle of the night?" he asked.

The raven spoke. "Are you ready, old man?"

"Ready for what?"

"You have lived many years," Raven said.

"Yes, I have seen many seasons."

"You must grow weary," said the bird.

"Sometimes."

"I have come to take you to the other side."

"Death?" Yixala asked.

"To another world. The spirit world."

"I am afraid," Yixala said.

The raven shimmered in the moonlight, and suddenly its image wavered. In its place stood Yixala's second wife. Yixala had outlived four wives and all six of his children.

"Do not be afraid," the woman said. She held out her hand. "We wait for you," she said.

Yixala felt the cool breeze as it brushed past her hair

and over him. The image changed. His fourth son, the young one who died of the coughing disease, appeared.

"We are waiting," the boy said. "Go with Raven."

The boy wavered like the heated air rising off black muck. The bird took back its natural shape. "It is not a far trip," Raven said. "There is no pain. Close your eyes and I will lead you."

Yixala lay back on his mat and closed his eyes.

Zinni curled her back against her husband. His arm went over her and she settled into the curve of his body. He was already asleep. Zinni smiled. He was still so warm, and she so moist from their lovemaking. Zinni snuggled closer. She was glad Ochopee did not remember that he had not been with her this way since Taska was conceived. She lay awake listening to him breathe, feeling the heat from him radiate to her back, dreading the day his memory would return.

Taska's eyes fluttered open. "Wake up!" he called. "Buhgo!"

Buhgo, startled from his sleep, sat straight up.

"It is Yixala! He is dying!"

"What do you mean?" Ochopee asked, also roused from his sleep.

"Yixala is dying this very moment! You must hurry," Taska said.

Buhgo rushed from the hut, followed by Ochopee. "Get Uxaam," Ochopee told Buhgo.

Ochopee burst across the village and into Yixala's hut.

"Yixala," he said. "Are you all right?"

There was no answer. Ochopee could barely see. The old man lay on his sleeping mat, his mouth agape, his breathing labored.

"Can you hear me?" Ochopee asked, lifting Yixala's head.

Uxaam and Buhgo entered the hut.

"Look," Buhgo said. "He smiles."

Uxaam and Ochopee stared through the dull light, but clearly they saw Yixala's mouth turn up at the corners.

"It is as if he has a pleasant dream," Uxaam said.

"But he is not dreaming," Ochopee said. "He would wake up from a dream."

Yixala took in a deep breath, his chest expanding upward. He let it out in a long sigh like the wind soughing through the trees.

"What is that noise?" Ochopee asked, looking up.

"The sound of bird wings," Uxaam said. "Raven has come."

They could feel the air the wings pushed, and it blew over their faces.

For an instant the village became eerily still, then the crickets resumed their chirping and the common night noises returned.

"He is dead," Ochopee said. "There was nothing we could do." He laid Yixala's head on the ground.

"The old man had a good life," Uxaam said. "He lived for a long time, saw many things change."

"Does he have anyone left?" Ochopee asked.

"He has outlived all his family," Buhgo said.

Ochopee rubbed his forehead. "I should know these things!" he said.

"Do not let it frustrate you so," Uxaam said. "In time your memory could be restored. If not, then you go forward each day and build new memories."

The men walked outside.

"How did you know something was wrong with Yixala?" Uxaam asked.

"Taska knew," Buhgo said. "He woke us up and told us Yixala was dying."

"This is not your brother's first premonition," Uxaam said.

"No," Buhgo answered. "It happens all the time."

"Why has no one ever really spoken to me about it?" Uxaam asked.

Ochopee looked to Buhgo for an answer. Buhgo stumbled over his words. "My father has not been proud of me, of what I am. He, um, Ochopee wanted . . ."

"Say it," Ochopee said. "I must hear."

"Taska was born with an imperfection, a physical abnormality. Though his body was imperfect, his mind is more than perfect. When he was four summers, he knew as much as I. Another deviation. Then as he grew, he experienced premonitions."

"The spirits make up for what they take away," Uxaam said.

Buhgo continued. "And I am more woman than man, even though my body is a man's. I did not choose that. I was born that way."

Ochopee looked confused. "But why has that kept you from going to the shaman?"

Buhgo hung his head. "We humiliate you. Taska's premonitions or mystical powers are just another aberration. He wants to shame you no more."

Ochopee looked away. "I do not know who I am," he said. "I do not know where those feelings came from, what made me who I was or who I am. I do not know what to say. There must have been reasons."

"Taska," Uxaam said. "I believe he may have the gift of the shaman."

Joog pushed off in his canoe. The men stood at the bank and wished him a safe journey. He took up the paddle and maneuvered the canoe parallel to the shore in deeper water. With the sun at his left shoulder, Joog headed south toward Jeaga territory.

Nyna stood down the beach, away from the crowd, where she could see him without interference. She watched his golden-brown arm lift the paddle, then with no splash, sink it in the blue water. His back was straight, the sun glinting off it, his hair blowing behind him. She wanted to feel him behind her, showing her how to swing the bola, his chest against her back.

Nyna felt a tingle travel through her. These were special feelings, but she didn't understand them. She closed her eyes and let the image of him fill her. The ocean sang to her, helping her drift away. It was easy for her to imagine things, as she had had much practice, imagining she was home so many times. Nyna pictured Joog standing behind her, his arm coming around her waist, his breath on her neck. She leaned her head back against his shoulder, and they were together gazing across the sea.

She opened her eyes and watched Joog until she could see him no more. Finally she dragged her gaze from the sea and wandered back toward the village.

A group of three men stood in the middle of the trail, just outside the village as Nyna returned. Guacana was one of them.

"Nyna," he said. "Come here."

Nyna kept walking.

"Ais women do what men say," he said. "Come here."

She stopped. "I am not Ais," she said. "Have you forgotten?"

Guacana laughed, as did the other two.

"What do you find funny?" she asked.

Guacana slapped his friend on the back. "She does not want to be Ais, wants to make weapons, does not want to be subject to Ais law! Is that not so, woman?"

Nyna clenched her jaw. "What do you want?" she asked.

"But you know what I want from you. You are good for only one thing. Relieve me."

Nyna glared. "What are you saying?"

"A man needs to relieve himself," Guacana said.

"You are disgusting," she said, taking up her walk again.

Guacana grabbed her arm and whipped her around.

"I said relieve me." He pushed her to the ground, spun her over and hoisted her hips.

Guacana shoved himself into her. "See, she likes it," he said. "She does not fight once she gets it."

One man laughed, but the other spoke. "Enough, Guacana. Get off."

Guacana pumped into her. "You can have her next," Guacana said. Furiously he thrust into her, rocking her whole body, her hair dragging in the dirt, her elbows scraping.

"Stop," she whispered. "Why do you do this?"

The man who objected pulled on Guacana's shoulder. "Get off her. Leave her be."

Guacana pushed harder, but the interference by his companion impaired him. He slipped out of her, stroked his failing part with his hand to bring more life to it, and tried to enter her again.

"Leave her!" the companion repeated. "Even your manpart does not want to cooperate."

Guacana rolled off her and onto the ground with a grunt. "Ah, you are taking the fun out of this," he said. He looked down at his organ shrinking before his eyes. "A man cannot concentrate."

"What is going on?" It was Etac who discovered them. Nyna was still on her hands and knees, and Guacana lay naked, his once tumescent manpart rapidly deflating in his hand.

"Having a little fun," Guacana said. "But the two of you spoil it."

Etac bent next to Nyna. "Are you all right?"

Slowly she got to her feet. She wiped the tears from her face, smearing it with the dirt on her hands.

"Go," Etac said.

Nyna fumbled with her skirt and ran toward the beach.

"What is the matter with you?" Etac asked. "I will bring this to Council!"

Guacana laughed. "That does not make me tremble,"

he said. "I tell you, Council will do nothing. You will see."

Etac stomped back to the village. "Call Council!" he told Chogatis. "Call the men together now."

At the sound of the conch horn, the men gathered. Buhgo stood close enough to overhear.

Guacana and his two companions strode into the circle and sat as Etac glared.

After everyone settled, Chogatis lifted the Talking Stick. "Etac has requested this meeting," he said. "Tell us what your concern is."

"I happened upon something that is intolerable," he began.

The men listened intently as Etac revealed what he had witnessed. "We have laws, rules that we follow, and there are punishments for men who break those rules. Our grandfathers made the laws in accordance with the spirits."

Guacana shifted and laughed under his breath.

"Even now he scoffs at our laws," Etac said.

"What do you say?" Chogatis asked Guacana.

"I am glad you ask. Did we or did we not decide that this woman, Nyna, is not Ais and not subject to Ais laws? We allow her to make weapons, to use them. We denied her a grandmother for just that reason. She is not Ais!"

"But there are laws that govern your behavior," Uxaam said.

Guacana smiled. "But the laws do not protect her, only Ais women. Is that not so? I have done nothing wrong, just as she did nothing wrong making the weapons." Guacana glanced smugly around the circle. "This is what you wanted, what Council decided is it not?"

Chogatis shook his head. "You are right. We made such a decision, but this was not the intention. Where is your dignity, your character, your decency? You squirm around the laws like a worm. Now I understand what you were doing in the last meeting. Have you no pride in being Ais?"

"I am a proud Ais warrior," Guacana said. "She is nothing. She should have been left to die on the beach, and everyone here knows that."

"Your tongue is not attached to your head!" Etac said. "I cannot believe what you say." He looked at the expressions on the men's faces. "Do you not see how you shame us all? We cannot condone this."

"You do not need to condone or disapprove of anything," Guacana said. "The law is the law."

Uxaam stood up. "If you think so poorly of Nyna, then why do you do this act? If she disgusts you, why would you join with her? What is your purpose to do such a thing in front of others?"

"To shame her, humiliate her as she humiliated me."

"When you were children?" Chogatis asked with disbelief in his tone. "You still carry that sourness? You retaliated. The lessons were learned when you were children. Now you are a man. Behave like one!"

"I do not believe it is the humiliation any longer," Uxaam said. He glared at Guacana. "If she did not arouse you, you would not be able to do the deed."

Guacana's face turned red. "She does not arouse me! She makes me sick."

"You have something wrong in your head," Chogatis said. "You dishonor the people, your heritage."

"We must do something," Etac said.

"And what will be done?" Guacana asked. "Nothing, because without doubt Council decided Ais laws do not apply to this woman. If I should decide to humiliate her again, I will."

"And I will raise my hand against you," Chogatis said.

"You are an old man, Cacique. Besides, there are laws about that. Ais do not harm Ais without consequences."

Chogatis dropped the Talking Stick and walked out of Council.

As soon as Chogatis left the meeting, Buhgo took off to find Nyna. Standing on the beach he spotted her swimming deeper and deeper.

He called her name and ran into the water. Buhgo's arms and legs moved in a frenzy as he swam to catch up to her.

"Stop!" he called, treading water for a moment. "Nyna, wait!"

She looked back. "Let me go, Buhgo."

He swam harder, finally closing the gap between them. "You let Guacana win if you do this," Buhgo said.

They faced each other in the deep water.

"I do not care about winning. I am tired. I want it over."

"No," Buhgo said. "How many times have you told me you were sent here for a purpose? One day you will return to your people and bring them the help they need. That is your destiny."

Nyna started to cry.

Buhgo wrapped his arm around her neck and began to sidestroke. Too exhausted to fight him, she allowed him to tow her to the beach. Finally both of them lay on their backs, their legs still in the shallow water, their eyes staring at the sky.

"You cannot give up," Buhgo said. "No matter what happens."

"It is so hard." She sighed.

"No one's life is easy," he said. "Look at Chogatis. How much has he lost? And Joog? It must have been terrible to see his father slain, to be captured by the enemy. Everyone has his burdens."

"You think I am self-indulgent, do you not?"

"That is not what I mean. You have great things to look forward to. These are mere trials to test you."

"Perhaps I am not worthy."

"And that is why you made such a long brave journey across the sea?"

"It is not just Guacana that is a complication. There is another. If I tell you, will you promise not to tell anyone?"

Buhgo sat up and looked at her. "You know I will not if that is your request."

Nyna sat up, too, and watched the waves. "I have had this strange feeling inside that I did not understand for a long time. Now I think I do." Her voice was soft as the wind, as if the breeze might catch the words and take them away to a safe place.

23

Joog watched the shoreline as it staggered dense mangrove with open white sand beaches crawling with creeping vines, flowers, and sweet cocoplums. He passed a sandbank where there had been a feast of some kind, the ashen fire pit now cool and gray. He was in Jeaga territory.

Joog beached his piragua and wandered over the dunes. The remains of the fire and feast indicated that it had been many days since the Jeaga were here. A fishing expedition he assumed. He moved past the dunes, deeper into pine and palmetto scrub. Before he would meet with the Jeaga he needed to meditate, to rest in the place of oneness.

In the thin shade of a pine he hunkered down and set his mind free. An osprey settled in a pine branch above him. Joog sank deeper into himself, just as Chogatis had taught him. Deeper still, he soon crossed the fourth curtain. His spirit lifted up and out, curling into the air as smoke might. As the osprey opened its wings, Joog flew with it into the shadow of memories, times long ago. He was there in the Jeaga village with Talli and her new husband Akoma.

The osprey spoke. "I am happy you have come," it said. Joog recognized the voice as that of Banabas, the man who had rescued him from the hands of another Jeaga. Banabas had pleaded for the boy to be spared, and had taken him back to the Jeaga village to live with him and his wife, Talli. Banabas still watched over Joog from the other side.

"Is that you, Banabas?" he asked.

With his spoken question, the vision quickly faded, and Joog passed up through the doors, back into the world of the first curtain.

He shook his head in disappointment. He knew better than to let thoughts and questions come into his mind. He thought he had mastered that.

Joog snatched a few cocoplums before pushing his dugout back into the water. He bit into the sweet white pulp of one of the fruits and hopped inside the canoe.

At the mouth of the river, Joog paused. There were scents and sights that brought back hazy memories and emotions. It had been so long ago. Who that knew him would still be amongst the Jeaga?

Joog paddled against the current, upriver. As he approached the village, he saw a boy at the landing.

"Ais!" the boy screamed, running away.

Joog remained off the bank and waited for someone to permit him to come ashore. In a few moments the landing filled with men, weapons in hand. The last meeting between Ais and Jeaga had been bloody, and neither people had forgotten.

Akoma stood in front of the crowd, and Joog recognized him.

"I am Joog," he said, standing in the canoe.

Akoma lifted his hand and gestured for him to bring in the dugout. As the canoe bow ran aground, Akoma stepped forward and grabbed the dugout. "Joog!" he said. "You have grown into a man."

Joog laughed as he got out of the dugout. The two men grasped each other's forearms in greeting. "You remember Ufala and Ocaab," Akoma said, meaning the two men who stood just behind him.

"Yes," Joog said. Moving to the front of the crowd

was another man. "Tawute!" Joog said. It was his child-hood friend.

"How good to see you again," Tawute said.

"So often I think of the time we spent together as boys. Happy and sad times."

"Come," Akoma said. "Welcome to our village. Talli will be so happy you are here. There is not a day she does not wonder how you are."

Word spread quickly about the village that Joog had returned. Talli jumped up and ran to the center of the plaza.

"Is it really you?" she asked as Joog made his way to her.

"It is me," he said.

Talli cupped his face in her hands. "A fine man," she said.

She had been much younger the last time he had seen her. He remembered her and Akoma walking into the Ais village to bring him home. How brave they had been to dare to walk into the enemy's village unarmed.

Fine lines were just beginning to etch about her eyes and corners of her mouth.

A young man came next to her. "My son, Mikot," she said. "I am sure you do not recognize him. He has grown a lot since you last saw him."

"Mikot!" Joog said. "You were so young when I left."

"I have a daughter, also," Talli said. "She has gone to dig coontie with several others. She should be back soon." Talli looked at her hands as she rubbed the knuckles. "We had another son, but he lived only two days."

Joog embraced her. "I am glad to see you again," he said. "Can we sit and talk?"

"I would like that," Talli said.

"While you two reminisce, there are a few things I must tend to. I will not be long," Akoma said.

Talli led Joog to a quiet space by her lodge. "Do you remember much?" she asked.

"Some," Joog answered. "I wish Banabas had lived," he said, recalling the day Banabas's bloody body had been brought into the village. Joog had thrown himself over the dead man and cried. "He was a good man."

"He was," Talli said. "I miss him."

"Come," Tawute said to Joog. "I want you to see my mother. She has been sick. She will be so happy to see you."

Tawute led him to his mother's hearth. Ceboni sat sewing, her hair straggling down her back. She looked so much older than Talli. He supposed the illness played a part in that.

"Look who I have brought to see you," Tawute said.

Ceboni did not look up. Joog squatted by her side, and Ceboni stared at him.

"Who are you?" she asked.

"Joog," he said. "Do you remember me?"

Ceboni clapped her hands in front of her face. "Joog!" She hugged him. "Let me look at your face again," she said. She studied it a moment, outlining his features with her fingertip. "Yes, it is you," she said.

"Tawute says you have been ill," Joog said.

"Ah, just getting older," she said. "What brings you here?" she asked.

"I am going to speak to Council," Joog said. "I wish the peace between the Jeaga and Ais to continue."

"That is good," Ceboni said.

"I suppose I should go and speak with Akoma about my visit," Joog said. "But I wanted to see old friends first."

"Yes," Tawute said. "You will have time to visit later."

Joog got to his feet and followed Tawute to the plaza where he sat and waited on Akoma.

Much had changed about the village. There seemed to be faces he did not know and supposed this was now a mixture of the Turtle and Panther clans. He had lived only with the Panther clan.

Akoma invited him close to the fire. Serious matters were often discussed after drawing sweat from the body.

"So, what brings you to visit?" Akoma asked.

"We have maintained peace for a long time," Joog said. "I know the old ones do not forget, none of us do. But we have learned to live in peace, and that has been good for both."

"I have great respect for your grandfather," Akoma said.

"Chogatis also has respect for you, and he admires you. He does not forget the risk you took to do the right thing for me."

"But you do not come for that reason alone," Akoma said.

"No," Joog answered. "We have had no rain since the big storm, and my people begin to fret that another drought may come."

"The river," Akoma said.

"Our Ais brothers, the Bobcat clan, Osprey, Anhinga, Gar, and others, have enough water to support themselves, but not enough to take on the Hawk Clan. If we push north, we tread on Mayaca or Jororo. To our south are you and the Yobe. You have the river. If we go west, we distance ourselves from the sea. We have few choices. I have come to ask for the Jeaga to consider a proposal. If there is a drought, the Jeaga would permit the Hawk clan of the Ais to temporarily live along the river, of course keeping a respectable distance."

"I cannot make that decision," Akoma said. "That is one the Council must make, and of course we must consult the other Jeaga clans who occupy the river."

"I understand," Joog said. 'I know there is no drought yet, but we must explore what we can do. Unlike the past, the Jeaga and Ais are on peaceful terms."

"That makes a difference," Akoma said.

"The Ais and Jeaga are not so different," Joog said. "And, there is a woman who lives amongst us that comes from a people we have never heard of. She says her people are Taino. She has also shown me that people, no matter the clan or tribe, are all the same. They find joy and pain in the same things."

"Taino," Akoma said. "I have not heard of them. Where do they live?"

"Far out in the sea. She spent days in a dugout crossing the water, fleeing the Carib, their enemy."

"I do not know the Carib either."

"The world changes as we speak," Joog said. "The more I learn, the more I realize how little I know."

Akoma laughed. "How wise," he said. "You are right." He paused a moment, then said, "I will bring this to Council, but I will not ask them to make a decision right away. The idea must settle in their minds first. If I ask for a quick decision, they will respond with all their old notions, from the gut. Give it time."

"That is good," Joog said. "I want to tell you a quick story. When I was a boy I tracked a raccoon, got so close I thought I could just reach out and touch him. The raccoon suddenly stopped, turned and looked at me. For that moment our eyes locked, then just as quickly he moved on. I wondered for a long time what had happened. It took many seasons to understand. For that instant that the raccoon held still and looked at me, he offered himself to me, the animal willing to give up his flesh for man. But I did not take the opportunity. I tell you this because the rains and peace give us this opportunity to enrich the amity between our two peoples. We do not want the opportunity to pass."

"That is a good point. We must be patient, but still not wait too long."

"If the drought comes, the people of the Hawk Clan of the Ais will suffer. You cannot tell a man he cannot feed his family or ask him to watch his children die. That is when the peace would end. He would have no choice but to fight for the land along the river. I do not want that to ever happen again."

"Nor do I," Akoma said. "We should not let this opportunity for continued peace pass us by, like the raccoon."

Sweat drenched the two men's bodies. "I believe my daughter Cian has returned by now. Talli is anxious for you to meet her."

They proceeded to Akoma's lodge. Talli stood nearby talking to a young woman whose back was to them.

"Ah, Joog," Talli said. "This is our daughter, Cian."

Cian turned around and smiled at him. "Is something wrong?" she said.

"You look like your mother," he said.

"That is what everyone says. I think it a compliment."

"It is," Joog said.

Council met late in the day, and Akoma did not ask for an immediate decision. Joog stayed in Akoma's lodge for the night. In the morning he went outside and followed the old trail to the river. The air was especially cold, and the water chilled him as he stepped into it. He splashed it on his face and rubbed. He rinsed the rest of his body, sinking to his neck in the cold water. Joog took a big breath and sank beneath the water. With an explosion he speared up through the water shaking his wet head, sending out a crown of water droplets into the air.

Akoma had come to the river. "Too cold for me," he said. "I will wait until the sun is higher."

Joog laughed. "Do you get old and soft?"

"I suppose I do," Akoma said.

Joog climbed from the water and redressed.

"Council came up with a proposition. I think it might be a good idea."

"What is that?" Joog asked.

"If she pleases you, and of course if you please her, I think it would be a good thing for there to be a marriage between you and Cian."

Nihapu took the hide from the large wooden trench where she had soaked it. Next to her were two forked posts that supported the horizontal beam. She draped the hide over the beam and used both hands to twist and wring out the excess water. The tail end of the deer hung slightly over the beam and the neck end nearly to the ground. Nihapu rubbed her hands a moment to warm them. Then she pulled the neck of the hide up over the tail end so it overlapped. Starting at one side she rolled the edges of the hide to the center, tucking in loose flaps of skin as she went. She rolled the other side the same way so both sides met in the center.

Cetisa came up to her. "The medicine has not worked," she said. "Can you make it stronger?"

"I told you only the spirits can breathe a life into you," Nihapu said. "The medicine allows the body to be ready. That is all it can do." She grabbed her heavy wood branch and stuck it through the loop of hide, twisting as hard as she could. Water streamed from the hide.

"I am getting too old," Cetisa said. "I have to do something!"

Nihapu looked up and let the hide untwist. She wiped her forehead with the back of her hand.

"You do not know how I feel," Cetisa ranted. "You cannot. You have everything."

Nihapu dragged her gaze from her sister back to the hide. She twisted it in the other direction, applying as much force as she could muster.

"I want a child! That is not so much to want!"

"Then I suggest you go home to your husband," Nihapu said.

Cetisa turned on her heel.

"She is an ill one," Nyna said, coming out of the lodge. "You gave her medicine to help her have a baby?"

"Yes, but she does not want Etac to know. She does not like to ask for my help. So say nothing to anyone."

"She talks so hatefully to you."

"Yes," Nihapu agreed. "But she is my sister." She wrung the hide again. Now only a dribble of water came from it. "You and Buhgo fetch the plants for her medicine. Tell him what it is for, but not who it is for. He will know which plants to gather."

Nyna went for her friend. As they wandered the forest, they talked. "The other day, when we were on the beach and I told you my secret, you had little reaction," Nyna said. "Why is that?"

"I am afraid it will not work out and you will be hurt."

"I said that I think I have special feelings for Joog, not any more than that. I do not expect him to feel the same for me."

"I am afraid for you, that is all."

"I know," Nyna said. "I should not have said anything. It is just a fantasy in my head. Of course I love him . . . like a brother."

"I do not think this revelation of yours was that you love him like a brother."

Nyna bent to pick some leaves. "I suppose not."

Buhgo let out a deep sigh. "I have secrets, too," he said.

"Really," Nyna said. "Are you going to share them with me?"

"You are the only one I can share it with."

Nyna sat and patted the ground next to her. "Tell me," she said.

Buhgo lowered himself next to her. "It is better not said."

"You know I will tell no one," Nyna said.

"But if I say it, somehow it makes it true. I do not want it to be true."

"Words cannot make things real or true. They are only words."

"Once spoken I cannot take it back," he said. "The words never die. They float in the air forever waiting to fall on someone else's ear."

"You are too mystical," Nyna said. "After I told you about my secret, I felt better. Now I have someone I can talk to about it instead of carrying it all alone."

"I am glad," Buhgo said.

"Now you tell me," she said. "It will lighten your burden."

"If you tell anyone, they will find it despicable."

"I said I would not tell anyone. Do you not trust me? If you really are not ready to tell, then do not. But if you worry if you can trust me, that should not be a concern."

Buhgo rubbed his eyes with the heels of his hands. "I fear Uxaam will send me on a vision quest very soon. I do not want to be a man. This thing," he said, looking down at his groin, "this part of me that declares me a man, is only an appendage. Inside I am a woman. I know that what they say about me is true. But I will have to go on this quest or I will shame my family. And if I go and fail, I will shame them. I cannot admit to Uxaam that I do not want to be a man . . . that I am a woman. Even though that is what everyone thinks and they ridicule me, a confession would never be tolerated."

"How horrible for you," she said.

"That is not even the worst," Buhgo said. "I am of the age where boys think of women . . . the joining. I hear them talk amongst themselves, laughing about the dreams and fantasies they have. I dream, too," Buhgo said.

"That is good," Nyna said.

Buhgo shifted, then cleared his throat as if the words might come easier. "It is a loathsome thing I am going to tell you." Buhgo sucked in a deep breath. "My dreams are not about women."

24

Chogatis rubbed his shoulder. "I do not hunt as well as I used to," he said.

"Your shoulder aches," Nihapu said. "Let me massage it for you."

Chogatis stretched out on his mat facedown. "I do not think I like this getting old."

"Do not call yourself old."

"Bah," Chogatis said. "That is what I am . . . old. I do not see as well or hear as well as I used to. My joints ache and my hair turns gray."

Nihapu spread a salve on his shoulder and began working it in.

"I know why I loved Tsalochee so much," she said. "He was like his father."

Her fingers rolled his shoulder muscles beneath the flesh, stretching them, massaging out the kinks.

"Tsalochee was lucky to have you as his wife, as am I."

"I am the lucky one," she said. Her hands worked his whole back now, kneading up his spine. She bent forward and kissed his shoulder.

Chogatis turned over and looked at her. Nihapu lay down next to him. "Nyna has gone to collect medicine plants for me. She will be awhile," she said. She played her fingers across his chest. "Chogatis, I want to be your wife."

"You are my wife," he said.

She kissed his neck. "Your *wife*," she said.

Chogatis held her close. "It has been a long time since I have held a woman," he whispered. "I do not know if . . ."

"Shh," Nihapu murmured. She moved over him, soft and airy like a whisper. She nibbled his neck, the lobe of his ear, then touched her mouth to his chest and belly.

Chogatis tried to speak, but Nihapu pressed a finger over his lips. He pushed his fingers through her hair and closed his eyes at the sheer pleasure she brought to him.

There was a commotion in the village. Nihapu moved aside and Chogatis got to his feet. "Untimely, whatever it is," he said, walking outside. He raked back his hair and looked about.

There was a crowd surrounding someone moving across the plaza.

Ochopee sprinted over to the cacique. "Your grandson has returned," he said.

"Gather the men at the hearth," Chogatis said. "Let us hear the news he brings back."

Ochopee gazed at Chogatis. "Are you all right? You look flushed."

"I am fine," Chogatis said. "I am very fine."

Cetisa drank her medicine and watched the backs of the men as they sat about the central hearth. Her eyes were fixed on Ochopee. It was a good thing he had lost his memory, she thought. Her gaze turned to her husband. If this medicine did not work, she would ask Buhgo to prepare something for her. Perhaps her sister purposefully did not make a good medicine. Maybe Nihapu did not want her to have a child! Maybe Nihapu gave her medicine that would prevent it!

She set the rest of the medicine on the ground. This was a good time to see Buhgo, while the men gathered. He could do no worse than Nihapu.

Buhgo sat with Taska and Laira.

"Where is your mother?" Cetisa asked.

"She does not feel well," Laira said. "She rests."

"I need to speak with Buhgo. Do you mind?"

"Do you wish to talk in private?" Buhgo asked.

"Yes," Cetisa said. "Can you do that?"

Buhgo got to his feet. "Let us talk at your hearth," he said.

"I am sorry to take you away, but it is a private matter," Cetisa said.

"I understand."

Cetisa sat and stirred the cook fire with a stick. "It is unusually cold, is it not?" she said.

"What did you want to speak to me about?" Buhgo asked.

"My sister has been preparing a medicine for me, but it is not working. I thought perhaps you might know of another."

"Nihapu is the expert. I learn from her."

"But maybe she does not remember something that you might." Cetisa's words were slow and thought out.

"I doubt that. What kind of medicine does she make for you? Are you ill?"

"I am not sick," she said.

"Then what?"

"Etac is such a good man, and he wants a child so badly. He would do anything for a baby. I want to give him that child."

"I know the medicine she prepares. I gather the plants for her. She gives you the only medicine there is for what you want."

Cetisa snapped the stick in half. "How do you know that? You collect the plants, but do you concoct the potion?"

"Why would she have me gather the ingredients and then not use them?"

"So you do not suspect that she gives me a weak medicine. She does not want you to know."

"You do not make sense," Buhgo said. "Why would Nihapu do such a thing?"

"Because she does not want me to have a child. She has always had to have all the attention."

"I have heard enough," Buhgo said, standing to leave. He looked behind him. "Council breaks up. I want to hear what Joog has said."

"You are not going to give me a medicine, are you?"

"Nihapu gives you what you ask for." Buhgo walked away.

"You have no gift!" Cetisa screamed. "You are nothing, just a perversion. Your father knows what you are!"

Buhgo kept on, ignoring Cetisa. Uxaam and Joog stood in the plaza. Uxaam called out to him.

"Are you ready to become a man?" the shaman asked.

Buhgo looked confused.

"Your vision quest," Joog said. "Uxaam has decided it is time."

"Oh," Buhgo said. He hesitated. "Yes, I am ready."

"You do not show much enthusiasm," Uxaam said.

"I am distracted," Buhgo said. "But I am eager." He was afraid to express his fears. It would be worse to have this rite forbidden to him. Uxaam could decide he was not worthy of becoming a man.

"Good, then," Uxaam said. "The new moon."

Buhgo blanched. The new moon meant there would be only starlight at night. He cringed as Uxaam joined another group of men.

Joog and Buhgo sat by the central hearth.

"You do not want to go on the quest," Joog said.

Buhgo looked in the distance. "I am not like you," he said. "I wish I was."

"It is not so bad. Do not be afraid."

"If I fail, think of the shame my family will suffer."

"You worry too much," Joog said.

"I know." Buhgo drew his hair back in a knot and

rethreaded the bone pins that held it in place. "Tell me the outcome of your visit with the Jeaga."

"I did not get an answer," Joog said. "But they are willing to listen and to give our request some thought."

"Amazing, isn't it?" Buhgo said. "What happened to your father and to you was so terrible at the time. But good comes of it. The spirits take us down paths we do not understand."

"Akoma and Talli have a daughter, Cian. They tinker with the idea of a marriage between us. That may be a good idea. She is quite pretty but I have only met—"

"No," Buhgo interrupted. "There is no need to go that far."

"I will court the girl if Council thinks it a good idea."

Buhgo wrung his hands. "This is not a good idea," he said. He wanted to tell Joog Nyna's secret, but he had promised to tell no one. But this would change things. He would tell Nyna right away. But there was something he needed to tell Joog first.

"While you were gone, a vile thing happened," Buhgo said. "Did anyone tell you about Guacana?"

"What has he done?" Joog asked.

Buhgo fumbled for the right words. "He is despicable. Do you recall all the ruckus about Nyna making weapons and her not being Ais. You said you were curious why Guacana stood with you and agreed to no punishment for her because she is not Ais. You told me he stated several times that laws do not apply to her. You thought that strange and did not like it."

"I recall," Joog said.

"Your instinct was right."

Buhgo related the story of Guacana's assault in public on Nyna and how Council could not punish him, as Ais laws did not protect her.

"How could he do such a thing?" Joog said. "And Nyna . . . is she all right?"

"She does not say much about it. The only reason she

keeps on is her determination to go home again and help her people. If not for that I believe she would have given up and done something awful to herself. I dragged her out of the ocean right after this happened. We talked about her going home one day."

"I want to talk to her," Joog said. "Bring her to my house."

"You want to see me," Nyna asked.

"Come and sit," Joog said.

"Inside? Is that proper?"

"It does not matter," he said.

Nyna entered the lodge and took a seat near the entrance.

"Buhgo has told me about Guacana. I am sorry this happened to you."

Nyna's eyes teared, and her bottom lip trembled. "I do not understand why he does this."

"It is his revenge for that day when you were children."

Nyna stared at him.

"What do you see?" he asked.

"A good man," she said.

Joog took her hand in his. "If you were Ais, it would be different." He threaded her hair behind her ear. "There would be many things different."

Uxaam prepared Buhgo, covering his body with ash. Taska assisted the shaman, sitting next to him in the special chair Buhgo had made for him. Uxaam implored the spirits as he always did when launching a young man on his first vision quest, and Taska repeated the prayers and incantations to himself, memorizing the shaman's words.

The shaman took Buhgo's hand and turned it palm up, drawing his knife across it. Buhgo bit the inside of his cheek, and he tasted blood, but he did not flinch.

Flinching would be a sign of weakness. He felt Ochopee's eyes hard on his naked back. The air chilled him, and he held back a shudder.

Buhgo watched his blood drip on the ground. Uxaam was speaking, but he did not listen, his mind on the days to come when he would be so cold and alone in a wilderness he knew only as a woman might. He had made several kills, rabbits, and raccoons, as was expected of him. But he prowled the forest for plants, not game. His hunting and survival skills were weak at best.

Uxaam continued the ritual, puncturing the flesh of Buhgo's chest with a thorn. He rubbed his black paste into the design, setting the tattoo.

"Here is the boy, Buhgo, who comes to you to know his future. All waters, all trees and animals, all creatures of the earth, all sacred ones of the universe, see him!" Uxaam chanted.

Uxaam cued Buhgo to set out on the trail.

"You will be safe, my brother," Taska called out.

When Buhgo had disappeared into the forest, Uxaam consulted with Taska.

"Did you listen carefully?" Uxaam asked.

Taska spit back the first prayer that Uxaam had said.

"How do you learn so fast? Perhaps the spirits gave you this physical limitation so you would use your mind more. And you surely have done that! Even as the smallest boy everyone was in wonder at your mind."

"I like to think that is why I was born like this."

"Tell me, how is your father?"

"I lost a father who resented me, but I gained a father who does not even remember me."

"You have had visions before, but you have never invoked them. The visions have been spontaneous, is that correct?"

"I do not know how to make them happen," Taska said.

"I will teach you," Uxaam said. "I believe you are the

one the spirits have chosen to take my place when I am gone. It is my responsibility to train you. You need to know how to call the spirits to you when you need them. Close your eyes and repeat what I say."

Taska did as he was told. Uxaam spoke in the old tongue and Taska repeated the words. It came easily to him, flowing from his tongue like a favorite song. Instinctively he knew the rhythm, the cadence, the melody. His body seemed lighter as his spirit gathered in a place near the crown of his head. He was caught in a cyclone of darkness, the wind roaring. Then he shed his body like a useless shell. The sensation was exhilarating, tingling his arms and legs, up and down his spine. Never had he had this kind of freedom to move, to not be shackled by his infirmity. The air flowed through his flesh, through his bones as he became lighter and lighter. A mist gathered before him, and now he could see without opening his eyes.

From somewhere in the mist Uxaam called to him. Uxaam's face appeared. He spoke, but his mouth did not move. "This is the realm of the shaman," Uxaam said. "Only a man of the spirits can attain this. Let your mind be free, and the spirits will bring you a vision."

Taska remained fascinated by this new freedom from his flawed body. He floated, weightless, one with the air. An image began to take form. Through the mist he saw a woman. He waited, watching the form come into focus. His mother? She stood with her back to him, long flowing hair, petite body. Slowly Zinni turned to face him. Taska's breath caught in his chest.

"No!" he screamed. Immediately his spirit was sucked back to earth and into his body, the wind howling in his ears.

25

Uxaam's eyes fluttered open. "What is it, Taska? What did you see?"

"My mother," he answered.

"You saw something bad?"

"She is ill, covered with lesions, and her mind is gone."

Uxaam wiped the back of his hand across his mouth. His wide face took on a grave expression. "Perhaps it is only a warning for her to take care of herself."

Taska shook his head. "That is not my impression," he said. "It was dreadful. What should I do?"

"There is nothing you can do. You see what is to be or a warning of something to come. You cannot change what is predestined by the spirits. Speak to your mother, see how she is feeling, encourage her to take care of herself. That is the most you can intervene."

Buhgo crouched beneath a scrub hickory. He was hungry and thirsty. His nose and mouth played tricks on him. He could smell and taste the oily beverage, *pocohicora*, his mother often concocted by grinding the nuts and brewing them in water. Darkness would be coming soon, and the night air would be colder.

Buhgo wore no clothes, leaving himself open and vulnerable to the spirits. He sat with his legs crossed, his hands on his knees, and said the prayers. He found it difficult to concentrate on the meaning of the words as his mind centered on his frailties. He rocked back his head and spoke aloud.

"I cannot do this alone," he cried. "Sacred ones, see me, guide me." He had no sense that this was the place he was to have his vision—rather his exhaustion had made him stop and rest beneath this tree. "How will I know where I am to go? I am Buhgo, an Ais boy who is to become a man." His voice trailed off as he spoke the last word. "Man," he repeated.

The wind blew from the northwest, and he shivered. A fallen log would help keep the wind from him. When he found one, Buhgo collected branches and propped them against it, making a flimsy wall. Over those branches he packed leaves, smaller debris, sabal palm fronds, and anything else he could find.

When night did come, Buhgo huddled behind his construction. The air was cold, but at least he was spared the wind. He wanted to sleep, to dig a pit beside the log, cover himself in it, and close his eyes. But if he did that, he might miss the vision. The spirits might come, and he would not be ready. That was all part of the quest, denying yourself.

"Here I am," he shouted.

This was only the end of the first day and he knew he had weakened already. How would he survive several days?

Through the night Buhgo sat, back straight, head up. He needed a fire, not only to keep warm, but to ward off animals. The dark night was full of strange sounds he had not noticed before. Every creak and croak seemed a threat. How many animals did not sleep in the night? Was man the only one who did?

The horizon line emitted a faint glow. Buhgo greeted Father Sun with thanks. The sky gradually changed from black to indigo, and then the brilliance of sunrise with all its glorious roses, oranges, and purples. Buhgo found tears streaming down his cheeks. Horrified at his weakness, he wiped them away.

Perhaps the spirits would not recognize him as a man. He could stay here forever and never have a vision. Was that what was to happen to him? Would a slow death from exposure, starvation, and thirst be the punishment for being the aberration that he was?

"I am Buhgo," he called out. "I am a creation of the spirits. I am what you gave life. You made me what I am. Do with me what you will!"

His belly growled with hunger, but something else rose inside him. Even in all the despair and tribulation, he saw more clearly that he had little control of his destiny. Only the spirits knew what was to become of anyone. If you did not go willingly down a path, they pushed. If you did not give them the reverence they wanted, then they brought you to your knees.

Buhgo left his simple shelter and stood naked in the open. He raised his arms, palms stretching toward the blinding blue sky. "Oh, Great Spirit, Creator, Sacred Ones of the four directions, Grandfathers, all the creatures and plants of the earth, my name is Buhgo. I come humbly to ask for spiritual guidance. I hear your voice in the winds. I am weak. I am small. I need your wisdom and strength."

Buhgo stretched his arms in front of him. He stared at his hands. "Make my hands respect the things you have made, my ears sharp enough to hear your voice and understand, my eyes clear enough to see the lessons you have hidden in each rock and leaf."

Again he looked at the sky. "I am Buhgo, your child."

The sun flared, and like lightning, it illuminated the forest with brilliance. Buhgo's eyes closed in response. He felt a rush of heat soar through his body and an enormous pressure swell inside his chest. Slowly, he opened his eyes, which burned and teared in the light. An image began to appear, translucent at first, as if having a difficult time forming. The obscure image faded in and out, gradually taking on a definite shape.

Buhgo fell to his knees. His vision!

The Great Spirit's hands, larger than the trees, came down from the sky. They began to sculpt something in front of Buhgo. Buhgo watched the formation of a beautiful woman, the soil her flesh, the rocks her bones, the wind her breath, the trees and grasses her hair, the rivers and streams her veins.

The Great Spirit laid her down, and she became Mother Earth, to nurture all that would live upon her. The hands of the Creator took some of her flesh up in his hands and molded the animals, and finally the people.

From Mother Earth's flesh sprang more trees and flowers and all kinds of plants. Buhgo could not name them quickly enough. A hummingbird lit on a fragile branch next to a cluster of yellow flowers. Suddenly a flock of blue jays darted about, circling the hummingbird. Buhgo thought the hummingbird was frightened, but the little bird did not take flight.

Again the sun blinded him and the vision ended.

He was a man!

"Can you help me?" Nyna asked. "I do not know how to use this atlatl."

Joog took the wooden handle with the hooked tip from her and examined it. "You have made a good one," he said. "I like it. It is simple and efficient."

"But I do not understand it. I need your help."

"Get your things," he said.

Nyna got several spears and followed Joog to the open beach where their practice would be out of sight of the villagers and unobstructed by brush and structures.

He moved up behind her and adjusted her arm, showing her how to hold the atlatl. "Shoulder high," he said.

"Like this?"

"Mm," Joog confirmed. He laid the stick on the top

of the atlatl and the hook held it in place. "When you throw it, whip it. Quickly."

Joog felt her smooth and sleek hair brush against him. It touched his face and shoulder. He pulled it back from her face so it did not get in her eyes.

"Thank you," she said.

The air was cool and the heat from her body radiated to him. He huddled even a little closer, liking the smell of her, the feel of his rough hand on her smooth skin.

"It is only like an extension of the arm," he said. "Think of it as part of your arm, a natural part of yourself."

Nyna shifted her head to the side so she could see him out of the corner of her eye. He stepped back a step, thinking he offended her.

"No," she whispered, leaning into his shoulder. "Stay close."

They stood still, afraid if they moved they would break the moment.

Finally, Joog stepped back. "I am sorry," he said. "I am here to help you learn to throw this—"

"Joog," Nyna broke in, "do not be sorry."

"Did he hurt you?" Joog asked.

"Who?"

"Guacana. Did he hurt you?"

"No," she said.

"I will kill him myself if he does it again. You will tell me. I do not care what Council thinks."

"He will not bother me again," she said.

"You do not say that with conviction in your voice," he said.

"Guacana has made his point. He does not need to repeat the deed. And why would he if he harbors so much hatred for me?"

Joog turned her so she would look at him. Nyna's raven-black eyes peered deeply into his. The words he wanted to say all collected in his head. He started to speak, his lips parting, but at the last moment he decided not to.

Seagulls squawked overhead and the tide pushed the waves onto the shore, spraying over a small outcrop of rocks.

"Do you want to say something?" she asked.

Joog did not want to make her life any more difficult than it already was. If things were different, he would pursue this woman he knew so well. She stirred his spirit with gentleness and a wonderful sense of adventure and mystery.

He finally dragged his eyes from hers. "Take up the spear," he said, noticing it had fallen to the ground.

Nyna retrieved the spear and readied it on the atlatl.

"Throw it," he said.

Except for the sea and the seagulls, everything seemed to grow still and silent. Nyna gripped the spear shoulder high, and with a sharp whipping, hurled the spear. Her arm fully extended in front of her, her hand still gripping the atlatl, she watched the spear zing through the air, going much farther than she could have ever thrown it on her own.

Nyna jumped with joy as the spear finally came to the ground far down the open stretch of beach.

"You master things quickly," Joog said.

"I have practiced before, but I needed your help. I swung it more sidearm without the whip. You do help me so with everything," she said.

"You would have learned on your own."

"Look," Nyna said, still staring down the beach. "Buhgo!"

Buhgo straggled down the shore. He waved, his arm high and proud.

"He has done it," Joog said. "I knew he would!"

Nyna and Joog ran toward him, their feet leaving depressions in the loose sand.

Fatigued and dirty, Buhgo sank to the ground in front of them, laughing and crying.

"One day!" Buhgo said. "They felt sorry for me and made me stay only a day. I had my vision! I had a vision!"

Joog reared back and thrust his arms up. "Ah, the spirits are such a wonder," he said.

Nyna crouched next to Buhgo. "Are you all right?"

"I am wonderful," he said. "Perfect. Splendid!

Joog knelt with them, and their arms wrapped around each other, their bodies forming a tight circle filled with joy, friendship, congratulations, and tears.

Guacana carelessly sharpened his stick, then put it in the fire to harden. He watched Zinni and Nihapu in deep conversation. Curious, he withdrew his stick from the fire and moved closer. Craftily, he pretended to test his new lance, moving closer still. He made certain he did not squarely face them, as they might become suspicious. He strained to hear, feigning an examination of the point of his stick. He rolled it in his hands and listened.

Zinni shook her head, not believing what Nihapu told her. "It cannot be," she said.

"Perhaps not," Nihapu said. "We will pray to the spirits that you do not have the sickness. Is this the first time the chancre has appeared?"

"Once before. But it went away."

"And Ochopee?"

"I have not noticed," she said.

"Wait and see," Nihapu said.

"Can you prepare medicines?"

"There are a few, but there is no cure, if indeed, this is the disease. Stay apart from Ochopee. If you have a child, it can be passed on."

Zinni put her face in her hands. "How long I have longed for my husband to come back to me, to my bed . . . his distaste for me finally gone with the rest of his memory. Now this."

"I cannot be sure," Nihapu said. "But if this sore has come again, it is something to consider. I do not know if the spirits in the sore contaminate another, or if when the sore is gone, the bad spirits have no power. Be careful, is all I say."

"Do you mean that when the sore heals, I can be with my husband as a wife?"

"I do not know. Like I said, be careful."

"By *careful*, you mean never let Ochopee . . ."

"Yes," Nihapu said. "Babies can be born with it if their mothers have the disease." Nihapu paused and breathed a deep breath. "I am sorry," she said. "Have Buhgo gather pokeberry and—"

"I do not want him to know," Zinni said. "Tell me what to do."

"I can get the plants," Nihapu said.

"I want to do it myself."

"Pokeberry," Nihapu said. "This is a good time of year. The roots must be gathered in winter. Boil them, then take several drops in a tea every morning and evening, but no more than several drops. Also, take the berries, pulverize them until thick and sticky. Apply that to the chancre."

"Is that all?"

"There is another medicine, but it is best if I prepare it. There are many ingredients: lobelia, sumac root, the inner bark of the pine. I think it better if I do that."

"Not when Buhgo is with you."

"I will be careful he does not see," Nihapu said. "But you must still understand these medicines are not a cure. They help ward off the bad spirits, keep them at a distance. The spirits are strong and will one day overtake the power of the medicine."

"But not tomorrow," Zinni said.

Guacana hurled his stick and chased after it. He had heard enough and he knew exactly what he would do with the information!

26

Days passed and still there was no rain. Buhgo's cross-over into manhood was properly celebrated with dance, music, and as always, Guacana's taunting. But Buhgo paid no mind. Guacana's mockery meant nothing to him any longer. The fury that grew inside him sprang from what Guacana did to Nyna, not Guacana's words.

The Hawk clan grew more and more anxious. Already there was less game in their territory. Fish in the sea were abundant, and they thanked the spirits for that. But game was more than food in their bellies. Quarry provided skins and pelts, sinew, bone, antler, claws, teeth, tools, and ceremonial objects. And if the cenote were to become tainted with saltwater, they would suffer even a greater loss.

Chitola and others from the Osprey Clan visited the Hawk. They came to see how badly their neighbors suffered, and Chitola came especially to court Laira.

Some of the sloughs and marshes already began to dry up, leaving a mosaic of gray, cracked, and hard-packed soil. The alligators grew sluggish from the cold nights, and sunned themselves in the daytime. In the marshes, those giant creatures wallowed their powerful bodies in sidestrokes, burrowing deep into the muck, digging out a hole where water collected. Willow seeds took hold along the perimeter of the holes, creating thick circles. Other animals relied on the alligator holes for their drinking water, and predators came to take advantage.

Taska, Uxaam, Chitola, Joog, and Buhgo sat near the stream. They looked at the waterline on the banks. The water had dropped low enough to alarm everyone. Soon the stream would be a trickle, and then a dry, crusted bed.

"This is not a good sign," Chitola said. "Do you negotiate with the Jeaga to move toward the river?"

"I have visited," Joog said. "The conversation has begun."

"They understand our brother Ais have only enough water to sustain themselves," Uxaam said.

"They will consider our proposal of temporary occupation during a drought," Joog said.

"The Osprey say they will do what they can. Even if the Hawk must split up into very small groups, the other clans will absorb you," Chitola said.

"We have spoken of that," Joog said. "But the clan wants to stay together. They fear families will be split. The Hawk will have no leader, no identity. And it would be a strain on the other Ais. First we will negotiate with the Jeaga."

Chitola scooped up a dusty handful of dirt. "I was hoping conditions would be better. I entertain the idea of asking Ochopee for his daughter."

Buhgo grinned. "Laira speaks about you all the time. She was smitten with you the first time she saw you."

Chitola's face lit with excitement. "Is that so? I thought perhaps in light of the situation I should postpone my request."

"I think it is an excellent time," Uxaam said. "It will bring a bit of joy and distract our thoughts from the lack of rain."

Chitola strolled the bank. He reached down and picked up a small dead gar.

"I will go and speak with Ochopee," Chitola said, dropping the dead fish.

"I will go with you," Joog said.

After Chitola and Joog left, Uxaam focused on Buhgo. "The grasshoppers in Joog's vision speak," Uxaam said. "If you are ready to understand your vision, Taska and I are prepared to help you."

Buhgo had disclosed his vision to Uxaam prior to his celebration, but put off the interpretation until after he told Taska. Uxaam agreed to give Taska the opportunity to contemplate the vision, so together they would render its meaning.

"I am ready," Buhgo said.

Taska began the explanation. "You are a healer, and so the spirits reminded you of the respect you must have for Mother Earth, knowing that all things spring from her flesh. She is the mother of us all."

Taska glanced at Uxaam, who approved.

"You are Hummingbird," he continued. "Hummingbird is a good sign. She is a good-luck messenger."

"She . . ." Buhgo said, his voice melancholy.

"Remember there is nothing about you that the spirits do not know," Uxaam said. "They created you. They formed you in their hands as you saw Mother Earth formed. The Great Spirit breathed life into you. If He and the sacred ones were not pleased with their creation, you would not exist. There is no shame before them for what you are."

Buhgo looked to his brother to continue. "Hummingbird takes our prayers to the heavens, the ancestors, and the spirits. She is a healer and has the power to travel long distances against great odds, just as you have done in your life. Her colors represent healing and balance."

Buhgo smiled. Thus far he was pleased with the interpretation and the image of himself as Hummingbird.

Uxaam took up the explanation. "The bluejays, though they are beautifully colored, have bad powers. They warn us about the people we see in our lives, the challengers and the negative ones. They are noisy, prideful, and full of gossip. They lie and steal. If one flies into your house, it means someone plots against you. You have met them. You know who they are."

Buhgo's head nodded. He recalled that Hummingbird had not flown away frightened by the jays. And certainly, Buhgo knew the bluejays in his life were many. The vision showed him a strength he did not realize he had.

"You will bring healing to the Ais. The spirits confirm your gift through your vision," Taska said. "It was a good vision."

Suddenly Taska shivered, and his eyelids fluttered. Buhgo reached for him.

"Be still," Uxaam said. "The spirits visit him."

"Taska's head dropped, his chin touching his chest.

"Is he all right?" Buhgo whispered.

"I have been helping him open himself to the spirits. He has always had the gift, but he learns to open the pathways for the spirits to enter him."

Taska lifted his head and his eyes opened. His face paled.

"Chogatis!" Taska said.

Chogatis studied the tree. It was a tall yellow pine. This tree would make a fine canoe. He put a ring of clay, like a dam, about waist high around the girth of the tree, then a hand's breadth above that another ring of clay. These would keep the fire from burning too high.

At the base of the tree he built small tented fires all the way round. He sat back as the tinder caught. He added small amounts of wood to the fires and let the flames lap at the bark of the tree.

The fire was as much a tool as his ax. The flames would not burn deep into the green wood, so after the fire had charred the tree, it was time to use the ax.

Chogatis swung his ax, biting into the burned wood, hacking away the charred masses. He chipped the dead wood away all around the tree, chopping with the shell ax.

He felt his muscles strain with the exertion, and he cursed them for weakening. Winded, Chogatis dropped the ax and fueled the fires again. He sat on his haunches, arms folded over his knees, watching it burn. His hands were still large, but the skin on them thinned and crinkled. He rubbed the first joint in his fourth finger. It was enlarged and sore. He did not grip things as firmly as he used to. He coughed from the tightness that arose in his chest. He really was old, he thought to himself. When had felling a tree been such an enormous task?

Chogatis's hand pressed on his breastbone, and again he coughed softly. Sweat broke out over his body. His hands and feet were cold, yet his body sweat profusely.

"Bah," he said, getting back to his feet with the ax. "Old man," he said aloud. He would not give in to aches and pains of age. He was still strong and able.

Chogatis lifted the ax to take another blow at the tree, but the rip of a sharp pain in his chest stopped him in mid-swing. The ax thudded to the ground and he bent over, his hands clutching his chest.

What was this? What was happening? He sat and propped himself against another tree. He scolded himself for attempting to chop down the tree by himself. Joog offered to help, but he had refused, his pride getting the best of him. He wanted Nihapu to still see him as strong and virile. As soon as this cramp in his chest and the shortness of breath left him, he would finish the job. But, he promised himself, it would be the last time he did something so foolish. His wife loved him, whether or not he still had it in him to take down a tree. Maybe it wasn't Nihapu he was proving something to at all.

He would just rest a moment. He would feel better as soon as he caught his breath. He closed his eyes. If he could get a short nap, when he awoke he would feel better. This growing pressure in his chest was most uncomfortable.

*   *   *

"Where is Chogatis?" Uxaam asked Nihapu.

"I am not sure," she answered. "He said he wanted to select a tree for a new dugout."

"Where is Joog?" Buhgo asked.

"Is something wrong?" she asked. "You look anxious."

Nyna came and stood close to Nihapu. "What is it?" she asked.

"We need to find Chogatis," Buhgo said.

"Let me ask Joog," Nyna said. "He talked with him this morning."

Nyna fetched Joog and brought him to speak with Uxaam and Buhgo.

"Do you know where your grandfather is?" Buhgo asked.

"I know the area," he said. "He wanted a tall yellow pine for a dugout. Tell me what is so important?"

Uxaam glanced at Nihapu and spoke carefully. "Taska has had a vision or premonition. It may be nothing."

Nihapu sucked in a breath. "Has something happened to Chogatis?"

"We do not know," Uxaam said. "We thought it prudent to check on him. Taska is untrained. He may have seen nothing of concern."

Buhgo patted Nihapu's shoulder. "Uxaam is right. But we will look for Chogatis just to make sure he is all right."

"I want to go with you," she said.

Uxaam objected, not knowing what they might find. "But Nihapu—"

"I am going," she said.

Joog led them to an area he thought his grandfather would have chosen. "Split up," he said. "Whistle if you find him. Nihapu, wait here."

"No," she said. "He is my husband. I will go with Buhgo."

A few moments later Joog discovered Chogatis slumped beside a tree. He signaled the others with a whistle.

"Do not call me a foolish old man," Chogatis said.

"You should have let me help," Joog said, squatting next to him. "You do not need to be cutting down trees and making dugouts."

"I wanted to," Chogatis said. He looked past his grandson and saw Nihapu coming. "I want to for her," he said.

Nihapu sat next to Chogatis and pulled him to lean on her. She stroked his head and put her lips to his forehead. "I am angry with you," she said.

Buhgo put his hand on Chogatis's chest, feeling his heart beat. "It hurts you here?" he said.

"A little," Chogatis answered. "It is better, now. I just needed to rest."

Uxaam touched the top of the cacique's head and closed his eyes. "The problem is in the heart," the shaman said.

"Let's get him back and Nihapu and I will make medicine for him," Buhgo said.

The three men started to lift Chogatis.

"I can walk," Chogatis said.

"Of course you can," Nihapu said. "But you are not going to. They are going to carry you back."

"It will cause such a commotion in the village," Chogatis argued.

"We are not going to listen to you," Joog said.

Joog got under one of Chogatis's shoulders and Uxaam under the other. Buhgo and Nihapu held his legs up.

Instead of going through the center of the village, they stayed behind it and circled around to Chogatis's lodge.

As discreet as they were, they still attracted attention and a crowd began to gather outside Chogatis's lodge.

Guacana watched from a distance. He saw that Zinni and Ochopee hurried across the plaza. Uxaam and

Buhgo carried Taska to the cacique's lodge. The time was perfect!

Guacana backed away slowly, shortening the distance between himself and Ochopee's house. He stood just outside the doorway and glanced around to see if anyone noticed him. Everyone appeared to gather near Chogatis's lodge.

Guacana darted inside the house. He looked around and picked up a sewing kit, but then put it back. He fumbled through a basket of ornaments, examining a shell pendant. It was etched with a design and strung on a sinew thread. He had seen Zinni wear this on occasion. Guacana put the pendant in a pouch attached to the waistband of his breechclout.

He eased out the door and went behind the hut. He would cut through the woods and emerge on the other side of the village.

"Guacana!" Laira said as he backed into her and Chitola.

Guacana jumped. "What are you doing here?" he asked.

She lifted her basket. "He helps me gather greenbriar roots," she said. "What is going on?"

"Nothing," Guacana answered. "I was going to check some traps."

"I mean over there," she said, looking toward the crowd.

"Oh," he said, letting out a full breath with his word. "I am not certain. Something is wrong with Chogatis."

Laira and Chitola went to the front of her hut and put down her basket. They started across the plaza. Laira looked back at Guacana.

"You are not going to see what is wrong?" she asked.

Nyna gathered torch-wort for Nihapu. She said a decoction made from it was good medicine for the heart.

She had not been in the forest long when Guacana intercepted her.

"Do it," he said.

Nyna's throat tightened. "There will be no need to hurt me," she said. "You give me no choice. I do not want Buhgo hurt, nor do I want Chogatis to have to fulfill his promise and come to my defense. He is ill. You are young, and he is old." Nyna dropped to the ground. "Get it over with so I can be on my way," she said.

"Are you not going to resist?"

"No," she answered. "Just hurry up. Nihapu waits for these medicine plants."

Guacana hesitated.

"What is wrong?" Nyna asked. "Is it no fun if I do not care? Or is it that you just cannot do it . . . like the last time."

Guacana knelt behind her and loosed his breechclout. He fumbled with himself for a few moments.

"Ah," Nyna said. "Now I understand. It is only exciting to you if I fight back. But you have made the rules so I cannot resist."

"Still your wagging tongue," Guacana said. "Be quiet!" He stroked his manpart until at last it was hard enough that he could enter her.

"What is taking you so long? I have things to do."

Guacana yanked her hair, pulling her head back. "Do not speak!"

"Do I distract you?" Nyna said.

He jerked the handful of hair again. His hips worked back and forth, and she could feel him banging inside her. He grunted and groaned, thrusting furiously. He kept at it so long that she thought perhaps he might give up.

His breathing was hard, and his sweat dripped from his face, down his chin and onto her back. With each thrust now, a gush of air rushed out his chest until it almost sounded as if he were in pain. The faster and harder he drove into her, the more he sounded as if he were in the throes of agony.

Suddenly he jerked, then his body went rigid like he was paralyzed. Even his breathing stopped. Finally Guacana fell in a sweaty heap against her back. Nyna rolled from under his weight and stood up. She smoothed her skirt and picked up the basket. "There must be something wrong with your manpart," she said. "It takes a lot of coaxing to get it to cooperate." She grinned at him. "And this time there was no one to blame for spoiling your fun. I tell you, your manpart is faulty."

Guacana lay with his cheek on the ground, looking up at her as he still heaved for air.

Nyna bathed in the cenote before returning to the village. As she entered the plaza, she saw Guacana talking to Ochopee. Ochopee glared at her as if he wanted to lash out at her about something. What could Guacana be telling him?

27

Guacana opened his hand. "Do you recognize this?" he asked.

Ochopee lifted the pendant. "Zinni's," he said.

"I thought so." Guacana glanced at Nyna as she entered the village. "I saw her with it. She was deep in the woods, saying strange prayers in her own language. She was conjuring some kind of spirits. When she finished, she hid this pendant in the brush. I was curious, so I retrieved it after she was gone. I think she wishes to harm your wife."

"Why? What would she want to hurt Zinni for?"

"To get at you, I suppose. You have stood against her from the very beginning. I think she has evil magic. I still say she is from another world, the sun, cast out because she is a sinister witch of some kind."

"She hurts my wife to get back at me," Ochopee said.

"She is a clever one. If she did something to you, no one would doubt it. But by harming Zinni, she eliminates any suspicion. I think you should talk to your wife."

Ochopee rubbed his jaw. "She has acted strange lately. Keeps her distance from me, if you know what I mean."

"You see! Something is wrong with her, and Nyna has caused it, invoked her evil spirits to visit upon your wife!"

Ochopee glowered at Nyna as she made her way across the village. "I will speak to my wife," he said. "I thought this was going to be a good day. Chitola spoke for Laira. Now that is spoiled."

Guacana looked over his shoulder and smiled as Nyna entered Chogatis's lodge.

When night came, Ochopee took Zinni aside. "Is there anything wrong with you?" he asked. "Anything strange?"

Zinni shook her head. "Nothing."

"You behave strangely," he said. "And I have reason to believe something is wrong."

"Nothing is wrong," she said. She stepped around him, but Ochopee took her wrist. "Perhaps I am excited that our daughter has a handsome suitor and she has agreed to be his wife," she said.

"I do not mean just today." He held out his hand. The pendant rested in his palm. "Guacana brought this to me," he said.

"My necklace," she said. "How did he get it?"

"Nyna had it. Guacana saw her saying peculiar incantations over it. He did not understand the words as she spoke in her language. When she was finished, she hid it in the brush. Guacana recovered it and brought it to me. He is sure she wants to cause you harm."

"That is absurd," Zinni said. "Why would she want to harm me?"

"Because of me," Ochopee said. "She knows how I feel about her. She gets to me through you. She has done something, Zinni. You must know what it is. Why do you not tell me?"

Zinni's hand went to her mouth, and her eyes filled with tears.

"I am your husband," Ochopee said. "What do you keep from me?" He squeezed her wrist. "It is bad enough that I have lost my memory, now you keep me out. Was I so terrible? If so, I am sorry. I love my wife and my children. I do not know what I did in the past.

I know only the Ochopee who exists after the storm. I do not want to live this way. If you cannot tell me—"

Zinni clutched her throat. She loved this man more than she loved anything. It was wonderful to have him back after so long, and now she was not allowed to have him. Her heart ached. What cruel tricks the spirits played.

Zinni knelt in front of him and held his hands in hers. She looked up into his face. "I did not want to tell you because I am not sure. I may be sick," she said. "Nihapu is not certain."

"Sick? You do not appear ill."

"I have a sore," she said. "A chancre. I keep myself from you because if I have the illness, I could pass it on to you or an unborn child. You cannot touch me there or the bad spirits jump from the sore to you."

Ochopee rocked with shock. He knew this illness. It was the scourge of the people. It thrived on love and joining, a perversity.

"I have had the chancre once before, but it healed and went away," she said. "It was before the storm. Before you lost your memory."

Ochopee massaged the back of his neck. "It is believed the evil spirits jump between two people during the joining."

"Yes," Zinni said.

"Then who did you get this disease from? Were you unfaithful?"

"I have never been with anyone but you," she said.

Ochopee paced. "Then Guacana is right. This is Nyna's doing."

His mind raced. Had his wife been a promiscuous one? Was he laughed about in men's circles because his wife enjoyed other men? But that did not seem like this woman, the wife he found love for even though he had no memory of her. Could he have had the disease? Did he ever have one of those sores? Zinni would have noticed.

"You would have known if I had had a sore like that," he said. "I could not have kept it a secret." He waved his hands, certain of his conclusion. "It has to be Nyna."

Zinni hung her head. "It could have been you. We had difficulties as man and wife before you lost your memory. You kept yourself from me most of the time. When you learned I carried Taska, you withdrew from me as a husband. You did not want another imperfect child. We were not together that way for most of the time. So, I would not have known if you had the sickness."

"But where would I get such an illness?"

"Oh, Ochopee, I loved you then as now, but you did not seek pleasure in me. Men have their needs," she said. "I understood that. You did not throw me out when Taska was born, so I believed you loved me even if we did not participate in that intimate part of marriage. I heard the rumors of your indiscretions when on journeys to other villages. I could live with that as long as you came home to me."

"No, no, no," Ochopee said. He shook his head in denial. "But Guacana saw Nyna with your pendant, chanting over it. He must be right."

Zinni's hands slid down her face. She propped her chin between the heels of her hands. "Maybe she was doing something else and this sickness has nothing to do with it. I do not know," she said. "Maybe I do not have the disease at all. It is such a strange illness. It makes itself known in stages. I can only wait to see what happens."

"I am not going to wait. Nyna will send the spirits away that she has summoned. I will take care of this," Ochopee said.

He turned on his heel and marched to the cacique's lodge.

"Chogatis," he called.

Nihapu appeared in the doorway. "Shh, he sleeps."

"Wake him!"

"No," Nihapu said. "What is it that cannot wait until morning?"

Ochopee pushed past her to Chogatis's bedside. "Cacique," he said.

Chogatis opened his eyes, barely able to see by the light of the tallow light that burned near him.

"What do you want, Ochopee?" His voice was fragile and had a wet sound to it.

"I told him you were sleeping," Nihapu said. "But he pushed his way inside."

"It is important," Ochopee said. "My wife is ill, and Nyna is to blame."

Ochopee explained what Guacana had told him.

"That is ridiculous," Nihapu said.

"Guacana saw her. She had Zinni's pendant. What else would she be doing with it in secret?"

"Sit down," Chogatis said. "Listen to reason."

Ochopee took a seat on the ground next to Chogatis.

"Before the storm, you were a different man. You had no tolerance for your sons, and you and Zinni had troubles. It could be that you gave her the disease, not Nyna."

"Then what did Guacana witness? It is only logic that she attempts to do something evil to my wife."

"I would not rely on anything Guacana says when it comes to Nyna. He has made his feelings about her quite clear."

"But she had the pendant! Everything fits, just as Guacana says."

Chogatis coughed, and Nihapu fed him some of her medicine.

"Go," she said. "Let him rest. We will speak to Nyna in the morning."

"I want her to get rid of the evil spirits that visit upon

my wife. If she summoned the illness, she can get rid of it. Tomorrow!"

The air was warmer than the previous few days, and the people shed their wraps. The luxurious rays of the sun fell welcome on their backs. Joog looked to the east, in the direction from which came the breeze. The sky was clear blue, blazing with the sun. No clouds. No sign of rain.

Chogatis had summoned Joog. He entered the lodge.

"Good day," Chogatis said. The cacique sat on a split-log bench. Nihapu tied his hair in a knot, locking it with two bone pins. From the knot she suspended a raccoon tail. "There," she said. "Now you look more like yourself."

Though Nihapu did her best to tend to Chogatis's needs and appearance, he still looked ill. His eyes sat deep in their sockets and his skin seemed to sag. He walked and moved slowly, and the strain of such exercise showed in his face.

Nihapu called for Nyna.

"Ochopee came to me last night," Chogatis said. "Guacana has prodded him to continue to cause trouble."

"I heard his words," Nyna said, coming before Chogatis. Her eyes were swollen from crying. "None of it is true."

Chogatis explained Ochopee's charges to Joog. "He will not let this go easily."

"Tell us about this, Nyna," Joog said.

"I never had Zinni's pendant. He never saw me do anything. He has made up the entire story."

"How would Guacana have possession of Zinni's pendant?"

Nyna shrugged and shook her head. "Perhaps he took it to make up this tale."

Nihapu massaged Chogatis's shoulders. "Zinni is sick. She confided in me and asked for medicines."

"But I did not make her sick," Nyna said. "Why would I do that? I have never set out to hurt anyone. If you had not taken me in, I would have died on the beach as a child." Her voice cracked, and her eyes filled with tears. "Zinni and her sons are my friends."

Joog pulled her to him, holding her head against his shoulder.

"I can stand no more," she said.

"This will not go to Council," Chogatis said. "Bring Etac, Ochopee, and Guacana here. We will resolve this privately."

Joog recalled only one other time Chogatis had held a meeting inside his lodge. It was a long time ago when he was a child.

"Nyna, you will stay and confront Ochopee and Guacana," the cacique said. "Etac is open-minded. We will rely on him."

Nyna's stomach churned. When would this misery end? Every day she prepared to leave, to find her people, but she was not ready yet.

The men assembled and sat quietly at first, as was the custom. No one rushed the discussion. Chogatis related the whole story to Etac, stating both what Ochopee claimed and Nyna's side of the story.

"We will not use the Talking Stick," Chogatis said. "There are few of us, and we will allow each of us to speak as necessary. Do we all understand?"

"Why is Nyna allowed here?" Guacana asked. "Women have no place in Council or any other meeting of men."

"Ais women," Chogatis corrected him. "Nyna is an exception to everything. She is not Ais, as you have so determinedly brought to our attention."

Chogatis let his statement hang in the air. Guacana shifted, and his left eye twitched.

"Nyna says that none of what Guacana says is true," Chogatis said. "She denies ever having Zinni's pendant.

And so we have to come to a decision about who is telling the truth."

Etac looked from face to face, trying to interpret the expressions in their eyes. "Let me ask a question," Etac said. "What would Nyna's motive be to hurt Zinni?"

"To hurt me," Ochopee said. "I have spoken against her."

"And what would Guacana's motive be?" Etac asked.

No one answered.

"Who do you want to respond to your question?" Chogatis said.

"Let Ochopee answer me. Do you think there is motive for Guacana to make up this story?"

Ochopee did not answer.

"You answer, Nyna," Chogatis said.

"There is a long history of his attempts to hurt and humiliate me," she said. "Everyone in this village knows that."

"Has anything happened recently?"

Nyna swallowed and looked away from the cacique. She did not want to lie to him, but neither could she tell the truth. "No," she finally said.

Guacana smiled. "You see," he said.

Etac spoke again. "Have you ever had the disease?" he asked Ochopee.

"No," he answered quickly and in a tone that made him sound offended.

"But how do you know?" Etac asked. "Your memory is gone."

"I would know," he said.

Everyone sat quietly for a few moments. Then Chogatis called on Etac. "Give us your wisdom," he said. "You are unbiased."

"I see no resolution. Neither admits to lying. I see more reason for Guacana to make up the lie, but it cannot be proved. I suggest that Uxaam examine Zinni and attempt to rid her of any evil spirits. And, also, to eliminate any more questions about Nyna, I suggest she be escorted wherever she goes. If she is always in the company of another, then no charges can be brought again. And if she conjures evil spirits to cause harm, she will no longer have the opportunity."

"Bah!" Guacana said. "Why do you not see what she is? She has caused the disease in Zinni. Is that not enough?"

Etac gazed at Ochopee. "I am not so sure," he said. "I know you wish to believe you did not pass this sickness on to your wife, but it is a possibility. You do not recall what kind of man you were. I find no satisfaction in having to tell you that you sought out many women whenever we traveled. All of us were aware."

"If you do not punish this woman," Guacana said, "then you are calling me a liar."

"Not true," Chogatis said. "We say that we do not know who tells the lie. It is very possible, even probable, that Ochopee passed the disease to his wife. If it cannot be decided who lies, we can justify punishing Guacana no more easily than Nyna. Etac's suggestion is a good one. He is fair. From this day, Nyna will have an escort wherever she goes."

Guacana stood, his nostrils flaring, his brows diving to the bridge of his nose. He shook his fist at Nyna. "I am not finished with you," he said.

"But you are," Chogatis said.

28

In barely another turn of the moon, Uxaam stood in front of the assembly with Taska sitting next to him.

Laira and Chitola listened as the shaman said the words that would make them man and wife.

Nyna stood in the background with Nihapu. Cetisa slinked away from the crowd and joined her sister. "I think the medicine has worked!" she whispered. She touched her belly. "My moon cycle has not come. I have not told Etac yet. I will wait a little for that, but I am so anxious!"

Nihapu's face brightened. "I hope it is true. How many moon cycles?"

"Just one," she said.

"Do not get too excited yet. You do not want to be disappointed."

"Do not spoil it, sister," Cetisa said. "Your medicine has worked!"

"If you are pregnant, it is because the spirits choose it to be."

Nyna thought about the last time she had been in the woman's hut. Cetisa had been there. She had been sad and short-tempered. Cetisa cried the first day and told Nyna how long she had wanted a child. Every moon, without fail, she was disappointed.

A rush of cold blood gushed through Nyna's veins. She had not been back to the woman's hut since then.

She looked up at the moon. She had lost track. If Cetisa's moon cycle was late, then so was hers.

Nyna felt sick. Guacana! Could she be carrying Guacana's child? What a horrible thought. "I do not feel well," Nyna said. "I am going back to the lodge."

"What is wrong?" Nihapu asked.

"Your face is drained of color," Cetisa said.

"I just need to rest," she said.

Nyna had not slept well, dropping off to sleep and jerking awake with the thought of having a part of Guacana inside her. When the pale yellow of early-morning light seeped into the lodge, Nyna stirred.

She crept outside, took a coal from the central hearth, and started the cook fire. Nihapu would probably scold her for going as far as the central hearth without an escort, but nobody had seen her. She understood and appreciated Nihapu's reasoning that if she were always escorted, then Guacana could not get to her to harm her, nor could he make false claims about her activities. But sometimes she wanted to be alone.

If she carried Guacana's child, she had to do something about it. Never could she bring a monster like that into the world.

Nihapu emerged from the lodge, surprised that Nyna already had the fire going and tea brewing.

"What has you about so early?" Nihapu asked.

"I awoke early."

"And you walked to the central hearth alone."

Nyna stirred the tea. "It is just in the center of the village. It is not like I wandered to the beach or the cenote."

"But if someone saw you, they might wonder where you had been."

"I know you are right," she said. "I wanted to do something nice for you and—"

"It has to be uncomfortable to be watched all the time."

Nyna changed the subject. "Chogatis seems to feel stronger each day. You must make him good medicine."

"He does look better," Nihapu agreed.

"How did you learn the medicines?" Nyna asked.

"When I was a child I sensed things about plants and healing. One day I was playing with a friend. She fell and cut her knee on a rock. I ran to the woods, plucked some pilosa leaves and hurried back to my friend. I do not know what told me to go get the pilosa. I just knew. When I reached my friend, her mother and an old woman, who was the healer in the village, were already at her side. The old woman looked at me and asked what I had in my hands. I held the pilosa out to her, and this look of amazement came over her. She said I was born with the healing gift, and from that day on she trained me."

"What about the medicine you gave Zinni that time?"

"Which medicine?"

"The one you prepared when she did not want to have a baby."

"She misused it," Nihapu said.

"How did you know what to give her?"

"The old woman taught me, like I teach Buhgo."

"Have you taught Buhgo the medicine you gave Zinni?"

"Yes," Nihapu answered. She ladled tea from the pot and sipped it. "Why?"

"That must be such a powerful medicine! What kind of plant could make the body expel a baby before its time?"

Nihapu offered Nyna the dipper. "It is a combination of plants and their parts."

"Like what?" Nyna asked, putting the dipper to her lips.

"Silver leaf roots, kernels from the tallowwood." Nihapu swirled the brew with a stirring stick. "That reminds me. I was going to ask Buhgo to gather some plants for me today. Maybe you would also enjoy the walk."

"I would," she said.

"You need to tell Joog," Buhgo said, stooping to pluck several stems of savory.

"What good would it do if I told him I think I love him?"

"He should know," Buhgo said.

"Why are you so determined that I tell him? I am not Ais. We could never be together. And one day I will leave."

"He cannot make decisions about his life if he does not have all the information." Buhgo stripped myrsine leaves and added them to the basket.

"You do not take the berries," Nyna remarked.

"They are of no use," Buhgo answered. "Will you tell him?"

"You do not let this subject die," she said.

Buhgo faced her. "The Jeaga speak of a possible marriage."

"Joog and a Jeaga woman?"

"The woman who cared for him has a daughter."

"Oh." Nyna sighed. "Then for certain I should not tell him."

"And you will not let me tell him or say that I suspect?"

"Let this go, Buhgo. Leave it alone."

"All right," he said. "I do whatever you wish."

They walked on in silence for a short distance, making their way toward the beach.

"Pick some of the stopper leaves," he said. "And dig some spurge nettle roots. I will look for dove plum and saffron."

Nyna took her basket and headed toward the small white stopper tree, but another plant got her attention.

The shrub came only to her knees, the branches vinelike and thorny. Since the winter cold had left, the tallowwood had fruited as it would again in the fall. She picked two of the bright yellow fruits and hid them under some other leaves in her basket. She glanced behind her. Buhgo was busy and did not look at her. She went on to the stopper and gathered the leaves.

As Nyna worked, she looked about. She saw no silver leaf. She had plenty of stopper leaves, probably too many, so she moved on. She knew where the spurge nettle grew, but she detoured, taking in a wider range. Still no silver leaf.

Nyna gripped the digging stick and dug sideways into the dune, careful the nettle did not touch her with its stinging hairs. She traced the long stem down to the tuber. After clearing away some of the sand, Nyna cut the tuber free with her woman's knife.

"Are you finished?" Buhgo said, coming up behind her.

Nyna sprang up. "Is that all?" she asked.

"I believe we have gotten everything Nihapu asked for."

On their way back, just before the trail opened into the village, Nyna spotted a silver leaf to her right. She stopped.

"What is wrong?" Buhgo asked.

Nyna looked back at him. "Nothing," she said, walking again. She took a last look over her shoulder. She had to remember exactly where this tree was. Perhaps ten long strides north of the trail. She counted her steps to the village. She used the fingers of both hands, ten times, and then three more times. The tree would be hard to locate in the dark.

The sounding of the conch horn surprised them. They trotted across the plaza. Buhgo escorted her to Nihapu's side, then joined the Council.

Chogatis appeared weary and weak, but still he took

command. "We welcome our visitors," he said, nodding at two men Buhgo had never seen before.

They bore markings that were different than any Ais's. They were Jeaga.

The language of the Ais and Jeaga came from the same mother language, many words sounding and meaning the same. The dialect was different, but not enough to interfere with communication.

"Akoma has sent us on behalf of our people to tell you we will talk to you about your proposal," the tallest of the two men said. He had a black stripe down the center of his chest and swirling tattoos on his arms. The other man was stockier and had fewer tattoos. He wore ear plugs made from shark vertebrae. "If the time comes, we ask that you send Joog."

"We would do that," Etac said.

The tall man spoke again. "That is the time we will decide where the Hawk Clan of the Ais can stay, and for how long . . . if it becomes necessary."

Chogatis peered up at another brilliant blue sky. "It does not look promising," he said.

Guacana indicated he wished to speak, and Chogatis acknowledged him, hoping he would not offend the Jeaga.

"I think someone should go with Joog. He should not go before the Jeaga alone."

Chogatis looked at Joog. "Tell us what you think," he said.

"It is not necessary. I am comfortable with the Jeaga."

Guacana shifted on his haunches, his hands scouring his thighs. "But perhaps there are some of us who think it would be in the best interest of the Ais if someone accompanied you in the Jeaga Council."

Chogatis stabbed the Talking Stick in the ground. His eyes, more gray than black, glared at Guacana. Guacana had just essentially told the Jeaga that some did not trust that Joog would negotiate completely in their favor. The worst was that Guacana insinuated the Jeaga would not negotiate in good faith.

"Guacana," Joog said, his voice edged sharp like his knife, "do you intend to insult our guests and me?"

Guacana did not have enough power in Council to go head-on with Joog. Even though there were those who harbored the faintest notion that Joog might be too favorable to the Jeaga because of his past, they would not express their concern now, not in front of the Jeaga. Ais did not brandish their conflicts in front of visitors, whether from another Ais Clan or an entirely different people.

Guacana glanced around the circle. Disapproval squirmed over their faces. Etac pulled his lips taut, and the muscles of his jaw worked behind a closed mouth. One of Joog's eyebrows arched, and his angry breathing lifted his chest. If Chogatis's eyes could have left his head, they would have flown through the air and pierced Guacana's heart like finely pointed darts.

"Perhaps I was misunderstood," Guacana said. "I will bring it to Council another time."

The Jeaga visitors were given shelter for the night in Buhgo's new hut. Cetisa slept close to Etac, her hand resting on her abdomen. Zinni stared at Ochopee in the darkness. The sore was healing and again she missed her husband.

Nyna waited until the noises in the village were silent. She heard Uxaam say his evening chant. He was usually the last to retire. The Fire Keeper pushed the logs that stoked the central hearth closer to the center. They would burn all night.

She lingered on her mat for a long time after the village was quiet. Not everyone fell asleep right away, she knew. Finally she rose from her mat and crept to the entrance of the lodge. Her foot bumped one of Nihapu's baskets and the drying plants rustled.

Nyna paused. When there was no response from Nihapu or Chogatis, she slipped out the entrance. She pressed herself against the trunk of a tree and surveyed the village. She had to stay out of the light of the fire and moon, hugging the shadows.

She moved behind the village, hiding in the trees and brush until she came to the path she and Buhgo had followed that day. She counted, remembering how many steps she had taken. Under the cover of the trees along the trail the night seemed to grow darker. In darkness the things beneath her feet felt odd and eerie. What living creature waited on the trail to bite her ankle or sting her heel? A spiderweb tacked to her face, and Nyna sputtered, brushing it away.

Suddenly she stopped. Now she had lost count. How many fingers and hands?

She stared through the blackness, trying to spot some kind of marker that would give her a clue. But everything looked the same: branches, trees, leaves, brush. Nothing special told her where she was on the trail.

Nyna backed up to the beginning of the path and started again. What if Nihapu or Chogatis awakened and looked for her? What if someone could not sleep and saw her come out of the lodge? Her heart thumped in her chest and her hands grew cold and sweaty.

She had to do this! She had to get the leaves of the silver leaf. That was part of the medicine Nihapu had given Zinni to get rid of her baby. It had not worked only because she did not use it right. Nyna would probe Buhgo about how to take the medicine, then it would be over. She would be rid of this foul thing that grew inside her.

She counted again, ignoring the creepy things of the night. Both hands ten times, then three more. Nyna stopped and faced north. The silver leaf should be just ten long strides ahead.

Nyna paced off the distance, but the route was not

straight. She found her path blocked by trees and shrubs she had not taken into account. Again she backed up, retracing her steps to the path. Directly at her back was a tall pine. She would use it as a marker. She took her ten strides again, moving back into line with the pine every time she had to vary from a straight path.

"It should be right here," she said. Just to her left she saw it and breathed with relief. Quickly she stripped some leaves. Suddenly she realized she had forgotten to bring a basket. She stacked the leaves straight in the palm of her hand, holding them down with her thumb. Her hand as full as she could get it, Nyna turned around.

Near her lodge she heard a noise and stopped, backing into the darkest shadow. She heard herself breathing and was sure if anyone was near, they would also hear. Her eyes strained in the darkness. The breeze-stirred leaves and branches created illusions. Was there someone there, moving slyly, or was it only the trees?

Nyna took in a shallow controlled breath and held it. If she were caught, Guacana would convince everyone she had been doing something bad. How would she explain the silver leaf? Cetisa would be certain the leaves were to be used in a medicine furtively fed to her.

Nyna squeezed her eyes shut and prayed. She had forgotten most of the prayers to the *zemis* her mother taught her as a child. She made it up, doing her best to recall the Taino words. She said the prayer in her head, afraid to whisper, hoping the *zemis* would hear her if she prayed hard enough.

After a while, when no one came through the trees, she decided to make her move. She could see the lodge. It was not far. She had two choices. She could dash in the open and expose herself a very short time to being caught, or she could continue to work her way behind the houses, which would take more time.

She chose to stay hidden. Every moment seemed much longer than it was, every breath louder. At last she stood just behind the lodge. Nyna's heart thudded against her breast, and her tongue searched her dry mouth for saliva.

She paused, then struck out and sped into the house. Inside she breathed hard and rapid. Careful not to wake Chogatis and Nihapu, she picked up her basket that contained the articles she took to the woman's hut during her moon cycle. Quietly she took the basket to her room and sat with it next to her mat. Nyna unpacked the basket and retrieved a pouch hidden in the bottom. She stuffed the silver leaf collection in the pouch with the tallowwood and returned it to the basket. Attentively she folded and replaced her woman things on top of the pouch. No one would go through those personal belongings.

Her eyes burned and she yawned. She would get up early and put the basket back where it belonged. It would be taking too much of a chance to do it now. No one would miss it, and if she had to, she could sneak it back in its place when everyone was out of the lodge. Nyna lay down on her mat and closed her eyes.

Her dreams came as they had not in a long time. She ran down the beach with her mother and father. Obaec was shouting for them to get in the Carib dugout. His blood streaked his chest and side. Her mother was crying.

Then suddenly she was in the piragua. The Carib lurched out of the water, his hideous face, with black outlined eyes, came so close to her she could smell his breath.

Nyna screamed.

"Wake up," Nihapu was saying as Nyna's eyes fluttered open. Perspiration soaked her.

"It was just a dream," Nihapu said. "Only a dream."

Nyna sat up.

"The Carib attack?" Nihapu asked. "The same dream you used to have when you were little?"

Nyna's fingertips worked her forehead, pressing, massaging away the dream. "Every time it is so real. It is like I am there again, reliving every moment."

Nihapu got to her feet. "Sleep, now," she whispered. She stepped back to leave and in the darkness stumbled over Nyna's basket.

29

Nyna's belongings spilled out of the basket, her leather strap, the soft packing for the strap, utensils, ladles, and the secret pouch that stuck out from under a wooden bowl. The tip of a silver leaf poked through the drawstring neck. Nyna hoped Nihapu did not see well in the darkness. She scrambled, shoving the pouch in the basket, and covering it as quickly as she could.

Nihapu bent to help. "I am sorry," she said.

"I will get it. Go back to sleep," Nyna said. Nyna swept the rest of her things into the basket. "There," she said.

"Is it time for your moon cycle?" Nihapu asked.

Nyna nodded briskly. "I made sure everything is ready," she said. "That is why the basket is here beside me. I checked it before going to sleep. I am sorry I awakened you. I am fine now, really."

Nihapu said she would see her in the morning and returned to her mat.

Nyna lay with her eyes staring at the roof. She did not like living lies. Not being truthful and sneaking about made her nervous and upset her stomach. The lies were like ropes tangled around her feet. Every step she took, she tangled them more.

Nyna stayed awake the rest of the night, thinking up a plan. She would have to go to the woman's hut. She had mentioned it was time for her moon blood to Nihapu and surely Cetisa would notice and ask questions. At least in the woman's hut she could prepare the medicine and not be watched so closely. That was the only place she was not required to have an escort. During her moon cycle everyone knew she was isolated. If she was seen anywhere but at the woman's place, there would be questions as to why she was not with an escort.

There were several things she had to do before confining herself to the woman's hut. She had to talk to Buhgo first. She needed more information than she could prod Nihapu for. She needed more specifics about the medicine. Then she would spend five days in isolation. Nyna hoped the medicine would work by then.

When morning finally arrived, she was eager to begin setting up her plan. She flit about the cook fire during the morning meal, but only nibbled at the food. Nihapu watched curiously.

"Are you not hungry?" Nihapu asked. "You barely ate anything."

"Not this morning," Nyna said. "Must be my moon cycle. I am restless, but still tired."

"You are fidgety," Nihapu said. "Be still, you remind me of a mosquito." She laughed. "You did not have a good night's sleep."

Nyna drummed her fingers on her knee while she sat and sipped at her tea. "Is there something you want me to do? Do you need me to collect anything with Buhgo?"

"Nothing that I can think of." Nihapu looked at Nyna. "I believe a walk would do you good. Do you need to get away for a bit?"

"I like it when I help Buhgo gather plants for you. Most of the time I have to sit right here. When I am in the forest I feel so much freer."

"Then I will send Buhgo for something, and you can go with him." Nihapu dug through her baskets. "I could use some sea grape leaves and porterweed. When Buhgo comes for his lessons, I will send him."

"Thank you," Nyna said. She could have asked Nihapu

more about the medicine, but she would probably grow suspicious since Nyna had already inquired about it. As soon as she got the information from Buhgo, she would leave for the woman's hut.

Joog watched Nyna as she and Buhgo crossed the village. She was clearly a woman now, her body filled out in the right places so she was a creation of soft flesh and curves. Her hair dropped to her waist and swished as she walked. Joog rarely thought of her as the child he had found on the beach. They had grown, seen so many things, shared so many things. She knew him better than anyone. He could not imagine her not being part of his life. He was most content when she was near, when he helped her with weapons or tools. Perhaps that was because he touched her during those times, stood close, felt her skin on his. He liked the sound of her voice, the way her eyes twinkled when she was amused.

Etac came next to him. "You have an eye for her?" he asked.

"She is a good friend," Joog said.

"Men do not have *good* female friends. There is more."

"She is amazing," he said. "Think of the things she has been through, yet she remains strong. I do not know if I would have been so strong under the same conditions."

"Nyna is remarkable," Etac said. "I only wish more of our people appreciated her."

The sun glinted off her bracelet just before she and Buhgo entered the trail.

"Do you ever wonder about her home . . . the Taino?" Etac asked.

"Frequently," Joog answered. "I wonder, did she live far out to sea, near the place where the sun rises? Was she so close that she could have a piece of the sun and form it into a bracelet?"

"Why do you not court her?" Etac said. "You have an interest."

Joog looked into the distance. "The people would never accept it. And now there is talk about a marriage to the Jeaga woman, Cian."

"Follow your heart. The people would adjust."

"There would always be some that would make her life miserable. If there were a marriage between us, she would be committed to stay here in this village and not return home. I could never ask her to give up her dream of going home. I would not do that to her. So why court her if it would only lead to heartache?"

"I see," Etac said.

The two men looked over the village. The earth beneath them was dried and caked. Grasses and leaves turned brown. They needed rain to come soon.

"Sit down," Etac said. "I have something to discuss with you."

"What is on your mind?" Joog asked, folding his legs under him.

"Guacana concerns me. He is dangerous."

"He is always out to hurt Nyna."

"Not just that. Look what he did before the Jeaga."

Joog realized his thoughts were still with Nyna. He was not thinking clearly. He focused on Etac.

"Guacana compromises his own people," Etac said. "I hear him talk to a few others that question your loyalty. He wants to unseat Chogatis. He lectures on the cacique's old age and his continued softening toward the Jeaga."

"But the Jeaga may be the ones to spare us from the drought. Peace is better than war."

"Guacana has some kind of poison in his gut. It spews out in his words and actions. He vies for Chogatis's position. We must make sure that does not happen. You are the natural choice to follow Chogatis."

Joog rocked back. "I have thought about that, but I

am not so sure. The Hawk need someone they have no doubts about."

"It is only Guacana and a few others."

"They are enough," Joog said. "And then if I marry a Jeaga, that will provide even more hesitancy, though it helps keep the peace. There are many things to consider. But they are right about one thing, Chogatis does grow old, and we will soon have to make a decision about who is to follow."

Sea grape trees formed clumps along the sandy soil near the shore. In cold weather the leaves turned yellow and red and dropped onto the white beach. In warm weather large clusters of fruit dangled from the branches, ripening only a few at a time. The large leaves made good temporary plates or wrappings to roast fish in.

"Do you remember the medicine your mother took a long time ago that made her so sick?" Nyna asked. "Laira also took some by mistake."

"I thought they were going to die," Buhgo said.

"Was it a tea?" she asked.

"It should have been just a few drops in the tea."

"She drank it all at one time?"

"She thought it would work faster or better."

"How often should she have taken it?" Nyna asked.

"Small amounts, several times a day, for several days. She made a big mistake."

"Everyone believes that is why Taska is the way he is," Nyna said.

"My father does. Who knows for sure?"

"So, if Zinni had taken the medicine right, Taska would not have been born."

"Everything works out for the best," Buhgo said. "I am glad my brother was born and not lost to the medicine. I am glad he was born the way he is. He is so incredibly smart, and he has the shaman's gift."

"The medicine was tallowwood and silver leaf?"

"Those were ingredients," Buhgo said.

"It must be a complicated medicine to do such a thing."

"It should be."

"Seems there would be other ingredients to such a powerful medicine. Just silver leaf and tallowwood seeds seems too simple."

"There are other ingredients."

"Really?" Nyna said. "What other ingredients?"

Buhgo looked into the air inquisitively. "It escapes me," he said. "It is a good thing you have brought this up. I will have to review with Nihapu. It is not a common medicine. I have never prepared it. If I did, I would remember everything that goes in it."

Nyna let out a sigh.

"Is something the matter?" Buhgo asked.

"Nothing," she said. "I am not feeling well. I think it is time for my moon cycle."

They headed back to the village. Nyna twirled her hair with her fingers in frustration. There were other ingredients to this medicine and she did not know what they were. She could not bring it up again to Buhgo or Nihapu. If she questioned Buhgo's mother, Zinni would surely ask her why she was inquiring. All she could do was rely on the silver leaf, tallowwood, and her Taino prayers.

After delivering the articles Nihapu had requested, Nyna announced that she needed to go to the woman's hut. She gathered her basket, an otter stomach pouch of water, and Nihapu escorted her to the hut, stopping along the way to take a coal from the central hearth.

"I will bring you coontie to grind later," Nihapu said.

Nyna settled in. There was no one else in any of the huts, which pleased her. She had brought with her a ball of clay kept moist inside a hide pouch. She took it out and kneaded it with her hands. When the clay was pliable she began to shape it.

"Yuchahu," she whispered. Her fingers worked the clay, forming a head and body.

With a stick she poked holes for the eyes and with a swift swoop of her fingernail she made a mouth.

She did not know if this was what Yuchahu looked like, she could not remember. But she did recall the name of the fertility spirit, as her mother had often prayed to it for another child. She said the name again with a lilt in her voice like a chant. "Yuchahu, can you hear me?"

She remembered that on special occasions her mother hung an extra hammock so the spirit would have a place to sleep. She had no hammock, but she offered Yuchahu her mat. She would sleep on the bare ground. Yuchahu would then see her sincerity, even if she did not meet all the Taino qualifications.

In her home, the Taino had a meeting place, an earthen platform, where the oldest and wisest men met. They were called *Cemetti*. Her mother's father, her grandfather, was a *Cemetti*. He gathered with the others in the meeting place to discuss the heavens, the sun, the stars, the traditions, and things ancient. For days they discussed and meditated, taking no food. They surrounded themselves with images of *zemis* during their discussions. Nyna recalled her mother holding her on her hip and pointing to the gathering of the *Cemettis*. She told her to be proud of her grandfather.

Nyna laid the *zemi* in the sun to dry. She would not fire it like a pot because it would not be something she would keep. Such a thing would anger the Ais.

Nyna started her fire and threaded a lashed pot over the cross pole above it. Before she took anything else from the basket, she checked to see no one was near. She could prepare this medicine before Nihapu returned later with coontie. She would not eat anything made from the starchy root, but she was to perform a woman's work while in isolation.

Nyna took her wooden bowl and a smooth stone she had taken from the stream. She sprinkled the silver leaf leaves in the bowl and ground them with the stone. They left a dull green residue in the bottom of the bowl.

Nyna tweezed a hot stone from the fire and put it in the pot of water. It sizzled and steamed.

The *zemi* dried quickly next to the fire. The face and body fissured as it did so.

Nyna sliced open a tallowwood plum and removed the kernel inside. She plopped the nut inside the wooden bowl with the silver leaf and began to crush it with the stone. Finally, satisfied with the medicine paste she had created, she scraped it together with a small lucina shell, then into the pot. She tweezed another hot stone and added it to the pot. When most of the water had boiled away she would drain the medicine off into a smaller vessel.

While she waited, Nyna carefully lifted the *zemi* and moved to the shade of a tree. She held the *zemi* in front of her and called to it.

"Yuchahu, I am Nyna of the Taino. I need your help."

She repeated her call several times. "Yuchahu, rid me of this child that is not Taino. This child is the seed of a monster, an evil man. Hear me, Yuchahu. I am Nyna of the Taino. I need your help." Some of the words she spoke in Taino and some in Ais. She could not remember all the Taino words. She hoped the spirit was strong enough that language would not be a problem.

Nyna removed the pot from the fire, and when it had cooled, she poured it off into a smaller pot. She rinsed the big pot and put water in it before hanging over the fire again. She added fresh greenbriar root to steep and brew into a tea.

Nyna wrapped the *zemi* in a soft hide cloth and gingerly laid it in her basket.

Now was the time to take the medicine. She put her hand on her belly and for a flashing moment wondered if she were doing the right thing.

Nyna used a whelk dipper to ladle the greenbriar tea. Then with the lucina shell she spooned up a small portion of the medicine and dropped it in with her dipper of tea. The aroma of the tea wafted to her nose as she held it near her lips. It did not smell different, she thought. She sipped, tasting a tiny bit. It was not foul, but when she swallowed, she did notice a slight aftertaste.

She sat sipping on the tea, wondering if it was going to work. What would it be like to be a mother? She pictured herself holding an infant who cooed at her. She saw herself holding the baby to her breast and closing her eyes with such contentment. A smile spread across her face.

Nyna put down the empty ladle. She could not think of babies and being a mother, not now! This was Guacana's child! She could not have second thoughts.

She closed her eyes and prayed silently to Yuchahu to give her strength and to take Guacana's child from her body. A voice made her eyes spring open. It was Buhgo.

"I bring the coontie for Nihapu," he said. "What were you doing?" he asked.

The small medicine bowl rested next to her. Nyna scooted in front of it.

"I just finished some tea and was daydreaming," she said.

"It did not look like you were daydreaming," he said. "Are you all right? Is anything wrong?" Buhgo circled her, his eyes giving away his curiosity over the small bowl and shell.

"Do you take medicine for your belly cramping?" he asked.

"Yes," Nyna answered feverishly. "Exactly." She avoided looking at the medicine.

Buhgo bent and picked up the bowl.

"Something I mixed myself," she said.

He sniffed. "What did you put in this?"

"Things I had in my basket from last time. Nihapu

gave me the ingredients. I chewed the leaf before, but I saw no harm in putting it in a tea." She reached for the bowl, but before Buhgo gave it up, he put his finger in it and tasted.

"What have you done, Nyna?" he asked. "This is not made from—"

"I added some other healing things. Just simple dried berries. Things like that. I made up my own."

Buhgo stared at her as she babbled. "I taste tallowwood seed."

"What would I do with that? I eat the fruit, not the seed."

"You are not telling me everything. Not the truth," Buhgo said. "I see it in your eyes and hear it in your voice."

"Everything is fine," Nyna said. She took the bowl and put it on the ground.

"Look straight at me," he said. "Look at my eyes." He lifted her chin with the tip of his finger. His eyes bored into hers. "You do not have your moon cycle. That is why all the questions about Zinni's medicine. You are pregnant."

"No!" Nyna said, pushing his finger from her chin.

"You want to rid yourself of the baby because it is Guacana's."

Nyna stood up. "All right, yes," she said. "I want no part of this child. I want it out of me. I hate him," she said.

Buhgo grabbed one of her hands. "Calm down," he said. "Let us talk about this."

"There is nothing to talk about. I have made up my mind." Tears filled her eyes, and slowly she lowered herself to the ground.

"Did you hear what you said?" he asked. "You said that you hate *him* . . . Guacana. You do not hate the child."

"They are the same," she said.

"No, no, they are not the same. Inside you grows a new spirit. The baby inside you carries your spirit, Taino spirit, not only Guacana's. This child has inside it a piece of your mother's spirit, your father's."

Nyna rested her hand on her belly. Tears streaked down her cheeks. "How can I have Guacana's child?"

"Do you really hate the child, the baby that grows inside you? Your body nourishes it, the Taino spirits look over it. They have breathed the life into you, not Guacana. You cannot choose to destroy it."

Nyna sobbed.

"That child is part of you and all your people."

Nyna nodded. "I have even imagined his face," she said. "I have seen myself holding him."

"The spirits, whether they are Taino or Ais, look over you and prepare you for motherhood. Let the love you have for this baby flow free. It is the natural and right thing to do. For all the lives destroyed by the Carib, you bring another into the world. The Carib have not defeated you."

"You are right, Buhgo," she said, crying into his shoulder. He held her and stroked the back of her hair.

"You were only confused because of the horrible way this baby was conceived. You mix your feelings for Guacana with the unborn child. They are not the same."

Nyna jerked her head up. "But the medicine. I drank it!"

30

"Tell me exactly what was in the medicine and how much of it you drank."

Nyna wiped her nose with the back of her hand and sniffled. "I only knew tallowwood and silver leaf. I hoped that would be enough."

"Nothing else?" he asked.

"I put it in greenbriar tea. I used this lucina shell," she said, picking it up. "But I did not fill it. I only dipped a little with the shell and added it to the ladle."

"I am not sure," Buhgo said. "I do not know what the effects might be. There are several other ingredients to the medicine."

"What do I do now?" she asked. "I cannot just pick up and leave the woman's hut and tell Nihapu I lied."

Buhgo rubbed the top of his head, then smacked his lips. "You could stay here, just as you planned. Then at the time you should have your next moon cycle, you will say it has not come."

"But if Guacana stays away from me, he will know it is not true. I am escorted all the time. Everyone will know it is not true."

"Let me think," Buhgo said.

The two of them sat thinking. The lies, she thought to herself. Once you told one . . .

Buhgo's head snapped up. "I have it," he said.

*   *   *

Laira and Zinni walked behind Nihapu so as not to come between her and the fire, as that would be impolite.

"Welcome," Nihapu said as they took a seat beside her.

"The sore is gone, completely healed," Zinni said. "A small scar, but that, too, might vanish."

"Nihapu's medicine is good," Laira said.

Nyna's approach distracted Nihapu and she stood up.

"Why have you returned?" she asked. "It is too soon. Only yesterday you took your things to the woman's hut."

"It is done," Nyna said. "The moon blood is gone, so I have come home." She put her things away and returned to join Nihapu and the others.

"I am glad to see you looking so well, Zinni," Nyna said.

Zinni smiled. "I was just telling Nihapu the sore is healed. Perhaps I am not ill at all."

"Yaya," Nyna said.

"What?" Nihapu asked.

"The Taino call the disease *yaya*. There is a tree in my homeland," Nyna said. "It is called the Holy Wood. It has another name, but I cannot remember it. Holy Wood cures *yaya*."

Nihapu's attention piqued. "Can you tell me what the tree looks like?"

Nyna grimaced, trying to remember. "Chalky white bark . . . and the leaves fold up in the day." She paused, hoping to get more of a picture. "I am sorry, that is all I remember. I do not recall anything about what the leaves look like or if it flowers." She hesitated. "And there was another herb . . . *digo*, I think it was called. But it was not as effective as Holy Wood."

"I am surprised you remember as much as you do," Nihapu said. "It is amazing."

"I helped my mother gather bark for my grandmother.

She told me all about the Holy Wood and *digo* and what a wonderful miracle medicine these two things made."

Zinni spoke up. "The *digo,* do you recall what that looked like?"

"I am afraid I was not that interested in the gathering part, only the legend of the tree."

"Tell us," Zinni said. "Maybe the tree grows here, too, and something in the story will be a clue."

"It may be a little sketchy," Nyna said. She tilted her head back and searched her memory. "Umm," she said, figuring out where to begin. "There once was a great chief . . . I cannot remember his name."

"That is all right. Go on," Laira said.

"The chief stands on the seashore, looking into the water. He wants a wife. He sees a beautiful woman beneath the water, but he does not speak to her this time. He travels from island to island, from village to village, searching for a wife. Along the way he collects women, but none of them are as perfect as the woman in the sea. They travel with him on his journey, but he is unhappy with all of them. The chief goes to an island where there exists only women. There are no men. He is certain that here he will find a wife, but is disappointed. Unhappy he has found no woman as perfect as the one he saw in the sea, he leaves all the women on that island and returns home. By now he is covered in the sores. *Yaya.* This time when he sees the woman in the water he dives in. The woman gives him four white stone beads and tells him to plant them in his garden, and from it he will regain his health.

"The chief begs the woman to come with him, but she says she can never leave the sea. He takes the beads and plants them in his garden and cries remembering the beautiful lady of the water. His tears fall on the soil and a tree springs up.

"The chief boils small pieces of the wood from the tree and drinks it for three days, only consuming the medicine tea, four bird eggs, and small loaves of cassava. For ten . . . no maybe twenty days after he can eat nothing sour and no fish. On the last day he soaks cloths in the residue of the Holy Wood decoction, then lays them on his body. The sores heal, and he is healthy again.

"He is so pleased that he travels the sea to different villages, planting the seeds from the Holy Wood. And that is how the Holy Wood came to grow in Taino villages."

Nihapu shook her head. "Is there anything else in the legend? Any description of the tree?"

Nyna closed her eyes. "I have forgotten so much. I remember that story because I always looked in the water in hopes of seeing the beautiful woman in the sea. I had my mother repeat the story many times. I remember some of the other stories, the legends, not many. The common things I forget. That time is so hazy."

"I do not recognize the tree from what you have told us," Nihapu said. "I am sorry, Zinni."

"One day I will go home," Nyna said. "I will bring back seeds and bark for the Ais."

Zinni hung her head. "It will be too late for me," she said softly.

That night over a dying cook fire, Nihapu and Nyna chatted. Chogatis excused himself and went in the lodge to sleep.

"I did not want to question you in front of Zinni and Laira, but you only stayed one day in the woman's hut," Nihapu said. "I do not understand."

Nyna shrugged. "The moon blood went away."

"That quickly? I do no see how that can be."

"There was not much blood to start with."

Nihapu studied Nyna. "There is one consideration," she said.

"What would that be?"

"You have not had many moon cycles. Sometimes it takes awhile for the blood to come at the right time. That might be it."

"Yes," Nyna agreed. "That is probably it."

"But," Nihapu said, "there could be another explanation."

Nyna looked up at her. "Tell me."

"I suppose it could be what I am thinking. Sometimes when a woman is first pregnant there is a staining of blood, but not a true moon cycle."

"Do you think that is what happened?" Nyna balled her hands nervously. Buhgo had told her what to say to lead Nihapu to the conclusion that she carried a child. His advice had worked.

Nihapu wrapped her arms around Nyna. "How wonderful! A baby! We will ask Taska in the morning what he sees."

"But I have no husband," Nyna said, pulling away.

"Chogatis and I will provide. His father is Ais, even if not your husband." Suddenly Nihapu flinched. "I do assume this is Guacana's child and it could be no others."

"Only Guacana," Nyna answered.

"That is why you do not smile . . . Guacana's child."

"The circumstances are not as I have dreamed." Nyna touched her abdomen and looked down. "If there is a baby, it is not the result of a man and woman's love."

"But this would not be only Guacana's child, it would be yours. The baby would be your baby!"

"A child," Nyna whispered, lovingly touching her belly. "My child. It is funny how a woman loves her child from the moment she realizes it grows inside her."

"That is the spirits' way of making you a mother. But I do not think a man feels the same until that child arrives and he holds it for the first time. A baby is not real to a man until it comes into the world."

"But maybe the moon cycle is mixed up because I have not had many of them yet."

"I would think that, but Guacana . . ."

"The baby is part Taino," Nyna whispered. "Part of my people will live on with him."

"You are right," Nihapu said, getting to her feet. "Watch the moon. Keep track of the days," she said. She walked about, picking up a suitable long stick about as large around as her two thumbs together. She would have broken the stick and fed the fire with it, but she now had a better use.

"What is this for?" Nyna asked as Nihapu handed her the stick.

"Make a big notch in it tonight. Then notch it every night with small slashes. When the moon looks exactly as it does now, make another big notch. Keep notching every night. If you do carry a child, around the time you cut the ninth big notch, the baby will come."

"I am going to be a mother," Nyna said.

"This is a time of celebration, to be happy."

"But the bleeding . . . is that a bad sign? Could something be wrong?"

The joyful expression on Nihapu's face narrowed to a more sober one. "There is that possibility. But even without blood, things can go wrong. You must be extra careful not to exert yourself. Give the child time to grow."

"I am afraid," Nyna said. "This baby will be the only thing in my life that is truly mine, that will love me without hesitancy."

"I will give you medicines that are good," Nihapu said. "But be careful with your body. You must watch everything you do now, as whatever happens to you, happens to the baby. The two of you are really one. If you had a husband, this would be a time he could have a second wife to help with the chores. But Chogatis and I will take care of that. Buhgo will help, and so will Joog."

Touched by Nihapu's gesture, Nyna's eyes filled with tears. "Thank you," she whispered.

*   *   *

Nyna's stomach was sour every morning, and she had difficulty keeping many meals down. Nihapu did her best to convince her that for some women this was normal, and that the sickness varied even from pregnancy to pregnancy. But Nyna feared that because she had taken the medicine, she had harmed her child, just as Zinni had hurt Taska. Her dreams filled with visions of the birth. Raven would appear in the doorway to the lodge, and the pains would begin. Soon she would be screaming with agony. Nihapu would catch the child and lift him up. Raven's wings would stir the air as he took flight. Then Nihapu would scream. Nyna would try to see what was wrong, but Nihapu would quickly wrap the child in rags, covering even the infant's face, and run out.

Many times she awakened in a sweat, crying aloud. She was careful not to stress her body, and she abided by all the Ais myths concerning her diet. She wished she knew the Taino traditions.

Nyna peered up at the moon. It was just right, big and bright with a crescent in its top right side that looked like a child had taken a bite from it. She carved a large notch in her stick.

She was glad Buhgo had come to her that day in the woman's hut. How could she have even thought of getting rid of this wonderful child? As much as she hated Guacana, she loved this child.

Nyna put the stick next to her mat and lay down to sleep. Tonight she slept soundly without the terrible dreams.

When morning came, she felt refreshed, better than she had felt in quite a while. She smelled Nihapu's berry cakes, and it did not offend her stomach. She thought perhaps she might eat a little.

Nyna stretched and ducked out of the lodge.

"Where is Chogatis?" Nyna asked. He was not in the lodge and was not with Nihapu.

"He has gone to greet the day by the sea," she said.

"He feels stronger every day. This morning he said he was always overwhelmed by the power of the spirits when he was near the sea. So, he decided he would give thanks and greet the day there."

"The sea is a special place for me, too. My village was right on the water. I was lulled to sleep at night by the surf and awakened by the seabirds." Nyna smiled at her recollection and gazed in the distance.

"We will dig coontie today," Nihapu said. "Do you feel well enough to go?"

"I feel wonderful," Nyna said. She pinched off a piece of berrycake and put it in her mouth. "My stomach cooperates this morning."

"That is a good sign," Nihapu said. "Your body adjusts to the new little one inside. Some women's bodies do not cooperate the entire pregnancy."

"The baby will be born when it is cold again. That is such a bad time."

"Joog was born when it was cold. It did nothing to him."

Several women, including Nyna, Cetisa, Laira, and Nihapu, carried empty baskets on their backs and trekked to the high piney woods that was cobbled with ancient coral rock. With their digging sticks, they pried up the brown coarse roots, packed them in the baskets, and carried them back to the village.

"Rest in the shade a moment," Nihapu said to Nyna. "Do not overdo."

Cetisa stood a short distance away. She plunged her stick in the ground, turning up the soil in search of the coontie root. She huffed when she heard her sister's words. What made Nyna so special? She pitched up the dirt and it sprayed onto Nyna's legs.

"Sorry," she said, without looking up.

"Go on," Nihapu said to Nyna. "Work a little, rest a little."

Nyna backed away and sat, her back propped against a tree. It was getting toward the middle of the day and the heat was intensifying. It was a good idea that she rested.

Laira offered Nyna water from her pouch, and Nyna gratefully accepted.

"I did not think it would be this hot," Nyna said. "I think the baby makes me less tolerant."

Laira sat back and smiled. "I have exciting news," she said. "You are the first to know, except for Chitola. My moon cycle has not come either!"

Nyna grinned, her eyes wide. "How quickly! The spirits must think you will be a great mother!"

"Perhaps that is what has taken so long for Cetisa to carry a child. She has so much bitterness inside. Just look at her."

Cetisa wildly jabbed her stick in the earth. She snorted with the effort. Then she looked up at her sister. "Is there something wrong with Nyna?" she asked Nihapu. "Something besides carrying a child, just like I do?"

"She should take it easy," Nihapu said.

"And me? You do not think I should?"

"Any woman who carries a child should not overwork her body. You know that."

Cetisa threw down her stick and moved under a tree and sat. She mumbled to herself, but no one could clearly understand what she said. Nihapu assumed it was a complaint against her.

When they had enough to fill their baskets, the women packed them and strapped them to their backs.

"Give me some of your load," Nihapu said to Nyna. "Do not carry a full basket."

"I am fine," Nyna said. "Really, it is not that heavy."

"Well, mine is heavy," Cetisa said. She plucked several roots from her basket and stuffed them in Nihapu's. "And yours is light?" she asked Nyna. She took two more roots from her basket.

"No," Nihapu said. "Nyna has enough."

"Give them to me," Laira said. "Stop all this bickering."

Cetisa rammed the roots back inside her basket and walked ahead of them toward the village.

"She has wanted this child a long time," Nihapu said.

Laira laughed. "You always make excuses for her. Her disposition is nothing new. Everyone knows how she is."

Nihapu's mouth attempted a weak smile. "I would be glad to help her, but she makes it so difficult."

In the village many of the other women joined them to help in the washing and preparing of the coontie. They distributed what they collected amongst the newcomers and began the task of cleaning the roots. When Nihapu finished washing her roots, she pared them, discarding the rough brown skin.

"Tell me about this Jeaga woman, Cian," Nyna said to Nihapu.

"She is the daughter of Talli and Akoma."

"Is she beautiful?"

"I have never seen her. Only Joog has been to the Jeaga village. Ask him."

"No, I could not," Nyna said. "Does he speak to you of her?"

"Not much."

Nyna finished her paring and now began to grate the coontie into a large wooden bowl. "When he does speak of her, what does he say?"

Nihapu pushed her root along her grater. "His heart does not speak, if that is what you mean. If there is a marriage, it is just a plan. But I do not think that will come to be unless Joog and Cian want it to be."

"Why is that?" Nyna asked, stopping her grating.

"It is a long story. Talli was born to the Turtle Clan of the Jeaga. The Panther Clan wanted all the power. There was a clash between the two caciques. To keep things honest between both clans, Talli was given to a man from the Panther Clan."

"Banabas?" Nyna asked.

"Talli's father gave her to Banabas to seal the peace between the two Jeaga clans. But Talli was in love with Akoma, the next in line to become cacique of the Turtle."

"But she married Banabas anyway."

"Yes. When the Ais and Jeaga were at war, Banabas was killed. The Jeaga found out that the cacique of the Panther Clan had betrayed them. He also died in the war. Akoma and Talli were finally united. I do not think they will want anyone else to suffer as they did. They will not endorse a marriage if it is not from the heart. At least that is my opinion."

Nyna sat back and stretched, putting her hands on the small of her back.

"It aches?" Nihapu asked.

"A little," she said.

"Do as I said, work a little, rest a little."

Nyna got to her feet. "Let me walk a bit," she said. "I will stroll across the village and come right back."

"Do you want me to go with you?" Laira asked.

"I will not get out of sight."

Cetisa looked up and glared at Nihapu.

"I am your sister. Why is it you do not worry about me as much as you do that . . . that outcast?"

Though Nyna was walking away, she was still close enough to hear.

"Quiet your tongue, sister," Nihapu said. "You sound like a bitter old woman."

The women fidgeted, but pretended not to pay attention to the altercation between the sisters.

Cetisa pressed the root hard onto the grater and pushed. "Ouch!" she cried, jerking her hand back and putting a bloody finger in her mouth. "I have cut myself."

"You should not get so agitated over nothing," Nihapu said.

"You call it nothing?" Cetisa asked, her voice rising.

Qitce became increasingly uncomfortable and left, explaining she would return in a few moments. Laira looked at Zinni out of the corner of her eye.

"You know how long I have wanted this child and you show me little concern," Cetisa said. "No attention! But that one," she said, glaring at Nyna, "the outsider, you dote on her."

Nihapu picked up her bowl and carried it to the long trough of water. Cetisa continued to rant.

"You tell her do this, do that, do not do this or it might harm the child, rest awhile. You give me no advice. You do not worry that I overburden myself!"

The tension amongst the women was apparent. Their eyes darted to each other, though they kept their heads down so as not to appear to stare at Cetisa and Nihapu.

Nihapu dumped her root starch into the trough and then turned on her heel to face Cetisa. "I would gladly give you advice if you would accept it, but you resent it. Tell me, sister, what do you want and I will happily do whatever you wish."

"I want you to favor me, not some stranger. Mother favored you. Everyone did. It was always you, you, you."

Nihapu gazed down in the water that had already turned red. The white starch collected in a sediment at the bottom of the trough.

"You are like the coontie," Nihapu said. "There is good inside, despite the poison that makes it so hard to get to. Why do you not let go of the poison? There is good inside you."

Nyna leaned her head back and massaged her shoulder. Digging coontie was grueling work, especially in warm weather.

She heard her name called and turned to the side. It was Guacana.

"What are you doing alone?" he asked.

"I am stretching my legs and back," she said. "I will stay within Nihapu's sight." She continued her walk.

Guacana looked at her belly. It still showed no signs. "Do not expect me to provide for the child," he said.

Nyna stopped in her tracks. "What makes you think I would allow you to do anything for my child?"

"I am the father. It is the custom."

"You are the father only because I say you are."

"Everyone knows," he said.

"No, I am the only one who knows. I say it is you, but is that the truth?"

"Do not expect anything from me."

"You are like the Carib," she said. "They steal the young Taino women and take them as slaves and concubines, and if they bear a child, the Carib kill the baby. They raise none other than their own. I would never have a Carib claim a child of mine."

"I am the father. I am the one who planted his seed in you. Everyone knows how I have had you."

"Ais fathers provide for their offspring. When you do not provide, everyone will realize you just make big talk. I can always say your manpart never would complete the job, though you certainly tried. I will say I let everyone think you were the father so you could save face. I want no more trouble."

Guacana's face reddened and cords in his neck bulged. "But I did it to you in public. Even Etac saw."

"They all saw that you could not complete the act. Remember? Perhaps I keep the secret of who the father really is because he is my secret lover."

Guacana spat on the ground. "It is not over between us."

"The less I say, the more people will doubt you were able to perform. I will act so sorry for you, embarrassed for you, when they ask. The more I deny that you could not rouse your manpart, the sadder a face I will put on. That will convince them all. And of course your own raving about not providing will seal it. Good day," she said and walked away.

Nyna felt victory inside. She had certainly put him in a difficult position. She could hear him grumbling as she passed. This was nearly as good as those many seasons ago when she had held his face in the dirt!

31

Council sat in a large circle around the central hearth. The air was laden with mosquitoes and gnats and deerflies. The gar oil they painted themselves with kept the mosquitoes off, but not the biting deerflies. Etac swatted at one as he watched the cacique approach.

Sweat cascaded down Chogatis's back as he walked into Council. His gait was strained, each step deliberate. He took the cacique's seat, bracing himself with the Talking Stick as he lowered himself. He waited an appropriate few moments before he opened the discussion.

"Still there is no rain," Chogatis said. "It is time we send Joog to the Jeaga again." Chogatis could not hold back the cough that gathered in his chest. Joog glanced at him as if to ask if he was all right. Chogatis returned a faint nod.

"I see no indications of rain," Uxaam said. "Since the big storm the only rain we have had were the small drizzles, but not enough to make a difference. The grapevines wither, and the ground-nesting birds do not favor higher ground."

"I have not forgotten my vision," Joog said. "The grasshoppers and the egret. It is my destiny to be the mediator. I am prepared to go. But," he said, "I only go with everyone's approval. I will not have our goodwill and efforts undermined by a dissident."

The men shifted nervously, knowing Joog spoke directly of Guacana.

"This leads to you, Guacana," Etac said, startling many with his candidness.

Guacana's face twitched as he attempted to smile, only one corner of his mouth lifting. "I do not know why you think it is only I who thinks perhaps we should send two representatives to the Jeaga. Ochopee agrees, and several others."

Chogatis coughed again. He handed the Talking Stick to Etac and left Council.

"And that is another thing we must address," Guacana said. "The cacique has never fully recovered. We must think of who will take his place. Someone aggressive, with the good of the Ais as his passion."

Ochopee fanned the gnats from his face. He picked up a twig and tapped it against the sole of his foot.

"First let us return to the issue we began to discuss," Etac said.

"I do not mean to offend you, Joog, but everyone knows that because of your past, you are sympathetic to the Jeaga," Guacana said. "If another accompanies you, then everyone will be assured the best interest of the Hawk will be served. That would eliminate any doubt."

"I am Ais first," Joog said. "And I am offended."

Ochopee snapped the twig. "As long as we are being forthright," he said, "let me put a question to you. Could you take up a weapon against the Jeaga, against those you knew as a boy, if it came to that?"

Joog did not answer at first. He let the question hang in the air. With the silence, the deerflies seemed more of a nuisance. The men waved them away and swatted those that landed on them.

Joog looked at each man, then said, "Circumstances always govern a man's choices," he said. "There could be circumstances that would provoke me to take up a weapon against you, Guacana. It would be the same for the Jeaga."

Etac arrested a smile that threatened to cover his entire face. "Well said, Joog," he said. "I think that answers Ochopee's question."

"The Jeaga requested Joog and only Joog," Uxaam said. "If we send another with him, we do not abide by their wishes. We ask them the favor, not the other way around."

"I agree," Etac said. "We would appear contemptuous."

"You must all decide," Joog said. "I will not pretend that I represent all the Hawk, if that is not so."

"Guacana, you must put your faith in Joog this time," Etac said. "There has been bad blood between you and Joog for a long time. Put away your personal feelings. If you are Ais in the heart as well as the head, you will see that to get what we want, we must honor the Jeaga's only request. They have imposed no other restriction. If, however, you cannot discard your personal feelings, then perhaps you should reevaluate your loyalty to the Ais. Is it the Ais you serve with this dissidence, or is it yourself?"

Guacana's fists tightened. His lower jaw slid back and forth, grinding his lower teeth against the upper.

Etac stood and drew the line in the dirt.

Two days after Joog had gone, Nyna awoke in the night. Her stomach cramped, just as if her moon cycle had come. Half-awake, she rubbed her belly and fell back asleep. The dreams came. She was delivering the child. Raven sat in the doorway as Nihapu urged her to push. Why didn't Raven go away? The pains were sharp and made her cry out. Her hands slid down the pole in the birthing hut as Nihapu kept telling her to push. But she could push no more. The pains were too awful. Her hands slowly slipped from the pole, and Nyna collapsed on the floor. She saw Raven take a last look at her and fly away. Nihapu was crying, saying the baby was dead.

Nyna whimpered and awoke long enough to realize it

was only a bad dream. She drifted back into a restless sleep. But just as the sun rose, the cramping awakened her again. This time she sat straight up on her mat. "The baby," she whispered.

She had only missed three moon cycles; there was no way it was time for the child to be born. Nyna swiped her hand between her legs to feel for blood, then held it up in the sunlight. Relieved there was no red stain, she got to her feet. She had to tell Nihapu. Nihapu would know what to do. Nihapu would help.

At Nihapu's side she bent quietly, not wanting to wake Chogatis. Nihapu's head rested on Chogatis's shoulder and his arm was wrapped around her. For an instant Nyna wondered if she would ever sleep so contentedly with any man.

Nyna whispered, "Niha—"

Suddenly she backed away. No, she thought. It was Buhgo she needed. He knew about the medicine she had taken. He would be the one who would know what to do.

Silently Nyna crept out of the lodge into the dawn. She slipped across the village, praying no one saw her. Outside Buhgo's hut, she called softly to him.

"Buhgo, wake up."

She waited, her gaze flying over the village, watching for anyone to come out of his hut.

"Buhgo!" she said louder. There was still no response. Nyna ducked inside the hut. Buhgo rested peacefully on his mat. She shook his shoulder.

"Wake up," she said.

Buhgo opened his eyes. "Nyna?"

"Wait a few moments and meet me where I used to hide my weapons . . . near the cenote. It is important."

Buhgo propped up on his elbows and nodded that he would do as she said.

Nyna hurried around the perimeter of the village. The sun was rising quickly, and so would the villagers. She steered deeper in the woods behind Guacana's hut.

A length of vine twisted around her ankle and tore at
it. Nyna reached down and pulled it off, leaving a tiny
burning slice in the skin. The vine had tangled the other
foot as well. She lifted her foot and shook it. When that
didn't work, she backed up to put tension on the vine.
She stumbled over a rotten fallen log. The dry old wood
collapsed under her, and she thudded to the ground.

Boat-tailed grackles roosted in a nearby tree. Startled
by her fall, they simultaneously burst into the air like
thick black smoke. Their rolling cries and flurry of wings
rang through the village.

Nyna bit down on her bottom lip. She sat very quietly
a moment, then scrambled to her feet and ran on toward
the cenote as fast as she could. Was someone following
her? Had the birds attracted someone's attention?

Winded, Nyna arrived at the designated place. She
shouldn't have run so hard, she thought to herself as
she paced, walking off the labored breathing and the
heated muscles.

She heard something, stopped, and cocked her head.
Buhgo was coming. She could hear the twigs snap and
grass crackle under his feet.

"Here," she called.

In an instant, Guacana's sick grinning face appeared.
"You are out here alone," he said. "No escort."

"You followed me," Nyna said. "Leave me alone."

"You scared the birds," he said. "Mistake."

"My escort is on the way." Her breath still came in
rapid spurts.

Guacana stepped toward her. "No one is coming." He
eased closer.

"Yes, Buhgo is coming."

Guacana laughed. "I am afraid," he chortled. He extended his arm and Nyna stepped back.

"The baby," she said softly. He could not do this now.
If the baby was in trouble, Guacana might make it worse.

"Get away from me," she said. "You cannot do this!" she said. "Not this time!"

A liquid smile oozed over his face. "You were right. I like it better when you resist." He grabbed her wrist.

Nyna yanked her arm, but he held fast. "That's it," he said. He gripped her other arm and wrenched it behind her, spinning her back to him. Nyna whimpered with the pain.

She kicked behind her, barely missing his shin.

"Yes, that's the way," he said, pushing down on her head so she was made to bend over. He tore at her skirt, ripping it off her.

He shoved her, and Nyna fell to the ground. Guacana flipped her over.

"This time you will watch my face and see what great pleasure there is in this for me," he said.

He kept one arm across her chest as he climbed on her, while the other hand unleashed his breechclout. Nyna squirmed beneath him, her legs kicking at the air. Her fists pounded his back.

"No!" she yelped. "Get off!"

Her cries only spurred him on. She felt his entry.

"Ah, yes," he sighed. "You are so warm inside."

Nyna thrashed, and Guacana grinned. He began to pump. Nyna's hands searched the ground for something, anything she could hit or stab him with. Her fingers shuffled across the earth, under the brush.

Her ax! Her first weapon! She had forgotten all about it. She clutched the short handle and carefully pulled it out of the brush. She glanced at Guacana's face. It made her feel sick.

Closing her eyes, Nyna swung with all her might, landing the shell ax blade on Guacana's head. Instantly he went limp.

His blood felt slick as it slid onto her shoulder. She dropped the ax, and with both hands pushed his shoulders up and off her. She finally pushed the weight of his lower half off and she wiggled from under. Lying next to Guacana, Nyna turned her head to see that his cheek rested in the dirt and his eyes were closed.

She lay there trembling. Had she killed him? Was he breathing?

Nyna's hands held her abdomen as she cried.

The shadow that came over her made her look up.

32

Buhgo knelt next to Guacana. "I think he is dead," he said.

Nyna sat up. "I came to you this morning because I was afraid there was something wrong with the baby, maybe because of the medicine I took. Guacana followed me here, and when he tried to . . . I was afraid it would hurt the baby. What am I going to do? I did not mean to kill him, just get him off me."

Buhgo pressed his forehead with the fingers of his right hand. He touched the gaping wound in Guacana's scalp, then wiped his hand in the dirt.

Suddenly Guacana rattled a low breath.

"He is alive!" Nyna said.

Buhgo stood and lifted Guacana's feet. "I will drag him to the cenote and throw him in."

"No," Nyna said. "You cannot do that. He will drown."

Buhgo tugged on Guacana. Nyna got to her feet. She put a hand on Buhgo's shoulder. "You cannot do this," she said.

"What else can you think of?" Buhgo asked. "If he disappears, then there will be no questions put to you. If he lives, then what? Do we just leave him here, let someone find him? What do you think will happen then? Use your head, Nyna."

"Then I am no better than the Carib. No, I will have to tell what I have done and face the consequences."

"Joog is not here and Chogatis is weak. There will not be much support for you in Council."

"Do you think he will recover?" Nyna asked.

Buhgo squatted next to Guacana again. He separated the bloody hair to see the actual wound, wiping away some of the blood with leaves and moss. "I think you have cracked his skull. I see a line, like a break. That is not good."

Nyna helped Buhgo heft Guacana's flaccid body over his shoulder. He did not look so intimidating now, his hair soaked in blood, his arms and head dangling down Buhgo's back. The thrill she held on to for so long from when she had held his face in the dirt, suddenly dissipated.

As they entered the village, the people turned to stare.

Nyna lowered her head and whispered what she had been thinking along the way. "I have decided not to go to Chogatis," she said. "He is weak and this would be so burdensome to him. He rests most of the day in his lodge. He may never know. I will go to Etac. He will take it to Council, and I know he will be fair."

"I agree," Buhgo said.

Ochopee accosted them. "What has happened to Guacana?" he asked.

"Go for Nihapu, but do not disturb the cacique," Buhgo said. "Hurry."

Ochopee turned and sprinted away.

Inside Guacana's lodge, Buhgo and Nyna gently maneuvered Guacana onto his mat.

"Roll up that hide and put it under his head," Buhgo said.

As Nyna rolled the hide, she heard a crowd gathering outside. "I can only tell the truth," she said.

"As soon as Nihapu gets here, I will go with you to talk to Etac."

"He may already know something is wrong," Nyna said. "Listen how they wait outside already."

Nihapu came through the doorway, followed by Ochopee.

"If you want to be helpful," Buhgo said to Ochopee, "go for Etac and have him wait for us in his lodge. Nyna and I will be there momentarily."

"How is he?" Ochopee asked.

"I do not know yet. See if someone has called for Uxaam."

"How did this happen?" Ochopee asked.

"There is no time now. Deliver my message to Etac. I will explain later."

Ochopee disappeared from the lodge.

Nihapu put her ear to Guacana's chest and listened. In a moment she sat up. "His heart is rapid and his breathing shallow. Not good signs."

"I did it," Nyna said. "He came at me again, and I hit him in the head with an ax. He would have hurt the baby."

"Ax?" Nihapu said.

"I had left it hidden under the brush a long time ago. It was the first weapon I made. I forgot about it until today."

"Nyna and I are going to Etac," Buhgo said.

They pushed through the crowd, avoiding questions. "What will they do to me?" Nyna asked. Buhgo did not answer.

Etac waited outside his lodge. Ochopee stood at his side.

"Only Etac," Buhgo said, ushering Nyna into Etac's lodge. The War Chief followed, leaving Ochopee outside.

The three sat, Nyna's heart thumping crazily in her chest.

"There has been an accident," Buhgo began.

Nyna sat alone in front of Chogatis's lodge. The cacique rested peacefully inside, and she did not want to disturb him. It would be better if he did not find out about this. He would be too distraught.

Nyna sipped some tea that was supposed to soothe her, but as she watched the men gather for Council, the brew lost its potency.

She noticed the cramping in her belly had stopped. She touched the upper swell of her left breast. The tenderness had diminished.

Could the baby be dead? Had Guacana's assault ended the pregnancy, tenuous as it was?

Nyna put down the ladle of tea and raked her fingers through her hair. Why would the spirits bother to give her this child, make her love it beyond anything she had ever loved, then take it from her? What had she done to displease them so?

Nyna put her hands over her face and cried into them.

Etac studied the faces of the men as they entered Council. Rumors and speculations had spread through the village like fire through dry muck.

Usually the men entered Council in silence, as these meetings were treated with great respect. Today they whispered to one another, even as they sat.

"We are gathered now because there has been an unfortunate accident," Etac said. He went on to tell them the details, just as Buhgo and Nyna had related them to him. When he finished, a stunned hush fell over them.

Finally Ochopee spoke. "There is no question what we must do. We have tolerated this woman long enough. Now she has caused grave harm to one of us. Her life, to pay for what she has done."

A rapid barrage of chatter shot through the men.

"If one of you killed another Hawk, that would be the consequence," Ochopee said.

"But Guacana is not dead," Etac said.

"But he might die. Is that not so, Buhgo?" Ochopee asked.

"It is possible," Buhgo said. "But she was responding in self-defense. Guacana attacked her. We all know how he has abused her time after time, and we have allowed it!"

"Guacana did not intend to kill her. There is no self-defense," Ochopee said. "She did not protect herself from death."

The men all began to talk at the same time, most agreeing with Ochopee. They were livid that this outsider had taken down one of their own.

A man in the back stood up. "I am with Ochopee. She does not belong with us and has caused nothing but misfortune. We have put up with it, permitted excuses to be made. Now is the time for it to stop."

Etac raised the Talking Stick and the men settled down.

Buhgo asked to speak again. "She was acting to protect herself and her unborn child. Nyna feared she might be losing the baby. That is why I was to meet her near the cenote. She feared Guacana's attack would harm or even kill the child."

Uxaam asked to speak. "Why did she not come to me? And why meet you in secret?"

"Right," Ochopee bellowed, standing again. "She broke the laws, wandered about freely with no escort."

"Quiet," Etac said.

Ochopee sat down.

"When Nyna first learned she carried Guacana's child, she did not want it. Think of how it was conceived! She made a medicine and attempted to destroy the child, but then had a change of heart. She could kill no baby and this child was part of her and her people. Nyna was afraid she had done harm. Taska was a constant reminder of what she might have done. She came to me this morning, frightened that something was wrong."

* * *

Chogatis emerged from his lodge. "Why are you crying?" he asked Nyna.

She wiped her face and straightened. "I am moody, I suppose. They say carrying a child does that to a woman."

Chogatis caught a glimpse of the central hearth. "Council gathers?"

Nyna did not answer. "Has something happened? Is that why you weep?" he asked.

Nyna's throat squeezed painfully as she held back more tears.

Chogatis hobbled across the plaza to the gathering of men.

Etac stood with respect. "Cacique," he said, handing Chogatis the Talking Stick.

Ochopee seized the moment to tell Chogatis what had happened. "She must pay with her life," he said.

"Banishment," Chogatis said, his voice raspy and low. "The spirits brought her here. Send her away. If the spirits want her, they will reclaim her."

"We abide by Ais laws, Ais spirits. Do we have the right to take her life . . . or should we give her back to the spirits that brought her here?" Etac asked.

"If we offend the Taino spirits, they may be vengeful," Chogatis said. "And the child, though not born, is Ais. If we take Nyna's life, we also take the soul of one of us. I say we leave it to the spirits to decide. Banish her. Send her out alone. If she is to live, the spirits will see to it. If she is to die, they will see to that also."

"I fear the baby is dead," Nyna told Buhgo as he helped her pack a basket she could carry on her back. "If the child is dead, let them have me. Drive a stick through my already dead heart."

"You must not think that way," Buhgo said.

"I cannot believe you would be asked to suffer any more," Chotgatis said. "There are no spirits that cruel."

Nyna embraced Nihapu. "I will remember you. You were my mother when I had none. And, Chogatis, you were my father," she said, palming his cheek.

Nihapu started to cry.

Nyna turned away, choking on her struggle not to cry. She forbade the tears, determined she would leave in dignity. There was time for crying later. Now she had to be strong, especially for Chogatis.

"I will walk you to the water," Buhgo said. "Follow the shore. It will keep you from wandering in circles."

"Tell Joog that I will miss him," Nyna said. She slid the bracelet off her wrist and handed it to Buhgo. "Give this to him so he will remember me," she said.

"Can I tell him more?" Buhgo asked.

Nyna shook her head.

Buhgo carried her hand basket and walked alongside her on the path to the beach.

"I do hope Guacana lives," Nyna said. "I hated him, maybe I still do. I even thought I wished him dead. I do not like that about myself. Such thoughts make me closer to the Carib than I like."

Atop the dune, Nyna gazed across the sea. "I have to survive to go home one day," she said. "But I am so afraid."

"You are not like other women," Buhgo said. "You have practiced with weapons and making tools. Other women would surely perish alone in the wilderness. You are strong, in your head and in your body."

"I have never really hunted, and I am not nearly as good with any of the tools and weapons as the men." Nyna took her basket from him. "If the baby is dead, nothing will matter anyway," she said.

Buhgo wrapped his arms around her, his eyes filling with tears. "You see," he said. "I cry like a woman." Buhgo took a deep breath and composed himself. "Go north," he said. "The Jeaga are to the south, and as the

Ais and Jeaga's futures are uncertain, you would not want to be caught in the crossfire by accident.''

Nyna pulled away, and they stared at each other for a moment. Then she turned her back and began her trek up the beach.

As the day wore on, the sand grew uncomfortably hot under her feet, and the basket on her back heavier. She stopped a moment and adjusted the basket. She decided to walk in the shallow water.

Near dusk she moved inland for the night. She realized it was too late to construct any kind of shelter, and she was too tired anyway.

Nyna picked some cocoplums as she passed, then found a spot she liked inside a cluster of sabal palms and oaks. As she watched the moon rise, she ate the cocoplums and a piece of coontie bread from her basket. She hung her water pouch from a low branch after taking a gulp. First thing in the morning she would look for a fresh water source.

As darkness fell, Nyna felt more and more vulnerable. The cries of the night-feeding animals sounded eerie and much different than they did when she was in the safety of the village and the lodge. She wished she had thought about starting a fire. Tomorrow she would be more prepared for nightfall.

Nyna curled under the sprinkling of starlight. With one hand she clutched her medicine bag that held Uxaam's drawing of her village. The other hand rested on her abdomen. She had to stay focused on those two things for strength. If not for them, she was willing to lie down tonight and wait for the spirits to come for her.

Void of dreams she slept through the night.

Daylight shone through her lids as if they were not even covering her eyes. Nyna squinted and peered at the sky through the branches and broad palm leaves. She lay on her back for a while, listening to the birds and the surf in the background.

She noticed something different in the air. It was not a smell she could describe, but she knew what it was. Nyna sat up, listening to the rustling trees. She moved to a clearing for a better view of the sky. A gathering of bloated dark clouds festered to the east and appeared to be moving in her direction. The air temperature dropped. It was going to rain!

Nyna quickly cut a few cabbage palm leaves and covered her baskets. She retrieved her water pouch and opened its neck.

The rain began with a drizzle and a distant rumble of thunder. A closer strike of lightning cracked the sky and generous large drops of rain splashed on the thirsty soil. Nyna watched where the water collected and spouted off the leaves of the trees. She held the neck of her water pouch open and let the water spill down the leaf channel and into the container, replenishing some of what she had used.

She closed her eyes, opened her mouth and lifted her face to the downpour. No water on earth tasted as sweet and clean and refreshing as rainwater. Nyna raised her free hand so her arm extended straight out from the shoulder.

Delicious, delicious rain!

Ochopee danced in the downpour, singing and waving his arms. Others joined him in the merriment.

"Rain!" he sang over and over.

Suddenly he stopped. "You see!" he said, jubilant in his revelation. "The woman from the sun is gone, and the rains return. The spirits reward us!"

The men whooped, their feet tamping down wet grass and splashing in the mud.

Chogatis sat outside his lodge. He did not have the strength to join the spontaneous celebration. He lifted his eyes to the clouds. His face drenched, he rubbed it with his hands. Nihapu jogged across the plaza to her husband. She stopped in front of him and danced, swaying, turning, waving her arms so gracefully.

"Rain, husband. Rain," she said, her voice quaking.

Chogatis nodded. "Do you hear what they say?"

Nihapu stopped her dancing and looked back. Her face took on a somber expression. "What do they say?"

Chogatis took her hand in his. "They say it rains because we have sent Nyna away."

Nihapu sunk to the ground next to Chogatis. She bowed her head and picked at her fingernails. "I do not think—"

"Of course not," Chogatis said. "It is simply the return of the rains, the Ais good fortune."

Though the storm ended quickly, the people continued to celebrate into the night. The men covered themselves in mud and danced in a circle around the central hearth. The women prepared food and set it all in the center of the village. Uxaam said prayers of thanks and made an offering of pine. He boiled down the fruit of the wax myrtle, coated a length of palm fiber in it, then set the fiber in the wax as a wick. Uxaam lit the wick and the myrtle candle glowed. The shaman breathed in the candle scent as it floated in the smoke.

Exhausted by all the excitement, the people slept hard through the night. In the morning, the dew that had collected from the humid air left everything and everyone damp.

The next day the people of the Hawk Clan returned to normal chores. They kept an eye on the sky, hoping another storm would brew during the day, but the sky remained crisp and clear.

In the late afternoon, Buhgo saw Joog enter the village. He stopped him.

"I am saddened that I must bear bad news," Buhgo said.

"What is it?" Joog's face slackened, and his brows dipped.

"Nyna is gone."

Joog cocked his head. "I do not understand," he said. "How can she be gone?"

"Guacana attacked her again, and fearing it might hurt the baby, she fought back. She struck him in the head with an ax. I do not know if he will recover. Council wanted to have her pay with her life, but Chogatis persuaded them to banish her."

Joog crouched and picked up a stone, turning it in his hand. "I was not here to help her," he said. "Where did she go? I will go after her."

"She cannot come back here. Ochopee will work the people into a frenzy, and surely they will have her impaled on a lance. If you brought her back, you would guarantee her death."

Joog pitched the stone. "I cannot believe this happened."

Buhgo squatted in front of him. "She wanted you to have this," he said, giving Joog the bracelet. "I told her to go north," he said.

As quickly as the storm had come, it dissipated. Nyna could almost hear the earth cry out for more, sobbing from the tease of being nourished.

She collected a few more drops of rain that trickled from the leaf. She wiped her face with the crook of her forearm, clearing the tiny shining droplets that her lashes had harvested.

This was not enough rain to end the drought, but perhaps it was a sign that the dry spell was coming to an end.

Nyna attached the water pouch to her waist, strapped one basket to her back and carried the other in her hand. She did not want to venture too far from the sea, as it was an excellent food resource. But she had to find drinking water, and that would be her task for the day. She watched for soft earth below her feet, which might indicate a spring beneath, and she listened for frogs and the sound of water birds.

Her bare feet tramped through the forest as she kept the sound of the ocean at her right shoulder. At midday, she rested in the shade. She put a thin strip of smoke-dried venison between her teeth and tore at it. She bit free a small tasty piece. When she settled, she would store food and cook, but not yet. As she propped against a tree, her eyes grew heavy. She rested her chin on her chest and dozed off.

She could not have slept long, she thought, but the short nap refreshed her. Nyna picked up her belongings and wandered on. Later in the afternoon, she noticed a change in the landscape ahead and to her left. There she saw a sprinkling of cypress and denser grass.

Water, she thought. As she got closer she was sure there was water ahead. Willows and cattails formed a circle, enclosing the sinkhole.

Nyna put down her baskets and pushed her way through the thick broad-bladed brush. Neatly laced in by all the cattails, rushes, and willows, sat a beautiful spring-fed sinkhole. Nyna stood at its edge and peered through the clear water. Caverns lay below, and she could see the current flow swiftly out of one. Fish, plump and healthy, more than she could count, swam freely through the light blue-green water.

She scooped a handful of water and brought it to her mouth. Water as sparkling and quenching as that of the Ais cenote.

Across the sinkhole the water spilled into a meandering stream that flowed east.

This was the place she would stay. Here she would live, give birth to her child, and when able, she would fashion a large seagoing dugout that would carry her on her journey in search of her home.

Nyna explored the cenote and the surrounding area.

Deciding on the best location, she cleared an area that would become the floor of her hut.

With her knife she cut bundles of willow and hauled them to the spot she had cleared. Nyna dragged the heel of her foot as she walked in a circle, leaving a gouge in the dirt. With the circle complete, she stepped back and observed. On this line in the dirt she would plant the framework of her house.

She took four of the largest willow branches and trimmed them to the same size. Then in each of the four directions she dug deep narrow holes. When the holes were finished, Nyna rested, drinking from her water pouch. Yes, she thought, here she would have everything she needed. She could hear the squawk of seagulls, so she was still close to the sea.

Nyna drove the larger ends of the willow branches deep into the holes and then covered them, tamping the dirt firmly around them. She bent all four branches to the middle and lashed them with cordage from a spool Chogatis had put in her basket. This would serve as the basic framework for her domed hut.

Next to one of the original branches, Nyna planted another stick half a hand away. She bent it away from the original pole she had planted it next to and lashed it to the second original pole. She crisscrossed another branch in the other direction, working back and forth down to the ground with shorter and shorter arches, finally closing in one quarter of the hut.

On one side she left a small opening. By the time she was done with the framework, twilight rapidly approached. She decided to stop work on the hut and start a fire.

The bow drill Joog had helped her make a long time ago sat straight up in the basket she had carried on her back. Cattail fluff, dried grasses, and other plant fuzz made good tinder. She also collected wood that had dry rotted. She rubbed it into a powder and added that to her tinder.

Nyna removed the bow drill and fireboard. She set the tinder beside the notch and rested the drill in the cavity in the fireboard. She looped the bowstring around the drill, put her left foot on the board, and began the sawing motion. When the notch began to smoke, Nyna smiled and sawed even faster until the hot black powder spilled out onto the small pile of tinder. When the spark ignited the tinder, Nyna gently blew. But as easily as she had forced her breath over the tinder, it was too strong, and the tiny glow died.

Nyna sawed the drill again, and this time when it was time to fan the ember into flame, she was even more careful.

Suddenly the tinder burst into a little flame. Slowly, Nyna pulled away the fireboard and, pinch by pinch, fed the weak fire. At last she had a fire big enough to add twigs to, and then larger pieces of wood.

Nyna sat on her heels, proud of her accomplishment. She added some spokes of heavier wood to the fire so during the night she could push them in and keep the fire glowing. That would ward off predators.

Beside the cenote she cut cattail blades, then laid them on the floor of her unfinished hut. They would be her bed for the night. Tomorrow she would weave a mat.

Her stomach growled. If she were going to cook any food, she best find something to eat.

Nyna unpacked her basket and took out the last piece of coontie bread and venison. She stared at the meat and decided to keep it. She would powder it and mix it with rendered fat and berries to make a nutritious cake she could save.

She did find some red mulberry and brewed a tea. Mother Earth provided plenty. She would not starve as long as she could harvest, fish, trap, and hunt.

Nyna touched her belly and wondered if the child was still inside her.

Quickly, she put the thought aside, took the small buckskin shawl from her basket and pitched it over the dome of her hut as a temporary roof. Tomorrow she would attach thatch, and if she had time, would build a trap for turtles and weave a basket to trap fish. There was so much to do, she thought.

As the sun sank below the trees, Nyna yawned. The moon was already in the sky, even though it was too light for the stars to twinkle.

She notched her stick, crawled into her open-frame hut and onto her cattail bed, closed her eyes and slept. During the night she rose twice to nurture the fire.

For many days she worked on completing her hut, making traps, gathering wood for her fire, drying fruits, and making baskets. She took several trips to the beach, bringing back whelks, conchs, shells, small shellfish, and crabs. She smoked them all and feasted on them for several days. As fast as she could make a basket she filled it with fresh or drying foodstuffs. She hunted rabbit with the bola, roasted part of it for a fresh meal, smoked some to keep longer, and prepared the pelt.

By the turning of another moon, she had become proficient at catching turtles with a trap she baited with fish or pieces of meat left from her meal. She captured snake with a noose at the end of a long stick, frogs with gigs, raccoons and other small game with deadfalls. She stayed clear of alligators and bears. She wove a basket that trapped fish and she harvested freshwater mussels.

Nyna had acquired nearly everything she needed, but every day her heart ached from loneliness. One afternoon, she sat on the beach thinking. She had to learn to hunt larger prey, like deer, to provide hides. She would need them for the baby and when the weather turned cool. And after the baby came, she would make a canoe from the giant cypress tree she had picked out. She decided that if she started now, doing only small amounts of work each day, she would have downed the tree by the time the baby came.

One afternoon, as she walked the beach she was staring at the sky, imagining herself and her child in the dugout arriving on a Taino beach. She could hear her people's voices ringing out in welcome.

Suddenly she realized the voices were not in her head. Coming from the north was a large dugout. She strained to see, but could not make out the occupants.

33

Quickly she climbed behind a dune and lay on her belly, peering over the crest of the sand hill.

The dugout came closer, paralleling the shore. Nyna looked behind her to see if smoke from her fire curled into the air, but she could not tell for all the trees, but they would be able to see from the water. Nyna watched, her breath catching in her chest as one of the men in the dugout yelled something. He was too far to make out the words, but even so, the language seemed unfamiliar.

Who were these men? she wondered. Nyna scampered farther from the dune and climbed a tree. From there she could see more clearly. Strangers indeed!

She stayed perched in the tree, breathing hard until the piragua passed. She watched until it faded in the distance. Maybe they were Jororo or Mayaca. Or perhaps they were people from the south who had ventured north and now returned home. She was not sure who they were, but she did realize she was not as safe as she thought.

Nyna scurried back to her camp. As she looked about, she realized that if anyone came ashore and wandered this way, they would realize this was someone's permanent camp. They would search for the occupant. She could always destroy the hut and build a lean-to that could be scattered quickly. And she could keep fewer supplies on hand so she could hide them in the brush.

But that was not going to be reasonable when the baby came.

Nyna lay back on the hard ground and put one hand beneath her head. As soon as she and the baby were able, they would have to travel and keep on the move. Her eyes teared as she thought about never seeing Joog again.

Suddenly Nyna reached for her round belly. She closed her eyes and smiled as she understood the fluttering beneath her hand. The baby moved inside her.

As days passed, the season eventually changed. The chill in the air made Taska shiver. He pulled his wrap around his shoulders.

Uxaam fanned the small fire in the center of the raised ceremonial platform. He withdrew a pinch of powder from a bowl and flicked it into the fire. Sparks flew out in a brilliant halo like a swarm of fireflies.

"Hear me, sacred ones. Here is the boy, Taska, who is to become a man. See the infirmity you have bestowed upon him so that he could devote all his time to you. And because of this infirmity, he cannot participate in the traditional vision quest. But he can have a vision. He calls upon you to lead him down the sacred path."

Uxaam tossed another dash of powder in the fire. "He has made himself clean with the smudge of the pine, and he has cleansed his body through fasting. He anxiously awaits you."

Uxaam began a trilling chant, summoning all the mysterious forces. The air vibrated with his song. So engaging was the shaman's chant that the birds and other creatures stopped to listen. The potency of his words, the rhythm and pitch of the melody, reached out with long fingers stroking the air, strumming it like a musical instrument. The stimulated air gave birth to a gusting wind that howled through the trees.

The villagers, stunned by the magic of the shaman,

stopped whatever they were doing. Something truly spiritual and powerful was taking place. They looked up onto the covered platform where Taska and Uxaam sat. Clouds, dark as soot, rolled in from the west, and lightning spiderwebbed across the sky.

The villagers gathered closer to the platform. This was not just a boy on a vision quest—this was the making of a shaman, a holy man, one who communicated with the spirits.

They stood rooted in awe as the earth responded to the gathering power. The icy wind crashed through the trees, lifting old leaves and twigs from the ground, chilling even the deepest fiber in the people.

Taska closed his eyes and checked his breathing. As he felt the air fill his lungs, he thought of his feet. Concentrating, he made all the energy stored in his feet flow out. Gradually, he moved up his body, releasing the tension until he was in a state of complete relaxation.

A faint mist wafted into his head, but Taska's mind was stubborn, and thoughts kept flitting through it. He told himself to let go, to give up control so the spirits could take over. Finally the sounds around him vanished, and a gray haze formed. So great and powerful were the spirits that his mind had to become an empty vessel. There would not be room for both Taska and the spirits.

A loud whooshing began, like wind blowing directly in his ear, only it was inside his head. He felt the pressure grow in his head as the spirits filled it. His skin prickled on the back of his neck. Taska's eyes burned right through his closed lids. Swirling about him were shapes, like wisps of clouds or white smoke. In through his nose, his ears, they swooped, curling around him, wrapping around him.

The face of a giant black ant appeared through the whirlpool of murky forms.

The ant put Uxaam's chant directly into Taska's head. Suddenly he understood the ancient words. The forgot-

ten language of shamans came easily to him as if he
had always known it, and Taska began to chant along
with Uxaam.

The black clouds burst open with a peal of thunder,
and wind-driven rain doused the village.

So stricken with the event taking place on the shaman's platform, the people did not seek cover. They shivered in the cold, shielding their eyes from the stinging
rain, and hovering close to the platform.

The rain pounded and splattered on the ground,
quickly forming rivulets and puddles. Zinni moved
through the slush, coming closer to the platform. Tears
streamed down her rain-soaked face. Taska was not only
a man, but a man of the spirits. It was so much more
than she had ever hoped for her son.

Cetisa held her swollen belly as she stood entranced.
The child inside kicked and rolled. He, too, must feel
the power, she thought. A slight tightening across her
back made her hand leave her abdomen and press the
small of her back. She had watched the moon. The child
could be born at any time.

Cetisa backed out of the rain and into her hut. Perhaps
this pain in her back was the beginning. She cursed the
rain and the extraordinary event that was taking place
with Uxaam and Taska. All that would take away from
the birth of her child.

Nyna wrung out the hide blanket. Almost everything
was soaked from the days of heavy rain. Only a few
articles had been spared the drenching. There would be
peace for the Ais, she thought. Joog would be pleased.

She wondered if the proposed marriage between him
and the Jeaga woman had taken place. She glanced at
her stick. There were nine big notches. A shudder of
trepidation ran down her spine. She would give birth to
this child alone.

Nyna checked the small blanket she had made from

rabbit furs. It was dry and soft. She pressed it to her cheek. It would not be long before this blanket enfolded a baby. In the beginning she thought the baby would die, that it would not grow. How wrong she had been. Her belly had swelled to unbelievable proportions, and the child kicked so furiously that many times she was unable to sleep.

Nyna let one finger touch the neatly folded stack of hide rags she would wrap the baby in. She was as ready as she could be, except for one thing.

Nyna grabbed her lance and atlatl. Once the baby came, she would not be able to hunt as readily. Babies needed attention every moment. She had already sewn a large hide sling for the baby that she could carry it at her side or on her back. With this she could take the child with her to check traps and the like. But little ones could not go on a hunt. Babies gurgled and cried. The creature Nyna hunted today would have to last awhile.

A stand of oaks nearby was a favorite feeding place for deer. Unable to carry her kills over her shoulders as stronger and larger men did, Nyna had built a travois, much like the one Buhgo had built to transport Taska. When she killed deer, she hauled them onto the travois and then dragged them home.

Pulling the travois behind her, Nyna trekked to the oak stand. She put the litter down and crept through the brush. It did not take long to spot a young white-tail buck. Its short tawny coat would make a good blanket or winter cape.

Nyna circled to make sure the wind came at her face and away from her quarry. This would ensure her scent was not carried to his nose. The deer would be especially nervous today because of the wind. With the wind blowing, its hearing would be impaired. Leaves and branches rattled, and debris blew across the ground, covering other sounds. A deer's hearing was acute, able to discern the nonthreatening movement of a raccoon or opossum, or the lighting of a bird in a tree from the cautious padded footfall of a panther. But with the wind blowing, the deer grew apprehensive because his ability to interpret threatening from nonthreatening noises became diminished. The deer could not go about his routine calmly. He was on alert. Though the deer was skittish, the wind favored the hunter, obscuring his sounds.

Nyna's experience had shown her that deer did not gather to drink where water rushed in the stream, but rather where it bubbled along almost silently. They depended too much on their hearing to be the first to alert them to danger. If any other sense joined in so that the deer saw movement or detected an unfriendly scent, the animal bolted.

Nyna waited for the deer to lower its head and feed. When it did so, she stepped from behind a tree. One small movement now and she could spook the deer. She stood perfectly still. The deer's head jerked up and he sniffed the air, testing for smells. When he looked away and continued his feeding, she slowly cocked her arm, ready to throw the lance with the atlatl.

She did not enjoy hunting, especially deer. She avoided looking at deers' eyes, as they appeared so childlike. But she needed to stock up on smoked meat and the mixed berry, fat, and meat cakes that would last for a long time. She needed the sinew, the antlers, the hide, even the shoulder bone that would make a good scraper. Time was running out before the baby came.

Sure the deer was not aware of her, she hurled the lance, sending it flying to her target.

The deer instantly slumped to the ground when the fire-hardened point of the wood lance penetrated it. Nyna thanked the *zemis* for such a clean kill. The last time she hunted deer, she had brought the animal down, but had not killed it right away. When she approached, she saw the deer pathetically watching her, the lance moving with every ragged breath, its eyes seeming to ask why. Nyna had pulled out the lance and cried as she plunged it into the deer's chest. The animal had quivered, its legs jerking, eyes wide. Finally the creature died. She had not hunted deer since.

Mostly she had lived off fish from the sea and the cenote, turtles, snakes, and shellfish, berries, and plants. Her traps provided her with many small animals, but she avoided hunting as much as she could.

Nyna took the deer home on the travois. She tied its back hooves together and hoisted the carcass over a low limb. The rest of the day she spent skinning and butchering her kill.

Just after dark, she feasted on a piece of meat she had skewered and cooked over her open fire. Though she hated the hunting, she did like the flavor of succulent deer meat.

Before going inside her hut to sleep, she checked the strips of meat that hung on grates above the smoke pit. She added more slow-burning green wood so it would continue to smoke through the night.

The processing of one deer was an enormous amount of work for one person. She looked about, pleased with all she had accomplished today. She was tired and her body ached. Nyna embraced her large belly, then ducked into her hut to sleep.

In the middle of the night, a twinge in her lower abdomen awakened her. Her eyes flew open and she wondered what that sharp pain had been. She lay still, waiting to feel it again. After a while, when the pain did not return, she turned to her other side. She curled up, one hand under her cheek, and drifted off to sleep again.

Later, another pain awakened her. This one was not as sharp, but it lasted longer and covered a larger part of her belly. She touched her tight abdomen. Nyna rolled to her back and caressed her belly with her fingertips. She felt a pressure low inside her abdomen, almost as if she needed to empty her bladder. The pressure grew steadily until there was a pain associated with it. Nyna held her breath and bit down on her bottom lip. But then the tightness and pressure let up, and the pain subsided. She blew out a long breath.

Through her doorway, Nyna saw the darkness lifting, giving way to the sunrise. So this would be the day her child would come.

Nyna got up and brewed some warm willow bark and mulberry tea. She could see her breath in the air, and the cold polished her cheeks. She sipped on the tea, cupping the ladle close to her for additional warmth.

Suddenly she panicked. A birthing pole! She had not thought of that! How could she have forgotten? As the time had gotten closer, not a day had gone by she had not checked her supplies and gone over the things she would need when the baby came. How could she have never given a thought to the birthing pole?

It was not long before another pain gripped her. Her head dropped to her chin and her hands squeezed the ladle of tea. When it passed, she took a deep breath of relief.

Nyna unwrapped the *zemi* figurine she had made when she first learned she carried this child. Crude and falling apart, she propped it in front of her.

A single tear fell from her left eye as she wished her mother were here to hold her hand. Nyna knew there would be blood and water, so she spread a large deer hide on the ground inside the hut. She would deliver the baby on the blanket, wrap the afterbirth in it, and dispose of it.

By late afternoon, the pains came regularly and were much stronger. She lay on her side, her body drenched in sweat, her hand clutching the edge of the blanket.

She focused on the dying fire outside her doorway. Suddenly a black shadow settled in the doorway.

A raven!

34

"No," Nyna screamed, remembering her nightmares.

The raven looked squarely at her, then opened its wings and flew away.

Another clamping pain wrapped around her, and Nyna struggled to stifle her cries. As the contraction declined, she retched, vomiting up a small amount of fluid. She had eaten nothing all day, only the tea in the morning. Nyna writhed and sobbed as another pain encircled her, wracking her body as it radiated across her back and spread around her.

By evening, she did not have enough strength to cry any longer. The pains swept over her like crashing waves. Still her water had not broken, and there was no midwife to do it. Her sweat-soaked hair clung to her face. Between pains, she pulled her hair from her eyes. She had to do something or both she and the baby would die. Nyna reached out for her sewing basket, but could not reach it. Moaning, she wriggled closer. Her hand fumbled through the basket until she found the long bone awl. Her fingers curled around it just as another contraction began. Nyna's body went rigid, her face wincing with the agony.

The spasm finally ended, and she rolled to her back. Her empty hand searched between her bent legs and guided her other hand as it inserted the awl. She probed gently, afraid she might hurt the baby.

A burst of water exploded from her, soaking her legs and the blanket beneath. Nyna withdrew the awl. The breaking of her water initiated a fiercely intense contraction. Before it ended completely, another began. She needed the birthing pole!

Nyna struggled to a squat. She wrapped her arms around her knees. Her body bore down so violently she thought her head might explode. Her arms squeezed her legs as she grunted. Again another pain took her breath from her. She was sure she was splitting in two, her bones shattering.

Nyna reached beneath her. The head! She felt the baby's head. She pushed harder, her breath exploding at the end. She had to lie down. There was no one to catch the baby.

She lay on her back, knees bent up. She pushed again, her face turning crimson with the effort. The baby erupted from her, followed by another gush of fluid. Nyna cried out, tears quickly streaking her face. She reached for the baby between her legs. It was slippery and warm.

She maneuvered the newborn to her abdomen and patted its back, but the child did not cry. Nyna lifted her head, and dizziness overtook her. She fell back. After all this, the baby had to be alive! Desperately she flicked the child's arm, bringing forth a soft mewling cry from the baby. Nyna sobbed aloud as the baby's first fragile cry turned into a squall. Her hands stroked the infant's back. She wanted to hold her baby, cuddle it close to her, but she knew she had to wait.

When the afterbirth was delivered, Nyna turned to her side. Her birthing basket sat in front of her. She extracted a piece of sinew and her knife. She tied off the umbilical cord, then cut it. Her head swam dizzily. Exhausted, she snuggled the baby to her breast to suckle and soon fell asleep.

Nyna awoke awash in blood. She had to clean herself

and the baby. She attempted to sit up, but the dizziness stalled her. She had not even looked to see if the child was a boy or a girl.

Gently she urged her baby from her breast. A girl. A beautiful baby girl. From the crown of her head that was covered with rich, thick black hair to her tiny toes, she was perfect. The baby had her grandmother's eyes, Taino eyes. A fleeting blurry image of her mother flickered in Nyna's mind. It had been so long since she could recall her mother's face. The eyes of her baby brought it back to her.

The baby closed her eyes and her tiny mouth puckered. Nyna propped herself on one elbow. She had to get up and take care of the mess. Her head swam when she first sat up, but then it cleared. She dipped a rag in a bowl of water and cleaned the baby, then wrapped her tightly in the swaddling and laid her on the ground, off the soiled blanket.

She cleaned herself, but as fast as she wiped the blood from her, there was more. She put on the leather strap and lined it with absorbent moss.

Nyna rolled up the blanket and put it outside the hut. Every step and movement she made hurt, hurt worse than after Guacana's first attack. She needed to bury the hide and its contents. Predators could sniff out the scent of a birth of any animal, hoping to prey upon the vulnerable newborn.

Her daughter stirred, and in a moment her arms flailed and she howled to be nursed. Nyna spread a new blanket on the ground. She was cold, so she covered them both with a rabbit fur blanket. Nyna watched in wonder as her baby suckled. There was no semblance of Guacana. This was her child. She wanted to follow the Taino tradition of putting the baby to rest against a cushion, to shape the skull. But she did not know exactly how it was done. Perhaps in a few days, when her strength returned, she would think about it some more.

Nyna and the baby slept into the night, the child waking every so often and nuzzling her mother's breast. Nyna would help the baby find her nipple and then she would drift back into sleep.

When the sunlight awakened her in the morning, Nyna was horrified at the amount of blood that pooled beneath her. She rolled up the soaked hide and placed another on the ground. She only had one more, and of course the deer hide she had not yet prepared.

Nyna cleaned herself and applied a new strap. Thirsty, she crawled to her water pouch. She turned it up and drank it dry. She would need more water, and she had to wash the blanket, strap, and swaddling.

She shivered with the cold. She needed to get to the cenote, but was not sure she could walk that far. Nyna bundled the baby in fresh rags and put her in the sling. She slung the strap over her head. She carried the dirty blanket and rags through the brush to the cenote. She dipped the blanket in the water. It was so much heavier, now that it was saturated with water, that she had difficulty swishing it to clean it.

Nyna pulled the blanket from the water and spread it out to dry in the sun. Her hands ached with the cold. She blew on them for warmth, then proceeded to clean the baby's rags.

Nyna filled her water pouch and left the cleaned articles beside the cenote. They were too heavy to carry back.

The baby fussed in the sling, and Nyna took her into her arms. The walk back seemed so long, her tired legs cramping. She laid the baby down inside the hut, then went outside. She couldn't leave the child alone in the hut to take the birthing blanket away. Afraid if she buried it close by, the scent still might attract a predator, she decided to burn it.

She had not tended the fire and it had gone out. She got her bow drill and worked tediously to start it again.

Beads of sweat broke out on her forehead, even though she felt chilled. She fed the fire until it blazed, then she cut swatches of the birthing blanket and burned it, piece by piece. She left the afterbirth wrapped in a small piece of hide, then put it on top of the fire. It was a slow process as everything was damp with the birthing fluids. As she waited for each piece to burn, she lay on her side in the dirt. She was so tired. How was she ever going to take care of both of them?

When the disposal task was complete, Nyna burned the bloody stuffing of her strap and replaced it with clean filling. Inside the hut, she lay down beside her daughter. She needed a name, Nyna thought. But she was too tired to think. She closed her eyes and sank into sleep.

She had only slept a few moments when the baby cried. Nyna opened her shawl and offered the baby her breast. The infant sucked furiously. Maybe in another day or so her milk would come in and the baby's hunger would be satisfied.

As days passed, the baby's vigorous sucking made her nipples so raw, they cracked and bled. Now each time the child cried, Nyna flinched with the anticipation of the baby's nursing. She coated her nipples with grease and fish oil, but it did not help enough.

The baby thrashed in her arms, and Nyna put her to her breast. Her body tensed as the baby started to suck. In an instant, the child stopped nursing and cried fitfully. Nyna knew that when the baby cried, her breasts should fill with milk in response. But that did not happen, and now the child got little if any nourishment from her. She supposed that her anxiety over the pain the nursing caused and her general weakness prevented the milk from letting down as it should. Ais women often shared the task of nursing babies if one mother was ill or needed relief. But here there was no one else. Nihapu would have prepared a soothing salve, and her breasts would have healed.

Nyna sat in the middle of her hut and cried, rocking her infant back and forth as it wailed from hunger. Her head reeled as she stood and a gush of warm blood streamed down her leg. She was not hungry and had not been since the baby was born, but she was going to make herself eat. She had to get stronger.

Nyna sat by the fire, chilled and nauseated. Flies gathered on the flesh-speckled deer hide of the prey she had killed days before. She still had done nothing to the hide, and now feared it was too late. At least she had smoked the meat and made the cakes.

Nyna bit into one of the cakes. Her mouth was dry, and the taste, which once pleased her, made her gag. She forced another bite and swallowed it. If she allowed herself to become poorly nourished, she would stop making milk altogether. She could not allow that.

The young mother pulled the fur away from the baby's face. How beautiful she was, even as her eyes screwed into little slits as she cried. She ran her finger across the little one's cheek. The baby turned to the touch, her mouth pursing in search of her mother's breast. Nyna tried to relax and think of pleasant things so her milk would come down. She eased her daughter to her breast and winced at the rasping pain.

Cetisa gently cradled her son next to her. Etac stood outside the door of the woman's hut. Cetisa would stay there for a few more days, totaling seven altogether.

"Uxaam waits on his platform," Etac said. Cetisa slowly got to her feet and emerged from the hut. She handed Etac the baby.

"What name do you think he chooses?" Cetisa asked, following behind. Her stride was short as each step caused her pain. But Nihapu's poultices were helping her heal quickly.

"One never knows what name the shaman chooses,"

Etac said. "The spirits visit him and reveal the name. There is no way to predict."

"But I thought perhaps he might have told you, or hinted to you."

"Do not be so impatient. You will know in a moment."

Etac carried the child up the ladder onto the ceremonial platform and handed him to the shaman. The villagers gathered below.

Uxaam disrobed the infant, who started to cry at the shock of cold air.

Cetisa, still considered unclean, waited farther in the distance. She strained to hear.

Uxaam waved the child over the fire four times while he prayed to the fire for special blessings. He put the baby in his lap and sucked on a small stone pipe he filled with magical herbs. Uxaam drew deeply on the pipe and then set it down. He lifted the child and blew into his nostrils a thin trail of cloudy smoke. The baby coughed and shuddered.

"Ocklawaha," Uxaam said.

Cetisa put a finger to her lips and said the name. "Ocklawaha." It was such a long, complicated name for such a small child, she thought.

Uxaam and Etac came down from the platform with the baby. Cetisa followed a safe distance behind so as not to contaminate anyone.

At the edge of the cenote, Uxaam dropped to his knees. He held his hand over the infant's nose and mouth and quickly immersed him four times. Ocklawaha squealed.

Cetisa swayed anxiously. The air was cold and so was the water in the cenote. She feared the dousing, no matter how much it pleased the spirits.

Uxaam stood and wrapped the screaming infant in the child's furs and handed him to Etac.

"He is a feisty one," Uxaam said. "He will always speak his mind."

"Not like Ochopee or Guacana," Etac said.

"No," Uxaam said. "He will not be like that."

"Guacana is fortunate he is alive," Etac said. "The wound to his head should have killed him. He should be more thankful than so bitter. He is rancid inside."

"Now he has no one to focus his venom on. Nyna was his target for so long, I think he misses her for that reason."

Etac handed the baby to Cetisa, who quickly offered him her breast and began a song.

They traipsed back to the village, Cetisa going to the woman's hut and the others to the plaza.

Guacana, bundled in blankets, warmed himself in front of the central hearth. The head wound had left him blind in the right eye, which remained in a permanent squint. His expression was locked into a squirming grimace. When he spoke, his lips only moved on the left side. The right side of his lower lip flagged, and he had to continually wipe drool from it. The scar on the back of his head was absent of hair and stood out clearly.

Another aftereffect of the injury made some people afraid of him. Without warning he would drop to the ground, his body would shake, then stiffen, and his eyes would roll back in his head. Sometimes he would vomit on himself. No matter how hard someone would shake him or call to him, he did not respond, not until the fit ended. When this happened, mothers would swoop up their children and run away in fright. Men would back away and feel ill themselves.

Guacana had become somewhat of an outcast as so many shied away from him. Every time he saw his reflection, he cringed and hate boiled inside him. He wished Nyna had not been banished so he could have delivered his own torture. Death was not strong enough. He wanted her to suffer every day, like he did. He prayed that she did.

35

Every day was a struggle for Nyna. A whole moon had passed since she had delivered the child. She had not anticipated this much weakness or this much difficulty in caring for herself and the baby. A simple trip to the beach or the sinkhole was overwhelming. Nyna's throat clenched as she realized she was not getting much better. Her strength had not returned and the bleeding kept on. She rocked gently, trying to soothe the child into sleep.

Were they both going to die? Nyna peered at her beautiful daughter. She could not wait any longer to give her a name. If something happened to them, the spirits would need to know her name.

"Mixya," she said aloud, seeing her mother's eyes so clearly in her daughter's. "You are called, Mixya, like my mother, your grandmother. I do not know how to present you to the spirits, but I will do my best."

Nyna carried the baby near the cook fire. She bundled green pine needles and lit them. She waved the smudge about, making certain some of the smoke wafted over Mixya, but she was careful not to bring it too close, afraid of the unpredictable sparks.

"This is my daughter, Mixya," she said, holding the baby up to the sky. "See her. Know her face, her voice, her soul."

Nyna lowered the baby and snuggled her close under the wrap of furs. For the last two days Mixya slept most

of the time. She had stopped the fitful crying and demanded Nyna's breast much less. The young mother un-
folded the fur and examined her child. She pinched up
the skin near Mixya's wrist. The flesh was not resilient
and seemed to lie closer to the bone. Was the baby
smaller than when she was born?

Though Nyna's nipples had toughened, they remained
chapped, and she supposed she had never made enough
milk, even from the beginning. She lifted her breast and
held the infant to it. Mixya's little lips puckered, but she
did not latch on. The child was growing too weak to
suckle. At that moment Nyna made the decision to return to the Ais village. They could do whatever they
wished with her, but her daughter had to be saved. Mixya
was half Ais. They would not deny that!

Her head swam in dizziness and confusion. What did
she need to take with her? One small basket only. She
wondered if she could even carry that and the child for
such a distance.

She needed her leather straps, skins to keep them
warm, and a water pouch. She had a little of the deer
meat still stashed and some dried fish.

She gathered her things in the basket, leaving behind
all her weapons, tools, and traps. She took no utensil
or cooking pots. If she left this morning, she could travel
nearly a whole day. She had to get Mixya to the village soon.

Nyna put the sling over her head and shoulder so
Mixya rested against her chest. She picked up the basket
and began her hike. The first wave of dizziness passed,
leaving her feeling weak and wobbly. How was she ever
going to reach the village? But she had to. She pushed
herself onward, almost mindlessly.

Several times she stopped to rest and offered the baby
her breast, but Mixya showed little interest. When the
sun went down, Nyna prepared no shelter or fire. She

curled beneath a tree and huddled Mixya close to her under a blanket.

When dawn came, she realized the baby had slept through the night without once waking to nurse. Nyna threw the covers away to check on the child. Fear collected in the pit of her stomach.

The baby lay still, undisturbed by the sudden loss of the blanket and its warmth. Nyna pulled the infant to her.

"Mixya," she cried.

The child was cold and her skin pale. Nyna forced a knuckle in the baby's mouth. "Mixya," she whispered. "Wake up."

Nyna held her baby close and got to her feet, pacing, talking to the child, gently shaking her. She thumped the baby's feet with her fingers. "Wake up!"

Nyna could not control her sudden need for air. She gasped, her breathing sharply painful in her chest. What was wrong with the baby? Was she dead?

Nyna frantically shook all the wraps off her baby girl. She sobbed aloud, calling the baby's name over and over.

Mixya finally whimpered, and Nyna plunged to her knees. "Sweet baby girl," she cried. "I am sorry." She was sorry for bringing such an innocent baby into her world. Sorry she was such a poor mother. There was no reason this tiny soul should suffer.

Nyna forced her nipple into the child's mouth. She pressed and squeezed her breast, expressing a weak stream of milk. Mixya sputtered, then swallowed and began to suck.

"Yes, yes," Nyna whispered through her tears. "Everything will be all right. I will take care of everything."

While the baby nursed, Nyna gathered up their things and trudged on. Her legs felt twice as heavy as they were. Her back ached, her head pounded. How far from the village was she?

Nyna's feet chilled in the ocean water as she moved

on, keeping the sea to her left shoulder this time. Her progress was slow and painful.

In mid-afternoon, Nyna lost her balance, stumbled and fell. The saltwater splashed in her eyes and stung them. Mixya started to cry.

Nyna tried to get up, but found herself too weak. She released the basket from her back and crawled over the sand. The protection of the coastal forest seemed so distant and her efforts to get there pitifully feeble. If she rested for a while, later she could take up the journey. But now she was so tired.

Nyna finally staggered to her feet. Another gush of warm blood trailed down her legs. The bleeding had let up days before. Now it returned with a vengeance.

She struggled over the dunes and collapsed in the shade of a large sea grape. She and Mixya slept, even though a large thunderstorm passed over them, soaking them.

The drizzle kept on even after the storm passed. Chogatis wiped the rain from his face.

"Come inside," he said to Uxaam and Joog. He gathered his blanket around his hunched shoulders. "We should talk."

Uxaam and Joog followed inside the cacique's lodge.

Chogatis leaned on his walking stick, and very gingerly lowered himself to sit on the bench. "I have not been the same since I got sick," he said. "When you get old once you get sick, you never come back to the man you were before. Nihapu fusses over me like I am a child and in some ways I am. The people need a leader."

"You will get stronger," Uxaam said.

"That is not going to happen. And I am tired, shaman. The time is right."

Chogatis stretched his legs out in front of him, rubbing his knobby knees. "What do you think, Joog? You are my grandson."

Joog took a deep breath. "I am not the one," he said.

"But you are the cacique's grandson," Uxaam said.

Joog rocked his head back and stared at the roof. "How can I begin?" he said. He looked back at Uxaam and then Chogatis. "A question was put to me once that I have since given much thought to. I was asked if I could raise a weapon against the Jeaga, against those I had known and lived with."

"And you answered that you could," Uxaam said.

"I can raise a weapon against anyone who threatens my life. But if the Jeaga and Ais come into conflict, could I attack my old friends? Could I creep up in the night and without warning hurl my lance into an old friend's heart?"

"That tells me you are a good, fair, and honest man," Chogatis said. "A man worthy of being the cacique."

"The people need a more objective cacique than I could be. And there would always be that fear in the men's hearts that in a critical moment of battle, I might hesitate, and that could cost lives. And they are right."

"Then who?" Uxaam said.

"Etac," Joog said.

Chogatis nodded. "I agree. Everyone respects the War Chief."

"Then Etac it will be," Uxaam said. "But there is no rush."

"Do not wait until the people must grieve a cacique," Chogatis said.

"We will take it to Council," Joog said. "Council will determine how many moons."

"Tell them they should not wait too long," Chogatis said, ending with a shallow cough.

"Rest, Grandfather," Joog said. "We will leave you to nap before the evening meal."

Joog and Uxaam ducked out of the lodge.

"Are you sure, Joog?" Uxaam asked.

"I have given it much thought," Joog said. "I did not come to this decision lightly."

"And the marriage to Cian?"

"She is not in my heart. I cannot do it."

"Before we announce your decision, I think it wise you go on a vision quest. At least you will find peace with your decision if it is the right one."

"I think you are right," Joog said. "Explain to my grandfather where I have gone."

Uxaam continued on to the central hearth and Joog followed the path to the beach. This was an enormous decision he had made, but he was certain it was the right one, the only one a loyal Ais could make. A vision from the spirits would confirm it.

Joog roamed the beach in the rain. He moved knee-deep in the water, then sank beneath the waves. When he came up, he held his arms in the air.

"Lead me where I am to go. Show me the way and make yourself known to me," he called out. He turned in circles in the water, his arms stretched overhead. "I am Joog, grandson of Chogatis, of the Hawk Ais. See me!"

He dragged himself out of the water. He plucked a strand of grass from the sand, held it out, then released it, letting the wind take it. The grass blew north. He would follow.

Joog trudged up the shoreline, ignoring his hungry belly as night closed in. He moved up the beach until the moon was high overhead. The young man took the egret feather from the leather case that hung from his breechclout sash. He said prayers over it, then laid down on the sand on his back, arms outstretched, legs straight. He watched the sky, the clouds crossing the moon, the twinkle of the ancestors' fires in the heavens.

He relaxed, sinking deep inside himself. Soon his mind was clear. Images began to form in his head. Dolphins arced up out of the sea, following the coast. Egrets flew overhead in the rain that washed grasshoppers into the sea. Next he was like the porpoises, swimming in the sea. Contentment swelled inside him, warm and satisfying.

One dolphin split from the group and disappeared in darkness. It called to him. Joog wandered in the blackness looking for the lost dolphin. Again he heard it call his name and ask for help.

Suddenly the images vanished, and his head cleared. Joog's eyes flew open. He sat up and looked over the dark water. The vision was vague in its meaning, as all visions were. He would sleep and perhaps some revelation would come in his dreams or in the morning.

The bright sunlight shone through Nyna's closed eyes. Her eyelids fluttered.

How long had she been asleep? She quickly turned to Mixya, touching her cheek. The infant opened her eyes. They appeared cloudy and unfocused, Nyna thought. She pulled the baby close and urged her to nurse. Mixya responded for a short while, then gave up.

Dried blood streaked Nyna's legs and caked beneath her. She needed to clean herself in the ocean and be on her way quickly. She did not know how long she had slept and how long Mixya had gone without nourishment. She attempted to stand, getting to all fours, then pushing herself up to sit on her knees. With her head erect, she swooned. She waited, hoping the dizziness would pass. She tried to stand, but it was too much for her, and she crumpled to the ground.

In a shifting dream Nyna saw her mother clearly for the first time in a very long time. Her mother and father stood on the most beautiful white sparkling beach. The palms, laden with coconuts of sweet flesh and milk, swayed in the gentle ocean breeze. The aroma of cassava cakes floated in the air. Beautiful red, green, and yellow plumed birds roosted in the trees. The lushly foliaged mountains jutted into the brilliant blue sky. She was home!

"Let me see the baby," her mother said.

"She is called Mixya, for you," Nyna said, handing the baby to her mother.

The grandmother smiled and looked up at Obaec.

"I am so happy to be home," Nyna said.

Nyna's mother handed her back the child. "You cannot stay," she said.

"But I want to," Nyna said. "I have spent my whole life trying to come home again."

Obaec's face frowned. "Not yet, my little one," he said. "It is not time."

"Please," Nyna said.

"Good-bye, Nyna," her mother said. "We love you, daughter."

"No!" Nyna cried. "Let me stay!"

"Nyna! Nyna!" a voice called through the fading dream.

Her pleading must have changed their minds. She caught a glimpse of her father's gleaming old bracelet as his strong warm hand came under her neck and lifted her head from the cold ground.

"I love you," she whispered.

Another arm slid under her knees, and she was lifted up.

"I am taking you home," the voice said.

Nyna smiled. She was not afraid anymore. She felt Mixya stir as the baby rested against her chest. She did not hunger or thirst anymore. She felt at peace. She and her daughter were going home.

36

Joog ran along the beach carrying Nyna and the baby. He was afraid she was going to die before he could reach the village.

His feet pounded the wet sand, and water sprayed up behind his heels. He cut through the forest and onto the path that led to the Hawk village.

Cetisa saw them and yelled for Etac.

Joog rushed across the plaza and to Nihapu.

"Oh my!" Nihapu cried.

A crowd immediately began to gather.

"Leave her be!" Joog said, turning to them. He was winded, and his voice sounded husky.

Guacana limped up to see why the people clumped together outside the cacique's lodge. Had the old man finally died?

"Joog has brought Nyna back," Ochopee said.

Guacana shoved his way through the crowd. His good eye glared at Joog. "You defile the Ais spirits," he said.

"Get back, Guacana," Joog said.

"I have a right to be here. She does not." Guacana took another step forward.

"Stay back," Joog said, lifting his fist. "Do not permit your putrid gut to force Ais hands to rise against each other. Back off."

Guacana looked down at Nyna. "She is good as dead anyway," he said. He began to edge away. "But if she lives, prepare yourself."

Chogatis came to the opening of his lodge, clutching his chest as he coughed. He looked at Nihapu tending to someone. He moved so he could see better. The old man's hand rushed to wipe tears from his eyes when he saw that it was Nyna and her baby.

"Bring them inside," Chogatis said. "Buhgo, fetch Uxaam. And the rest of you be gone. Do not seek your enjoyment here."

Buhgo hurried to find Uxaam, but the rest of the crowd stayed in place.

"I am still the cacique," Chogatis said. "Do as I say. Be gone, all of you."

The people began to back away. Ochopee's voice rang out over them all. "She cannot stay, Cacique. We are done with the woman from the sun."

Nihapu bathed Nyna and the baby. She put clean wraps on both of them.

When Buhgo and Uxaam arrived, Nihapu told Buhgo what medicines to prepare.

Uxaam stood back.

"Start your prayers," Chogatis said, irritation etching his frail voice.

Uxaam looked first at the cacique, and then Joog.

"What is it?" Joog asked. "Why do you hesitate?"

"She is not Ais."

"It does not matter what she is," Joog said.

"Ais spirits will not recognize her," the shaman said. "They will not visit their powers on her."

"But they will recognize the baby," Chogatis said. "The child is Ais. Now do what you do best. You are the shaman."

"Go for Taska," Uxaam said. "It might take the power of both of us to help them."

Chogatis's head jerked up when he heard the call of the conch horn. He hobbled outside. Guacana blatantly stood at the central hearth, sounding the horn. It was not his place to do such a thing.

Chogatis felt the fury blossoming in his chest, his breathing becoming heavier.

Nihapu looked up. "I will take care of Nyna, no matter what," she said. "She is our daughter."

Chogatis caught his breath, Nihapu's words soothing him. Joog took him by the arm and led him to the Council meeting.

As he passed, Chogatis snatched the conch horn from Guacana.

"He is the one who defiles everything that is Ais," he said to Joog.

Joog picked up the Talking Stick and handed it to his grandfather. Etac shifted sideways, leaving an open space for the cacique.

Chogatis sat, his eyes piercing each face that looked at him. "We will wait for Uxaam, Buhgo, and Taska."

"There is no reason to wait," Ochopee said. "We all agree what must be done."

"We will wait," Chogatis said. The pale skin of his face was taut over the bones and was crisscrossed with a net of fine lines. His thin lips ended at the arced creases that cut deep at the corners of his mouth. His hair hung in silvery strings to his shoulders. He was old, but still imposing.

Council sat quietly at first. The Fire Keeper nourished the coals to a blaze. As the time passed, the men grew anxious. They shifted and mumbled.

Finally the three men entered Council.

"You should not have wasted so much time on them, while we sit here and wait," Guacana said.

Chogatis nodded to Joog to begin.

"Yesterday the cacique, shaman, and I discussed who would take Chogatis's place when the time came," Joog said. "This discussion was at the cacique's request."

"What does that have to do with the woman?" Ochopee said.

Chogatis pounded the end of the Talking Stick on the

ground. He glowered at Ochopee, warning that if he interrupted again, he would be excused from Council.

Joog continued. "We concluded that I am not the best candidate." A burst of muttering followed his statement.

"We will discuss that later. Uxaam suggested that before I made that final decision, to confirm it, I should go on a vision quest. And so I followed his advice.

"I followed the spirit's direction, going north up the shoreline. When the vision came, it was of dolphins. One of them got separated from the pod and called to me for help.

"I slept on the beach last night, not understanding the vision. But now I do. When I awoke this morning, I heard crying. Following it, I found Nyna and the baby.

"Do you recall the totem Uxaam gave her when she was a child? Porpoise. The spirits have seen to it that she is brought back. They came to me in a vision and showed me. These are Ais spirits that minister to me, not Taino, not witches, not outcast souls!"

The crowd fell silent.

"It is true," Uxaam said. "The spirits want her returned. We cannot question."

Guacana chucked a stone into the fire. "How do we know Joog tells the truth?"

"I was with him yesterday," Uxaam said. "I did suggest the vision quest."

Joog took in a deep breath and let it out slowly. "The vision does confirm my decision. There will always be this devisiveness surrounding me, whether it be linked to my past with the Jeaga or with Nyna."

"Hmm," Etac said. "I see what you are saying. We cannot ignore the spirits' desire. They brought her here we sent her away, and now without a doubt they have brought her back to us. We cannot pretend to understand why. Only the spirits know what they do."

"But when she left, the rains returned," an old man said.

"Perhaps they would have returned anyway," Uxaam said. "We cannot say if Nyna had stayed, we would have surrendered to a drought."

"I did not go in search of Nyna," Joog said. "The spirits led me to her, arranged every event from my birth to this point. Yesterday's conversation was the final event that led to Nyna's return. The divine hand moves us all, directs every step we take, though we cannot see our destination."

The luster of the bracelet shone into Guacana's one good eye. He squinted harder, nearly unable to see. "Look at me," he said. "Can you forget what she has done to me? I should be a constant reminder of her evil."

Chogatis stood up. "Your disfigurement reminds us all of the evil in you. Now we see you as you really are. And Ochopee," Chogatis added, "look upon Guacana's face. See how the rotting gut inside sits upon his face. Do not let that happen to you. You are a new man since the big storm. The spirits have spoken clearly to you." Chogatis paused and let the men think for themselves. Finally he said, "Uxaam, draw the line."

Nihapu lifted Nyna's head onto a hide pillow. "Drink this," she said, holding the decoction to Nyna's mouth.

Nyna sipped the medicine and shuddered at its taste.

"It does not taste good, but it will help stop the bleeding. Then you will start to gain your strength."

"Where is Mixya?" Nyna whispered.

"Ah, you named the baby for your mother," Nihapu said. "It is a beautiful name." She repeated it. "I like the way it sounds. Musical almost. She sleeps over there. She is bundled snugly."

"I do not have enough milk," Nyna said. "I had so much pain and got so weak I never produced enough to nourish her properly."

"Do not worry about anything," Nihapu said. "I will take care of everything. All you need to do is take the medicines, eat a little, and drink a lot. Let me worry about the rest."

Nyna closed her eyes. She had not felt so safe for a long time.

When both Nyna and Mixya were sleeping soundly, Nihapu left the lodge. She stood outside the men's Council. Chogatis noticed she was there.

Uxaam stood next to Chogatis and drew the line in the dirt. Joog was the first to stand on one side. Buhgo followed, bringing his brother in the travois.

As Ochopee took his place, a collective hush fell over them all. He hesitated, straddling the line.

"Do not be a coward," Guacana said.

Ochopee stepped next to Guacana. They were the only two on that side.

"She stays," Chogatis said. "That is what most of us say."

The men dispersed, and Chogatis joined his wife.

"Nyna does not have enough milk. The child is very weak, much worse than Nyna. We must ask for someone to help nurse the baby."

"I do not think we will have volunteers for that," Chogatis said. "The men have agreed to let her stay, but I doubt they will permit their wives to suckle her offspring."

"But the child is Ais," Nihapu said. "We have to try."

Chogatis agreed and sent word for all to gather in the plaza, both men and women.

When the entire village assembled, Chogatis put the problem to them.

"This is outrageous," Guacana said.

"You speak of your own blood and flesh, your child!" Nihapu said. "You deny her life!"

Nihapu held the baby so all could see. "She is a beautiful Ais child. Is there one among you who can suckle this precious spirit?"

Silence shrouded the plaza. Women with babies, held

them close and looked away, not wanting Nihapu to look at them. Cetisa backed away from the crowd, trying to use the trees to hide herself. Surely her sister would not ask her to care for Nyna's child as a return favor for her medicine?

"There must be a woman among you whose heart aches for this infant," Nihapu said. "No mother with a conscience can stand by and see an innocent child die from starvation."

Someone moved through the crowd. People stepped aside to let her pass.

"I have more than enough milk," Laira said. "Give her to me."

Days turned. Moons turned. The cold air departed and would stay away until the season changed again. Nihapu nursed Nyna back to health, thought it was a slow journey. Mixya stayed with Laira most of the time at first. Because Mixya did not nurse from her mother, Nyna's milk dried up. Her complete inability to suckle her daughter was an emotional disappointment. Finally, when Nyna was strong enough to care for the baby, Mixya was returned, but Nyna still had to take the baby to Laira to nurse. How she missed that intimacy with her daughter. When Mixya cooed during the nursing, Nyna always felt like crying.

Laira was sensitive to Nyna's feelings, and as soon as the baby was done suckling, she handed Mixya to her mother.

As time passed, Mixya nursed less often. She crawled, investigated her toes and everything around her.

"Do you think she confuses us?" Nyna asked Laira one day after nursing.

"Do not be silly," Laira said. "See how she looks at you. Mixya knows you are her mother."

Those were the words Nyna needed to hear.

"She looks at you like my son looks at me," Laira

said. "Is there anything more wonderful than being a mother?"

"Nothing," Nyna said. "I have so much to thank you for. Without you, Mixya would have died. And if she died, I would have also from a broken heart."

Buhgo stopped and played with the babies. He held Mixya up and she pulled at his eyebrows. "She is so inquisitive," he said.

Something across the way drew Buhgo's attention. "Guacana pays an unusual amount of attention to Cetisa's boy. Have you noticed?"

"I suppose I am too busy with Mixya to pay attention," Nyna said.

Laira put her son in her lap and put a small bit of coontie bread in his mouth. "I have noticed," she said. "I even mentioned to Chitola that I thought it peculiar that Guacana paid so much attention to Ocklawaha."

"What did Chitola say?" Buhgo asked.

"He thought it was because Guacana realizes he will probably never have a wife, and so he will never have a son."

Nyna hung her head. She was responsible for his disfigurement. "I am sure it is difficult for him."

Buhgo was shaking his head. "I am not so sure," he said. "I will pay more attention. Something eats at me, but I do not know what it is."

Buhgo gave Mixya back to Nyna and strolled across the plaza.

"Good day, Guacana," he said.

"Buhgo," Guacana said.

"Cetisa's boy is a handsome child," Buhgo said. "And where is his mother?"

"She had some things to do. I told her I would watch Ocklawaha for her."

"Umm," Buhgo said. "What a kind gesture."

Guacana bounced the boy gently. "That bothers you," he said.

"Yes," Buhgo answered slowly. "Such charity does not fit you."

"We all grow old and mellow," Guacana said. "It happens to all of us."

"You seem to take good care of the boy, considering your lack of experience."

Guacana smiled broadly . . . sickly, Buhgo thought.

"Cetisa trusts me." He paused a moment, then cocked his head, his good eye flaring with a baneful spark. "She would never forgive me if something happened to her son."

37

Buhgo approached his brother. "Taska, have you had any premonitions lately? Anything about Guacana or Ocklawaha?"

Taska shook his head. "Do you think I should have?"

"Perhaps," Buhgo said. "Perhaps you could call upon the spirits. Inquire about Cetisa's child and Guacana."

"Uxaam has more experience," Taska said.

"No, I do not want anyone else to know. I have this uncomfortable feeling, but nothing to base it on. I cannot go to Uxaam or anyone but my brother."

"Then I will do it," Taska said. "I will tell you whatever the spirits reveal to me. Come to me after the evening meal."

Buhgo busied himself with routine tasks the rest of the day, but his mind kept returning to Guacana. From his cook fire, where he brewed medicine for Chogatis, he could see Guacana. He kept track of him during the day. At one point Guacana hiked into the forest. He did not appear to be going on a hunt, and Buhgo's curiosity was aroused.

Buhgo carried the medicine to Nihapu.

"Thank you," she said. "Chogatis comes out of the lodge less and less. He chants, and prays, and sleeps. I fear he is preparing for death. He seems ready, but I am not."

Buhgo set the container of medicine on the ground.

Uxaam, Joog, and Etac gathered at his side this morn

ing. Their faces were solemn. "When the new moon comes, Etac will become the cacique."

After the evening meal, Buhgo visited his brother. "Have you spoken with the spirits?" he asked.

"I do not understand what they showed me. If I could consult Uxaam—"

"No," Buhgo said. "Not yet."

"It was very strange," Taska said. "Guacana's face was not real . . . he was not what he seemed. He looks at Ocklawaha with his ordinary ugly face, but when he turns away and I see him, his face melts like fat over a fire. His face slides off and beneath it is revealed one that is blackened and eaten away by death rot. He has no flesh on his nose nor any lips, just bone and teeth. He smiles, then that which melted away comes back together and his face returns. He looks back at the child." Taska shrugged. "I do not understand the two faces."

Buhgo raked his fingers through his hair. "I think I saw a glimpse of that other face today."

The new moon brought the darkest night, and the fire in the central hearth blazed high into the blackness. Uxaam, dressed in full accoutrement, stirred his special elixir. He donned a cape of white feathers and a fox headpiece. Necklaces and bracelets of shells and the treasured white beads draped his body. Black and white paint streaked his face and chest in finger-wide bands.

Uxaam skimmed the top of the liquid to rid it of the herbal residue. He closed his eyes and chanted over it in the ancient tongue. Carefully, so as not to spill a single drop of the sacred tea, he brought the elixir to his lips and drank. He traced the liquid by its warmth as it glided down his throat and into his stomach. Beads of sweat broke out across Uxaam's forehead. In a moment, he lifted his head and looked out into the night.

Taska watched in awe as the shaman became lost in

the spirit realm. The center of Uxaam's eyes seemed to glow like dark coals.

The shaman descended the ladder. Buhgo lowered Taska in his sling that was strung over a pole attached to Uxaam's ceremonial platform.

"He is amazing," Taska said, switching into the travois. In front of the people, Uxaam let his voice ring out.

The village seemed cloaked in the mystery of the spirit man. When Uxaam opened his arms, the cape lifted into a wing shape. So entrancing and charismatic was the shaman that people thought he might take flight at any moment.

The drummers kept their rhythm as if it were Uxaam's heart until everyone's heart beat in unison. Even the earth vibrated to the same throbbing pulse. There was definitely magic in the air.

When Uxaam's voice stopped, the drums ceased on the same beat.

Chogatis crept feebly to Uxaam's side. He braced himself with a walking cane and the Talking Stick.

"Etac, come forward," the cacique said.

Cetisa stroked Ocklawaha's back as she watched her husband move through the crowd. At last she had her child, and a husband whom all admired. Women were jealous of her, not Nihapu!

The baby fretted on her hip. Cetisa shushed him and swayed back and forth, but Ocklawaha did not seem comforted. Cetisa lifted him up higher. "See your father," she said. "Look there," she said, jiggling him. "In a moment he will be the new cacique. This is a proud moment, so stop your fussing."

Ocklawaha rubbed his face on his mother's shoulder. His little legs stretched out straight, then drew up as he let out a cry. Cetisa bounced and patted him. "Shh, shh," she whispered.

Ocklawaha's crying intensified. Cetisa could not find

anything to soothe him. His wailing was disturbing the ceremony, so reluctantly she moved out of the crowd.

"What is the matter?" she asked. "Why have you been so miserable lately?"

Ocklawaha bellowed, then coughed and threw up.

"Are you sick?" She cleaned him up and just as she finished, his stomach heaved up more of its contents.

Cetisa looked back over her shoulder as she carried Ocklawaha to her hut. Etac was being proclaimed the cacique. She heard a cheer as she wiped Ocklawaha's mouth and chest. She cleaned herself and put the baby in a fresh wrap.

"There, there," she said. "Too much excitement for one day. You did not even have a chance to nap," she said.

Ocklawaha's cries turned to gasps and whimpers. He closed his eyes as his mother stroked his back with her fingertips. Cetisa sang a sleeping song and in a moment, her son was sleeping.

She crept outside and stood in front of her lodge. She wished she could see and hear it all. The women would be envious and gather about her if she was in the crowd.

Tomorrow, she thought. They will have their chance tomorrow. She would be the woman held in the highest esteem. Nihapu would no longer have that claim.

The men of the village would begin on the new cacique's lodge early in the morning. It would be the grandest of all!

Usually, if the cacique died, he would be buried beneath the floor of his lodge, but not before his leg bones were removed and cleaned. The people would venerate the bones, and they would be stored inside the lodge. The new cacique would move in.

But Chogatis was not dead. He would remain in his lodge and a newer lodge would be built for Etac.

At last Cetisa had everything she ever wanted.

*   *   *

The new lodge had been under construction for two days. The men worked on it during the daylight, and the women gathered in circles to socialize. Laira visited the new cacique's wife to pay her respect. She brought Ocklawaha a rabbit fur blanket.

"It is very nice," Cetisa said, examining the gift.

"He seems quiet today," Laira said. "Ocklawaha is usually so full of energy. Is he not feeling well?"

Cetisa looked at her son, who slept at her side on a soft buckskin. "He has not been himself lately. A little cranky and upset stomach."

"If they could only tell us what is wrong it would make it so much easier on mothers," Laira said. "Why do you not take him to your sister? Let her make a medicine."

"I might do that," Cetisa said.

Ocklawaha opened his eyes and rubbed them. He sat up and scooted against his mother, leaning his head on her arm.

"Here," Cetisa said, offering him a ladle of fish stew.

The boy turned his face away and whined at her effort to make him eat.

"I am sure he will feel better in a day or two," Laira said.

After Laira left, Guacana took a break from the work and stopped to speak to Cetisa.

"The lodge is nearly done. It is impressive."

"I am anxious to move into it," she said.

Guacana looked at Ocklawaha. "Where is all his energy?" he asked, tousling the child's thick black hair. "Let me take him for a little walk in the woods," he said. "It will be good for him. Fresh air improves the appetite. Then you can take a moment to do things you need to do."

"I suppose that would be all right," she said. "But do not be too long."

Beside the new lodge, Buhgo put down the bundle of thatch he was lashing and watched Guacana carry Ocklawaha down the trail and into the forest. *Two different faces,* Taska had said. *He is not what he seems.*

He walked over to Cetisa. "Guacana spends a lot of time with your son."

"Oh yes," Cetisa said. "It is so good of him. He is a lonesome man." Cetisa wiped her brow. "I am grateful he takes my son for a walk. Ocklawaha has not felt well for the last few days, and I have not had much rest. At least I can get a few things done while he is gone. He has been so whiny all I have done is hold him and rock him."

Buhgo's face darkened. "Ocklawaha is not well?"

"He is fine, just an upset stomach. You know how little ones are."

"Have you asked Nihapu to look at him?"

"If he does not feel better later today, I will take him to her."

Ocklawaha did not feel better as the day went on. He became even more lethargic. Cetisa gathered him up and took him to Nihapu.

"He vomits occasionally and does not eat. He cries, and I think his stomach cramps," Cetisa said.

Nihapu stripped the wrappings off the child and examined him. She looked closely at his eyes and pulled down his lower lid to see the color there. She felt his forehead with the back of her hand, and then her lips. He was not feverish, but clammy. She pushed on his stomach and put her ear to his chest.

"Is he all right?" Cetisa asked.

Nihapu rested two fingers on the side of his neck to feel the child's pulse. Even as she examined him, he slept, except to complain now and again with a weak whimper.

"I am puzzled," Nihapu said. "His body is not hot, but he behaves as if he is sick. Nyna," she called, "boil some tubers of groundnut, elder, and cattail. After it comes to a boil, cover it and let it steep."

Nyna hiked Mixya higher on her hip. "Is something wrong with Ocklawaha?"

Cetisa nervously pulled at her necklace as she looked between Nyna and Nihapu.

"His stomach is upset," Nihapu said. "We will prepare a soothing tea for him."

Guacana walked up to them. "The boy is sick?"

"Nyna is preparing a medicine for him," Cetisa said.

"Nyna? She is not a healer."

"I told her what to prepare," Nihapu said.

"She has stopped me several times lately when I have had Ocklawaha and offered the boy some tea. Was that your medicine, also?"

"I have prepared no medicines for the boy until now. She must have shared some of Mixya's berry teas with Ocklawaha."

"Yes, that must be it," Guacana said. As he turned his back and walked away, a smile spread over his face. Everything was so perfect he had to fight back his urge to thrust his arms in the air and whoop.

38

Over the next several days, Ocklawaha grew weaker despite Nihapu's medicines. Cetisa did not sleep. Etac offered to hold their son and tend to him while she rested, but his wife refused. Etac gathered their belongings and settled his family in the new lodge, but the excitement of the move lost its meaning for Cetisa. Her eyes sunk in her head, and dark circles rimmed them.

"I do not understand," she said, frantically rocking Ocklawaha. "Nihapu gives him medicines and still he gets worse. Uxaam says his prayers and administers his medicines. He has tried to suck the evil spirits from his breath, but . . ." She broke into tears.

Etac put his arm around her. His eyes, too, filled with tears. He looked at Ocklawaha, and as much as he wanted to console his wife, he knew they were losing their son.

Nyna left Mixya with Nihapu and visited Cetisa. Her heart ached for the distraught mother.

"He is no better?" she asked.

Cetisa strangled on her tears and could not answer.

"Nothing seems to be working," Etac said.

"What can I do to help?" Nyna asked.

Cetisa's head shot up. "Get me Buhgo," she said. "I want to talk to him. Maybe my sister does not give my son the best medicine. Maybe both of you conspire against me. Nihapu does not want me to be happy."

Etac embraced his wife. "You know that is not true," he said.

Cetisa burst into tears and ranting. "I do not know anything!" she said. "Our son drifts farther from us every day. We are watching him die right before our eyes. He looks at me like he is asking why I do nothing to help him. How do I answer him? I hear his cries, even when he sleeps. Why? Why is this happening? Someone must be able to do something!"

Nyna looked painfully at Etac. "I am so sorry."

Cetisa sobbed into her husband's shoulder as Nyna left.

Inside her lodge, Nyna reached for Mixya and picked her up. She held her daughter close, breathing in the sweet scent of the child's skin. She carried her outside into the sun. She could not imagine the fear Cetisa was feeling.

Joog came behind her. "You look so distant," he said. "Where are you?"

She turned to see his face. For a moment she imagined that Joog was Mixya's father and that they were a family. She wanted to back into his shoulder and feel his arm reach around her waist. She closed her eyes for a moment, reveling in her fantasy.

"Nyna?" Joog said. "Are you all right?"

"If anything happened to my daughter, I would not be able to bear the pain," she said.

"Nothing will happen to her. What is wrong?"

"Ocklawaha is not getting better, and no one seems to be able to help or even decide what is wrong with him. I was thinking how horrible it must be for Cetisa."

Joog put his hand on her shoulder. Her head tilted toward it so she felt the top of his hand against her cheek.

"Nyna," he whispered.

She waited to hear what else he was going to say, holding her breath, but he did not speak.

Joog took his hand from her shoulder and tugged on Mixya's toes, making the girl laugh.

"You need this back," he said, starting to remove the bracelet.

"No," she said. "It is yours. I want you to keep it. It will insult me if you return a gift."

Joog brushed her cheek with his fingertips and threaded a strand of hair behind her ear.

Nyna curled next to Mixya in the dark, thankful her nightmare had only been a dream. She smelled the delicate fragrance of her daughter's hair and smiled. She closed her eyes and drifted back to sleep.

Suddenly she was jolted awake by a loud shrieking. Nyna sat up. She heard Nihapu scramble out the door. She grabbed Mixya and ducked outside.

"What is it?" Nyna asked.

The screams screeched through the village, drawing most everyone outside. Chogatis shuffled out of the lodge.

"What is happening?" he asked.

Nyna shook her head just as a jagged bolt of lightning lit the sky. A booming thunderclap followed ushering in a downpour. Buhgo ran through the plaza. Nyna shielded her eyes with her hand and watched to see where he went, straining to see in the dark.

A flash of lightning briefly illuminated the village. There was Buhgo standing next to Cetisa who held a limp Ocklawaha in her arms. Etac's arms were wrapped around her as she wailed.

Cetisa crumpled to her knees, holding her son snugly to her as she rocked back and forth, screaming his name. The rain pounded down.

Nyna did not need to see more. Ocklawaha was dead.

Nyna had trouble sleeping the rest of the night, but near dawn she finally drifted off. A commotion outside the lodge awakened her. She sat up. Mixya was not at her side.

Nyna sprang to her feet and ran outside. Nihapu held her daughter in her lap. Guacana stood with several others in front of Chogatis. His voice was loud.

"We cannot bring this to Etac. He is grieving. It was her," Guacana said, pointing to Nyna. "She killed the boy."

Nyna's eyelids fluttered. What was he talking about?

"This is absurd," Joog said. "Leave Chogatis alone. The boy is dead because he was sick. You just look for something to punish Nyna."

"She poisoned the child," Guacana said. "I told you she often offered Ocklawaha special teas, but never when his mother had him, only when I watched the boy."

Nyna's stomach lurched to her throat. What was he saying? Her mouth gaped in shock.

"But why would she do such a thing?" Chogatis asked.

"Go back to your chores," Joog said. "Chogatis will hear no more of this."

"She favors Nihapu," Guacana said. "Cetisa has never accepted Nyna. Cetisa was finally getting all she deserved, and Nyna could not stand it. She felt she owed Nihapu something."

"This is it," Ochopee said. "There will be no banishment for this. For this she will die."

"You have decided on her guilt only on Guacana's word," Joog said.

"Guacana has seen her feed the child teas," Ochopee said. "Guacana says Nyna even prepared the boy's medicine. Is that not true, Nihapu?"

"Under my direction," Nihapu answered.

Buhgo joined the group. Chogatis explained the accusation Guacana made.

"Did the child have a sickness that either you or Nihapu could recognize?" Guacana asked.

"We did not determine what was wrong with Ocklawaha."

"Because he was slowly poisoned," Guacana said. "No one else is ill, no adults, no children. The boy died as a result of Nyna wanting to punish Cetisa for her unkindness to her sister. Everyone knows her feelings toward Cetisa. It has been no secret."

"My sister and I were not close, but we had mended some of our wounds," Nihapu said.

"Council cannot meet until Etac has had several days to grieve and the child is buried. It would be disrespectful," Ochopee said. "But in four days we will meet and the recommendation will be death!"

Guacana pushed past Nyna and went inside Chogatis's lodge. When he emerged a few moments later he held a fistful of crab's eye and machineel.

"The proof," he said, throwing it on the ground in front of everyone. "We all know what these are . . . poisons. I found them in one of Nyna's baskets."

Nyna shook her head. Where did Guacana get those things? Neither she nor Nihapu stored machineel or crab's eye. There was no medicinal use for them.

"For now she will be tethered to the post at the central hearth," Guacana said.

Nyna flinched. How could this be happening?

"I have heard enough," Buhgo said, backing away.

"Take her, Ochopee," Guacana said.

Nyna could not move, horror rooting her to the spot where she stood.

Ochopee grabbed her wrists and tied them behind her.

Joog stepped up to him and thumped into Ochopee. "Council has not found her guilty," he said. "Turn her loose."

Ochopee laughed. "She will run," he said.

"She will be my responsibility," he said. "If she runs, then it will be my life you take."

"That is reasonable," Chogatis said. "We are not a

cruel or unfair people, Ochopee. Punishing her before Council decides on her innocence or guilt is not our way."

Ochopee backed away. "If Nyna leaves, Joog will pay the price."

While the men still festered, Buhgo sneaked behind the lodges until he came to Guacana's. He took a quick look to see if anyone saw him. Satisfied that he was unnoticed, he darted inside.

Buhgo rifled through Guacana's belongings. "It has to be here," he whispered to himself. "He has it here somewhere."

Buhgo dug through baskets and pouches. Nothing. Finally he reached his hand beneath Guacana's sleeping mat. He sat back on his heels and pulled out a parfleche from under Guacana's bed. He unlaced it and peered inside.

He had been right! Buhgo stuffed the parfleche back where he had found it and bolted out of the lodge. He knew what he had to do!

The men sat about the central hearth late into the night, discussing the horrible death of their new cacique's son. Guacana did most of the talking. Buhgo sat himself next to Guacana and did not speak much. He focused on something other than the conversation. Guacana got to his feet as he orated, leaving his tea on the ground. He continued riling the others with his emotionally charged accusations and propositions.

Taska raised an eyebrow at his brother. He watched Buhgo carefully, while all other eyes focused on Guacana and Ochopee. Slowly, Buhgo's hand moved over Guacana's tea, then came back to rest in his lap. Only Taska saw.

Joog did not sit with the others around the hearth. He stayed with Nyna and Mixya in his lodge.

"I will not run," she said to him. "Go and join the others."

"I stay not because I do not trust you, but rather because I prefer your company."

Mixya had fallen asleep in Nyna's arms. She laid her on a sleeping blanket.

"If I am put to death—"

"Stop," Joog said. "We will not even discuss it."

"But we have to. I need to know that someone will take care of Mixya. Nihapu grows older. What will happen to Mixya when Nihapu dies? I cannot ask Laira. Would you take Mixya?"

"You need not even ask such a question."

Nyna bit down on her bottom lip. "Between you and Buhgo, I think she would be well taken care of. I need that assurance."

Joog pulled her to him, cradling the back of her head. His other hand smoothed her long hair, then ran up under it.

Nyna breathed a deep sigh.

Both of Joog's hands reached under her hair, lifting it until he held her head in both hands. He directed her face so she would look at him.

"I will not let them harm you," he said. "If the decision is made that they want your life, we will escape." His mouth was suddenly all over her face, her eyelids, her mouth. He whispered her name.

Nyna's breath was taken from her. She melted into his arms, listening to the sound of her name come so huskily from him.

"I love you," she whispered.

In the morning, the village was unusually quiet. Joog stared at Nyna while she slept. She was his woman. He kissed Nyna's bare shoulder and pulled the blanket over her. Quietly he slipped outside.

Everyone felt the grief that gripped Etac and Cetisa. It

seemed almost disrespectful to go on with their everyday chores. For Cetisa and Etac, the forward momentum of their lives had come to an abrupt halt.

"Where is Guacana this morning?" Ochopee asked, sipping on a ladle of tea that Zinni had prepared for him earlier.

"He exhausted himself last night with all his ravings," Joog said.

"Perhaps someone should check on him," Buhgo said.

"Yes, brother," Taska said. "Perhaps Ochopee should check on his friend."

Ochopee took another sip. "It is early yet. Guacana will be along."

The morning had nearly passed before Guacana emerged from his lodge. He stumbled to his cook fire to find it had gone out in the night. He cursed it, then staggered to the central hearth for an ember.

"What is wrong with you?" Ochopee asked.

Guacana appeared ashen. His hair, wet from sweat, clung to his scalp and hung in long strings.

"I woke in the night with my stomach churning. I must have eaten too much."

Buhgo eased next to Guacana. "Let me fix a stomach medicine for you," he said. "The potion always works."

Guacana didn't answer. He bobbed his head as if to agree and scooped a hot coal into a sand-tempered pottery bowl.

Buhgo watched him ramble back to his hearth. "I suppose I should fix his medicine now. He does not seem to feel well at all."

"The sooner he drinks your elixir, the better," Taska said.

Later, Buhgo appeared in front of Guacana's hut. "I have your medicine," he called.

"Come in," Guacana muttered.

"My goodness, you do not look well," Buhgo said. "Drink all of this, and I promise you things will resolve."

Guacana propped himself up on one elbow and took the bowl from Buhgo. He tasted the medicine and drew back. "This is bitter," he complained.

"It is not the taste that has the power," Buhgo said. "Go on and drink it down. It will be easier if you just down it all, instead of sipping on it."

Guacana groaned and put the bowl to his mouth. He tilted it up and drank, some of the liquid spilling out of the corners of his mouth. When the bowl was empty, he thrust the bowl at Buhgo. "It had better make me feel better. That is nasty tasting."

"I will be back later to check on you and see how you are feeling," he said.

Guacana flopped back on his mat. As the day wore on, Guacana felt worse. He scratched a hole in the dirt floor to vomit in. The taste of Buhgo's medicine lingered on his tongue.

"One more dose should do it," Buhgo said, walking into Guacana's dank hut. He coughed in response to the stench of vomit and feces.

Guacana moaned. "Get Nihapu and Uxaam. Your medicine does not help."

"This should be the last dose. I will be here first thing in the morning with others. But first, drink this."

Buhgo knelt beside Guacana and helped him lift his head. He touched the bowl to the sick man's lips. "Drink," he said.

Guacana's lips parted, and Buhgo tipped the bowl. Guacana sputtered.

"No, no," Buhgo said. "Like I told you, drink it down fast and get it over with."

Guacana opened his mouth, and Buhgo poured. Much of it spilled out of his mouth, but Buhgo was satisfied that Guacana drank enough.

Buhgo stood. "I will be back in the morning. Sleep well."

39

Near dawn, Buhgo decided the time was right. He emerged from his lodge and stared up at the dark sky. "My ancestors," he said to the stars. "Your hearths burn brightly. Your voices are clear. I have done the right thing."

Buhgo crossed the plaza to the old cacique's lodge. Nihapu heard him calling. She slipped from her bed and went to the entranceway.

"Wake Chogatis," Buhgo said. "He needs to come with me."

"What is all this about?" Nihapu asked. "Chogatis needs to rest."

"Just do as I say." Buhgo lifted the pitch torch to see her face. "It is important. It means Nyna's life," he said.

Nihapu disappeared in the darkness of the lodge, and in a moment Chogatis came outside.

"Follow me," Buhgo said, waving the torch.

They stopped at Etac's hearth and Buhgo called his name.

Etac rubbed his eyes as he came through the doorway. "Shh," he said. "Do not wake Cetisa. She has not had much sleep."

"Come," Buhgo said. "It is important that you come with me."

"Where are you taking us?" Chogatis asked. "What are you up to?"

Buhgo did not answer. How could he tell them he had

poisoned Guacana? They would understand when he was finished. He led the two men to Guacana's hearth just as the sky began to lighten.

Buhgo stooped to enter, and Chogatis spoke. "Are you not going to ask permission to enter?"

"I already have permission," Buhgo said. "Come inside. In a moment everything will be clear to you."

The three men entered and stood at Guacana's feet.

"Do you sleep, Guacana?" Buhgo asked.

Guacana groaned. "Your medicine is no good," he said.

Buhgo moved the torch so they could see the sick man's face better. Guacana's face was pale, his lips blanched white, his eyes dull with dark circles beneath.

"I want Nihapu and Uxaam. Your medicine has done nothing to help me."

"You are mistaken, Guacana. My medicine works exceptionally well. Tell me how you feel."

"You know I am sick," Guacana said, his voice thready with exhaustion and infirmity. "I am so weak I cannot get up, and my stomach holds nothing. I grow worse, not better."

"Hmm," Buhgo said. "Interesting symptoms." He knelt next to Guacana and looked back at Chogatis and Etac. "This sounds familiar, do you not think so?"

"Help me," Guacana said. He retched, but his belly was empty.

Buhgo touched Guacana's forehead and neck. "Your body is not hot at all. Your skin is cold and sweaty . . . like Ocklawaha's. Do you think you caught the boy's illness? You did spend so much time with him."

"Get Nihapu," Guacana said. He squinted into the light of the torch. "Where are Nihapu and Uxaam? You said you would bring them."

"Neither of them can do you any good," Buhgo said. "Do you recall how they failed to help Ocklawaha?"

"I am not Ocklawaha," Guacana said.

Buhgo's eyes flashed and his mouth curled with dramatic curiosity. "But it seems you have the same illness."

"No," Guacana said. "That is impossible."

Buhgo propped up the sick man's head, then opened his fist. "What do you suppose this is?" he asked.

Guacana's eyes bulged at the sight of his parfleche, which contained the crab's eye and machineel. Buhgo had found it beneath his bed! "You have poisoned me!"

"You recognize the symptoms, do you not? They are the same as Ocklawaha's, but your illness came on much faster as your dose was much higher. I did not have the time to waste."

Guacana struggled to sit up, but he was too weak. "He has poisoned me," he moaned.

"What have you done?" Chogatis asked.

"I have the antidote," Buhgo said. "It is too late to save Ocklawaha, but Guacana has a chance if he takes the antidote. I have it here in this water pouch."

"Give it to me," Guacana said. "You cannot let me die." He reached for the pouch that Buhgo dangled in front of him.

"First you must admit to what you have done. You know what that is, do you not, Guacana?"

Guacana did not answer.

"Confess and the antidote is yours. Remain silent and the three of us leave. Nihapu and Uxaam will treat you as they did Etac's son. You know how that will end."

Guacana's lips thinned into pale lines as he pressed them together.

"Your choice," Buhgo said, rising to one knee.

Chogatis thought he was beginning to understand. "What does Buhgo want you to confess? Tell us, Guacana."

Guacana reached for Buhgo's hand. "I did it," he whispered.

"You did what?" Chogatis asked.

"Yes, tell them what you did," Buhgo said. "Look at Etac when you speak. He will want to see your eyes."

Spasmodic retching seized Guacana again. His whole body shook and contorted. When it was over, his body went limp.

"You will die without the antidote," Buhgo said.

"I poisoned Ocklawaha," Guacana mumbled. "I gave the poison to him slowly, over a long time."

Etac lunged toward the sick man, but Chogatis and Buhgo held him off.

"Wait, and he is yours," Buhgo said. "One more thing, Guacana. Did Nyna have anything to do with Ocklawaha's death?"

Guacana shook his head.

"Say it," Buhgo said.

"She had nothing to do with the boy's death," Guacana said.

"Why?" Etac said. "Why did you hurt my boy?" His face twisted as he fought not to cry out.

"He deserves an answer," Buhgo said.

Guacana moaned. "To get rid of Nyna. To hurt her."

Buhgo looked at the witnesses. "Enough?" he asked them.

Chogatis nodded. Etac slammed his fist into a support post, then walked out the door.

"I have said what you want, now give me the antidote," Guacana said. "Help me," he pleaded.

Buhgo poured a small amount of the antidote into a shell dipper. He lifted Guacana's head and put the dipper to his lips.

"The antidote will work?" Chogatis asked.

"He will be fine by tonight," Buhgo said. "Perhaps a little weak, but he will recover."

Buhgo tilted the dipper, and just as Guacana opened his mouth, Chogatis kicked the dipper from Buhgo's hand.

"He will suffer the same as Ocklawaha," Chogatis said.

*   *   *

Cetisa watched Uxaam draw a line down her son's forehead with yellow ocher. The shaman uttered prayers that she did not understand. To her ears his voice was a jumble of noise. Etac gently clasped her hand and looked in her face. His mouth moved, but his voice, too, was nothing but a muddled medley of sounds.

Uxaam lowered Ocklawaha into his grave. Cetisa knelt and scattered a handful of flowers and herbs over her son's small chest. The pain in her tightening throat prevented her from saying what she wanted to say. She ached to tell her child one last time how much she loved him, how he had brought such joy to her life.

Instead, Cetisa talked to Ocklawaha in her head. If he were a spirit, he could hear her, she hoped. Her thoughts poured through her mind, all the time the image of his little face before her. When the words inside finally ceased, she felt her strength rush from her body. Suddenly her shoulders shook with sobs, and Cetisa let out a painful cry.

"Why?" she cried. "My baby, my son!"

Etac took her by the arm and helped her up. She buried her face in his shoulder, her body heaving with her sobs. "I should have known! I let this happen, let Guacana—"

Etac stroked the back of her head. "You could not know," he whispered. "You were a good mother."

"No," Cetisa said. "I was blinded by my bitterness. I killed our son!" Cetisa rammed her fingers through the tangle of her hair and sunk to her knees, crying.

Uxaam covered the grave and put a stone on top. The villagers backed away, leaving only Etac and Cetisa.

Etac kissed his wife's face, her forehead, her cheeks, her hair, as he held her, desperately attempting to comfort and soothe her.

"I have to ask Nyna to forgive me," Cetisa whispered. "And my sister. She was right . . . has always been right."

"Nyna does not want you to ask for forgiveness and neither does Nihapu."

"I have to," she said. "For Ocklawaha. It will help make it right."

Suddenly Cetisa's eyes grew large. "Do not let them bury Guacana beside our son. Promise me!" Her voice sounded frantic.

"He will be burned and his bones buried apart from the village," Etac said. "Come, now," he said, again stroking her hair, "let us go home."

As the days passed, the villagers came to grips with the horror of Guacana's deed. For Ochopee, it was especially difficult.

"You will not feel better until you talk to Nyna," Zinni said. "You were wrong, but you know that now. And your son is a hero. He should hear from you also."

Ochopee arched his neck and glared up at the sky. "What do I say to Cetisa? Her grief is so profound. How do I tell her I am sorry, that I did not know what Guacana was doing?"

"You must try," Zinni said. "With each of them. Start with Buhgo."

Ochopee wiped a hand over his mouth. "I will talk to him now," he said, getting to his feet.

Ochopee looked about the village as he walked. He finally spotted his son with Nyna.

"Let me go with you in search of your people," Buhgo was saying. "You will need someone with the intuition and experience I have."

Nyna laid her hand on Buhgo's shoulder. "You are so good and kind," she said. "I would love for you to go with us, but this is a dangerous journey. I do not know if we will ever find my people or return. And if you did not come back, who then would look after the Ais? Nihapu must continue to pass on her knowledge to you.

You are the one the spirits chose to take her place. You cannot turn your back on them or your people."

Buhgo's head dropped. "I know that you are right, but it is difficult to imagine my life here without you and Joog."

Tears formed in Nyna's eyes. "You have been a wonderful friend. I owe my life to you." Nyna stepped forward and embraced him. "How can I ever thank you?"

"Buhgo," Ochopee said. "I am glad I have found you with Nyna. There are things I must say to you both. This is not an easy thing for me, but it must be done."

Buhgo gazed at his father.

Ochopee cleared his throat. "I . . . I have been wrong and it has taken the death of an innocent child to bring me to my senses. You deserved a father different from me and I am ashamed."

"The past is past," Buhgo said. "We cannot change anything. Let the door close on the past."

"It is not as easy as that," Ochopee said. "I must speak first. I have been a poor father and I regret it. I could not see all the goodness in you, the gift, the blessings. I was too concerned with what others might think. I should have focused on what my son needed from me. Buhgo, my heart fills with pride that you are my son. I know that is hard to accept, but it is true. It has always been true, but I feared that if I showed it, others might think I was less of a man. My heart aches when I think of how I let you down."

Ochopee brushed away a tear.

"We are only what the spirits make of us. Everything is for a reason," Buhgo said. "We go on from here. We need not speak of this again, Father."

Ochopee's head bobbed in understanding. "I humble myself before you also, Nyna."

"Buhgo's advice is good," Nyna said. "We go on from here. Let the past lie quiet."

Ochopee did not speak, afraid his voice would crack.

When Cetisa would see him, he would ask her forgiveness as well.

"Mixya is finally asleep," Nyna said, coming out of the lodge.

"Good," Joog said. "Come and sit by my side."

Nyna lowered herself to the ground, and Joog put his arm over her shoulder, pulling her close. "I think I have loved you since I found you, all huddled in the brush, so scared, so weak. There was something about you from the moment I saw you, even though I was a child myself."

"I tried not to let myself think of you," she said. "I never thought it could be . . . a Taino woman and an Ais man."

"We are fortunate," Joog said. "The spirits have brought us together. There is no other explanation."

"Yes," she whispered. "I will miss my Ais friends . . . my family. I do not want to think I will never see them again. I know that when we leave tomorrow, it will be the last time I see Chogatis and Nihapu."

Joog slipped his hand under her buckskin shawl, cupping her breast. He nuzzled her ear. The fleshy weight of her breast in his palm, the soft skin and the nipple that drew taut at his touch, the distinct scent of her hair, ignited a fire inside him.

Nyna sighed in response. She pulled away and got to her feet. "Come inside," she said, offering her hand to him.

Nyna gathered her baskets. Chogatis carried her bow and lance.

"Are you ready?" Joog asked.

Nyna smiled and hoisted Mixya up into her arms.

The villagers followed them to the beach and watched as Joog put their things in the large dugout.

Nyna reached in her totem pouch and took out the

drawing Uxaam had done for her. She handed it to the shaman. "Keep this to show others," she said. "I want others to know of the Taino. When I was alone, I saw a canoe filled with strangers. They were not Ais or Jeaga. So others come, maybe not today, but one day."

Uxaam took the drawing.

Nihapu hugged Nyna and started to cry.

"This is not a time to be sad," Nyna said. "I am going to find my people. I promise to come back one day."

Nihapu pressed her lips to Mixya's forehead.

"Take good care of them, Joog," Chogatis said, moving toward them with the aid of a walking stick. His old face, scored with furrows, expressed his emotions. He stared as if he were trying to take in as much as he could, realizing that this image would have to last him until his death.

Nyna's arms flung around Chogatis in a firm embrace. He patted her back.

"I will miss you so," Nyna said softly.

"And I, you," Chogatis answered.

She fought back her tears as they broke the embrace. "Thank you for everything you have done for me," Nyna said.

"May your journey be safe," Chogatis said, with a wave of his hand.

Nyna looked to the back of the crowd. Zinni stood there, her eyes dark, her skin pale.

"I will bring back the Holy Wood," Nyna said.

Zinni smiled and put her hands over her mouth.

Nyna's eyes locked on Cetisa's for a moment. It would be a long time before the grief did not rip at Cetisa's heart every moment of every day. "I will think of you," Nyna said.

Joog helped Nyna and Mixya into the canoe, then pushed off. He raised the paddle high, then plunged it into the water.

"I wait your return!" Buhgo called out. "I will see you again, child of the sun!"

Nyna watched the beach where the Hawk Ais stood until they grew to mere specks in the distance. She felt a hollow spot inside where she left behind a piece of her heart. Yes, she would return one day.

Nyna looked at Joog, and a tear streaked down her cheek. How fortunate she was.

Nyna held Mixya close and whispered to her, "We are going home."

Author's Note

Most everyone is aware of Christopher Columbus's discovery of San Salvador, the New World, on October 12, 1492, but few know of his landfall on Haiti's northern coast on December 6, 1492.

There is great debate as to how many Taino inhabitants existed on the island of Hispaniola when Columbus arrived. Some early Spanish historians claim there were as many as 3,000,000 to 4,000,000, but that is regarded as a gross overestimate. The current thinking is in the neighborhood of 400,000.

Early Christmas morning in 1492, the *Santa Maria* went aground off what is now Cap Hatien. The bottom of the ship was so badly damaged that it had to be abandoned. The *Pinta* was lost, and the *Nina* could not accommodate all the sailors. With the help of the Taino, Columbus salvaged the timber from the *Santa Maria* and used it to build a small fort he named La Navidad. The sailors begged Columbus to stay, as they were certain that here they would find their fortunes in gold. Columbus chose thirty-nine to stay behind.

The Taino were recognized as a gentle people, described as happy, friendly, and highly organized. Each small kingdom was ruled by a leader called the cacique. When Columbus arrived, there were five known kingdoms in Hispaniola.

The Taino lived in circular buildings with poles as the supporting framework. These huts were covered in woven straw and palm leaves. The caciques' housing was different. Their houses were larger, rectangular, and had porches. Furniture was limited to wooden stools, chairs, cradles, and couches. The people slept in hammocks woven from cotton or on mats made of banana leaves.

For the most part the women and men went naked except for short skirts and adornments, especially those made from shells. They wore some small, hammered gold ornaments and painted and tattooed their bodies.

Their diet consisted mostly of meat and fish as the source of protein. On the island there were only a few small animals to hunt. They did hunt ducks and birds, and turtles in the lakes and the ocean. They practiced an agricultural technique of raising their crops in a *conuco*, a large mound they packed with leaves to guard against soil erosion. Their primary crop was cassava or manioc.

There is a discrepancy amongst scholars as to how severely the Taino were terrorized by the Caribs. Some say the evidence is abundant that the Caribs were warlike cannibals who consistently raided the Taino, stole their women, killed the men, and fattened the young men to eat. So horrid was the Carib reputation that even the Europeans gave the Caribs a wide berth when traveling through that part of the world. Others protest that the tales of the Caribs are exaggerated.

The Taino worshipped gods called *zemis*. The *zemis* had the power to control everything in the universe. The Taino carved stone figures to represent their gods, in the forms of toads, snakes, and other animals with distorted human faces.

The demise of the Taino on Hispaniola is credited to several factors. When Columbus returned to Hispaniola, he found the men he had left behind on the island had been killed. The sailors had raped and violated the Taino women and destroyed their property. Outraged by the sailors' dreadful deeds, the kindly Taino finally rose up against them. The Spanish methodically hanged and otherwise murdered the caciques, burning the people and the villages.

By 1507, the Taino had shrunk to 60,000, and by 1531, the number was down to 600. Within 50 years of Columbus's arrival all the Taino had died from Spanish attack, overwork as slaves in the gold mines, starvation, and disease.

The Hispaniola gold the Spanish sought so feverishly, and at such tragic cost of human life, was exhausted by 1530. Spain lost interest in Hispaniola and eventually moved on.